UNFORGIVABLE
STORIES

By the same author:

The Bloody Red Baron
Jago
The Night Mayor
Bad Dreams
Life's Lottery
Dracula Cha Cha Cha
Seven Stars
Anno Dracula
The Quorum
The Original Dr Shade
Famous Monsters
Orgy of the Blood Parasites (as Jack Yeovil)

UNFORGIVABLE STORIES

Kim Newman

POCKET BOOKS

LONDON · SYDNEY · NEW YORK · TOKYO · SINGAPORE · TORONTO

First published in Great Britain by Pocket Books, 2000
An imprint of Simon & Schuster UK Ltd
A Viacom Company

1 3 5 7 9 10 8 6 4 2

Simon & Schuster Ltd
Africa House
64–78 Kingsway
London WC2B 6AH

Simon & Schuster Australia
Sydney

A CIP catalogue record for this book is available
from the British Library

ISBN 0-671-02221-0

Typeset in Sabon by SX Composing DTP, Rayleigh, Essex
Printed and bound in Great Britain by Cox & Wyman Ltd

For Ramsey, Dennis and Charlie.

In Memory of Karl.

CONTENTS

Acknowledgements   ix

Introduction *Eugene Byrne*   1

Further Developments in the Strange Case of Dr Jekyll
    and Mr Hyde   11
    Story of the Photograph   13
    E. H.   17
    The Broken Key   23
    The House of Dr Jekyll   29
    Henry Jekyll's Further Statement of the Case   35
    In the Fog   50

Amerikanski Dead at the Moscow Morgue, or:
    Children of Marx and Coca-Cola   53

Just Like Eddy   83

A Victorian Ghost Story   99

Dead Travel Fast   111

Une Étrange Aventure de Richard Blaine   121

Great Western   135

Alternate Majors   165
    Slow News Day   167
    The Germans Won   176

Completist Heaven   185

Coastal City   199

Quetzalcón   209
     Introduction: A Message from Coatlicue   211
     Friday Night   213
     Guest of Honour Biography *Jack Yeovil*   215
     Saturday All Day   217
     I'm the Kingston, Me   218
     Saturday Night   220
     Kingston Dunstan: An Appreciation *Kim Newman*   221
     Sunday   222

Residuals *With Paul J. McAuley*   225

Teddy Bears' Picnic *With Eugene Byrne*   253

ACKNOWLEDGEMENTS

Thanks to Ellen Datlow, Gardner Dozois, P. N. Elrod, David Garnett, David Hartwell, Maxim Jakubowski, Stephen Jones, David Pringle, Nicholas Royle, Al Sarrantonio, John Skipp, Michael Marshall Smith, Craig Spector, Mark V. Ziesing. And, especially, to Eugene Byrne and Paul J. McAuley for permission to appropriate work written in collaboration.

'Further Developments in the Strange Case of Dr Jekyll and Mr Hyde' was first published in *Chronicles of Crime: The Second Ellis Peters Memorial Anthology of Historical Crime*, edited by Maxim Jubowski (London; Headline, 1999). 'Amerikanski Dead at the Moscow Morgue, or: Children of Marx and Coca-Cola' was first published in *999: New Stories of Horror and Suspense*, edited by Al Sarrantonio (New York; Avon Morrow, 1999). 'Just Like Eddy' was first published in *Interzone* magazine, 1999. 'A Victorian Ghost Story' was first published in *Interzone*, 1998. 'Une Étrange Aventure de Richard Blaine' was first published in *The Time Out Book of Paris Short Stories*, edited by Nicholas Royle (Penguin, 1999). 'Great Western' was first published in *New Worlds*, edited by David Garnett (Clarkston, Georgia, USA; White Wolf/Borealis, 1997). 'Alternate Majors: Slow News Day' was first published as 'Slow News Day', in *Interzone*, 1994. 'Alternate Majors: The Germans Won' was first published as 'The Germans Won', in *A Game of Two Halves*, edited by Nicholas Royle (London; Gollancz, 1996). 'Completist Heaven' was first published in

The Mammoth Book of Frankenstein, edited by Stephen Jones (London; Robinson, 1994). 'Coastal City' was first published in *The Time Out Book of New York Short Stories*, edited by Nicholas Royle (Penguin, 1997). 'Quetzalcón' was first published as a chapbook for the World Fantasy Convention (London; Airgedlámh Publications, 1997). 'Residuals', written with Paul J. McAuley, was first published in *Asimov's Science Fiction*, 1997. 'Teddy Bears' Picnic', written with Eugene Byrne, was first published in *Interzone*, 1997.

INTRODUCTION
Eugene Byrne

When Kim invited me to write the introduction to this latest collection of his short stories, my heart sank. Well, okay, only a little bit, but it took a southward turn all the same. I'll happily tell you that this is a wonderful collection of stories, well worth shelling out your hard-earned for, but it'd be harder to tell you why because I'm no literary critic. I don't know how to criticise anything except other people's driving.

At the time of writing (November 1999), Kim's novel *Life's Lottery* has just come out to some deservedly rave reviews. The man is at the peak of his abilities, but not yet, I'll bet, the peak of his career. So why don't I tell you what he was like at school? Then, when others come along in the future to write biographies of him, I can say that I got in first.

Kim James Newman was born in London in 1959, but when he was still quite young his artistic parents decided to forsake Brixton for rural Somerset. The family moved to the village of Aller, on the Somerset Levels, in pursuit of rural tranquillity, space in which to think and create.

The pair of us spent one weekend in February 1998 driving around the Levels. This was close to the end of years of thinking about, and researching for, a series of novels set in Somerset in an alternate world in which the Germans have won the Second World War. As research, it was time usefully enough spent. The first novel, *The Matter of Britain*, now complete but as yet unpublished, bears quite a few of the fruits of two and a bit days of getting lost on B-roads. For me, though, the experience was more valuable than that. First, it made me realise how easy it is to find the history in a landscape if you only look carefully enough. It also confronted me with what a strange, mysterious place the Levels are. Though I was brought up in a small town on the edge of them, though I went to school in a big town in the middle of them, I had never really noticed, never engaged with, this land before.

Kim grew up in a village – hamlet really – slap in the middle of the Levels. To the back of his parents' house is a long, wooded hill, but most of the rest of the landscape is flat – on, and often below, sea level. Until a few hundred years ago, much of it was under water all year round. Even nowadays, the fragile ecology of the Somerset Levels depends on an intricate system of pumps, ditches and canals, and upon the strength of the sea walls at Burnham-on-Sea. Even then, many of the fields look more like rice paddies for much of winter.

This is not wealthy country and never has been. The farm-land is of indifferent quality and there are few local industries. In much of England, we are resigned to the notion that pleasant villages within an hour's drive of major cities will be colonised by the middle classes. The Old Schoolhouse and Ye Village Smithy have long since lost their original purpose and are now home to Mark and Caroline, the two kids, a four-wheel-drive and a small emergency back-up Metro. The Levels are a little too far from any major centre of economic activity for that kind of nonsense. When Kim, his parents and his sister arrived there in the 1960s, Aller was even more remote. And yet it was the making of him.

While he knows this, he has a deeply ambiguous relationship with Somerset in general and Aller in particular.

Ambiguous negative because small communities aren't usually the best places for gifted kids to grow up. There aren't too many other like-minded folk around and you have to look hard for stimulation and entertainment. Living in the sticks with a wretched bus service (yes, Virginia, things were just as bad before privatisation), there was little to do.

Ambiguous positive because of the consequences; it forced

him back on to what resources were available – television (especially movies), books and his own imagination. These and the occasional company of his parents' visiting friends, and the art students who came to sit at his potter father's feet to learn the secrets of wheel and kiln.

Ambiguous positive and negative because for anyone with half a brain, and a lot of others who haven't, the Somerset Levels are awash with history and mythology. A few miles from Aller one way is Sedgemoor, site of the last battle on English soil, of the Duke of Monmouth's failed attempt to seize the crown. The tragic consequences of this – the monstrous injustice of the execution or transportation of thousands in the subsequent Bloody Assizes – are still a source of local resentment. A few miles in another direction is the hamlet of Athelney. A thousand years ago, it was a tiny island in the middle of marshlands, the last refuge of King Alfred before he launched his successful counter-attack against the Danes. 'Then came the men of Somerset all', it says in *The Anglo-Saxon Chronicle* of the preparations for the battle of Edington in which Alfred defeated Guthrum and forced him to get baptised – at Aller – before the two of them and their retainers sat down to a heroic ten-day piss-up at Wedmore. It was right here, on the Somerset Levels, that Alfred, the only English King to be awarded the title of 'The Great', founded the Anglo-Saxon kingdom of England.

A few miles from Aller in yet another direction is Glastonbury. Now, whatever your take on religion, Glastonbury is one of the most important spiritual centres in the Western world. Nowadays, it's an uneasy mix of local market town and place of pilgrimage for everyone from the straightest born-again evangelicals all the way to 57 different flavours of pagans, wiccans and New Age types. The two camps are in a state of incipient civil war. Throw in the Arthurian connections and it's clear that this place has very special powers, whether there is real magic or simply that its influence is all in the mind.

What does all this have to do with the stories in this book?

Quite a lot. Kim is one of the few true agnostics I know. In many of his stories, the magical and the rational have noisy, energetic, honest arguments. In the astonishingly clever 'Just Like Eddy', he takes the tragic life story of Edgar Allan Poe and gives it a terrific spin which you can ascribe either to supernatural forces or to madness closing in on the man. In 'A Victorian Ghost Story' a rich, greedy, ruthless Victorian businessman gets lost in a London pea-souper and finds himself in a very squalid part of town among ragged, desperate, dangerous creatures who cannot merely be The Poor. Or are they? Then there's 'Further Developments in the Strange Case of Dr Jekyll and Mr Hyde', a very cheeky sequel indeed with a lovely modern/modernist 'explanation' of what really happened.

On a more mundane level, Aller is the model for the fictional Alder, the setting for a number of Kim's stories, notably his early novel *Jago* as well as *The Matter of Britain*. The rural setting for his forthcoming novel *An English Ghost Story* is a variation on Alder, too, though nowhere is it mentioned by name. In this collection, Alder is the setting for 'Great Western', a splendidly tense little yarn that takes many of the themes and conventions of classic cowboy films and plays them in a small English village in the aftermath of an imagined civil war.

Young Kim had passed the eleven plus (naturally). For boys in that part of Somerset at that time, this meant Dr Morgan's Grammar School in Bridgwater. He and I were in different forms and I can't clearly remember when I first became aware of him. Maybe in the first year, maybe the second. But lordy, was he a weird kid.

This weird: if you can remember the fashions of the 1970s, you'll recall that in winter, chaps wore anoraks, crombies or parkas. Kim wore an opera-cape.

You'd hear stories about how he was obsessed with horror films, about how he'd corrected the English teacher on a literary or grammatical point, or of a wisecrack he'd made that

4

paralysed the lesson for a full five minutes. The teachers by and large gladly tolerated this insufferable little smart-Alec because he was the one exceptionally bright kid you only get every two or three years.

Oh, yeah, and by the time I knew him he had memorised 'all' of Poe's 'The Raven' and at the slightest prompting would stand on a desk and recite the whole bloody lot in a convincing Vincent Price accent. Like I say, you don't do that kind of thing if you live in a town with street-corners to hang around on, mates to hang around on them with, and girls to laugh at your pathetic efforts to get off with them. By the time he was fifteen, Kim had read his way through the whole of the Gothic canon and a whole lot else besides. He'd watched every Hammer film as it came up on the telly, not to mention every other classic movie, horror or otherwise. And he'd written his first novel. He worked on the manuscript in lunch-breaks. The following term he proudly showed us his growing collection of rejection slips.

All of which goes some way towards explaining his comfortable familiarity with Poe, with Jekyll and Hyde, with every vampire tale ever, and with old movies. Read 'Une Étrange Aventure de Richard Blaine' for his insight into how stories – movies, novels, opera, local mythology – influence the physical landscape of a place, in this case Paris. It's the product of a huge amount of reading, watching and learning that flatters you, the reader, by giving you the impression that you know as much as the author does.

A lot of the tales in this book are stories about stories. Our joint effort, 'Teddy Bears' Picnic', can certainly be read that way. It's one of a series we wrote over about ten years (we started in November 1989 when the Berlin wall fell) set in an alternate twentieth century in which America is Communist and Russia remains Tsarist/capitalist. The series has been published as *Back in the USSA* in the States but has yet to find a British publisher, perhaps because it's so weird. Weird because they're not your conventional alternate history stories, but because they're also alternate story stories. These are as much literary constructions as historical ones. In 'Teddy Bears' Picnic', we've got the Likely Lads doing their National Service, going through basic training with a lot of other characters from 1970s British TV sitcoms and then being sent to the Vietnam War (Russia and Britain are fighting the commies there in this world) for an adventure that borrows riffs from *The Deer Hunter* and *Apocalypse Now*. Ian McDonald pointed out a few years back that in the early and middle 1990s there was a big fashion in music for sampling and re-mixing, and that the USSA stories were the literary equivalent thereof.

Collaborative writing like this is not unique, but it doesn't happen too often. People ask me how we manage to write together, whether there aren't 'artistic differences' or clashes of personality or ego. After all, some of them add, Kim can be a rather 'forceful' personality. And you can be a pain sometimes, too, Byrne.

In fact (and, if I'm honest, to my continued surprise), we don't argue much. I think this is partly because we've been working together since we were teenagers. Much of our communication happens by osmosis, the product of over two decades of habit. By the time we were in the third year at school there was a little gang of us who put on plays, or formed bands and got into various other creative ventures. What brought us together was a shared taste for showing off and a shared aversion to much of the small-minded, authoritarian culture of our provincial grammar school. When it went comprehensive in our fourth year there, things got a whole lot better. We were given rather a lot of slack by teachers who themselves found the new regime immensely liberating. We went from being a bunch of weirdoes and geeks to being, um, well, a bunch of weirdoes and geeks who had a lot more fun than previously.

Kim works very successfully with other people, too. Turn to the last story in this book for his collaboration with Paul McAuley, a tale of close encounters in the Californian desert.

Before he started writing full-time, Paul was a scientist, who also happens to have spent some time living in Los Angeles. On the surface, his background and interests appear very different to Kim's, but they have worked together on a few projects. Many people, when they first meet Kim, find it odd that so many of his credits include other folks – he's co-edited collections of stories, contributed to reference and critical works as well as writing scripts and stories with other people.

The reason, I think, why he can work so well with others is that he has a very powerful sense of right and wrong. He has, as it were, a very low centre of moral gravity which can instantly focus a story's theme, spot the tensions and give it a strong goodies-and-baddies framework. That's half the graft done before you've either of you had to write a single word. Kim makes this stuff easy by knowing how to keep a story under control. This is also one reason why he is capable of turning out such an astonishing volume of high-quality work. While other writers spend months wrestling with the best way of telling the story that's half formed in their heads, Kim can have the whole thing roughed out from start to finish in a couple of days. Hours, even.

Kim has always been a great exponent of horror-as-morality-tale, but this moral vision goes beyond mere vampires and zombies. He has always taken an active interest in politics, and there are three fine examples here. 'Amerikanski Dead at the Moscow Morgue' is a dark poke at the incursion of American consumerism into the Soviet Union. But hey, it's got zombies in, too (they're called 'Amerikans'), as well as one of Kim's all-time Top Ten Historical Characters, Grigori Yefimovich Rasputin. The Mad Monk is the very epitome of that magical-versus-rational tension in Kim's work; it's possible that this joker was just a clever fraud, but if he was he was abominably clever. Meanwhile, there's more politics in 'Slow News Day' and 'The Germans Won', two funny-but-thoughtful takes on some of the Conservative politicians who cast their shadows over almost the whole of his adult life.

But no matter how many stories he does about John Major – and Kim was writing him up as dull-but-decent-and-deluded long before his autobiography confirmed as much – a lot of Kim is still that solitary kid in the sticks reading H. P. Lovecraft or desperately copying out the end credits on Hammer films off the telly. What liberated him in the end from Aller and his term-time schoolmates was being old enough to travel on trains and coaches on his own. Kim joined the ranks of Fandom, travelling to conventions and the meetings of clubs and societies, finding that there were a few other people out there who had the same interests as he did.

My two favourite stories in this collection are about fandom. 'Completist Heaven' is an uproarious satire on the kind of folks who become obsessed with cult or genre TV or movies to the point where it screws their lives up. Lest anyone take offence – and for all I know, he may have had one or two people in mind when he wrote the story – Kim would be the first to admit that he was once that fan. Kim has freeze-framed the vid to note down the names of technicians on movies and TV programmes. He knows more about *Dr Who* than would be considered appropriate by the headmaster of Dr Morgan's Grammar School for Boys. But then he managed to get it down from obsession to healthy, informed interest and made it the basis of a very successful career as a film critic.

It's best not to give too much away about the other fandom story, 'Quetzalcón', except to say that it's a hoot and that it gets the tone of convention programmes off to a tee. Now you can probably read all manner of hidden meanings about the nature of fans and literary celebrity into it, but I'm sure he's just kidding.

Isn't he?

Oh.

Right.

Well, anyway. Kim grew up some, went to Sussex University and never permanently resided in Somerset again after that. He's very fond of cities these days. Anywhere with lots of people will do, really. And if you tell him you're thinking of moving to the country because you've seen this wonderful old schoolhouse in the middle of Nether Scrotum which you could *just* about afford, he'll beg you, for your children's sake, not to do it. But as this book and a whole load of others demonstrate, it did him no harm in the long run.

FURTHER DEVELOPMENTS IN THE STRANGE CASE OF DR JEKYLL AND MR HYDE

Story of the Photograph

Through the lawyer Mr Utterson, who placed the documents before the public, all the world knew the facts in the strange case of Dr Jekyll and Mr Hyde. The slaying of the Member of Parliament Sir Danvers Carew was laid at the door of Edward Hyde, whose self-poisoned corpse was discovered by Utterson in Jekyll's private laboratory. With the publication of the posthumous accounts known as 'Doctor Lanyon's Narrative' and 'Henry Jekyll's Full Statement of the Case', attempts to search for the missing Jekyll were abandoned and his obituary published in *The Times*. Initial scepticism evaporated, to be replaced by a species of affrighted credulousness. Though much of the affair remained as murky as the brown fog that clung to London during the months when the murderer was at large, one thing was agreed upon: Jekyll was Hyde, and Hyde Jekyll.

Of all the wonders and horrors of a wondrous and horrid age, the transformation of Jekyll into Hyde was the most wonderful and the most horrible. The sensation press sponsored attempts to repeat the experiment; to compound again that drug which enabled the respected middle-aged scientist Jekyll to become the young brute in human form, Hyde. Thus far, as Jekyll himself found, it had proved mercifully impossible to duplicate the impurity of a vital salt which seemed the key to his tragic success. The term 'a Jekyll-and-Hyde character' entered common parlance to denote a duality of personality inherent to some extent in all souls. The doctor's sad example epitomised a struggle between higher and base instincts that makes battlefields of all hearts, and was used to explain the cruelties of archbishops and the kindnesses of thieves.

It was Utterson's intent in publishing the statements of Hastie Lanyon and Henry Jekyll to end the storm of speculation surrounding the death of Hyde and the disappearance of Jekyll. Once the solution was known to the public, he assumed the mystery would cease to be of interest. He would no longer be beleaguered by newspaper reporters or Scotland Yard investigators. He soon realised the assumption was unworldly: in this case, the solution was more fascinating than the mystery, and interest increased tenfold.

Never a clubbable man, Utterson withdrew even from his few involvements in society, to escape the confounded questions that accompanied him everywhere. It seemed a boom time for his practice, but fully nine-tenths of those who secured appointments were revealed as sensation-seeking busybodies. Dramatists wished to present the strange case as a blood-and-thunder production for the stage – with a woman or two written in, of course, to spice the pudding. Clergymen were eager to save each and every divided soul by securing an endorsement for some species of new apostasy. And alienists wanted to claim Jekyll for their own, naming a new-discovered strain of lunacy for him.

Utterson was forced to disengage almost entirely from his practice but could not shuck off the burdensome task of managing Jekyll's estate. The chore was complicated by successive and discredited wills that left the bulk of Jekyll's substantial fortune 'in the event of my death or disappearance' to Hyde or to Utterson himself. Distant relatives of the doctor put in claims against the estate, as did a horde of low people with real or imagined cases for compensation against debts of dissolution run up by Edward Hyde. The lawyer had first heard of Hyde in connection with the trampling in the street of a little girl, an incident witnessed by his cousin Richard Enfield and settled by a sizable cheque to the child's family drawn on Jekyll's account at Coutts'. Now it seemed every urchin in London had been under Hyde's loose-fitting boots, and their families were righteously determined to make Jekyll's estate pay through the nose for the injury.

His house became his prison, Utterson lamented. While the shut-up mansion of Jekyll was shunned by the superstitious, the lawyer's less impressive town castle was besieged. Even on

Sunday nights, when he was wont to divide his attention between a book of divinity and a bottle of gin, he was not unmolested, though now there was a moment of peace. For perhaps the first time in eight months, he was not thinking exclusively of Jekyll and Hyde but of that most English of all concerns, the weather. Tonight the fog was again thick, a gaseous sea eddying through the city. Rising up above the hats of the unwary pedestrian and freezing the knees of the huddled cabbie, fog made reefs of the meaner dwellings and archipelagoes of the streets of detached houses. Fog was a curse, to be sure, a numbing thing that crept through cracks and wisped even in gaslit and coal-warmed homes, but it could be a mercy, a blanket upon the mind and heart, a killing of pain. The book of sermons was closed and the bottle of gin unopened. Utterson heard the ticking of the long-case clock in his study and the beating of his own heart. All else was fog.

An urgent knocking came at the door. A hand of dread closed upon Utterson's heart: it would be Jekyll and Hyde again. A new claimant or some fresh crank. One madman, having allegedly duplicated Jekyll's formula, had drunk a bubbling phial of it on Utterson's doorstep; his convulsions climaxed not with physical transformation but with extensive dyspepsia.

Utterson's instinct was to shout, 'Away to the Devil with you!' and have done with it. The knocking ceased and was not renewed. Yet he had not shouted. No sooner did he wish not to be bothered than fog swallowed up his botherer. He would have thanked providence and allowed himself a rare smile but experience had taught him to be wary of answered prayers.

He stirred himself from his armchair and ventured out into the hallway. A packet lay upon the mat by the door. His caller had made a delivery. Again, this was not unusual. For every blockhead who assailed him in person, another half-dozen put inane proposals or wild theories in writing.

Bending down to pick up the packet, he felt his age in his back and limbs. Some pains were heightened, not dulled, by the fog. He carried the prize back into his study – his name was printed in an ill-formed hand on the label, misspelled 'Uterson' – and used his pen-knife to sever the pink string and break the sealing wax. Within brown paper, he found a rough oblong of wood with a sepia-tone photograph pasted to it. The wood was planed as a mount. He recognised a cheap, home-made species of framing. A child might fashion such a thing to preserve a favourite picture from the illustrated press. Yet the photograph was a studio-posed family portrait.

At first, he could see nothing extraordinary in the picture. A man in a sergeant's uniform stood erect by a seated woman in a wicker chair. She was gathering a boy in a sailor suit to her lap while an older girl knelt at her feet. The father's moustache was waxed to points and his eyes were fixed. The boy's hands were blurred because he had not kept them still throughout the exposure. The mother and daughter had identical, rather sad expressions.

From the style of the ladies' dress and the unfashionable stiffness of the pose, Utterson judged the portrait to be about fifteen or twenty years old. He turned the block over and found nothing of interest. There was no note of explanation in the packet and no photographer's card to indicate the studio in which the picture had been taken. He was puzzled, though something nagged at him, nastily.

He looked again at the photograph, wondering what message was being sent to him. He did not know this family.

The fog lifted and terror rushed in. One face was familiar, horribly so.

The boy, who seemed eight or nine, was a monkeyish lad, his cap twisted off-centre. There was nothing truly misshapen about the face or the limbs, but he gave an impression of irregularity, even deformity. His young face already reflected a malformation of his soul.

The boy in the picture was Edward Hyde. Mr Hyde as a child. But Jekyll was Hyde. There had never been a boy Hyde. And yet here he was.

E.H.

Two days after the arrival of the photograph, Utterson received in the morning post a note in the same hand – and with the same misspelling – as the address on the packet. It announced that the sender would call on the lawyer that afternoon, and was signed with the initials 'E. H.'

His caller was a small woman of perhaps thirty-five. He admitted her into his home and saw her in his study. She was obviously not entirely of the gentle classes, but neither was there anything in her dress or manner to suggest complete degradation. Her clothes were not new but were neat.

'My name is Ellen Hyde,' she announced.

Utterson looked at her face and saw the resemblance. He had once confronted Edward Hyde and tried to warn him away from his friend Jekyll. Ellen Hyde had the same eyes and the same undefinable cast to her features. She was not unattractive but there was something about her face, her very posture, that was hostile, sly, repulsive. Yet he could not but pity her.

'I am the girl in the photograph,' she said.

'And the boy . . . ?'

'Is my brother Ned.'

He had thought himself prepared for this but his knees gave him gyp. He had to sit down.

'Edward Hyde,' she underlined.

The woman stood over him, merciless. She was barely five feet tall, but there was a wiry strength to her. Her hands were habitually knotted into fists.

He felt obliged to explain.

'Attempts were made to uncover Hyde's past,' he insisted, 'by Inspector Newcomen of Scotland Yard and later by myself. We made every effort to trace any family.'

'I am all that's left of us. And I made every effort not to be found, Mr Utterson. You know what it means to be associated with Mr Hyde. Imagine what it means to bear his name. Not that it's the one he was born with. He took it from me, the devil. From my husband, rather. Then he took my husband. He was like that as a boy. If I had a toy, it had to be his to break. If I had a pet, it was for his pleasure to torment. My husband, the real Mr Hyde, is dead now. Just like Ned.'

He imagined the lad in the photograph breaking a doll or throttling a cat, building a sand-castle or whipping a spinning top. Even before reading Henry Jekyll's statement, Utterson had never considered what Edward Hyde might have been like as a child. Since the fantastic story had come out, he had believed Hyde to be a creature without a childhood. New-born in Jekyll's laboratory, instilled from his first consciousness with a singular and malign intellect, he had not grown and developed like others.

'And your parents?' he prompted.

He handed her the photograph, which she looked at and slipped into a pocket.

'Father died months after this was taken,' she said. 'In India, of some disease. Mother was never the same. It wasn't as if he'd been killed in a war. Then there'd have been medals and a pension. Some disgraceful thing caught from a native girl fetched him away. Or maybe something he had all along, that he bequeathed to us all. Mother . . . well, I needn't say how it took her, or where Ned and me were left. I sometimes think it might have been best to be born in the depths rather than descend to them. We always had the memory, you see, of how things had been, and knew there was a better life than the one we were reduced to.'

'You have my deepest sympathy, Mrs Hyde.'

The woman grimaced as if to laugh bitterly, then accepted his sentiment.

'It's no use blaming anyone or anything, Mr Utterson. We have all made of ourselves what we would. Plenty have gone down Ned's road with the encouragement of a father and the love of a mother. It doesn't matter whether it was in his nature or he was driven to it. It was always a toss-up as to whether he would end up on the gallows for some other poor devil, or whether the other poor devil would end up on the gallows for him.'

Utterson was puzzled, almost beyond enduring. A pain in his head joined those in his limbs.

'Mrs Hyde, I can't put this all together. You must appreciate how difficult this has been for me, to learn of my good friend Henry Jekyll that he was involved in such a bizarre affair, that he was *transformed* somehow into this Hyde. And now, you come forward, with the revelation that there was an *original* Mr Hyde, an individual independent from Dr Jekyll. Are you suggesting your brother was the model for what Jekyll became? Did Jekyll's Hyde apprentice himself to your Ned, perhaps murder and replace him?'

'I read what that man Lanyon wrote and the confession Jekyll left. I can't account for what either of those *gentlemen*' – she bit down on the word – 'might have meant. But there was only one Ned I know of, and the world is well quit of him. His very name has justly become a byword for the beast in man. The illustrated papers always depict him as a monster, as a fanged human ape in fancy clothes that don't fit. He was a monster all right, just not the sort you read about in penny dreadfuls. Somehow, people like it when a person is all good or all bad. They don't want to hear about reasons. Jekyll-and-Hyde mixes all that up but still doesn't make it any clearer. If *anyone* was all bad, it was Ned. But he had a hard life and he was always afraid. He wasn't just the fiend in the fog. He was a frightened man, a *little* man. He hurt people because he had been hurt. He was weak and without power, so he looked for those weaker than himself to be master over. If he hadn't done the things he did, you'd be sorry for him.'

Utterson recalled Enfield's description of Hyde after the trampling of the child, a small man seized by an angry mob, 'with a kind of black, sneering coolness – frightened, too, I could see that – but carrying it off, sir, really like Satan'. Utterson had found Hyde pale and dwarfish, giving the

19

impression of deformity without any nameable malformation, with a displeasing smile and a bearing that was a murderous mixture of timidity and boldness. In retrospect, the worst of Hyde was his insignificance; he seemed a man without even the courage of his vices, the sort of small boy who acts the bully and then hides behind tears. Only when he bludgeoned a Member of Parliament did anyone really take notice of him.

'But I'm not sorry for him,' Ellen Hyde continued. 'And I'm not sorry for myself, either.'

Utterson saw the woman's determination, and recognised in it a sibling to Hyde's fixed nature. He had no conception of Ellen Hyde's morals or behaviour, no idea whether she earned her keep as the worst harlot in Soho or the most angelic nurse in a charity hospital. Yet he discerned a reflection of her brother in the eyes, in the set of the shoulders, the unconscious darting of her tongue, the movements of her large hands. Elements of the likeness were evident even in the photograph, not only in the children but in the parents.

'You will forgive me my puzzlement and must allow that you have further muddied waters which were far from clear in the beginning. Of the many things I do not understand, the most paramount is to do not with Mr Hyde but with yourself. Mrs Hyde, what service may I perform for you?'

She smiled and for a moment the evil of Edward Hyde burned fully in her eyes. Except it wasn't evil, really. Just slyness.

'Now we come to it,' she said. 'You are the executor of Dr Jekyll's estate. I know what that means because I have taken pains to find out.'

'Indeed. There are many things not yet settled.'

'It is my understanding that Dr Jekyll left everything to my brother. What was the phrase, "in the event . . ."?'

'". . . of my death or disappearance or unexplained absence". It is an unusual clause.'

Ellen Hyde extended a bony finger, making a point.

'My brother was found dead in Jekyll's laboratory, *after Dr*

20

Jekyll's disappearance. I am my brother's only living relative. When he died, he should have inherited Jekyll's fortune. Now, that money is due to me.'

Utterson could not have been more surprised if Ellen Hyde had kissed him. In an instant, he wondered why he had not seen this coming. The case had always been so wrapped up with the weird that he had quite forgotten that, at bottom, it was about money.

Without mirth, he barked laughter.

Ellen Hyde glared death at him.

'And what do you find so amusing, Mr Utterson?'

'It is time I retired,' he said, shutting off his laughter as if it were a flowing tap. 'That I could have been so taken in. In the case of Jekyll and Hyde, we are so desperate for an *explanation*. Not just a solution, but an explanation. It was so hard to accept the truth when it came out that you were able to open it all up again, to unpick all the answers and throw me back to all the questions. And yet, in the end, you overplayed your hand. You are quite the most entertaining of the many claimants, Mrs Hyde. Is that indeed your name? I rather think it might be. Your story has touched my flinty old heart and darts in and out of the established facts so cunningly that I admit I am shaken by it, but its conclusion undoes all the good work. You ask for money.'

'Only what is legally mine.'

'Not necessarily. Even if you are who you say you are and bear the relationship to Edward Hyde that you claim, your entitlement to the Jekyll estate is moot. Quite apart from the existence of a later though equally disputable will in which I am myself the sole legatee, the fortune was to go to Hyde only if Jekyll's disappearance exceeded three calendar months. Jekyll was seen only days before the time of Hyde's death. Hyde was dead long before he could have inherited the estate and with him died any claim you might have made.'

'Another lawyer may disagree with you.'

'Perhaps. But most judges would not.'

21

Ellen Hyde left Utterson's house. Only now did he allow himself a glass of gin. He wished fervently never again to hear the names of Jekyll and Hyde but knew that was in vain. Whether or not he was ever bothered by the woman again, she had re-opened the case. It would have to be raked over and with each new examination the business became more painful.

The Broken Key

One of the sadnesses brought into Utterson's life by the case of Jekyll and Hyde was the curtailment of the weekly rambles he had been wont to take with his cousin, the man-about-town Enfield. Neither had called a halt to their meetings but both were jarred out of their orbits by their parts in the now-famous story. He felt Enfield rather resented being roped into the tale: as a witness to Hyde's first recorded crime, the trampling of the girl. As an indication of a connection between the good doctor and the disreputable villain, Enfield's testimony was the beginning of the thread that had led to the revelation that they were one and the same.

Since publication of the truth, Enfield had been travelling abroad. Utterson knew his cousin had lately returned from the South Seas and reopened his London house. He had intended to make overtures towards the resumption of their association as soon as he was himself free of the entanglements of Jekyll and Hyde. Ellen Hyde having forced his hand, he found himself on Enfield's front steps. A footman opened the door and admitted him into a warm, well-lit hallway.

'Why, it's Gabriel Utterson,' declared Enfield, from the landing above. 'Good old Utterson come to call. This is a cause for celebration.'

Enfield's reception was warm and sincere and made Utterson sorry he had stayed away. His cousin clapped him on the shoulders and dragged him into a comfortably appointed den. The walls were liberally decorated with exotic fetishes and other souvenirs of Enfield's voyages.

Wine was poured and toasts drunk.

'I see at once that something troubles you, Utterson,' said Enfield. 'It is Jekyll and Hyde again, isn't it? Curse their memory. Or should it be his memory?'

'I can keep nothing from you, Enfield.'

Utterson told his cousin of his meeting with Ellen Hyde and of her claim to a prior relationship with Edward Hyde.

'There was a photograph, you say? I've heard tell they can play tricks with plates and exposures.'

It was not Utterson's impression that the family portrait was manufactured from whole cloth, but it was reassuring to hear Enfield's opinion that it might have been.

'The rummest thing is that your caller posed as Hyde's sister. If she'd presented herself as his wife, she could have made her claim without asking you to discredit everything we've learned of Jekyll's double life. Then again, who'd have married Hyde? I knew at once he was a fellow with no use for women. You come across chaps like that from time to time. In the islands, all sorts of degenerates and outcasts gather. They pester the native youths.'

Utterson was disturbed by Enfield's line of thinking. It was, apart from its distastefulness, a distraction.

'I no longer know what to think,' Utterson confided. 'When I read what Lanyon and Jekyll wrote, I didn't believe it. Who *could* believe something like that? I'm not a scientist, but it seemed impossible that a drug could change one man into another, twist his soul from the good to the bad. Then, with the evidence before me, I was forced to believe. All questions, every aspect of the mystery, were answered. If Jekyll was Hyde, it made sense. Now if Jekyll and Hyde were two separate people, mystery returns like the tide crashing over a pebble beach.'

Enfield refilled Utterson's glass and lit a long pipe with a coal from the fire.

'You're a good lawyer, Utterson. Look to the evidence, argue the case, pick it apart. Consider the clues: what proof do you have to support Jekyll's confession?'

'Many minor matters and one very great one. To state the obvious, no one has come forward to testify that they saw Henry Jekyll and Edward Hyde at the same time. The first clue that was presented was that Jekyll showed me a letter which purported to be from Hyde. Questioning Poole, the butler, I later discovered this could not, as Jekyll had told me, have been

24

delivered to him by special messenger. Furthermore, Mr Guest, my head clerk and an expert in these matters, believed the letter to be the work of Jekyll himself, disguising his hand.'

'So we think Jekyll wrote a letter, pretending to be Hyde,' Enfield said, puffing on his pipe. 'At the time, your assumption was that Henry Jekyll was forging for a murderer, trying to throw the police off the track by making it seem as if Hyde had fled the country. That might still be the case, if there was some other tie between them – blackmail, as I at first assumed – without needing to involve fabulous potions or miraculous transformations.'

'Indeed,' Utterson said. 'Other circumstances could be open to similar explanation. The evidence for the transformation comes to us in Jekyll's statement, which is at least partially corroborated by a log-book of his experiments. The book certainly concerns a series of trials with a drug of his own devising, and the desperate attempts later made to reduplicate the impurity that led to his first successes. The most convincing corroboration, however, is the statement left by Dr Lanyon.'

'Ah yes, the fellow who *saw* Hyde turn into Jekyll.'

'That is correct. Lanyon was Jekyll's old mentor, before breaking with him after a quarrel which, as Lanyon had it, "would have estranged Damon and Pythias". Hyde, wanted for murder, barged into Lanyon's house with a note from Jekyll, demanding Lanyon secure from Jekyll's laboratory the ingredients for a potion. Hyde mixed up the solution in Lanyon's presence and drank it. Lanyon says Hyde turned into Jekyll before his eyes and swore him to silence. Lanyon left a memoir of this incident, but never spoke of it. Three weeks later, he was dead of shock.'

'I suppose Jekyll or Hyde couldn't have forged Lanyon's narrative?'

Utterson considered the suggestion. 'The document, marked for my attention alone and to be read only after the death or disappearance of Dr Jekyll, was included with other papers in Lanyon's hand and passed to me upon his death. The same Mr

Guest who adjudged Hyde's letter to be the work of Jekyll cast an eye over the narrative and declared it to be in the hand of Hastie Lanyon. Besides, it was entrusted to me – though not of course opened – before I came into possession of the Jekyll statement which corroborates its account of that incident and enlarges upon its circumstances, giving a full explanation not only of Hyde's fatal visit to Lanyon but of the whole course of experimentation that led Jekyll to compound his drug and become addicted to its effects.'

Enfield was thoughtful. 'Even so,' he rejoined, 'you've only the word of two dead men. They can't go into a court and be cross-examined. Could Lanyon and Jekyll have cooked the whole thing up between them?'

'It is my judgement that the estrangement between them was genuine. It was, as you know, awkward for me to be so close professionally and personally to them both during the period of their virulent quarrel. I always had the sense of being excluded on the grounds that they were explorers in a country I could never visit. Their conversations were full of queer leaps and ellipses a layman like myself could never follow. They were like a father and son or an old married couple who have their own private history and language. This mystery also was something that seemed settled by the revelation of Jekyll's experiments. I had thought that at last I understood what it was they could never discuss when I was there, what secret passions they shared. The root of their quarrel was Lanyon's inflexibility in the face of Jekyll's unwise daring, his devotion to scientific truth, to the demonstrable. It would have been completely out of character for him to collaborate in a hoax, no matter what the reason for it.'

'Don't you see, Utterson: all you've proved is that Lanyon believed what you came to believe when you read Jekyll's statement, what we've all come to believe. Damn it, man, forget belief; give me evidence. What makes *you* so sure Jekyll was Hyde?'

The comfortable warmth of Enfield's den receded as a fog of

memory drifted in, dimming the gaslight, throwing into relief the hideous faces of carved idols that snarled like Edward Hyde. Sharksteeth eyes glittered like those of Ellen Hyde. Utterson was taken back to the end of it all, when it seemed Jekyll was held hostage within his laboratory by Hyde. With Poole, the butler, and Bradshaw, the footman, Utterson had broached the door and found Hyde still twitching but dead, apparently poisoned by his own hand, shrouded in Jekyll's clothes, leaving behind Jekyll's confession.

'Before I read that document, my fear was that Hyde had murdered Jekyll before ending his own life,' Utterson said. 'We searched for a body or a grave but found neither. Then, hoping that Jekyll had escaped his tormentor and lived still, we tried to find another way out. As you know, we found none. The only other door to the laboratory was locked, and curtained over with cobwebs. There was undisturbed dust and filth everywhere, around the windows, covering every possible place of concealment. Then, I read Jekyll's statement, and all seemed clear.'

'Hyde could not have killed Jekyll and concealed his body, or thrown him out of the laboratory?'

Utterson shook his head. 'The most important item of evidence was the broken key. By his own account, Jekyll tried to banish Hyde from his life. He broke the key to the back door – through which Hyde was wont to come and go – shutting his other half out of his house. This symbolic rejection did not keep Hyde down for long, but it did in the end serve to trap him in the laboratory. At the conclusion of his statement, Jekyll asks, "Will Hyde die upon the scaffold, or will he find courage to release himself at the last moment?" My assumption is that Jekyll carried the thought of suicide through the transformation. Hyde took Jekyll's last advice and poisoned himself.'

'Did the doctor leave the poison out for his other self? Like the cat's milk?'

Utterson thought of it, imagined the final metamorphosis.

Hyde must have been desperate again, the little man trapped but with his protector gone. Was it courage or cowardice that drove him to the poison?

'It is definite that Jekyll went into his laboratory and that Hyde was found dead there,' said Utterson, repressing a chill. 'If Jekyll was not Hyde, the question would remain: where is he, alive or dead? The only solution to this, which we must consider a "locked-room mystery", is that Jekyll and Hyde were one. Jekyll's statement confirms this.'

'And so your mystery is solved again?' asked Enfield.

'In my mind, yes,' said Utterson. 'But this affair goes beyond the reach of my mind. In the light of day, we know Jekyll was Hyde, but in the dark of night, with the fog rising around everything, the mystery stands.'

'Talk is all very well, Utterson, but we need action. We must visit the scene of the crime. You still have the keys to Jekyll's house?'

It was what he had been expecting, and dreading. His cousin was right. They would have to go back to the place where Jekyll had lived and Hyde died.

The House of Dr Jekyll

Utterson and Enfield walked again, not with the aimlessness of their former rambles but with purpose. Their course took them through the by-street where Enfield had first encountered Edward Hyde. The infamous back door was nailed shut: Utterson had commissioned the job himself, to keep the curious and the morbid from breaking in. A fearful obscenity was chalked upon the door, but a single red rose had been laid on the step as if on a grave. Those were the tributes rightfully earned by the odious Mr Hyde and the sainted Dr Jekyll. Or was the rose intended – by Ellen, perhaps – for the monster and the oath for the good doctor?

'You recall the last time we passed this way?' prompted Utterson. 'Not when you told me the story of the child, but later.'

Enfield nodded. He took a draught of whisky from a flask, cursorily offering it to Utterson for his refusal.

'We saw Jekyll at his window,' Enfield said. 'He was on the point of inviting us in when something struck him and he withdrew suddenly.'

Utterson, stepping out of character, took the flask and – to his cousin's surprise – indulged in a healthy swallow. The liquor was a fire in his throat, but didn't keep out the chill of the fog.

'I've often dwelled upon that moment. It was the last time I saw the face of Henry Jekyll. It seems we narrowly avoided witnessing one of his transformations. The seizure which made him bar us from his house was the beginning of the frightful metamorphosis.'

Enfield took the flask back. The two men emerged from the side-street and stood before the impressive frontage of Dr Jekyll's mansion. Beside the door was a shining brass plate, announcing 'Dr Henry Jekyll, M.D., D.C.L., LL.D., F.R.S., &c.' Some of the upper windows were broken. The place had stood empty since the disbanding of Jekyll's household.

Faithful Poole was retired on the small legacy left by his master and the others gone to fresh situations.

Utterson took out the ring of keys. As executor, it was his duty to take care of the house until the estate was settled. He had already arranged for the repair of one set of windows, and was now irritated that more had been broken. This must be the district's haunted house, he thought, the lair of the monster. It would be a place of fascination and horror for children, and for not a few who should be more sensible.

'Are we going in?' ventured Enfield, not quite managing to sound intrepid.

Utterson found the long key to the front door and turned it in the lock. The gas was shut off, so it was necessary to hunt around by the light of a lucifer for a candle left in the hallway. He had himself placed the candle there, having once before been required to be in the house after dark to pay the glazier. The candle was not where he had thought it would be, but Enfield discovered it and touched a flame to the wick.

'That's odd,' Enfield said, looking down at the doormat.

'What?'

'When I opened up my house after returning from abroad, I had to wade through a sea of circulars and letters piled up in the hallway.'

Utterson proceeded down the hallway. If answer there was to the case, it would be found here.

The two men passed through the house and, unlocking more doors, crossed the dismal courtyard to the building at the rear of the mansion that had served Jekyll as a laboratory and Hyde as a last redoubt. The door hung slightly ajar, its lock burst the night Hyde died. Utterson pushed the door open, and they stepped into the laboratory.

Enfield whistled. Utterson realised his cousin had never been here before.

Candlelight was reflected in dozens of glass surfaces. Cases of instruments lined the walls, complex arrangements of retorts and tubes stood on the benches and a full-length cheval glass was erected in a frame in the middle of the large room. Utterson remembered Hyde, dead but writhing at the foot of the mirror. His position on the floor was still clearly marked by a stained rug that had been disturbed by his death throes. Here, the monster had turned upon himself. Here, Utterson had thought, the monster was born.

Enfield was taken with the cheval glass, which was angled so that anyone laid out on a divan could study his own reflection. He held up the candle and looked at himself. Shadows moved on his face, lending his features strange expressions.

'When he changed, he observed the process?' Enfield ventured.

'That's what we assumed,' Utterson agreed. 'Poole said the glass "had seen some strange things".'

'Maybe Jekyll liked looking at himself. He had more than a touch of vanity, wouldn't you say? D'you remember that string of degrees trailed after his name on the plate outside? Even on his calling cards? That "et cetera" tells a lot. And Hyde was full of himself, too. That sort always is. Like a woman, obsessed with looks, and not averse to a spot of paint and powder.'

They came at last to Jekyll's desk, where his full statement had been left for Utterson, along with a will cutting out Edward Hyde and making Utterson himself beneficiary of the estate. It had not proved valid and Utterson could not say he was sorry: he had no need of a fortune, and the temporary custodianship of this house was burden enough without the strain of actual ownership.

'This is where you found it? Jekyll's story?'

'Indeed.'

Enfield held the light over the desk. Everything was neat and tidy. There wasn't even any dust. Utterson had arranged for the house to be cleaned, but had neglected the laboratory. Madame Tussaud's had made an offer for the contents, which he had rejected out of hand.

Utterson had a crawling feeling. Someone must have been here.

'Supposing your lady caller' – Utterson blushed at Enfield's allusion to Ellen Hyde – 'to be telling the truth, previous searches of this place have missed something. Either Jekyll is still here, or there is some way of escape. The doctor is dead or fled.'

'We made an extensive search. Every inch was gone over, as we looked for loose flagstones, or a grave.'

'Could Hyde have killed Jekyll and disposed of him completely? Dissolved the corpse in acid, perhaps?'

'No acid was found. And no evidence of such butchery.'

'You considered the floor. What about the ceiling?'

'The attic cabinet above the laboratory is windowless. There is no possible egress through it.'

'Not the roof, the ceiling. I scent an old tiger-hunter's trick. You don't need an escape hatch to pull off a locked-room mystery if you can contrive a place of perfect concealment. If Jekyll is dead, he might be there still. If he is fled, he would merely have had to *hide* and emerge later when you had all departed.'

Enfield raised the candle. The laboratory was a high-ceilinged space. A network of pipes and gas-jets had lit it from above. These cast a grid-like shadow on the painted ceiling. It was not hard to imagine Hyde swinging from the pipes like a monkey, as a servant had described him.

'Take the candle a moment,' Enfield said.

Utterson did so.

'Now leave the laboratory and come back.'

Irritated by his cousin's frivolity, which betokened a childish streak he had often found as irksome as it was endearing, Utterson complied with Enfield's request. He stepped out into the courtyard, where thick fog pooled waist-deep and misty strands spiralled upwards in a draught, and closed the laboratory door behind him. After a few moments, he turned round and opened the door again, crossing the threshold.

Enfield was gone. Utterson felt no panic, no terror. His cousin had seen through the trick and duplicated it. He would bound back in again soon, having slipped out somehow to the street. Utterson turned, expecting Enfield to make his way round the house and in through the front door.

He looked up at the ceiling. That was where Enfield had found the clue.

A minute or so passed. Enfield did not return. Utterson had a pricking of irritation. His cousin was showing off more than was seemly, prolonging the moment of his triumph.

Utterson peered again up beyond the network of gas-jets. The shadows on the ceiling were strange, swelling like the fog. There was a straining sound.

The ceiling cracked open and a heavy, loose bundle fell on to him. The candle-flame was snuffed and complete darkness obtained within the laboratory.

Utterson lay under the dead-weight of a man.

There were quick footsteps and a boot trod on one of his hands. He heard the door open. Fog and the faintest traces of light crept in.

He threw off the weight of the warm body and took out his lucifers. He struck one; its flare showed him the red, swollen face of Richard Enfield.

He felt his cousin's neck and found a pulse. Enfield had been throttled to unconsciousness but still lived.

Hyde was back, to plague the memory of Henry Jekyll.

Utterson found the candle and lit it again. His shoulders were shaking but he forced his hands to be steady. He knew another had been in the laboratory, concealed in the bolt-hole Enfield had spotted. When Enfield clambered up to the ceiling and discovered the trapdoor – which Utterson now saw was hanging down like an idiot's tongue – the interloper assaulted him and kept him close. Only their shared weight exploded the hiding-place.

Along with footsteps, Utterson had heard a rustle of skirts. He knew who had been in the dark with them, who had trodden on his hand.

It always came back to Hyde. This time, it was the sister.

Enfield coughed and spluttered out of his swoon. He tried to sit up.

'Some devil was lying in wait,' he got out. 'Some long-fingered devil.'

'You've had a near thing,' Utterson said. 'I was afraid you'd gone the way of Sir Danvers Carew.'

He set the candle down on Jekyll's desk and a talon scraped his spine. In the exact spot where he had found the envelope containing Dr Jekyll's Full Statement of the Case lay an identical packet. On it, in a familiar hand, was written his own name.

The last envelope had promised a solution but left only more mystification. What would this contain? Utterson turned it over in his hands. Would it be best to touch its corner to the candle-flame and let its contents burn unread? He knew he could never take that measure.

Whatever was within, he must know.

Henry Jekyll's Further Statement of the Case

I ask you to consider again the opening words of my original statement:

'I was born in the year 18—— to a large fortune, endowed besides with excellent parts, inclined by nature to industry, fond of the respect of the wise and the good among my fellow-men, and thus, as might have been supposed, with every guarantee of an honourable and distinguished future. And indeed, the worst of my faults was a certain impatient gaiety of disposition, such as has made the happiness of many, but such as I found it hard to reconcile with my imperious desire to carry my head high, and wear a more than commonly grave countenance before the public. Hence it came about that I concealed my pleasures; and that when I reached years of reflection, and began to look around me, and take stock of my progress and position in the world, I stood already committed to a profound duplicity of life. Many a man would have even blazoned such irregularities as I was guilty of; but from the high views that I had set before me, I regarded and hid them with an almost morbid sense of shame. It was thus rather the exacting nature of my aspirations, than any particular degradation in my faults, that made me what I was, and with even a deeper trench than in the majority of men, severed in me those provinces of good and ill which divide and compound man's dual nature.'

Further, let me draw your attention to the phrase 'a certain gaiety of disposition'. Men like myself often wink at their audiences, flirting with revelation but stopping just short of the outright declaration of our nature. It is a harmless trait, even endearing. However, the time for such flirtation is ended, and I wish in this statement finally to set the record straight. I am well aware that what I have to say of my life – though far less outlandish than the improbable fiction I was forced in haste to compose – will not be publishable. Many will accuse me of hypocrisy in the life I have led and the actions I have taken, but ask yourselves: what manner of society is it that will concede the possibility of one man transforming entirely into another through the agency of a magic potion, but shuts minds to the actuality of love, in the fullest senses of the word, between one man and another?

I loved Edward Hyde. I love him still.

I have never had any use for women. For many years, I was forced to compound the duality of my life with a further duality. While I was for decades friend and companion to my old mentor Hastie Lanyon, physical intimacies between us were unsatisfactory to my tastes. Lanyon introduced me to my nature, opened for me the book of uranian desires, but was a timid explorer of his own potential. From an early age, as I suggested in the statement quoted above, I have searched elsewhere for a form of love that can be purchased in any city in the world. There are houses in London, districts even, that cater to the tastes of men like myself.

It is not my purpose to justify my predilections, but experience has taught me that they are shared by many. Members of Parliament, Ministers of Religion, Captains of Industry, Officers of the Armed Forces. Our secret history is written between the chapters of the lives of the great and the good. Even monarchs have not been immune from the lusts that sparked – and spark still – in my heart.

When I first met Hyde, singling him out from a knot of gay loiterers in Piccadilly and exchanging a few paltry coins for his favours, I was well past youth. I stood towards the end of the middle of my life having experienced a variety of physical forms of love, but my heart was essentially untouched. I had once thought I could love Lanyon, but my mentor's crankiness, his periods of desperate clinging, had become as irksome to me as the nagging of many a cold wife is to her husband.

Hyde did not return to his fellows. Having first bought him – cheaply – I kept him. He was the first of his kind I allowed into my home, though I kept him closeted in the cabinet above my laboratory out of sight of the servants. Later I gave instructions to my butler, Poole, that my friend and benefactor was in my absence to be obeyed as if he were myself. Hyde took a delight in bossing my servants; their bitter resentment of taking orders from so low a person accounts for descriptions they have left of him as less than human and worse than a brute. It was a quirk of our relationship that we took care never to be seen in each other's company – Hyde even establishing an address in Soho separate from my own house – and excluded the whole world from our intimacies.

How could I love Hyde? Reports of his person and character suggest him to be a creature beyond the reach of gentle emotion. I concede that what the world knows of Edward Hyde is not distorted. He was cruel, twisted inside, capricious, petty, dishonest, common. Yet, from the first I caught his glittering eye and selected him from a cluster of far prettier fellows, he was inside my heart like a worm in an apple. Gentle emotion could not contain him, but our love was not gentle: it was a violent need, a storm of possession, a fervid hunger that would not be satisfied.

For his part, Hyde returned my love. How could he not, to be taken from the streets and set up in a flat, to be coddled and dressed like a doll, to be a part of the life of the great Dr Henry Jekyll? He loved to wear my clothes, not minding how loose they were on him, just as he loved to bark orders at my servants or gamble and drink away my money.

Lanyon, of course, quarrelled with me over Hyde and shut me out of his life, babbling of Damon and Pythias. He blustered that I would be hurt by Hyde as he had been hurt by me, and that I would crawl back into his house a ruin. Hyde and I laughed when I reported the old fool's words. Others would never understand.

In love, it is impossible to tell master from slave. I was vulnerable, for I had much to lose from exposure; throughout everything, my position was of almost paramount importance to me. Yet Hyde too was on perilous ground; he had in the distant past suffered a fall from grace and, having found security in my person as much as my fortune, was terrified of its loss.

We were both cruel. Hyde would threaten to leave me. I would threaten to cast him out. Then our quarrels – which often extended to exchanges of blows – would become caresses, and we would redouble our love, our conjoined search for physical expression of what was in our hearts.

There were periods of remorse. I would turn to books of religion or good works as a way not of assuaging guilt over my nature or my love, but of filling the void where I had been taught – by Lanyon, for instance – that guilt should be. The paradox was that I was ashamed of not being ashamed. At these times, Hyde would abandon me for his Soho rooms and try to excite my jealousy by affecting an interest in others.

Hyde was used to bad treatment. His body was marked with the scars of the lash. His peculiar gait, which witnesses have remarked upon, was the result of bones broken and ill set by a band of drunken sailors who once abducted him and used him for rough pleasures over the space of three days. He bore rope-burns on his wrists from this ordeal, which varied in its titillating particulars with each retelling.

The worst I could do to Hyde was laugh at him. I discovered this early in our association and was unable to refrain from the joy of this especial torment. Was he not, after all, ridiculous? With my fine clothes flopping over his hands and boots, he looked like an organ grinder's monkey dressed up. His ignorance could not but be amusing to one with my education; each mispronounced word tickled my humour, each defence of something he mistakenly understood to be true – that Asia was in Egypt, Scotland over the sea, the bumblebee a small bird – was a prompt to cruel hilarity. When I laughed at him, he became stone-faced, indignant, and stuck by his doomed position, until I ended the game with a hungry kiss.

The walls of our world were the walls of the laboratory. I gave Hyde a key to the back-door, an expression he found apt, and he would always return. The world knows of the night he barged in, terrified, and demanded money to settle an account with the family of some street drab he had knocked over. He told me the child had offered to lift her skirts for him for a penny and that he had trampled her in instinctive disgust. I do not necessarily believe that, nor does the girl's character excuse her treatment. It is my belief that Hyde was vicious, in this instance, because he saw in the girl his own face, saw the wretchedness from which he had so lately come and to which he could so easily be forced to return.

There was never an idyll for us. Our love was not an oasis but a jungle. Together we explored, deliberately throwing ourselves into the lairs of dangerous beasts. The slowness that had come over me in my middle years fell away, and I was as enthusiastic as my young adventurer. He was physically smaller than I, and I could always wrestle him to the mat. I came to adore his sobs of pain and joy as he thrust his face against the pillow, tearing the cover with his stubby teeth, while I was his master and lover and tormentor.

Yet my years weighed me down. After our exertions, Hyde was frisky and flushed, eager to take to the streets, while I was drained and exhausted, heart pounding like a hammer against an anvil. Once or twice, I was physically incapable of the basic necessity of the act of love. Hyde seized mercilessly on my failure, pawing and jeering at my limpness, grinning like a baboon.

Other men, like Lanyon, might have accepted. But I am a medical doctor, a researcher, a chemist. I knew there were drugs which could help me, would help us. In my position, I had access to many substances unknown even in the opium dens of Limehouse. We experimented with compounds of many different elements. More than once, we were almost poisoned and spent a night in each other's arms, retching. But still we persisted, delighted with our successes.

Eventually, we found our perfect potion.

We shared it. I would take a mouthful, swallow a little, and pass it into Hyde's mouth through a deep kiss. Under the influence of this tonic, we were invincible and tireless, free of all physical and moral restraints. The effects were as much mental as physical, inducing first a dreamlike period of hallucination then a sudden vivid clarity of the senses accompanied by overpowering urges and the ability to act upon them. I installed a large looking-glass in the laboratory, so we could look upon our reflections as we became one two-faced creature. It seemed to me that in the act of love we became a single being, a giant pulsating heart.

Our exertions were acrobatic and cacophonous enough on one occasion to wake the household. In my delirium, I discerned Poole's tapping at the laboratory door. We had smashed glasses and given vent to screams of passion. As my servant pestered us, we were naked together, hanging like copulating apes from the gas-pipes. I do not remember which of us ordered the fool away but his interruption was a gnat-bite soon forgotten.

Of course, we became slaves to this drug of my devising. A shared need is a terrible thing. Each was affected in his own way and would recover at a different time. To come to and find Hyde still under the influence was to feel cast out from Eden and to be possessed by a desire to return. And returning was a simple matter of a little mixing and heating. At times, Hyde pleaded with me to make up a new batch of our delight – for it was beyond his talents to do so – and I would withhold acceding to his needs until he had abased himself. At others, I would snap out of a daze filled with panic that he had died of the effects of the drug, and he would titter at me like a girl, gnawing at my nerves. In a rare moment of mutual clarity, he forced me to show him exactly how to mix up the potion, and I tutored him in its making. For an instant, I saw the native intelligence in him that had been dulled by the life he had led, and a new strain of love, sentiment tinged with pity, joined the rapturous addiction that gripped my brain.

In this period, when we were equals, I wrote Hyde into my will. On occasion, he showed himself to my servants. My acquaintances Enfield and Utterson encountered him, and Utterson warned me against him. I listened to reason, for I was never so blind as to think my monster any species of angel, but could not break free of my need. Hyde became more devoted, more clinging, more of a pest. I tried to ration our sessions with the drug, but vows of abstinence never lasted, as one or other of us would break down.

Once, Hyde tried without my assistance to mix the potion. He nearly died, but did not learn his lesson.

The laboratory that had been our world became our prison. In trances or crazes, we only had each other. Eventually, one night in October, one or other of us suggested we venture out into the city to see the metropolis with new eyes. The fog was very beautiful and in it all things were possible.

A maidservant was witness to the unfortunate event. That she did not see my part in it was due to the fact that I was leaning in a daze against the wall directly below her window, a spectator though in some sense also a director.

We found ourselves in a spot Hyde knew from his previous life and to the spot came a man he knew well, Sir Danvers Carew, M. P. You recall the maid's description of Carew as 'an aged and beautiful gentleman with white hair' and may be interested to know that Carew's beauty was not altogether the gift of nature but had been augmented by feminine tricks.

Our shared indulgence in the drug was not an excuse for our actions. As I said in my earlier statement, the drug set free what was always inside us, let loose a part of our nature. Carew approached us and ventured a proposition. It strikes me as horribly funny that the servant, who admitted to being 'romantically given', described his face as he spoke words she could not hear as seeming 'to breathe such an innocent and old-world kindness of disposition, yet with something high, too, as of a well-founded self-content'. Hyde and I were of course beyond moral disgust at Carew's suggestion, but he was an intruder into our haze. Suddenly his presence seemed the spur for a final test of Hyde's devotion.

I told Hyde to kill Carew. As the maid said, 'The old gentleman took a step back, with the air of one very much surprised
and a trifle hurt; and at that Mr Hyde broke out of all bounds,
and clubbed him to the earth. And next moment, with ape-like
fury, he was trampling his victim under foot, and hailing down
a storm of blows, under which the bones were audibly
shattered and the body jumped upon the roadway.' Then,
unknown to us, the maid – our audience – fainted dead away.
She did not see Hyde hand me my own stick to finish the job.
It was my blows which snapped the stout cane and caved in the
old queen's skull. We were exultant in our shared adventure
and returned to my laboratory, heedless of all consequence, to
renew our caresses. Sticky with Carew's blood, we rutted until
insensibility came over us.

While we slept, the body was discovered and the identity of
the murderer became generally known. The maid recognised
Hyde as an occasional visitor to the house in which she was in
service; which calls into question the nature of the house in
which she was employed and perhaps clarifies precisely what
she meant by 'romantically given'. Just as we had no idea there
had been a witness to our exploit, it was no contrivance of
mine that Hyde should take the blame for our shared crime.
When I learned of the circumstances and communicated them,
Hyde – who seemed peculiarly to be suffering spasms of
remorse from which I was myself immune – immediately
informed me he had no intention of hanging alone and would,
if cornered, do his best to rope me in on the gallows.

'Who would believe you?' I asked him.

He was struck silent and terrified. It might have been the
after-effects of the drug, but suddenly he was pathetic again,
nagged by a realisation that he alone of all the world was
sufficiently wretched to suffer for his crimes while one as
respected as I would naturally be allowed free. If the maid had
actually seen me take my cane to Carew's head, she would not
have believed it. Everyone so wanted Jekyll to be a saint and
Hyde to be a monster that any evidence to the contrary would

simply not be credited.

He became almost comatose with panic.

When Utterson came to my doorstep, I was obliged to fob him off with a letter of my own writing – in a disguised hand – that purported to be from my 'friend and benefactor' Hyde, claiming to have fled the country. It was not the first time I had written something for him. At the time we met, he was almost a complete illiterate though he had a surprising talent for sketching. To amuse myself, I had taught him the alphabet but the only words he was disposed to set down were the obscenities he was wont, in the throes of a drug-fit, to scrawl in my books of theology.

Hyde then became my charge and prisoner. Having broken his key to the back-door, it was a simple matter to secrete him in the cabinet above my laboratory. At this time, we collaborated on the construction of a priest's hole to be used in the event of a thorough search. A false section of ceiling was put up, creating a space into which a small body could be crammed – when it came to be used, my longer limbs were confined uncomfortably – for an hour or two.

Months passed. I concluded the programme of experiments and shut the book on our drug. There was no more to be learned from it. Hyde squealed and protested but I locked away the ingredients. He, far more than I, felt the murderous tug of need as we withdrew from the addiction. Yet he was terrified, far more than I, of the monster the drug had made of him.

I endeavoured to order my life. It seemed that just as I no longer needed the drug, I no longer needed Hyde. It was not that I cared any the less for him, but the first burning of our love had run its course. Had he not been an obligation, I might have cut him loose.

He was a thorny problem. In concealment, he became clinging. As the only soul he saw, I became his master and keeper. He desired me in a way I no longer desired him. He made himself available to me with the sickening devotion of a small dog. He wheedled, trying always to keep on my right side. That in him which had been defiant and cruel and needling was stifled. With this change, I found he became as repulsive to me as to the rest of the world.

When he conceived his project, I misunderstood it entirely. I thought it an indulgence to pass the time, a desperate reversion to some long-forgotten need to better himself. He implored me to help him again learn how to read and write. The letter I had forged as from him was his inspiration. It became an obsession with him, and in two months of study – to which he applied himself with sweaty tenacity – he was capable of producing his own letters. It is an irony that his hand became an approximate match for the altered script I had used on his letter, but that should have alerted me to his purpose. To him, this was not an end in itself but part of a trick, a need to simulate.

I was lulled.

In January, I had cause to be away from town for some days. This, I decided, was the time for Hyde to go. To my surprise, he agreed entirely. I gave him money for cheap lodging rooms and a ticket for the boat-train the next day, assuring him that the search had died down and that he should be able to make his escape from the country. There was more grief on my side and less on his than I had expected, but this would be a clean break and a conclusion to my involvement with Hyde.

From henceforth, there would be only the good Dr Jekyll.

Upon my return, satisfied that Hyde was out of my life but also aware of a certain hollowness, I swept through my house to the laboratory and found the door hung open. Also forced by a locksmith was the safe in which my most dangerous chemicals were kept.

My head spun. Hyde had played a trick, I knew.

At the lodging I had arranged for him, I found imperfectly burned papers, successive drafts of two letters – one to Poole, and one to Lanyon. The hand was a fair forgery of my own. This was what Hyde had been learning. I remembered his knack for sketching, and realised what a good eye he had.

Once he was beyond earning a living with his body, he would have the trade of forgery to fall back on.

He had presented himself to Lanyon as my messenger and had Lanyon's man despatched to my own house, where Poole was under orders he supposed to be from me to break into my laboratory and secure the ingredients for our drug.

For months, Hyde had been planning this. And all to secure a supply of the potion to which he was addicted.

Some of this I was able to deduce as I made my way to Lanyon's house, some I learned later. I entered Lanyon's house not by the front door but through french windows at the rear, and came upon the scene just as Hyde had prepared a dose of the drug and was raising it to his lips.

Catching sight of me over Lanyon's shoulder, Hyde was exultant with triumph. He had tricked me at last and become the master. At this moment, he chose to demonstrate his mastery with a gesture of extreme cruelty.

'Lanyon,' he sneered, addressing myself as much as the old man, 'you who have so long been bound to the most narrow and material views, you who have denied the virtue of transcendental medicine, you who have derided your superiors – behold!'

He took a swig of the potion and embraced Lanyon, squirting the drug into his mouth. I stepped forward to protest, but my old friend was seized by the effects of the potion. Well I remembered the burning of the brain, the strange hallucinations, the burst of clarity, the unfettering of desires.

Hyde laughed and held out the bubbling retort to me.

Lanyon was clearly thunderstruck. Had Hyde again mixed a lethal, impure dosage? At that moment, I cared not. The mere whiff of the drug reawakened in me an overpowering need, just as Hyde had known it would.

I took some of the liquid and surrendered to the spell.

Hyde and I tore off our clothes, and Lanyon's. Hyde and I spent our lusts in every way upon my old tutor, forcing him to the indulgence of every pricking desire suppressed over the years. He was maddened, I know, and resisted us, but there was a part of him that joined willingly in our debauch, that was at last freed from the shackles he had placed upon himself.

Exultant, we left Lanyon a wreck. I smuggled Hyde back into my laboratory and slept. When I awoke, I needed more than anything to take another draught of my drug. As I mixed and stirred in a frenzy, Hyde laughed like the Devil. When I threatened to withhold from him the blessed potion, he went down on his knees and begged.

We were chained to each other and to the drug.

The full horror of our situation was soon brought home to us. Supply of vital elements ran low, and I endeavoured to replenish my stock of a certain ingredient. As I have said, 'My provision of the salt, which had never been renewed since the date of the first experiment, began to run low. I sent out for a fresh supply, and mixed the draught: the ebullition followed, and the first change of colour, not the second; I drank it and it was without efficiency. You will learn from Poole how I have had London ransacked; it was in vain; and I am now persuaded that my first supply was impure, and that it was that unknown impurity which lent efficacy to the draught.'

Then, truly, Hyde became the monster he is believed to be. He raged and raved, venting his destructive urges on my person and anything to hand. His plan to ensnare me had succeeded, but had further trapped him as well. As each new experiment failed to produce results and our supplies of the original drug – doled out like water in the desert – dwindled, Hyde took to blaming me for his misfortunes.

If we had been thinking rationally, we should have worried about Lanyon. A message came to me from him and I assumed we were about to be exposed to the world. Though it meant shameful revelations about himself and what he had suffered under us, he would tell the truth.

Those familiar with Lanyon's account of Hyde's visit to his home and of the effects of the potion can imagine my puzzlement upon first reading it. Hyde and I read and re-read

Lanyon's demented fantasy, in which Hyde transformed into Jekyll. We were both familiar with the hallucinations that came with the first rush of the drug and of the strange liberation that followed, and I remembered again my theory that many people – especially self-deluded prigs like Lanyon – will strain to believe all manner of incredible things rather than face the truth about themselves or any other outwardly respectable person.

It is plain that Lanyon believed what he wrote: 'He put the glass to his lips, and drank at one gulp. A cry followed; he reeled, staggered, clutched at the table and held on, staring with injected eyes, gasping with open mouth; and, as I looked, there came, I thought, a change – he seemed to swell – his face became suddenly black, and the features seemed to melt and alter – and the next moment I had sprung to my feet and leaped back against the wall, my arm raised to shield me from that prodigy, my mind submerged in terror.

' "Oh, God!" I screamed, and "Oh, God!" again and again; for there before my eyes – pale and shaken, and half fainting, and groping before him with his hands, like a man restored from death – there stood Henry Jekyll!'

The key phrase is 'my mind submerged in terror'. From his experience with the drug and his participation in what followed, he had mixed up Jekyll and Hyde, imposing one upon the other, refusing to admit his own part in our union. The world owes much to Hastie Lanyon, for he is the creator of the myth of Jekyll and Hyde. His mind, affected by our potion, dreamed up the bogey tale for which we are remembered.

What Lanyon sent me was a copy of a letter to Utterson, which was not to be opened by the lawyer until my death or disappearance. His narrative was the inspiration for all that followed.

Starved of the potion, I was in hell. Awful pains coursed through my abused body. Hyde was always by my side, insistent, a fellow-sufferer, a merciless torturer. I knew, long before he did, that it was hopeless. The drug could never be duplicated.

I would have to be rid of Hyde, in such a way as to conceal the true nature of our relationship. It would be easy to poison him. He drank every experimental potion I handed him, draining it down with a desperate glee that turned instantly to bitter disappointment.

Soon after I heard of the death of Hastie Lanyon, his body and mind too shocked by what we had done to survive, I wrote the memoir which has become known as 'Henry Jekyll's Full Statement of the Case'. A key to my success in this fiction is how close to the truth I stayed, straying only to drag in Lanyon's fantasy of metamorphosis. My true feelings for Hyde and the drug, of the addiction I have to both, are plain for all to read. In composing the statement, I forced myself to an understanding of my own divided soul.

Then, on that last night, Hyde flew out of control. He determined I was concealing from him the last dosage of the original drug – which was true – and endeavoured to beat it out of me. Knowing this was the last of him, I surrendered at once to mercy and murder and yielded the vial of the drug, admixed with a dose of poison.

From the commotion in the courtyard, I knew my servants had at last paid attention to the sounds of violence from within the laboratory. Soon, they would breach the door.

Hyde kissed me with real love and drank the potion. He paused with the vial half empty, and – displaying character and generosity with which I would not have credited him – offered me the remainder. I declined and he finished the draught, crushing the glass in his hand as the killing seizure took him.

As he fell, the door jarred.

I concealed myself in the priest hole and heard my servants and Utterson searching the building. I thought I might die in my lightless, airless space. However, in my confinement and in all the months of hiding that have followed, I have often wished that I had accepted Hyde's last, unwitting offer of the poisoned drug. To have departed this world in ecstasy hand-in-hand with the other half of my soul would have been a more fit conclusion to my dual life than has been this assumption of living death. Cut off from my fortune, a trespasser in the abandoned ruin of my house, bereft of even my grave (in which Hyde lies), I am become a ghost.

The world believes I died with Edward Hyde. I now think this is the truth. My mind has been permanently affected by my involvement with Hyde and with the drug we compounded for ourselves; and it seems to me that Hyde is with me still, as much a phantom as myself, and that until I rejoin him I shall not be a complete person. Sometimes I see his smooth face, hear his high voice, transformed again, imploring me to come away from this place. Outside there is only fog.

In the Fog

Further search of the property uncovered evidence that a tramp or some other low person had been camping out in what had once been the laboratory of the great Dr Jekyll. However, that person was now fled and all efforts to trace him came to naught. Ellen Hyde, too, disappeared into the fog, never in person to trouble Utterson again.

It seemed Jekyll and Hyde were together again. Without his Hyde, Jekyll was an incomplete person. Had the pathetic remnant of the doctor gone willingly with his victim's sister? Or was there an element of abduction involved? Ellen Hyde remained as much a mystery as her brother. It seemed she had known all along where Dr Jekyll was to be found. It occurred to Utterson that her attempt to come into the inheritance might partly have been for the doctor's benefit, to secure funds for their escape. Yet it was impossible to decide whether 'Sister Hyde' was the rescuer or tormentor of Dr Jekyll.

Drawing on funds from the estate, Utterson commissioned a fresh headstone. Hyde had been buried under the name of Jekyll, but it was not too late to change that. The disgust he had felt for Hyde was if anything increased by what he had learned from Jekyll's second statement, but it was accompanied by a wave of pity that would not be denied. When he thought of Hyde, he remembered the snarling, strutting degenerate, but also the little boy in his mother's lap.

One morning, Utterson and Enfield paid a ritual visit to the grave. The sun was entirely unable to penetrate the gloom of the fog, and they spent some minutes searching the churchyard for the newly erected stone.

'Perhaps we should have had the grave dug up,' Enfield suggested. 'To make sure.'

'Of what?' Utterson asked.

'That there's anyone there. It occurs to me that we might have been hoodwinked again. Or perhaps for the first time. Who knows what effects that damnable drug might have had? Is it not possible Jekyll-and-Hyde only seemed to die, and that he has returned, clawed his way out of the earth? Is it not conceivable that the transformations have become more extreme, more violent, more radical? If Henry Jekyll could become Edward Hyde, could he not also become Ellen?'

In some strange way, it would be more comfortable to believe that.

When they found the headstone of Hyde, they were unsurprised to see it defaced with a blasphemy. However, below the obscene epitaph, a fresh rose was laid upon the grave.

This backdoor homage to Robert Louis Stevenson was first published by Maxim Jakubowski in his *Chronicles of Crime: The Second Ellis Peters Memorial Anthology of Historical Crime*. Here are the notes on the story, and on the genre, I prepared for that appearance.

The historical mystery is too often cosy and tidy; horrible crimes have taken place, admittedly, but in a remote past, idealised through nostalgia or colourful historical detail. Of course, the game is to project a modern mystery sensibility into the past, to turn someone into an avatar of the twentieth-century figure of the official or private detective – hence those mostly asinine efforts in which Jesus Christ, Jane Austen or Benjamin Franklin crack cases. In the future, will we see 'historical mysteries' about Adolf Hitler, Madonna or Tony Blair? But crime and history wind round each other in a far more interesting manner than this suggests, as writers as diverse as Charles Dickens, Wilkie Collins, Ross MacDonald and James Ellroy understand only too well. In this story, I'm obviously evoking one of the major mystery writers (if unappreciated as such) of the nineteenth century. The stories are so well known by now that it's easy to forget that *Treasure Island* and *The Strange Case of Dr Jekyll and Mr Hyde* are mysteries, that their first readers didn't know what the Black Spot was, whether or not Long John Silver was a villain (that's still open for debate) and that – gasp! – Dr Jekyll was Mr Hyde. Like Jim Rockford, a detective from one of my favourite historical periods (the

1970s), I prefer to work on closed cases, and no case in literary history would seem to be more closed than that of the Good Doctor and the Mad Mister. But, perhaps . . .

AMERIKANSKI DEAD AT THE MOSCOW MORGUE
or: Children of Marx and Coca-Cola

At the railway station in Borodino, Yevgeny Chirkov was separated from his unit. As the locomotive slowed, he hopped from their carriage to the platform, under orders to secure, at any price, cigarettes and chocolate. Another unknown crisis intervened and the steam-driven antique never truly stopped. Tripping over his rifle, he was unable to reach the outstretched hands of his comrades. The rest of the unit, jammed half-way through windows or hanging out of doors, laughed and waved. A jet of steam from a train passing the other way put salt on his tail and he dodged, tripping again. Sergeant Trauberg found the pratfall hilarious, forgetting he had pressed a thousand roubles on the private. Chirkov ran and ran but the locomotive gained speed. When he emerged from the canopied platform, seconds after the last carriage, white sky poured down. Looking at the black-shingled track-bed, he saw a flattened outline in what had once been a uniform, wrists and ankles wired together, neck against a gleaming rail, head long gone under sharp wheels. The method, known as 'making sleepers', was favoured along railway lines. Away from stations, twenty or thirty were dealt with at one time. Without heads, Amerikans did no harm.

Legs boiled from steam, face and hands frozen from winter, he wandered through the station. The cavernous space was sub-divided by sandbags. Families huddled like pioneers expecting an attack by Red Indians, luggage drawn about in a circle, last bullets saved for women and children. Chirkov spat mentally; America had invaded his imagination, just as his political officers warned. Some refugees were coming from Moscow, others fleeing to the city. There was no rule. A wall-sized poster of the New First Secretary was disfigured with a blotch, red gone to black. The splash of dried blood suggested something had been finished against the wall. There were Amerikans in Borodino. Seventy miles from Moscow, the station was a museum to resisted invasions. Plaques, statues and paintings honoured the victories of 1812 and 1944. A poster listed those local officials executed after being implicated in the latest counter-revolution. The air was tangy with ash, a reminder of past scorched-earth policies. There were big fires nearby. An army unit was on duty, but no one knew anything about a timetable. An officer told him to queue and wait. More trains were coming from Moscow than going to, which meant the capital would eventually have none left.

He ventured out of the station. The snow cleared from the forecourt was banked a dozen yards away. Sunlight glared off muddy white. It was colder and brighter than he was used to in the Ukraine. A trio of Chinese-featured soldiers, a continent away from home, offered to share cigarettes and tried to practise Russian on him. He understood they were from Amgu; from the highest point in that port, you could see Japan. He asked if they knew where he could find an official. As they chirruped among themselves in an alien tongue, Chirkov saw his first Amerikan. Emerging from between snowbanks and limping towards the guard-post, the dead man looked as if he might actually be an American. Barefoot, he waded spastically through slush, jeans-legs shredded over thin shins. His shirt was a bright picture of a parrot in a jungle. Sunglasses hung round his neck on a thin string. Chirkov made the Amerikan's presence known to the guards. Fascinated, he watched the dead man walk. With every step, the Amerikan crackled: there were deep, ice-threaded rifts in his skin. He was slow and brittle and blind, crystal eyes frozen open, arms stiff by his sides.

Cautiously, the Corporal circled round and rammed his rifle-butt into a knee. The guards were under orders not to waste ammunition; there was a shortage. Bone cracked and the Amerikan went down like a devotee before an icon. The Corporal prodded a colourful back with his boot-toe and pushed the Amerikan on to his face. As he wriggled, ice-shards worked through his flesh. Chirkov had assumed the dead would stink but this one was frozen and odourless. The skin was pink and unperished, the rips in it red and glittery. An arm reached out for the Corporal and something snapped in the shoulder. The Corporal's boot pinned the Amerikan to the concrete. One of his comrades produced a foot-long spike and worked the point into the back of the dead man's skull. Scalp flaked around the dimple. The other guard took an iron mallet from his belt and struck a professional blow.

It was important, apparently, that the spike should entirely transfix the skull and break ground, binding the dead to the earth, allowing the last of the spirit to leave the carcass. Not official knowledge: this was something every soldier was told at some point by a comrade. Always, the tale-teller was from Moldavia or had learned from someone who was. Moldavians claimed to be used to the dead. The Amerikan's head came apart like a rock split along fault lines. Five solid chunks rolled away from the spike. Diamond-sparkles of ice glinted in reddish-grey inner surfaces. The thing stopped moving at once. The hammerer began to unbutton the gaudy shirt and detach it from the sunken chest, careful as a butcher skinning a horse. The jeans were too deeply melded with meat to remove, which was a shame; with the ragged legs cut away, they would have made fine shorts for a pretty girl at the beach. The Corporal wanted Chirkov to have the sunglasses. One lens was gone, or he might not have been so generous with a stranger. In the end, Chirkov accepted out of courtesy, resolving to throw away the trophy as soon as he was out of Borodino.

Three days later, when Chirkov reached Moscow, locating his

unit was not possible. A despatcher at the central station thought his comrades might have been reassigned to Orekhovo Zuyevo, but her superior was of the opinion the unit had been disbanded nine months earlier. Because the despatcher was not disposed to contradict an eminent Party member, Chirkov was forced to accept the ruling that he was without a unit. As such, he was detailed to the Spa. They had in a permanent request for personnel and always took precedence. The posting involved light guard duties and manual labour; there was little fight left in Amerikans who ended up at the Spa. The despatcher gave Chirkov a sheaf of papers the size of a Frenchman's sandwich and complicated travel directions. By then, the rest of the queue was getting testy and he was obliged to venture out on his own. He remembered to fix his mobility permit, a blue luggage-tag with a smudged stamp, on the out-side of his uniform. Technically, failure to display the permit was punishable by summary execution.

Streetcars ran intermittently; after waiting an hour in the street outside central station, he decided to walk to the Spa. It was a question of negotiating dunes of uncleared snow and straggles of undisciplined queue. Teams of firemen dug methodically through depths of snow, side by side with teams of soldiers who were burning down buildings. Areas were cleared and raked, ground still warm enough to melt snow that drifted on to it. Everywhere, posters warned of the Amerikans. The Party line was still that the United States was responsible. It was air-carried biological warfare, the Ministry announced with authority, originated by a secret laboratory and disseminated in the Soviet Union by suicidal infectees posing as tourists. The germ galvanised the nervous systems of the recently deceased, triggering the lizard stems of their brains, inculcating in the Amerikans a disgusting hunger for human meat. The 'news' footage the Voice of America put out of their own dead was staged and doctored, footage from the sadistic motion pictures that were a symptom of the West's utter decadence. But everyone had a different line: it was . . . creeping radiation from Chernobyl . . . a judgment from a bitter and long-ignored God . . . a project Stalin abandoned during the Great Patriotic War . . . brought back from Novy Mir by cosmonauts . . . a plot by the fomenters of the Counter-Revolution . . . a curse the Moldavians had always known.

Fortunately, the Spa was off Red Square. Even a Ukrainian sapling like Yevgeny Chirkov had an idea how to get to Red Square. He had carried his rifle for so long that the strap had worn through his epaulette. He imagined the outline of the buckle was stamped into his collar bone. His single round of ammunition was in his inside breast pocket, wrapped in newspaper. They said Moscow was the most exciting city in the world, but it was not at its best under twin siege from winter and the Amerikans. Helicopters swooped overhead, broadcasting official warnings and announcements: comrades were advised to stay at their workplaces and continue with their duly delegated tasks; victory in the struggle against the American octopus was inevitable; the crisis was nearly at an end and the master strategists would soon announce a devastating counter-attack; the dead were to be disabled and placed in the proper collection points; another exposed pocket of traitors would go on trial tomorrow.

In an onion-domed church, soldiers dealt with Amerikans. Brought in covered lorries, the shuffling dead were shifted inside in ragged coffles. As Chirkov passed, a dead woman, bear-like in a fur coat over forbidden undergarments, broke the line. Soldiers efficiently cornered her and stuck a bayonet into her head. The remains were hauled into the church. When the building was full, it would be burned: an offering. In Red Square, loudspeakers shouted martial music at the queues. John Reed at the Barricades. Lenin's tomb was no longer open for tourists. Sergeant Trauberg was fond of telling the story about what had happened in the tomb when the Amerikans started to rise. Everyone guessed it was true. The Spa was off the Square. Before the Revolution of 1918, it had been an exclusive health club for the Royal Family. Now it was a morgue.

He presented his papers to a thin officer he met on the broad steps of the Spa, and stood frozen in stiff-backed salute while the man looked over the wedge of documentation. He was told to wander inside smartly and look out Lyubachevsky. The officer proceeded, step by step, down to the square. Under the dusting of snow, the stone steps were gilded with ice: a natural defence. Chirkov understood Amerikans were forever slipping and falling on ice; many were so damaged they couldn't regain their footing, and were consequently easy to deal with. The doors of the Spa, three times a man's height, were pocked with bullet-holes new and old. Unlocked and unoiled, they creaked alarmingly as he pushed inside. The foyer boasted marble floors, and ceilings painted with classical scenes of romping nymphs and athletes. Busts of Marx and Lenin flanked the main staircase; a portrait of the New First Secretary, significantly less faded than neighbouring pictures, was proudly displayed behind the main desk.

A civilian he took to be Lyubachevsky squatted by the desk reading a pamphlet. A half-empty vodka bottle was nestled like a baby in the crook of his arm. He looked up awkwardly at the new arrival and explained that last week all the chairs in the building had been taken away by the Health Committee. Chirkov presented papers and admitted he had been sent by the despatcher at the railway station, which elicited a shrug. The civilian mused that the central station was always sending stray soldiers for an unknown reason. Lyubachevsky had three days of stubble and mismatched eyes. He offered Chirkov a swallow of vodka – pure and strong, not diluted with melted snow like the rat poison he had been sold in Borodino – and opened up the lump of papers, searching for a particular signature. In the end, he decided it best that Chirkov stay at the Spa. Unlocking a cabinet, he found a long white coat, muddied at the bottom. Chirkov was reluctant to exchange his heavy greatcoat for the flimsy garment but Lyubachevsky assured him there was very little pilferage from the Spa. People, even parasites, tended to avoid visiting the place unless there was a pressing reason for their presence. Before relinquishing his coat, Chirkov remembered to retain his mobility permit, pinning it to the breast of the laboratory coat. After taking Chirkov's rifle, complimenting him on its cleanliness and stowing it in the cabinet, Lyubachevsky issued him with a revolver. It was dusty and the metal was cold enough to stick to his skin. Breaking the gun open, Chirkov noted three cartridges. In Russian roulette, he would have an even chance. Without a holster, he dropped it into the pocket of his coat; the barrel poked out of a torn corner. He had to sign for the weapon.

Lyubachevsky told him to go down into the Pool and report to Director Kozintsev. Chirkov descended in a hand-cranked cage lift and stepped out into a ballroom-sized space. The Pool was what people who worked in the Spa called the basement where the dead were kept. It had been a swimming-bath before the Revolution; there, weary generations of Romanovs had plunged through slow waters, the tides of history slowly pulling them under. Supposedly dry since 1916, the Pool was so cold that condensation on the marble floors turned to ice-patches. The outer walls were still decorated with gilded plaster friezes and his bootfalls echoed on the solid floors. He walked round the edge of the pit, looking down at the white-coated toilers and their unmoving clients. The Pool was divided into separate work-cubicles and narrow corridors by flimsy wooden partitions that rose above the old water level. A girl caught his eye, blonde hair tightly gathered at the back of her neck. She had red lipstick and her coat sleeves were rolled up on slender arms as she probed the chest cavity of a corpse, a girl who might once have been her slightly older sister. The dead girl had a neat, round hole in her forehead and her hair was fanned over a sludgy discharge Chirkov took to be abandoned brains. He coughed to get the live girl's attention and inquired as to where he could find the Director. She told him to make his way to the Deep End and climb in, then penetrate the warren of partitions. He couldn't miss Kozintsev; the Director was dead centre.

At the Deep End, he found a ladder into the pool. It was guarded by a soldier who sat cross-legged, a revolver in his lap, twanging on a jew's harp. He stopped and told Chirkov the tune was a traditional American folk song about a cowboy killed by a lawyer, 'The Man Who Shot Liberty Valance'. The guard introduced himself as Corporal Tulbeyev and asked if Chirkov was interested in purchasing tape cassettes of the music of Mr Edward Cochran or Robert Dylan. Chirkov had no cassette player but Tulbeyev said that for five thousand roubles he could secure one. To be polite, Chirkov said he would consider the acquisition: evidently a great bargain. Tulbeyev further insinuated he could supply other requisites: contraceptive sheaths, chocolate bars, toothpaste, fresh socks, scented soap, suppressed reading matter. Every unit in the Soviet Union had a Tulbeyev, Chirkov knew. There was probably a secretary on the First Committee of the Communist Party who dealt disco records and mint-flavoured chewing gum to the High and Mighty. After a decent period of mourning, Chirkov might consider spending some of Sergeant Trauberg's roubles on underwear and soap.

Having clambered into the Pool, Chirkov lost the perspective on the layout of the work-spaces he had from above. It was a labyrinth and he zigzagged between partitions, asking directions from the occasional absorbed forensic worker. Typically, a shrug would prompt him to a new pathway. Each of the specialists was absorbed in dissection, wielding whiny and smoky saws or sharp and shiny scalpels. He passed by the girl he had seen from above – her name-tag identified her as Technician Sverdlova, and she introduced herself as Valentina – and found she had entirely exposed the rib-cage of her corpse. She was the epitome of sophisticated Moscow girl, Chirkov thought: imperturbable and immaculate even with human remains streaked up to her elbows. A straggle of hair whisped across her face, and she blew it out of the way. She dictated notes into a wire recorder, commenting on certain physiological anomalies of the dead girl. There was a rubbery resilience in the undecayed muscle tissue. He would have liked to stay, but had to report to Kozintsev. Bidding her goodbye, he left her cubicle, thumping a boot against a tin bucket full of watches, wedding-rings and eyeglasses. She said he could take anything he wanted, but he declined. Remembering, he found the bent and broken sunglasses in his trousers pocket and added them to the contents of the bucket. It was like throwing a kopeck in a wishing-well, so he made a wish. As if she were telepathic, Valentina giggled. Blushing, Chirkov continued.

He finally came to a makeshift door with a plaque that read 'V. A. Kozintsev, Director'. Chirkov knocked and, hearing a grunt from beyond, pushed through. It was as if he had left the morgue for a sculptor's studio. On one table were moist bags of variously coloured clays, lined up next to a steaming samovar. In the centre of the space, in the light cast by a chandelier that hung over the whole Pool, a man in a smock worked on a bust of a bald-headed man. Kozintsev had a neatly trimmed beard and round spectacles. He was working one-handed; long fingers delicately pressing hollows into cheeks; a glass of tea in his other hand. He stood back, gulped tea and tutted, extremely dissatisfied with his efforts. Instantly accepting the newcomer, Kozintsev asked Chirkov for help in going back to the beginning. He set his glass down and rolled up his sleeves. They both put their hands in the soft face and pulled. Clays came away in self-contained lumps: some stranded like muscles, others bunched like pockets of fat. A bare skull, blotched with clay, was revealed. Glass eyes stared hypnotically, wedged into sockets with twists of newspaper. Chirkov realised he had heard of the Director: V. A. Kozintsev was one of leading reconstruction pathologists in the Soviet Union. He had, layering in musculature and covering the results with skin, worked on the skulls tentatively identified as those of the Former Royal Family. He had recreated the heads of palaeolithic men, murder victims and Ivan the Terrible.

Chirkov reported for duty and the Director told him to find something useful to do. Kozintsev was depressed to lose three days' work and explained in technical detail that the skull wasn't enough. There had to be some indication of the disposition of muscle and flesh. As he talked, he rolled a cigarette and stuck it in the corner of his mouth, patting his smock pockets for matches. Chirkov understood this was one of Kozintsev's historical projects: high-profile work sanctioned by the Ministry of Culture, unconnected to the main purpose of the Spa – which, just now, was to determine the origins and capabilities of the Amerikans – but useful in attracting attention and funds. While the Director looked over charts of facial anatomy, puffing furiously on his cigarette, Chirkov picked up the discarded clays and piled them on the table. On a separate stand was a wigmaker's dummy head under a glass dome: it wore a long but neat black wig and facsimile wisps of eyebrows, moustache and beard. Once the skull was covered and painted to the correct skin tone, hair would be applied. He asked Kozintsev to whom the skull belonged, and, off-handedly, the Director told him it was Grigori Rasputin. There had been trouble getting glass eyes with the right quality. Contemporary memoirs described the originals as steely blue, with pupils that contracted to pinpoints when their owner was concentrating on exerting his influence. Chirkov looked again at the skull and couldn't see anything special. It was just bare bone.

Each evening at nine, the Director presided over meetings. Attendance was mandatory for the entire staff, down to Chirkov. He was billeted in the Spa itself, in a small room on the top floor where he slept on what had once been a masseur's table. Since food was provided (albeit irregularly) by a cafeteria, there was scarce reason to venture outside. At meetings, Chirkov learned who everyone was: the ranking officer was Captain Zharov, who would rather be out in the streets fighting but suffered from a gimpy knee; under Kozintsev, the chief coroner was Dr Fyodor Dudnikov, a famous forensic scientist often consulted by the police in political murder cases but plainly out of his depth with the Spa's recent change of purpose. The Director affected a lofty disinterest in the current emergency, which left the morgue actually to be run by a conspiracy between Lyubachevsky, an administrator seconded from the Ministry of Agriculture, and Tulbeyev, who was far more capable than Captain Zharov of keeping greased the wheels of the military machine.

Chirkov's girl Valentina turned out to be very eminent for her years, a specialist in the study of Amerikans; at each meeting, she reported the findings of the day. Her discoveries were frankly incomprehensible, even to her colleagues, but she seemed to believe the Amerikans were not simple reanimated dead bodies. Her dissections and probings demonstrated that the Amerikans functioned in many ways like living beings; in particular, their musculature adapted slowly to their new state, even as surplus flesh and skin sloughed off. Those portions of their bodies that rotted away were irrelevant to the functioning of the creatures. She likened the ungainly and stumbling dead creatures to a pupal stage, and expressed a belief that the Amerikans were becoming stronger. Her argument was that they should be categorised not as former human beings but as an entirely new species, with its own strengths and capabilities. At every meeting, Valentina complained she could only manage so much by examining doubly-dead bodies and that the best hope of making progress would be to secure 'live' specimens and observe their natural progress. She had sketched her impressions of what the Amerikans would eventually evolve into: thickly muscled skeletons like old anatomical drawings.

Valentina's leading rival, A. Tarkhanov, countered that her theories were a blind alley. In his opinion, the Spa should concentrate on the isolation of the bacteriological agent responsible for the reanimations, with a view to the development of a serum cure. Tarkhanov, a Party member, also insisted the phenomenon had been created artificially by American genetic engineers. He complained the monster-makers of the United States were so heavily financed by capitalist cartels that this state-backed bureaucracy could hardly compete. The one common ground Valentina held with Tarkhanov was that the Spa was desperately under-funded. Since everyone at the meetings had to sit on the floor, while Director Kozintsev was elevated cross-legged on a desk, the procurement of chairs was deemed a priority, though all the scientists also had long lists of medical supplies and instruments without which they could not continue their vital researches. Lyubachevsky always countered these complaints by detailing his repeated requests to appropriate departments, often with precise accounts of the elapsed time since the request had been submitted. At Chirkov's third meeting, there was much excitement when Lyubachevsky announced that the Spa had received from the Civil Defence Committee fifty-five child-sized blankets. This was unrelated to any request that had been put in, but Tulbeyev offered to arrange a trade with the Children's Hospital, exchanging the blankets for either vegetables or medical instruments.

At the same meeting, Captain Zharov reported that his men had successfully dealt with an attempted invasion. Two Amerikans had been found at dawn, having negotiated the slippery steps, standing outside the main doors, apparently waiting. One stood exactly outside the doors, the other a step down. They might have been forming a primitive queue. Zharov personally disposed of them both, expending cartridges into their skulls, and arranged for the removal of the remains to a collection point, from which they might well be returned as specimens. Valentina moaned that it would have been better to capture and pen the Amerikans in a secure area – she specified the former steam bath – where they could be observed. Zharov cited standing orders. Kozintsev concluded with a lengthy lecture on Rasputin, elaborating his own theory that the late Tsarina's spiritual adviser was less mad than popularly supposed and that his influence with the Royal Family was ultimately instrumental in bringing about the Revolution. He spoke with especial interest and enthusiasm of the so-called Mad Monk's powers of healing, the famously ameliorative hands that could ease the symptoms of the Tsarevich's haemophilia. It was his contention that Rasputin had been possessed of a genuine paranormal talent. Even Chirkov thought this beside the point, especially when the Director wound down by admitting another failure in his reconstruction project.

With Tulbeyev, he drew last guard of the night; on duty at three a.m., expected to remain at the post in the foyer until the nine o'clock relief. Captain Zharov and Lyubachevsky could not decide whether Chirkov counted as a soldier or an experimental assistant; so he found himself called on to fulfil both functions, occasionally simultaneously. As a soldier he would be able to sleep away the morning after night duty, but as an experimental assistant he was required to report to Director Kozintsev at nine sharp. Chirkov didn't mind overmuch; once you got used to corpses, the Spa was a cushy detail. At least corpses here were corpses. Although, for personal reasons, he always voted, along with two other scientists and a cook, in support of Technician Sverdlova's request to bring in Amerikans, he was privately grateful she always lost by a wide margin. No matter how secure the steam bath might be, Chirkov was not enthused by the idea of Amerikans inside the building. Tulbeyev, whose grandmother was Moldavian, told stories of *wurdalaks* and *vryolakas* and always had new anecdotes. In life, according to Tulbeyev, Amerikans had all been Party members: that was why so many had good clothes and consumer goods. The latest craze among the dead was for cassette-players with attached headphones; not American manufacture, but Japanese. Tulbeyev had a collection of the contraptions, harvested from Amerikans whose heads were so messed up that soldiers were squeamish about borrowing from them. It was a shame, said Tulbeyev, that the dead were disinclined to cart video-players on their backs. If they picked up that habit, everyone in the Spa would be a millionaire; not a rouble millionaire, a dollar millionaire. Many of the dead had foreign currency. Tarkhanov's pet theory was that the Americans impregnated money with a bacteriological agent, the condition spreading through contact with cash. Tulbeyev, who always wore gloves, did not seem unduly disturbed by the thought.

Just as Tulbeyev was elaborating upon the empire he could build with a plague of video-players, a knock came at the doors. Not a sustained pounding like someone petitioning for entry, but a thud as if something had accidentally been bumped against the other side of the oak. They both shut up and listened. One of Tulbeyev's tape machines was playing Creedence Clearwater Revival's 'It Came Out of the Sky' at a variable speed; he turned off the tape, which scrunched inside the machine as the wheels ground, and swore. Cassettes were harder to come by than players. There was a four-thirty-in-the-morning Moscow quiet. Lots of little noises; wind whining round the slightly warped door, someone having a coughing-fit many floors above, distant shots. Chirkov cocked his revolver, hoping there was a round under the hammer, further hoping the round wasn't a dud. There was another knock, like the first. Not purposeful, just a blunder. Tulbeyev ordered Chirkov to take a look through the spy-hole. The brass cap was stiff but he managed to work it aside and look through the glass lens.

A dead face was close to the spy-hole. For the first time, it occurred to Chirkov that Amerikans were scary. In the dark, this one had empty eye-sockets and a constantly chewing mouth. Around its ragged neck were hung several cameras and a knotted scarf with a naked woman painted on it. Chirkov told Tulbeyev, who showed interest at the mention of photographic equipment and crammed around the spy-hole. He proposed that they open the doors and Chirkov put a bullet into the Amerikan's head. With cameras, Tulbeyev was certain he could secure chairs. With chairs, they would be the heroes of the Spa, entitled to untold privileges. Unsure of his courage, Chirkov agreed to the scheme and Tulbeyev struggled with the several bolts. Finally, the doors were loose, held shut only by Tulbeyev's fists on the handles. Chirkov nodded; his comrade pulled the doors open and stood back. Chirkov advanced, pistol held out and pointed at the Amerikan's forehead.

The dead man was not alone. Tulbeyev cursed and ran for his rifle. Chirkov did not fire, just looked from one dead face to the others. Four were lined in a crocodile, each on a different step. One wore an officer's uniform, complete with medals; another, a woman, had a severe pinstripe suit and a rakish gangster hat; at the back of the queue was a dead child, a golden-haired, green-faced girl in a baseball cap, trailing a doll. None moved much. Tulbeyev returned, levering a cartridge into the breech, and skidded on the marble floor as he brought his rifle to bear. Taken aback by the apparently unthreatening dead, he didn't fire either. Cold wind wafted in, which explained Chirkov's chill. His understanding was that Amerikans always attacked; these stood as if dozing upright, swaying slightly. The little girl's eyes moved mechanically back and forth. Chirkov told Tulbeyev to fetch a scientist, pre-ferably Valentina. As his comrade scurried upstairs, he remembered he had only three rounds to deal with four Amerikans. He retreated into the doorway, eyes fixed on the dead, and slammed shut the doors. With the heel of his fist, he rammed a couple of the bolts home. Looking through the spy-hole, he saw nothing had changed. The dead still queued.

Valentina wore a floor-length dressing-gown over cotton pyjamas. Her bare feet must be frozen on the marble. Tulbeyev had explained about the night visitors and she was reminding him of Captain Zharov's report. These Amerikans repeated what the Captain had observed: the queuing behaviour pattern. She brushed her hair out of the way and got an eye to the spy-hole. With an odd squeal of delight, she summoned Chirkov to take a look, telling him to angle his eye so he could look beyond the queue. A figure struggled out of the dark, feet flapping like beached fish. It went down on its face and crawled up the steps, then stood. It took a place behind the little girl. This one was naked, so rotted that even its sex was lost, a skeleton held together by strips of muscle that looked like wet leather. Valentina said she wanted that Amerikan for observation, but one of the others was necessary as well. She still thought of capturing and observing specimens. Tulbeyev reminded her of the strangeness of the situation and asked why the dead were just standing in line, stretching down the steps away from the Spa. She said something about residual instinct, the time a citizen must spend in queues, the dead's inbuilt need to mimic the living, to recreate from trace memories the lives they had once had. Tulbeyev agreed to help her capture the specimens but insisted they be careful not to damage the cameras. He told her they could all be millionaires.

Valentina held Tulbeyev's rifle as a soldier would, stock close to her cheek, barrel straight. She stood by the doorway covering them as they ventured out on her mission. Tulbeyev assigned himself to the first in the queue, the dead man with the cameras. That left Chirkov to deal with the walking skeleton, even if it was last in line and, in Moscow, queue-jumping was considered a worse crime than matricide. From somewhere, Tulbeyev had found a supply of canvas post-bags. The idea was to pop a bag over an Amerikan's head like a hood, then lead the dead thing indoors. Tulbeyev managed with one deft manoeuvre to drop his bag over the photographer's head, and whipped round behind the Amerikan, unravelling twine from a ball. As Tulbeyev bound dead wrists together, the twine cut through grey skin and greenish-red fluid leaked over his gloves. The rest of the queue stood impassive, ignoring the treatment the photographer was getting. When Tulbeyev had wrestled his catch inside and trussed him like a pig, Chirkov was ready to go for the skeleton.

He stepped lightly down to the skeleton's level, post-bag open as if he were a poacher after rabbit. The Amerikans all swivelled their eyes as he passed and, with a testicles-retracting spasm of panic, he missed his footing. His boot slipped on icy stone and he fell badly, his hip slamming a hard edge. He sledged down the steps, yelping as he went. A shot cracked and the little girl, who had stepped out of the queue and scrambled towards him, became a limp doll, a chunk of her head dryly gone. Tulbeyev had got her. At the bottom of the steps, Chirkov stood. Hot pain spilled from his hip and his side was numb. His lungs hurt from the frozen air, and he coughed steam. He still held his bag and gun; luckily, the revolver had not discharged. He looked around: there were human shapes in the square, shambling towards the Spa. Darting up the steps, unmindful of the dangers of ice, he made for the light of the doorway. He paused to grab the skeleton by the elbow and haul it to the entrance. It didn't resist him. The muscles felt like snakes stretched over a bony frame. He shoved the skeleton into the foyer and Tulbeyev was there with his ball of twine. Chirkov turned as Valentina shut the doors. More Amerikans had come: the skeleton's place was taken, and the little girl's, and two or three more steps were occupied. Before bolting the doors, Valentina opened them a crack and considered the queue. Again, the dead were still, unexcited. Then, like a drill team, they all moved up a step. The photographer's place was taken by the officer, and the rest of the line similarly advanced. Valentina pushed the doors together and Chirkov shut the bolts. Without pausing for breath, she ordered the specimens to be taken to the steam baths.

Breakfast was a half-turnip, surprisingly fresh, if riddled with ice-chips. Chirkov took it away from the cafeteria to chew and descended to the Pool to report to the Director. He assumed Valentina would make mention at the evening meeting of her unauthorised acquisition of specimens. It was not his place to spread gossip. Arriving at the cubicle before the Director, his first duty was to get the samovar going: Kozintsev survived on constant infusions of smoky tea. As Chirkov lit the charcoal, he heard a click, like saluting heels. He looked around the cubicle and saw no one. All was as usual: clays, wig, shaping-tools, skull, samovar, boxes piled to make a stool. There was another click. He looked up at the chandelier and saw nothing unusual. The tea began to bubble and he chewed a mouthful of cold turnip, trying not to think about sleep, or Amerikans.

Kozintsev had begun again on the reconstruction. The skull of Grigori Yefimovich Rasputin was almost buried in clay strips. It looked very much like the head of the Amerikan Chirkov had secured for Valentina: flattened reddish ropes bound the jaws together, winding up into the cavities under the cheek-bones; enamel chips replaced the many missing teeth, standing out white against grey-yellow; delicate filaments swarmed round the glass eyes. It was an intriguing process and Chirkov had come to enjoy watching the Director at work. There was a sheaf of photographs of the monk on one stand but Kozintsev disliked consulting them. His process depended on extrapolating from the contours of the bone, not modelling from likenesses. Rasputin's potato-like peasant nose was a knotty problem. The cartilage was long gone, and Kozintsev obsessively built and abandoned noses. Several were trodden flat into the sloping tiled floor. After the Revolution, the faith healer had been exhumed by zealots from his tomb in the Imperial Park and, reportedly, burned; there was doubt, fiercely resisted by the Director, as to the provenance of the skull.

As Chirkov looked, Rasputin's jaw sagged, clay muscles stretching; then, suddenly, it clamped shut, teeth clicking. Chirkov jumped, and spat out a shocked laugh. Kozintsev arrived, performing a dozen actions at once, removing his frock-coat and reaching for his smock, bidding a good morning and calling for his tea. Chirkov was bemused and afraid, questioning what he had seen. The skull bit once more. Kozintsev saw the movement at once, and asked again for tea. Chirkov, snapping out of it, provided a cupful and took one for himself. Kozintsev did not comment on the appropriation. He was very interested and peered close at the barely animated skull. The jaw moved slowly from side to side, as if masticating. Chirkov wondered if Grigori Yefimovich were imitating him and stopped chewing his turnip. Kozintsev pointed out that the eyes were trying to move, but the clay hadn't the strength of real muscle. He wondered aloud if he should work in strands of string to simulate the texture of human tissue. It might not be cosmetically correct. Rasputin's mouth gaped open, as if in a silent scream. The Director prodded the air near the skull's mouth with his finger and withdrew sharply as the jaws snapped shut. He laughed merrily, and called the monk a cunning fellow.

The queue was still on the steps. Everyone had taken turns at the spy-hole. Now the line stretched down into the square and along the pavement, curving round the building. Tulbeyev had hourly updates on the riches borne by the Amerikans. He was sure one of the queue harboured a precious video-player: Tulbeyev had cassettes of *101 Dalmatians* and *New Wave Hookers* but no way of playing them. Captain Zharov favoured dealing harshly with the dead, but Kozintsev, still excited by the skull activity, would issue no orders and the officer was not about to take action without a direct instruction, preferably in writing. As an experiment, he went out and, half-way down the steps, selected an Amerikan at random. He shot it in the head and the finally dead bag of bones tumbled out of the queue. Zharov kicked the remains and, coming apart, they rolled down the steps into a snowdrift. After a pause, all the dead behind Zharov's kill took a step up. Valentina was in the steam baths with her specimens: news of her acquisitions had spread through the Spa, inciting vigorous debate. Tarkhanov complained to the Director about his

71

colleague's usurpation of authority, but was brushed off with an invitation to examine the miraculous skull. Dr Dudnikov placed several phone calls to the Kremlin, relaying matters of interest to a junior functionary, who promised imminent decisions. It was Dudnikov's hope that the developments could be used as a lever to unloose vital supplies from other institutions. As ever, the rallying-cry was *chairs for the Spa*!

In the afternoon, Chirkov napped standing up as he watched Kozintsev at work. Although the jaw continually made small movements, the skull was cooperative and did not try to nip the Director. He had requisitioned Tulbeyev's jew's harp and was implanting it among thick neck muscles, hoping it would function as a crude voicebox. To Chirkov's disgust, Rasputin was becoming expert in the movement of its unseeing eyes. He could suck the glass orbs so the painted pupils disappeared in the tops of the sockets, showing only milky white marbles. This was a man who had been hard to kill: his murderers gave him poison enough to fell an elephant, shot him in the back and chest with revolvers, kicked him in the head, battered him with a club and lowered him into the River Neva, bound in a curtain, through a hole in the ice. The skull bore an indentation which Kozintsev traced to an aristocrat's boot. In the end, men hadn't killed the seer; the cause of his death was drowning. As he worked, the Director hummed cheerful snatches of Prokofiev. To give the mouth something to do, Kozintsev stuck a cigarette between the teeth. He promised Grigori Yefimovich lips would come soon, but there was nothing yet he could do about lungs. His secret dream, which he shared with the skull (and, perforce, Chirkov), was to apply his process to a complete skeleton. Regrettably, and as he had himself predicted while alive, most of the monk had been scattered on the wind.

Lyubachevsky barged into the cubicle, bearing a telephone whose cord unreeled through the maze of the Pool like Ariadne's thread. There was a call from the Kremlin, which Kozintsev was required to take. While Chirkov and

Lyubachevsky stood, unconsciously at attention, the Director chatted with the New First Secretary. Either Dr Dudnikov had tapped into the proper channels or Tarkhanov was the spy everyone took him for and had reported on the sly to his KGB superior. The First Secretary was briefed about what was going on at the Spa. He handed out a commendation to Kozintsev and insisted extra resources would be channelled to the morgue. Chirkov got the impression the First Secretary was mixing up the projects: Kozintsev was being praised for Valentina's studies. The Director would be only too delighted to employ any funds or supplies in furthering his work with the skull.

Following the telephone call, the Director was in excellent spirits. He told the skull a breakthrough was at hand, and insisted to Lyubachevsky that he could hear a faint twang from the jew's harp. Grigori Yefimovich was trying to communicate, the Director claimed. He asked if he remembered eating the poisoned chocolates? After the jaw first moved, Kozintsev had constructed rudimentary clay ears, exaggerated cartoon curls which stuck out ridiculously. Having abandoned any attempt to simulate the appearance in life of the monk, he was attempting instead to provide working features. Since Rasputin's brains must have rotted or burned years ago, it was hard to imagine what the Director aspired to communicate with. Then, over the loudspeaker, Dr Dudnikov reported that there were soldiers outside the Spa, setting up explosives and declaring an intention to dynamite the building. Grigori Yefimovich's glass eyes rolled again.

Engineers were packing charges around the foyer. Entering the Spa through the kitchens, they had avoided the Amerikan-infested steps. It appeared a second queue was forming, stretching off in a different direction, still leading to the front doors. The officer in command, a fat man with a facial birthmark that made him look like a spaniel, introduced himself as Major Andrey Kobylinsky. He strode about,

73

inspecting the work, expressing pride in his unit's ability to demolish a building with the minimum of explosive matter. As he surveyed, Kobylinsky noted points at which surplus charges should be placed. To Chirkov's unschooled eye, the Major appeared to contradict himself: his men were plastering the walls with semtex. Kozintsev and Captain Zharov were absorbed in a reading of a twelve-page document which authorised the demolition of the Spa. Dr Dudnikov protested that the First Secretary himself had, within the last minute, commended the Spa and that important work to do with the Amerikan invasion was being carried out in the Pool, but Kobylinsky was far more interested in which pillars should be knocked out to bring down the decadent painted roof. As they worked, the engineers whistled 'Girls Just Want to Have Fun'.

Satisfied that the charges were laid correctly, Major Kobylinsky could not resist the temptation to lecture the assembled company on the progress and achievements of his campaign. A three-yard square map of Moscow was unfolded on the floor. It was marked with patches of red as if it were a chessboard pulled out of shape. The red areas signified buildings and constructions Kobylinsky had blown up. Chirkov understood the Major would not be happy until the entire map was shaded in red; then, Kobylinsky believed the crisis would be at an end. He proclaimed that this should have been done immediately the crisis begun, and that the Amerikans were to be thanked for prompting such a visionary enterprise. As the Major lectured, Chirkov noticed Tulbeyev at the main desk with Lyubachevsky, apparently trying to find a pen that worked. They sorted through a pot of pencils and chalks and markers, drawing streaks on a piece of blotting-paper. Under the desk were packages wired to detonators. Kobylinsky checked his watch and mused that he was ahead of his schedule; the demolition would take place in half an hour. Lyubachevsky raised a hand and ventured the opinion that the explosives placed under the main staircase were insufficient for the task of bringing down such a solidly constructed structure.

Barking disagreement, Kobylinsky strutted over and examined the charges in question, finally agreeing that safe was better than sorry and ordering the application of more explosives.

While Kobylinsky was distracted, Tulbeyev crept to the map and knelt over Red Square, scribbling furiously with a precious red felt-tip. He blotched over the Spa, extending an area of devastation to cover half the Square. When Kobylinsky revisited his map, Tulbeyev was unsuspiciously on the other side of the room. One of the engineers, a new set of head-phones slung round his neck, piped up with an observation of a cartographical anomaly. Kobylinsky applied his concentra-tion to the map and gurgled to himself. According to this chart, the Spa had already been dealt with by his unit: it was not a building but a raked-over patch of rubble. Another engineer, a baseball cap in his back pocket, volunteered a convincing memory of the destruction, three days ago, of the Spa. Kobylinsky looked again at the map, getting down on his hands and knees and crawling along the most famous thoroughfares of the city. He scratched his head and blinked in his birthmark. Director Kozintsev, arms folded and head high, said that so far as he was concerned the matter was at an end; he requested the engineers to remove their infernal devices from the premises. Kobylinsky had authorisation to destroy the Spa but once, and had demonstrably already acted on that authorisation. The operation could not be repeated without further orders, and, if further orders were requested, questions would be asked as to whether the engineers were as efficient as Kobylinsky would like to claim: most units needed to destroy a building only once for it to remain destroyed. Almost in tears, the bewildered Major finally commanded the removal of the explosives and, with parental tenderness, folded up his map into its case. With no apologies, the engineers withdrew.

That night, Valentina's Amerikans got out of the steam bath and everyone spent a merry three hours hunting them down. Chirkov and Tulbeyev drew the Pool. The power had failed again and they had to fall back on oil lamps, which made the business all the more unnerving. Irregular and active shadows were all around, whispering in Moldavian of hungry, unquiet creatures. Their progress was a slow spiral; first, they circled the Pool from above, casting light over the complex, but that left too many darks unprobed; then they went in at the Deep End and moved methodically through the labyrinth, weaving between the partitions, stumbling against dissected bodies, ready to shoot hatstands in the brain. Under his breath, Tulbeyev recited a litany he claimed was a Japanese prayer against the dead: '*sanyo, sony, seiko, mitsubishi, panasonic, toshiba . . .*'

They had to penetrate the dead centre of the Pool. The Amerikans were in Kozintsev's cubicle: staring at the bone-and-clay head as if it were a colour television set. Rasputin was on his stand under a black protective cloth which hung like long hair. Chirkov found the combination of the Amerikans and Rasputin unnerving and, almost as a reflex, shot the skeleton in the skull. The report was loud and echoing. The skeleton came apart on the floor and, before Chirkov's ears stopped hurting, others had come to investigate. Director Kozintsev was concerned for his precious monk and probed urgently under the cloth for damage. Valentina was annoyed by the loss of her specimen but kept her tongue still, especially when her surviving Amerikan turned nasty. The dead man barged out of the cubicle, shouldering partitions apart, wading through gurneys and tables, roaring and slavering. Tarkhanov, incongruous in a silk dressing-gown, got in the way and sustained a nasty bite. Tulbeyev dealt with the Amerikan, tripping him with an axe-handle, then straddling his chest and pounding a chisel into the bridge of his nose. He had not done anything to prove Valentina's theories; after a spell in captivity, he simply seemed more decayed, not evolved. Valentina claimed the thing Chirkov had finished had been a model of biological efficiency, stripped down to essentials, potentially immortal. Now, it looked like a stack of bones.

*

Even Kozintsev, occupied in the construction of a set of wooden arms for his reanimated favourite, was alarmed by the size of the queue. There were four distinct lines. The Amerikans shuffled constantly, stamping nerveless feet as if to keep warm. Captain Zharov set up a machine-gun emplacement in the foyer, covering the now-barred front doors, although it was strictly for show until he could be supplied with ammunition of the same gauge as the gun. Chirkov and Tulbeyev watched the Amerikans from the balcony. The queue was orderly; when, as occasionally happened, a too-far-gone Amerikan collapsed, it was trampled under by the great moving-up as those behind advanced. Tulbeyev sighted on individual dead with binoculars and listed the treasures he could distinguish. Mobile telephones, digital watches, blue jeans, leather jackets, gold bracelets, gold teeth, ball-point pens. The Square was a paradise for pickpockets. As night fell, it was notable that no lights burned even in the Kremlin.

When the power came back, the emergency radio frequencies broadcast only soothing music. The meeting was more sparsely attended than usual, and Chirkov realised faces had been disappearing steadily, lost to desertion or wastage. Dr Dudnikov announced that he had been unable to reach anyone on the telephone. Lyubachevsky reported that the threat of demolition had been lifted from the Spa and was unlikely to recur, though there might now prove to be unfortunate official side-effects if the institution was formally believed to be a stretch of warm rubble. The kitchens had received a delivery of fresh fish, which was cause for celebration, though the head cook noted as strange the fact that many of the shipment were still flapping and even decapitation seemed not to still them. Valentina, for the hundredth time, requested specimens be secured for study and, after a vote – closer than usual, but still decisive – was disappointed. Tarkhanov's suicide was entered into the record and the scientists paid tribute to the colleague they fervently

77

believed had repeatedly informed on them, reciting his achievements and honours. Tulbeyev suggested a raiding-party to relieve the queuing Amerikans of those goods which could be used for barter, but no one was willing to second the proposal, which sent him into a notable sulk. Finally, as was expected, Kozintsev gave an account of his day's progress with Grigori Yefimovich. He had achieved a certain success with the arms: constructing elementary shoulder joints and nailing them to Rasputin's stand, then layering rope-and-clay muscles which interleaved with the neck he had fashioned. The head was able to control its arms to the extent of stretching out and bunching up muscle strands in the wrists as if clenching fists which did not, as yet, exist. The Director was also pleased to report that the head almost constantly made sounds with the jew's harp, approximating either speech or music. As if to demonstrate the monk's healing powers, Kozintsev's sinus trouble had cleared up almost entirely.

Two days later, Tulbeyev let the Amerikans in. Chirkov did not know where the Corporal got the idea; he just got up from the gun emplacement, walked across the foyer, and unbarred the doors. Chirkov did not try to stop him, distracted by efforts to jam the wrong type of belt into the machine-gun. When all the bolts were loose, Tulbeyev flung the doors back and stood aside. At the front of the queue, ever since the night they had brought in Valentina's specimens, was the officer. As he waited, his face had run, flesh slipping from his cheeks to form jowly bags around his jaw. He stepped forwards smartly, entering the foyer. Lyubachevsky woke up from his cot behind the desk and wondered aloud what was going on. Tulbeyev took a fistful of medals from the officer, and tossed them to the floor after a shrewd assessment. The officer walked purposefully, with a broken-ankled limp, towards the lifts. Next in was the woman in the pinstripe suit. Tulbeyev took her hat and perched it on his head. From the next few, the Corporal harvested a silver chain identity bracelet, a woven leather belt, a pocket calculator, an old brooch. He piled the tokens behind him. Amerikans filled the foyer, wedging through the doorway in a triangle behind the officer.

Chirkov assumed the dead would eat him and wished he had seriously tried to go to bed with Technician Sverdlova. He still had two rounds left in his revolver, which meant he could deal with an Amerikan before ensuring his own everlasting peace. There were so many to choose from and none seemed interested in him. The lift was descending and those who couldn't get into it discovered the stairs. They were all drawn to the basement, to the Pool. Tulbeyev chortled and gasped at each new treasure, sometimes clapping the dead on the shoulder as they yielded their riches, hugging one or two of the more harmless creatures. Lyubachevsky was appalled, but did nothing. Finally, the administrator got together the gumption to issue an order: he told Chirkov to inform the Director of this development. Chirkov assumed that since Kozintsev was, as ever, working in the Pool, he would very soon be extremely aware of this development, but he snapped to and barged through the crowd anyway, choking back the instinct to apologise. The Amerikans mainly got out of his way, and he pushed to the front of the wave shuffling down the basement steps. He broke out of the pack and clattered into the Pool, yelling that the Amerikans were coming. Researchers looked up – he saw Valentina's eyes flashing annoyance, and wondered if it was not too late to ask her for sex – and the crowd edged behind Chirkov, approaching the lip of the Pool.

He vaulted in and sloshed through the mess towards Kozintsev's cubicle. Many partitions were down already and there was a clear path to the Director's work-space. Valentina pouted at him, then her eyes widened as she saw the assembled legs surrounding the Pool. The Amerikans began to topple in, crushing furniture and corpses beneath them, many unable to stand once they had fallen. The hardiest of them kept on walking, swarming round and overwhelming the technicians. Cries were strangled and blood ran on the bed of the Pool.

Chirkov fired wildly, winging an ear off a bearded dead man in a shabby suit, and pushed on towards Kozintsev. When he reached the centre, his first thought was that the cubicle was empty, then he saw what the Director had managed. Combining himself with his work, V. A. Kozintsev had constructed a wooden half-skeleton which fitted over his shoulders, making his own head the heart of the new body he had fashioned for Grigori Yefimovich Rasputin. The head, built out to giant size with exaggerated clay and rubber muscles, wore its black wig and beard, and even had lips and patches of sprayed-on skin. The upper body was wooden and intricate, the torso of a colossus with arms to match, but sticking out at the bottom were the Director's stick-insect legs. Chirkov thought the body would not be able to support itself but, as he looked, the assemblage stood. He looked up at the caricature of Rasputin's face. Blue eyes shone, not glass but living.

Valentina was by his side, gasping. He put an arm round her and vowed to himself that if it were necessary she would have the bullet he had saved for himself. He smelled her perfumed hair. Together, they looked up at the holy maniac who had controlled a woman and, through her, an empire, ultimately destroying both. Rasputin looked down on them, then turned away to look at the Amerikans. They crowded round in an orderly fashion, limping pilgrims approaching a shrine. A terrible smile disfigured the crude face. An arm extended, the paddle-sized hand stretching out fingers constructed from surgical implements. The hand fell on to the forehead of the first of the Amerikans, the officer. It covered the dead face completely, fingers curling round the head. Grigori Yefimovich seemed powerful enough to crush the Amerikan's skull, but instead he just held firm. His eyes rolled up to the chandelier, and a twanging came from inside the wood-and-clay neck, a vibrating monotone that might have been a hymn. As the noise resounded, the gripped Amerikan shook, slabs of putrid meat falling away like layers of onionskin. At last, Rasputin pushed the creature away. The uniform gone with its flesh, it was like

Valentina's skeleton, but leaner, moister, stronger. It stood up and stretched, its infirmities gone, its ankle whole. It clenched and unclenched teeth in a joke-shop grin and leaped away, eager for meat. The next Amerikan took its place under Rasputin's hand, and was healed too. And the next.

Once, long ago and far away, John Skipp and Craig Spector edited an anthology called *The Book of the Dead*, of mostly fine stories set more or less in the world of George A. Romero's 'Living Dead' films. It was so well received that the editors produced a further volume, *Still Dead*. Then, remembering that there were three Romero dead movies, they set out to do a third volume, which may well have been called *Deader Than Ever* or *Deadest Yet*. Since, in my other life as a movie critic, I had written extensively about Romero in my book *Nightmare Movies*, I was pleased to be asked by John to come up with something for this third book. I did a little rewriting at Craig's suggestion, got paid (as I remember it) and waited for the story to appear.

Years passed. I'm not really privy to what happened, but various publishers and editors fell out with each other and, though the third Dead book nearly happened at least twice (I once received page proofs of the story) it never managed to stumble into print. If you've been picking up recent anthologies of original horror stories, you've already read quite a few ship-jumping tales from the collection (Douglas E. Winter's wonderful 'The Zombies of Madison County' is one). For a while, 'Amerikanski Dead' was due to come out as a chapbook – but that never happened, either. Then, with the bogus millennium looming, I was asked by Al Sarrantonio if I had anything he might look at for what was then called *999: The Last Horror Anthology*, intended to be one of those genre-summing, über-collection doorstops that the field needs every so often to stay alive. I dug out this, and it wound up as the lead-off story in the somewhat more modestly titled *999: New Stories of Horror and Suspense*. For that appearance, the story lost its subtitle (a quote from Jean-Luc Godard) to keep the list of contents tidy, but I'm restoring it here.

Though the rising of the dead is supposed to be a global phenomenon, Romero's movies – *Night of the Living Dead* (1968), *Dawn of the Dead* (1979) and *Day of the Dead* (1984) – are all about America. One or two of the stories in the Dead collections are about foreign parts (Poppy Brite's 'Calcutta, Lord of Nerves') and Clive Barker was connected with a comic book spin-off that had dead folks (including the Royal Family) in London. But Romero's films belong now to the era of the superpower face-off, and I thought it would be interesting to see what might be happening in the then-Soviet Union during the time between *Dawn* and *Day* and, more importantly, what it might mean. The title is a riff on *The Living Dead at the Manchester Morgue*, the British release title of the Spanish-Italian movie *No profanar el sueño de los muertos* (1974) – known in America as *Don't Open the Window* or *Let Sleeping Corpses Lie* (rarely has one film had so many great titles).

The business about reconstructing faces from skulls is mentioned in Martin Cruz Smith's *Gorky Park*, but I remembered it from a 1960s BBC science documentary (*Tomorrow's World*?) in which the skull of Ivan the Terrible was used as a template to recreate his head. For Rasputin details, I drew on Robert K. Massie's *Nicholas and Alexandra*, Sir David Napley's *Rasputin in Hollywood* and various unreliable movie and TV performances by whiskery scenery-chewers like Lionel Barrymore, Boris Karloff, Tom Baker and Christopher Lee.

JUST LIKE EDDY

L[...] myself, for the present, Edgar A. Poe. The fair scr[...]ining before me need not yet be sullied by my full app[...] his has been already too much an object for the scor.., for the horror, for the detestation of my soul. To the uttermost region of the globe have not the indignant winds bruited its unparalleled infamy? Oh, outcast of all outcasts most abandoned – to the earth art thou not for ever dead? to its honours, to its flowers, to its golden aspirations? – and a cloud, dense, dismal and limitless, does it not hang eternally between thy hopes and heaven?

Upon my writing-desk is a gruesome object in the form of a volume: cheaply produced, ill set, carelessly glued; issued not a year or two gone, but misdated through ignorance of the correct use of roman numerals. Less an edition than a falling from the presses, this book – for such we must call the damned thing, though so to do assaults our sensitive bibliophile vitals – is cast out to stalls and stores, for the penurious and the ignorant. It might be gawped over for an hour or two before its pages loosen like the leaves of October and are spilled in the streets. Upon its thin, ready-warped board cover is a rough, ugly woodcut: a grinning skull with eye-sockets too small, a downcast black bird with wings too large. And the title of this gathering of butcher's paper, as given on the ready-yellowed, coarse frontispiece, is:

TALES AND POEMS
by Edgar Allen Poe

Tales and Poems need not concern us. The texts are a mish-mash, lifted entire through ingenious photographic process from several other editions so the face and size of type changes from page to page, from story to poem. Of course, many errors and misprintings are carelessly scattered throughout the copy, like seed strewn for chickens.

And there, on the frontispiece is the arch-error, the primal misprint, the eternal slip of the pen. Since I second ventured into the arena of print, dropping the dignified anonymity of 'A Bostonian' – for so I signed my first published work, *Tamerlane and Other Poems* – to speak up for myself and proudly state my own, true name, to stand by my work and dare the world to take it and myself as they would, this has plagued me.

Edgar Allen Poe

Allen! Edgar Allen Poe! All-damned Allen! Always Allen, always. Allen! Allen! Allen! Though it is the work of a devil of the printer's variety, I cannot but think it also the product of the machinations of another of his breed, of more sulphurous and princely-yet-tenebrous mein.

Never am I rid of this phantom of my own making. The dreadful double has dogged me through the allotted span of my life and persisted even beyond the supposed release of widely reported death. Edgar Allen Poe mocks my aspirations to Art and Science, unpicks the threads of my tapestry, gnaws ratlike at the foundations of my endeavour.

Allen is my imp of the perverse, my goblin damned, my ravening ghoul, my frightful fiend.

For the love of God, shall I never be rid of E. Allen Poe!

I concede that the Allen is my own fault, that he is my creation. All evil that he is comes from within me, and he is all that is base and degraded in my person. Yet he has a damnable life of his own, beyond my conscious influence, and directed entirely towards the destruction of my self, my reputation.

What is a man's name if not his reputation, his soul?

Each time *his* name appears in print, my own is devalued, trodden into charnel filth and forgotten.

The appearance of Allen is not confined to cheap, pirated editions that skim my most renowned works and pass them off as the ravings of a madman and a degenerate. Allen appears in learned commentaries, obituaries, scholarly histories, popular lectures, biographies and bibliographies, broadsheets and magazines, the credits of motion pictures and television programmes, the collections of major universities, articles in every manner of publication, private letters that have strayed into the public purview, numberless schoolboy essays and compositions, plaques and honours and monuments. Immortalised a thousand thousand times, he is carried abroad through media undreamed-of at the time of his, and my, first fame. The thousand-and-third tale of Scheherezade is of his rise to prominence in this fabulous age of futurity.

Edgar Allen Poe rules, as the graffito has it; and I, *le vraisemble* Edgar Poe, am lost, forgotten and impugned, cursed and doomed.

Like many of my sorrows, this has its beginning in the actions of the man who was never my father and acted, indeed, as no father to me.

I write, with distaste bitter still after more than a century and a half, of John Allan, of the trading house of Allan and Ellis. Upon the deaths of my true parents, David and Eliza Poe, I was taken as a babe into the house of Allan, a golden orphan, an ornament for the philistine businessman. With the death of his own wife, the devoted Frances, Allan began a programme of calculated torture by hope, dangling before me the prospect of wealth enough to support my literary endeavours but always snatching it away. My early failures, at university and West Point, can all be laid at the door of this Torquemada of the Modern Age, who mockingly refused either to cut me off and cast me out entirely or to finance properly my launch upon the literary world to which unasked-for poetical genius fit me.

When I was but two years of age, this creature prised apart my given name – Edgar Poe, honest and simple Edgar Poe of distinguished lineage – with prehensile fingers like those of a great orang-outan, and spat in his own patronymic, marking me for ever as a man with three names (one invariably misspelled).

This is the most hideous irony of the situation. I care not for the name Allan and wish it were not mine. Truly, he had no right to force it upon me. In railing against the malforming error of Allen-for-Allan, I defend not myself but the man who more than any other mortal sought to ruin me, to stand between me and my rightful position.

Allan! John Allan! I only ever signed myself Edgar Allan Poe when communicating with my *soi-disant* stepfather, usually in signing missives stating my desperate need for funds, in the hope of pricking his elephant-hide to awaken a conscience that was in him stillborn. Such letters were invariably unanswered, perhaps left in the rack for weeks on end as John Allan pursued his own mean pleasures. I understand that, in the writings composed during what is generally reckoned my lifetime, there survive only two minor instances of my use of the name Edgar Allan Poe, both from a period when I was unwisely tossing good emotional currency after bad by attempting reconciliation with a man beyond all decent feeling.

Many tales and poems and publications did I sign Edgar *A*. Poe. This, I admit, in mournful and never-ending remembrance. This, even, was a grievous, a ruining error. I was born Edgar Poe. I am known as such to this day in that congenial country France – the only blessed dominion where American geniuses on the scale of myself and the estimable Mr Lewis are fully understood and appreciated.

I should never have succumbed to the temptation of a middle initial. It is a sheer puffery, whereby many authors of mediocre reputation and talents attempt to inflate their own by-line to something with cachet, with status.

He speaks a profound truth who warns you to beware

authors – and especially *authoresses,* most especially my countrywomen – with three names. It seems these thrice-named ones are often afflicted with a peculiar and unwholesome compulsion to foist upon the public their maunderings in as many volumes as they have names, and indeed to pile upon such trilogies with additional instalments unpromised and unsought-for until the shelves of the book-sellers groan with heartfelt pain.

I should have abandoned even the token of Allan's name, that odious initial, that alien and alienating A. I am and was proud of the Poes that came before me, the Revolutionary general and the great star of the stage. I found my only safe harbour amongst the circle of their relatives, my cousin-wife Virginia Clemm (my own darling Sissy) and her mother, Maria Clemm (my devoted Muddy). Yet – I curse my weakness and vanity, my shameful need for cash and the acute embarrassment of living always in a state of genteel beggary – the Poes were much reduced in circumstances, through no fault of theirs, and John Allan was, through no endeavour of his own, colossally rich. A wealthy uncle died and left him a hoard of Croesus, a fabulous treasure beyond even that secreted by the pirate Captain Kidd. The gold tempted me, prevented me from breaking fully with this cruel man.

With money, what might I not have done? My cherished project, a true literary magazine for America, might have come to fruition and proved a very great success, much to the benefit of the culture of my homeland, which has – for the want of an influence such as *The Stylus* might have provided – descended into a barbarous, illiterate and nightmarish stew of ignorance and vulgarity beyond even the blackest of my black imaginings. *The Stylus* would have proved a forum for the highest of artistic and political debate: it could have presented reasoned, definitive answer to those abolitionist fanatics who so dreadfully sundered the country but a decade after I passed from public notice, inflicting upon it a rapine from which it has never fully recovered and elevating to wasteful mastery the brutish and barely human blacks who were in my youth so properly and mercifully chained. If we had been blessed with an income, my Sissy, rare and radiant maiden whom the angels name Virginia, might have received proper medical attention and survived beyond her tragically brief lifespan, to bear me sons and daughters who would have carried on my name and done me honour.

Allan denied me, denied *America*, these blessings.

Yet, each time I was on the point of abandoning entirely all hope of aid from that quarter, some crumb, some trickle, would come from John Allan. By keeping the ghost of his name within mine, and with each appearance of my name in print above a tale or a poem or an article or a work of criticism, I maintained the limping, lagging last of our relations.

John Allan passed out of my life, married again and with fat, bawling new heirs for his fortune. But, as he rode off in his gilded carriage to undeserved bliss, another appeared and crept from the shadows to torment me.

Edgar Allen Poe.

I cannot remember when he first appeared. It could not have been in any periodical for which I laboured in an editorial position: *The Southern Literary Messenger*, *Graham's Magazine* or *The Broadway Journal*. I was a proofreader of unmatched skill, as even those of my colleagues who became my bitterest foes would have been forced to acknowledge. When the matter was within my influence, I insisted upon the initial only, not the full name. Edgar A. Poe was safe, but Edgar Allan Poe was a dangerous venture which so often rebounded upon me.

No, Edgar Allen Poe must have been born in some other connection. Scratched on an envelope by a barely-literate tradesman, over one of the damnable reminders that elaborately bought to my attention some debt as if it were possible that I could with honour forget such a matter. Or perhaps it was printed above one of the many, *many* – mostly anonymous with the full cowardice such implies – attacks upon my work and character issued in publications that were the despicable organs of that canting gaggle of fools, knaves, toadies and dunderheads who then – as now! – made American letters their own frogpond, croaking at each other and their pitifully few indentured readers; all the while contriving to do down and push under any truly original, important voice.

Was there initially malign intent? Surely, the first to have made the mistake – the *common* mistake, I have heard it called, though how such a lingering and deadly blight could ever be a commonality is beyond the confines even of my notoriously fevered brain – could not have known. No, it was *repetition* that had the power to bring into the world the fiend who built upon the foundations of John Allan and worked so devotedly towards my utter degradation and ruin.

At first, when grotesque tales reached me, I was indignant, certain that lies were being propagated by my so-called friends and acquaintances. Of course, none dared repeat such calumnies to my face, but I was always sensitive to whisperings, perhaps unnaturally so. His voice, Allen's, is always a whisper, a low, distinct and never-to-be-forgotten whisper which thrills to the very marrow of my bones, the whisper of a man dead yet unable to depart his mummifying corpse.

The world knows, or thinks it knows, my story. After my final break with Allan, I was forced to embark upon a perilous and rarely remunerative career in the employ of the periodicals of the day, all the while hoping in vain to combine pursuit of literary excellence with the plebeian necessity of earning a daily buck. Sole support of my sickly wife and her helpless mother, I took a succession of positions with a succession of publications, making fortunes for bloated and idle owners but not myself, and losing through my drunkenness or stubborn pride each employment, leaving behind only tales and poems that have lasted to this day, and bad debts. It has been said, over and over, that I was a slave to the demon drink, that my condition was such that even a single glass of wine was enough to spin my brain into a frenzy, to send me on a binge that might last days and during which I was as one possessed, capable of any vice or insult, a terror to my friends and foes alike, yet so addicted to such stimulus that I would continue imbibing even to the point of physical collapse and, finally, death.

That, I maintain, was him.

Edgar Allen Poe.

Not I. Not Edgar Poe. Not, and it pains me to type the name to which I should never have laid claim, Edgar Allan Poe.

It was in Philadelphia, or perhaps New York, and after my Sissy had suffered the terrible onset of consumption, a vein in her throat exploding as her voice was raised in song, but before that dread disease took her away from me and robbed me of all hope for future happiness. I was writing so much and so fast that my fingers were permanently grooved by the pen and my hand was wrung with constant pain. Suddenly, without premonition, I was no longer welcome in the offices of publications with which I had hitherto enjoyed a cordial connection. The private homes of many were similarly closed to me, and the staff of certain hostelries or stores began to give me a wide berth in the street.

Had I somehow, unknown to myself, been transformed into a pariah?

I overheard stories of my exploits. I had assaulted this prominent novelist with a savage fury, importuned the wife of that noted editor with unbelievable licence. More than once, I found Sissy in tears and had to coax from her the substance of some misdeed she had overheard ascribed to me. I found myself dunned by bills – yes, in that hated phantom name, but with my actual address – that I knew for certain I had never run up.

There was only one possible conclusion, the impossibility that I might unknowingly be the subject of these fantastic tales having been justly excluded.

My double was at large, wrecking my life.

My *Doppelgänger*, as the Germans put it. Identical in every outward aspect, but inside a prodigy of evil, a warped mirror of my own self.

Many times, I was driven from home and position by Edgar Allen. He was a brawler and a drunkard, but possessed of the same canny intelligence that fired my own genius. I might be a pioneer among poets, but he was first among degenerates, as devoted to his calling as I to mine.

I set out to find him, and put an end to this sorry business between us. I knew he could be no more than a projection, a ghost before his time, escaped from my body but attached by a golden thread. If I were to snap him back, I would be free of him and he of me. We would be one mind, one soul. I was confident that I had the force of intellect and strength of character to deal with any ill influence he might have upon my thoughts.

It seemed that he was always just out of my sight. I might arrive at a place mere moments after his passing, which often put me in the position of answering for his misdeeds. My pursuit was dangerous, leading me to the receipt of many an unearned thrashing. Sissy and Muddy would tend my wounds, and worry over me, but my beautiful Sissy – her life leaking slowly, agonisingly away in a poetical tragedy of the first water – was in no condition to consider my poor health before her own. The walls appeared to be closing in on me and mine, and the scythe of death swished closer, ever closer, above the head of her whom I loved the most in all the world. It became paramount that I finish with this Allen, for only when he was a barely discernible heartbeat within the tomb of my mind would I be free to devote full energies to my husbandly duties and to the higher work of literature.

As dogged and perspicacious as any detective, I traced the impostor through reasoning. He led me from place to place, to other cities, and I apprehended that Allen was as intent on evading as Edgar was on ensnaring. In clues – the torn corner of a page scrawled with words in a caricature of my own hand, a button that upon examination I found missing from my own army greatcoat, lines of obscene verse scratched on the underside of a table in a low grog-shop – I found messages from him to me, from Edgar Allen to Edgar Poe. He could not bring himself to vanish into the mists, for he needed me at his heels to give his life purpose. Eventually, in dreadful and depthless despair, I realised he had almost won his final victory. In following him, I was compelled to venture into the dens of vice he frequented, and forced into many of the wretched habits that were his. Stories went back to Sissy and Muddy of me being seen in such-and-such a sinkhole of drunkenness and depravity; now, these tales were, in all particulars, sadly true.

The worst came when, after weeks in search of Edgar Allen, I decided finally to abandon the pursuit entirely. I purged myself of the obsession, and determined to let my rival go his own way. I would elevate my name so far above his that he could do me no harm. I returned to our poor home, bedraggled from my adventures and in a sorry state, to discover from Muddy that I was already in residence, closeted with Sissy, and that I had been so for some days.

Oh terror beyond imagining!

My home, shared with such tender and innocent souls, I had thought inviolate, 'off-limits', as we said at West Point. Yet now it was transformed at a lightning-strike into a haunt of horrors, each familiar item of furniture or crockery become a mocking grotesque. My limbs would not serve me as I dashed for the stairs, and I seemed to plunge into a maelstrom of churning darkness. Our cat, a wise and humorous presence suddenly become a fire-eyed imp, was between my ankles, stretching out to undo my balance. Muddy, full as ever of concern for her Eddy, rushed to support me. At first bewildered by what she took to be my bilocation, that good woman became affrighted that I had fallen from an upstairs window and received ill-treatment, perhaps under the hooves of a horse, in the street. I found myself struggling with my wife's mother, a true mother to me, and terrifying her with my cries. The cat joined in with the sounding of ferocious mewls, rendering my already taut nerves like the strings of a violin sawed at by the devil's fiddler.

Breaking free of Muddy, I ventured upstairs, dragging myself up by the banister, conscious of a growing terror that made my heart a bellows and caused the blood to pound in my temples like a pagan drumbeat.

The door of the room I shared with Sissy, my wife-daughter-lover-child-muse-sister, hung open. Within, a candle burned with sickly greenish flame.

I stepped across the threshold, and found Sissy sprawled atop the covers of our bed, night-clothes rent, scarlet blood discharging from her mouth. Other flowing wounds, open and intimate, marred the whiteness of her tiny form. She had been sorely abused. I am convinced that it was on that night she truly began the long, slow, heart-breaking business of dying. This was the worst the fiend Allen could do, the crime that was beyond all forgiveness.

Howling, I glimpsed my own two evil eyes as I smashed the mirror on the wall. That was the nearest I came to seeing him, until much later.

After that, I lost some days to hysteria.

Sissy, of course, died. I had opportunities after that and continued to write as ever, but my darker double had the upper hand. He grew bolder, taking advantage of my increasing reluctance to venture beyond my hearth, to perform ever more fantastic and appalling acts in my approximate name.

Edgar Allen Poe was busy in those years.

His name was everywhere. My own was quite eclipsed. I lost a deal of money and alienated a publisher who might have advanced my cause greatly by insisting a printer destroy an entire edition of my two-volume *Tales of the Folio Club* because the hated Edgar Allen Poe had signed the introduction to this collection of my greatest stories. With that abortion was lost an original tale of mystery – in which the Chevalier Auguste Dupin penetrates the tangled puzzle of 'The Suicides of Saint-Germain' – which would doubtless have been ranked among my finest pieces.

Allen even trespassed into print.

Now, I could not tell you which of my later works were his and which mine. Most of the famous pieces, the stories and the poems, are and remain mine. Too much of the journalism, the fillers and the canting reviews of unreadable books, are his. The worst tragedy is *Eureka*, an unwilling collaboration. The original manuscript of this essay was mine, a clear-sighted and visionary work which would have placed my name alongside not merely Milton and Shakespeare but Newton and Galileo. After a period of protracted study and insight, a single-theory-of-everything came to me and I was able to contrive no less than an explanation in a manner that could not be mistaken of the material and spiritual nature of the universe itself. When the work appeared in print, it had been tampered with by my rival. Whole passages were rewritten so that the meaning was horribly obscure, and the grand, beautiful design marred beyond repair by pernicious nonsense and stretches that crudely imitated my own style and manner as if composed by a trained ape with a nasty knack for mimicry. My critics, firmly in the Allen camp, were savage and merciless. It was a set-back I endeavoured to correct through lecturing and footnotes, but he had again lured me into evil ways and I could never reassemble my original version, could never recapture that moment of pure understanding that had prompted me to append such a thundercrack of a title to the book that should have been my finest but which became an embarrassment on a par with the poetry I tortured out of myself as a schoolboy.

The *Eureka* affair determined me to recommence my search for my enemy. Without a wife, I was less hampered by fear for my own safety. I was in my fortieth year, and the wrongs done me were stamped on my features. Implacable, purified by burning memory of the crimes against my soul, I turned about and looked for the trail.

It was late in the year of 1849 that I found him.

For months, I went from city to city, taking work as a lecturer and scribbler, capitalising on a fame which was now as much his as mine. I realised many who came to see me perform were hoping for a display of Edgar Allen-like madness and degeneracy rather than Edgar Poe-like sense and artistry. They were, for the most part, disappointed, though as before, the nearer I came to my quarry, the more like him I became.

I was unwelcome everywhere. Reports of my double came in from all quarters. He had engaged in fist-fights with editors and critics and common sots. He had approached literary ladies as if they were gutter drabs. He had declaimed his genius – my genius! – in such a manner as to alienate all who might have supported me. He had made fantastical claims of the wonders of the coming ages, misrepresenting as prophecy those fictions of mine presented as cautionary tales. He had delighted in the morbid and ghastly aspects of my work, but scorned the beauties and wonders I sought also to realise. He made bad jokes, undermining my once-prized reputation as a delightful wit; he even had the temerity to pass off as mine 'X-ing the Paragrab', a leaden failure at humour on the subject, no less, of *misprints*.

Sometimes, I would lecture and *he* would take the money owed me, scattering it in the worst dives. He made a will that ensured the permanent blighting of my name, appointing my worst enemy – Rufus Griswold, Rough Rufus, Griswold the grisly – as my literary executor. For near a century, my works were always republished, ascribed as often as not to Edgar Allen, with a libellous biographical sketch by the ghastly Griswold which attributed to me all the misdeeds and imperfections of character of my foul persecutor.

We played tag throughout the cities of the eastern United States, Philadelphia, Boston, New York, Baltimore. I realised things had changed between us. He was hunting me, as I was him, and I feared he intended to do away with me, perhaps to wall me up living in a cellar, and take my place.

I contrived in small ways to thwart him. In New York, certain I was in danger of being murdered, I shaved off my moustache to make a difference between us, so I would no longer be blamed for his crimes. That was a mistake; it made me, Edgar Poe, less the real man, and he, Edgar Allen, more the original.

It was night in the lonesome October, in the worst year of the century, and Baltimore was in the throes of a corrupt and hard-fought election. Then and there, I caught up at long last with my nemesis. I came upon him, and knew him for who he was, in an alley-way between taverns, steaming with the discharges of chronic inebriates, caked with a filth of loathsome putrescence.

Edgar Allen Poe was in a sorry state, a grotesque caricature of myself, having accepted many bribes of drink for each of the many votes he had cast for either of the candidates. At last, he was collapsed, shortly before sunrise, a tiny slug of a man. His clothes were shoddy, more threadbare even than those to which I was reduced, and he was as he had always been, a living spectre with a broken mirror for a face.

'Thou art the man,' I croaked.

It was but a moment's work to wring the life out of him. But as I choked, he uttered words.

It was Edgar Allen; but he spoke no longer in a whisper, and I could have fancied that I myself was speaking while he said: 'You have conquered and I yield. Yet, henceforward art thou also dead – dead to the World, to Heaven, and to Hope! In me didst thou exist – and, in my death, see by this image, which is thine own, how utterly thou hast murdered myself.'

These were my own words, cast back to me like an echo in my skull. They shook me to the core, and I hurried away, unseen by those who gathered about the stinking body on the cobbles.

Or was I the one gasping his last? And the shadow fleeing, my enemy?

He is buried, under my name. My miserly cousin Neilson Poe had me interred without marker. Later, he raised a subscription for a tombstone which was smashed – by a derailing locomotive – before it could be erected.

What was carved on that stone? His name, or mine?

I am what I am called, am whichever of us is invoked, and I shall be Edgar Allen as often as Edgar Poe. Each time the pernicious misspelling creeps into print the true Poe is beaked in the heart and the impostor reigns in illimitable triumph.

This is as it shall be, evermore.

I wrote this for the 150th anniversary of Poe's death in October 1849, and it duly appeared (very carefully proofread) in the issue of *Interzone* for that month. I keep being drawn back to Poe, who features as a viewpoint character in my hard-to-find Jack Yeovil novel *Route 666* and, more extensively, as a vampire in my *The Bloody Red Baron: Anno Dracula 1918*. Of the great many books on Eddy, the two I most consulted were biographies by Kenneth Silverman (*Edgar A. Poe: Mournful and Never-ending Remembrance*) and Jeffrey Meyers (*Edgar Allan Poe: His Life and Legacy*). Poe remains the most consistently misspelled great author of all time.

A VICTORIAN GHOST STORY

'Among the blessings of civilisation,' began Ernest Virtue, his shrewd glance passing over us, one by one, 'can any be more profound and yet simple than oak panelling? Its humble stoutness, derived from the most English of trees, serves us as our forefathers were served by the blockstones of their castles. Observe the play of firelight upon the grain. Does it not seem like armour? In a room lined with oak panels, one is safe, shielded from all harm, insusceptible to all fear. Were it not for oak panelling, I would not have the fortitude to tell you this story.

'Wondrous indeed is it to plump oneself in a comfortably stuffed leather armchair in the heart of a metropolis and find oneself at peace, the raucous sounds of the outside world muffled, the pestilential fogs of the capital banished. Add to the picture a roaring fire providing both light and warmth, the after-effects of a hearty meal, generous measures of fine old brandy and healthy infusions of pungent cigar smoke, and one might think oneself transported from the cares of the quotidian world to a higher realm even than that ruled over by our own dear Queen, God rest the soul of her beloved Prince Consort Albert. Without such an Elysian refuge, a man might be maddened by London. For this city is the most haunted place on Earth.'

In the club-room, the topic of the evening had turned to the beyond, and we were telling ghost stories. Colonel Beauregard had conjured the hill-spirits of far-off India, detailing the unhappy fate of a degenerate officer who meddled with the native women and incurred the wrath of a little brown priest.

The Reverend Mr Weeks had countered with a story of phantoms in a ruined abbey on an abandoned isle in the Hebrides, and of an unwary delver after treasure driven out of his wits by an intelligence that seemed composed of creeping, writhing kelp.

We were pleasantly stirred from the torpor that follows a substantial meal, awakened by brandy and terror, thirsty perhaps for more of both.

I had not expected Virtue – Mr Ernest Meiklejohn Virtue, of the brokerage firm of Banning, Clinch and Virtue – to enter the field and contribute a story. I had written him up for the illustrated press some months earlier and had formed the opinion that he was a man entirely of this world. Somewhat past middle age, with a barrel of a body and a generosity of grey whiskers about his chops to compensate for a growing expanse of baldness upon his dome, he was a man of substance. Had it not been for the quality of his clothes, he might have passed as an ageing prize-fighter or the chucker-out in a rowdy hostelry. It was said that many who confronted him on the floor of the Exchange yielded for fear that he would extend his financial attacks into the arena of physical assault. Needless to say, away from the bear-pit of the stock market, he had a reputation as the most charitable and mild-mannered of souls.

'I have in these last months become victim to a particularly pernicious species of apparition,' Virtue continued. 'Gentlemen, you see before you a man persecuted beyond endurance, persecuted by spectres.'

I drew in breath. From his solemn countenance, I could tell Virtue was not joshing us. The Colonel and the Reverend had passed on tales given them by colleagues who were themselves not the primary parties in the events recounted. Both had endeavoured, in the spirit of the thing as it were, to embroider, to add their own details, increasing the horripilating effects of their anecdotes. In comparison, Virtue seemed to offer the uncut, unpolished stone of experience.

Even in the warmth of the club-room, I felt a chill. The brandy I sipped stung my mouth.

'London is full of fog,' Virtue continued. 'Sulphurous, clinging, lingering, choking fog. As you know, it makes the streets seem like river-beds and turns us all into bottom-crawlers, probing blindly, advancing step by step. A moment's lapse of concentration and one is lost. All this is familiar to you. But I tell you there are creatures in the fog, unperceived by all but a few. These entities harbour a singular hostility, a resentment almost, towards those of us who enjoy the comforts of the living.'

The Reverend Weeks nodded sagely. Colonel Beauregard's hand went to his thigh, where, were he in uniform, his pistol would have been.

'I first became aware of these infernal spirits some months ago. I was, I confess, particularly pleased with myself that day. I'd concluded a nice piece of business, manipulating the market in an especially cunning manner so that my own cause was victorious and my rivals routed. I need not trouble you with details, but Weeks – who profited not a little from being let in on my machinations – can testify to the neatness of the trick. It would not be overstating the situation to say that fortunes changed hands that afternoon. *The Times* noted, somewhat predictably, "Virtue is Triumphant".

'While I indulged in a celebratory tot with my allies, accepting in all good grace the muttered tributes of fallen foes, the first real fog of autumn gathered in the streets. It rose like a tide of soup round scurrying pedestrians, washing against the thighs of the cabmen perched on their seats, closing over the backs of their horses. It is my custom to walk from the Exchange to my house in Red Lion Square, abjuring the comfort of a hansom for the sake of exercise. It is important to maintain the body, for flesh is the cloak of the soul and clothes should always make a statement, testifying to the man who wears them. I set out, flushed with my success—'

'—and with good spirits, I'll be bound,' said Beauregard.

Virtue inclined his head. 'A dram of whisky, no more. I have, of course, considered that my experience might have been shaped by an intoxication unperceived by myself. Indeed, this is what I later tried desperately to tell myself. However, that came afterwards.

'I am familiar with my route home. I was often given to expressing the sentiment that I daresay I could find my way to my front door blindfold. This sudden fog, which you may remember being of remarkable consistency, put my rash boast to the test.

'I must have made a misturn, for I walked for some considerable time, far longer than it should have taken me to return safely to my own doorstep. The outlines of the buildings that I perceived through the yellow wafting curtain of the fog did not resolve themselves into the familiar contours of Red Lion Square. I was going over and over in my mind the triumph of the day, allowing myself something of the sin of pride in appreciating my own cleverness. Strategic minor purchases like the opening feints of a fencing-match diverted those who opposed my interests until I was ready to deliver the elegant killing thrusts that secured my victory. I saw columns of figures piled up like heavenly bricks, and neglected to pay attention to the earthly stones beneath my feet.

'At length, I brought myself up short and looked around.

'It is a very queer sensation indeed to find oneself utterly alone in the middle of London. The fog hung so thickly as to be impenetrable, seeming almost to have coalesced about my person. If I reached out, my hand grew indistinct and then disappeared entirely from my sight. The effects of the fog were by no means restricted to the obscuring of my sight. It was of that singular texture, that dampness and stickiness, that clings to one's clothes and can sometimes not be washed away, that gums up your eyes and makes your nostrils flow, that tickles the throat, that seems to invade your anatomy and clog your chest and heart. That taste we Londoners can never entirely be free of was strong in my mouth, to the point of vileness. It was as if the fog had targeted me of all the millions of the city, and wrapped me in its woolly, stinking shroud, isolating me from my fellows, holding me fast in one spot.

'I would have continued to walk, but in my unlovely gloating I had lost all sense of direction. The sun was setting, and the yellow of the fog turning to a darker hue, tendrils of brown and black winding through it. But this change of light was general, not from a specific direction that would have enabled me at least to fix a compass-point. Dread fingertips touched my heart, coldly caressing. Terror sparked in my brain. It was my impulse to move, to run from the spot, to career blindly into the opaque cloud that clung to the streets, to keep running until I was free of this gathering gloom. Yet I was still Ernest Meiklejohn Virtue, Lion of the City, Master of the Exchange. I have iron in my soul. I resisted the impulse to panic, recognising it from many a hairy moment on the market floor, knowing that if I held fast I would prevail.

'I *felt* them, first.

'Something brushed past me, about the size of a big dog but clad in damp, ragged cloth, not sleek, smooth fur. Something that went on two shod feet, yet was not what I would consider a child. Something that was all bones and hurry. I was molested slightly, poked and prodded, and had good cause to clamp a protective fist about my gold watch. Then the creature was gone. All I saw of it was a mop-head of twiggy hair, like a flying bird's nest, at about waist-height, zooming away into the fog. I heard footfalls clatter, and then it was gone.

'What had it been?

'There were others. I was at an intersection, it seems, and these creatures passed every which way at will, jostling me one way and another. I glimpsed sparkling eyes, and felt hard little shoulders. I heard their mewlings, which were not the cries of animals and yet bore little resemblance to the patterns of civilised speech. I was possessed, I admit, with a loathing that went deeper than my intellect. An instinctive revulsion that made me shrink inside my clothes with each rude touch. I was sure their touch left deposits upon my person, and that these substances would prove even less susceptible to cleaning away than the miasmal filth of fog. They chattered and stank and jeered and passed by.

'It could only have taken a minute or so. The creatures were soon gone. I found myself breathing hard, sucking into my lungs yet more of the ghastly fog, which made me cough and splutter all the more. I bent double. I was drowning in the city's visible stench.'

Virtue took a swig of brandy and sloshed it around his mouth, trying to wash away the remembered taste. He had become quite agitated in the recounting of his experience, offering none of the eye-rolls and leers with which the Colonel and the Reverend had punctuated their tales. His ghost story was of a different quality. I found myself feeling a little of the horror Virtue claimed to have felt, but tempered by a distance, a quarrelsome need to question. I bit my tongue, and let him continue.

'When I straightened up, a miraculous transformation was taking place, as if in answer to a prayer I had not dared to voice. The fog was thinning. Good clean transparent air rushed in from somewhere and diluted the muddy clouds, reducing it to streamers of ropy substance and a ground-covering of thin white mist. A draught hurried the worst of the stuff away, and I could again make out something of the situation in which I found myself.

'Naturally, I felt a surge of joy at my deliverance. But it froze in my breast. The scene disclosed was not that which I had expected.

'Simply put, I was transported. From the London we know to another realm entirely, a Stygian parody of the city, entirely loathsome in its crepusculence.

'I stood on a street washed with filth. More mud than stone, more ordure than mud. Buildings stood all around, walls stooped over to make a tunnel of this thoroughfare. The ill-fitting bricks bulged in places, allowing foul water to dribble.

There were smashed street-lamps, none lit. Fires burned in the night, within the buildings or in barrels set on the street, but heat and light were swallowed by the darkness and cold of this unnatural place. A nearby sign was splashed with dirt, unreadable. I knew that I was, in a more profound sense than I could imagine, lost.

'This place was inhabited. That is the worst of it.

'The first ghost I got a good look at inspired me not to horror but to pity. It was a waif-like thing, with huge liquid eyes and a tiny knot of a mouth, clad only in a vest-like singlet that disclosed wasted arms and grubby bare feet. I was unsure of its sex, for it wore a shapeless cap of some rough material over its hair, but I knew that it was not alive as we are. This was some poor lost soul, wandering.

'It saw me and stretched out a hand, palm up, beseeching.

'I had much this creature wanted, I was sure, but nothing I could give. Its eyes grew wetter and its head angled to one side. I heard its painful moan, a wordless begging. I stifled the pity that sprang up unwanted in my breast, and was on my guard against this ghostly thing. I fancied malice in its eye. This creature loved me not, would do me harm if it could, was not to be trusted.

'There were others, roughly in the shapes of men and women, but clad as even the lowest savage of India would never clothe himself, in the meanest of rags. I was assaulted by details. Rotten teeth, marbled eyes, grimy claw-nails, fungus swatches of hair, great scabs, mismatched buttons.

'Had these once been people?

'They came out of their dwellings and gathered around me, like a pack of dangerous dogs.

'"You are spirits," I declared, "and you cannot harm a Christian soul. Begone!"

'My words gave them pause. My mental strength returned. I was better than these creatures. I was alive. They could touch me only if I let them. My moment of weakness was past.

'I still had to escape from this place. And to do so I would have to turn my back. I believe this is the most courageous thing I have ever done.

'I turned and walked away, loudly reciting the Lord's Prayer. As I knew they would not, the ghosts did not rush at me from behind. I was too strong for that, and they knew me for their better.

'But I heard barks of laughter, horribly close to human mirth. As I plunged into a bank of thickening fog, returning I hoped to the world of the living, my cheeks burned with an inexplicable embarrassment. The ghosts mocked me, jeering at my back, possessed by a cruel hilarity that cast me out of their region as surely as my feet carried me away, into the fog again.

'Now, I was running almost, at least walking briskly. I began on the psalms. After some interval, I collided with a police constable in Farringdon Road and was able from there to make my way home.'

The Reverend Mr Weeks nodded sagely, and Colonel Beauregard scowled in sympathy. I felt as if I had myself been transported beyond the rational world, into Ernest Virtue's hellish half-city.

'I thought, that night as I prepared for my bed, my horrible experience was at an end. I imagined this moment, when I would retell it to good friends within a room of stout oak and know I was beyond the reach of those ghosts. I slept soundly, untroubled by what had occurred. The world was back as it should be, and my place in it was fixed and secure.

'But that laughter had followed me.

'Three days later, in the street outside the Exchange, I heard it again. I looked about, startled, rudely breaking off a conversation. It was broad daylight, if overcast. A great many brokers stood about in groups, discussing the day's business. Amid so many frock-coats and top-hats, it was hard to catch a glimpse of the tattered cloak. But it was there, I was sure. The quality of the laugh was not human. It came from the beyond.

'That was not the only incident. I have been certain, always when outside, when on the street, that I have seen a shadow or heard a cry which could only betoken the presence of one or more of that ghostly crew, escapees from that dreadful place abroad in the city of the living. Have they followed me back? Or have they always been among us, unseen by the many, maddening the few cursed souls who have awoken to their presence?

'I have been touched again. Their hands sometimes grip the skirts of my coat as I pass. Their fingers poke and prod. My watch is lost to them. I don't know when it was stealthed away, but when I found it was gone I also found a blue bruise on my belly, where the watch must have pressed.

'They love us not, these ghosts. They envy the life we have. They are needy, with a hunger we cannot understand. They would take everything from us if they could. And if they cannot have what we have, they will tear us down and destroy all we hold dear, out of spite. I must be strong, must remain strong. Else the world will spin out of its orbit and be lost in the darkness.'

'Now, now, old man,' said the Colonel. 'Chin up.'

'Yes, Colonel. I keep my chin up. I keep my back straight. I keep my heart closed. I can resist.'

I expected our clergyman to have something to say, but the Reverend Mr Weeks had nodded sagely off to sleep. In itself, that gave me a chill none of the stories had raised.

'For a while, it was dreadful,' Virtue continued. 'Even in broadest daylight and in the most respectable thoroughfares, I was aware of them. They slouch among us, clinging to their gutters and alleys, boldly meeting our glances, trying with their guttural noises to harry our minds. London is thick with these monsters. I was woken up to their presence, and wondered what spell had been cast over me so that I should be cursed with the power of seeing those things that should decently remain invisible. They are parodies of life, loathsome and pitiable, despicable and damned. Their corruption is complete, and yet they yearn, even as we do, for the light, for the warmth.

I know you must find this hard to credit, for had another tried to persuade me of this before my experience in the fog I would have deemed him mad. But these ghosts are among us. All the time.'

An excitement, almost a rage, had built up in me as Virtue spoke. I had expected one of the others to cut him off, to rend apart his strange misconception. And yet it fell to me.

'Surely,' I began, 'your ghosts are nothing supernatural. The place you have described is simply a slum. Sadly, many such are to be found in London. Your ghosts are just the poor, no more.'

Virtue's eyes fixed me like the lights of a hostile gunboat.

'The poor!' he exclaimed. 'The *poor*?'

There was a terrifying force inside him.

'The unfortunate,' I continued. 'Beggars and wastrels, no doubt. The human detritus of our city, those who through birth or inclination have found themselves settling on the bottom.'

'This is London,' Virtue said, with a ferocious certainty, 'the most prosperous city in the world. No such creatures exist, not naturally. My dear friend, of this I am sure as eggs is eggs. For me, the curtain has lifted and I have seen a hellish world beyond.'

I was horrorstruck by something new in Virtue's tone. A spark of pity, for me that I could be so deluded as to believe his phantoms to be people like ourselves.

'Colonel Beauregard, Mr Weeks,' I appealed.

Neither worthy – for Mr Weeks was now awake again – joined my position.

'This is a case of spectral persecution,' Virtue insisted. 'It will be resisted. If you ignore them, I have found, they go away. For I am winning my private war. This last week, they have been fainter presences. I can still see them, but I have to weaken and to direct my gaze at a fixed shadow to be sure. I have been successful in willing myself free of persecution. By ignoring the ghosts, I deny them substance. Within days, I shall have banished these apparitions entirely. Oak panels are my armour. My mind is my sword.'

Somehow, his conviction swayed me. I came to see his experience as he did himself. I still held in my mind my original assumption, but in my heart I knew I relied too much on my mind.

There were ghosts. This city was spectre-plagued. Mr Ernest Meiklejohn Virtue was haunted.

I added my own story to the collection, to conclude the evening. It was hurried, I confess, a confection of hooded monks and a hook-clawed madman, with lovers united beyond the grave and a villain harried over a cliff by the bloodied, floating faces of his victims.

The company broke up, and departed the club to the quarters of the compass.

It was not a foggy night, but it was moonless. I watched Virtue stride off vigorously, down a street ill-lit by faint gaslight. He almost marched, swinging his cane like a lance, looking straight ahead and not into any of the alleys that fed into the street, whistling a hymn that spoke of the rich man in his castle and the poor man at the gate, He made them high and lowly and ordered their estate. In some of the alleys were huddles that breathed and stretched out empty hands. He walked past, unseeing.

For Virtue, the haunting was almost over.

But a horror worse than all the crawling severed hands, floating green shrouds, chattering skulls and ambulant scarecrows pitched in together clung to the stones of this prosperous city, impinging when it had to on the main thoroughfares but festering always in the shadows beyond the gaslight, wrapping the hearts of men and women like you and me in a misery more profound than the sufferings of any wailing spectre bride or seaweed-dripping wrecker's revenant. I remembered Virtue's conviction of his own rectitude and of the strength of oak panels.

I resolved to model myself on him, and walked home,

holding my breath in the darks between the pools of lamplight, arriving safely at my own oak-lined fortress.

That night, I saw no ghosts.

In reviewing a collection of Victorian ghost stories, I once noted that writers of the period looked at ghosts exactly as they looked at the poor – as waifs to be pitied or rogues who deserved their fate. Years later, I elaborated the point.

DEAD TRAVEL FAST

In the great shed, a waterfall of molten iron poured into a long mould. Today, the undercarriage of a new engine was being cast, for the Great Western Railway, the Plymouth-to-Penzance line.

Massingham was confused for moments by the infernal glow, the terrific roar and the insufferable heat. No matter how many times he might be brought to the foundry, it was not an environment a man could become accustomed to. Those who worked here often ended up deaf or blind or prostrate with nervous disorder.

He looked around for the Count de Ville, and saw the foreign visitor standing much too close to the mould, in danger of being struck by spatters of liquid metal. The soft red drops were like acid bullets. They would eat through a man's chest or head in a second. In twenty years' service with the firm, Massingham had seen too many such accidents.

Whoever had let the visitor venture so close would answer for it. It was bad enough when one of the workers got careless and was maimed or killed, but to let an outsider, who had pulled strings to get a tour of the works, suffer such a fate would bring unpleasant publicity. The Board of Directors would most certainly hold Massingham responsible for such a catastrophe.

De Ville was a black silhouette, fringed with bitter crimson. He seemed to look directly at the white hot iron, unaffected by the harsh glow that ruined others' eyes. All Massingham knew about the Count was that he was a foreign gentleman, with a great interest in railways. The Board scented an opportunity, assuming this toff was well enough connected in his own country to put in a word when it came to the purchase of rolling-stock. Two-thirds of the world ran on rails cast in this shed, riding in carriages made in the factory, pulled by engines manufactured by the firm.

'Count de Ville,' Massingham coughed.

He had spoken too softly, above the tinkle of teacups in a drawing-room, not the roaring din of the casting shed, but the Count's ears were as sharp as his eyes were hardy. He turned round, eyes reflecting the burning red of the furnaces, and bowed slightly from the waist.

'I'm Henry Massingham, the under-manager. I'm to show you round.'

'Excellent,' said the Count. 'I am certain to find the tour most enlightening. My own country is sadly backward by comparison with your great empire. I am anxious to be introduced to all the marvels of the age.'

He made no especial effort to raise his voice over the racket, but was heard clearly. His elongated vowels gave him away as someone whose first language was not English, but he had no trouble with his consonants save perhaps for a little hiss in his sibilants.

With no little relief, Massingham left the casting-shed, followed by the tall, thin foreigner. The noise resounded in his ears for a few moments after they were out in the open. Though it was a breezy day, he could still feel the intense heat of the foundry on his cheeks.

Out in daylight, under thick clouds that obscured the sun, the Count was a less infernal figure. He was dressed entirely in black, like a Roman Catholic priest, with a long coat over tight swathes of material that bespoke no London tailoring, and heavy boots suitable for harsh mountains. Oddly, he topped off his ensemble with a cheap straw hat of the type one buys at the sea-side to use for a day and lose by nightfall. Massingham had an idea the Count was inordinately and strangely fond of the hat; his first English-bought item of clothing.

It occurred to Massingham that he didn't know which country the Count was from. The name de Ville sounded French, but a rasp in his voice suggested somewhere in Central Europe, deep in that ever-changing patch of the map caught between the Russias and the Austro-Hungarian Empire. Running rails up and down mountains was an expensive business, and a solid contract to provide a railway system for such an area could be a long-term high-earner for the firm.

Massingham escorted the Count about the factory, following the creation of an engine by visiting all the stages of the manufacture, from the primal business of casting through to the fine detail-work on the boilerplate and the polishing of the brass finishings. The Count was especially delighted, like a little boy, with the steam whistle. The foreman fired up an engine on the test-bed, purely so de Ville might have the childish joy of pulling the chain and making the shrill toot-toot that would announce the coming of an iron giant to some out-of-the-way halt.

The Count de Ville was a railway enthusiast of great passion, who had from afar memorised his Bradshaw's guide to timetables and was merely seeing for the first time processes he had read of and imagined for many years. He probably knew more about trains than did Massingham, whose responsibilities were mostly in overseeing the book-keeping, and who wound up delivering more lectures than he received.

'What a world it shall be, when the globe is encircled round about by steel rails,' enthused the Count. 'Men and matériel shall be transported in darkness, in sealed carriages, while the world sleeps. Borders shall become meaningless, distances will be an irrelevance and a new civilisation rise to the sound of the train whistle.'

'Ahem,' said Massingham, 'indeed.'

'I came to this land by sea,' de Ville said sadly. 'I am irretrievably a creature of the past. But I shall conquer this new world, Mr Massingham. It is my dearest ambition to become a railwayman.'

There was something strange in his conviction.

The tour concluded, Massingham hoped to steer de Ville to the board-room, where several directors would be waiting, hiding behind genial offers of port and biscuits, ready to make casual suggestions as to possible business arrangements and privately determined not to let the Count escape without signing up for a substantial commitment. Massingham's presence would not be required at the meeting, but if a contract were signed, his part in it would be remembered.

'What is that building?' de Ville asked, indicating a barn-like structure he had not been shown. It stood in a neglected corner of the works, beyond a pile of rejected, rusting rails.

'Nothing important, Count,' said Massingham. 'It's for tinkering, not real work.'

The word 'tinkering' appealed to de Ville.

'It sounds fascinating, Mr Massingham. I should be most interested to be allowed inside.'

There was the question of secrecy. It was unlikely that the Count was a spy from another company, but nevertheless it was not wise to let it be known what the firm was working on. Massingham chewed his moustache for a moment, unsure. Then he recalled that the only tinkerer in residence at the moment was George Foley, of the improbable contraption. There was no real harm in showing the Count that white elephant, though he feared a potential customer might conclude the firm was foolhardy indeed to throw away money on such an obvious non-starter and might take his business elsewhere.

'We have been allowing space to an inventor,' said Massingham. 'I fear we have become a safe harbour for an arrant crackpot, but you might find some amusement at the bizarre results of his efforts.'

He led the Count through the double doors.

Several shots sounded, rattling the tin roof of the shed. Bursts of fire lit the gloom.

Immediately, Massingham was afraid that de Ville was the

victim of an assassination plot. Everyone knew these Balkan nobs were pursued by anarchists eager to pot them with revolvers in revenge for injustices committed down through the centuries by barbarous ancestors.

A stench of sulphur stung his nostrils. Clouds of foul smoke were wafting up to the roof. There was a slosh and a hiss as a bucket of water was emptied on a small fire.

The reports had been not shots but small explosions. It was just Foley's folly, again. Massingham was relieved, but then annoyed when he wiped his brow with his cuff to find his face coated with a gritty, oily discharge.

Through smoke and steam, he saw Foley and his familiar, the boy Gerald, fussing about a machine, faces and hands black as Zulus', overalls ragged as tramps'. George Foley was a young man, whose undeniable technical skills were tragically allied to a butterfly mind that constantly alighted upon the most impractical and useless concepts.

'My apologies, Count,' said Massingham. 'I am afraid that this is what one must expect when one devotes oneself to the fantastic idea of an engine worked by explosion. Things will inevitably blow up.'

'Combustion,' snapped Foley. 'Not explosion.'

'I crave your pardon, Foley,' said Massingham. 'Infernal combustion.'

Foley's written proposals were often passed round the under-managers for humorous relief.

'Internal,' squeaked Gerald, an eleven-year-old always so thickly greased and blackened that it was impossible to tell what the colour of his hair or complexion might be. 'Internal combustion, not infernal.'

'I believe my initial choice of word was apt.'

'That's as may be, Massingham, but look.'

The device that had exploded was shaking now, emitting a grumble of noise and spurts of noxious smoke. A crank was turning a belt, which was turning a wheel. Massingham had seen such toys before.

115

'Five times more efficient than steam,' Foley said. 'Maybe ten, a dozen . . .'

'And five times more likely to kill you.'

'In the early days of steam, many were killed,' said the Count. He gazed into Foley's engine, admiring the way the moving parts meshed. It was a satisfyingly complicated toy, with oiled pistons and levers and cogs. A child's idea of a wonderful machine.

'I'm sorry, sir,' said Foley, 'and you are . . . ?'

'This is the Count de Ville,' explained Massingham. 'An important connection of the firm, from overseas. He is interested in railways.'

'Travel,' said the Count. 'I am interested in travel. In the transport of the future.'

'You have then chanced upon the right place, Count,' said Foley. He did not offer a dirty hand, but nodded a greeting, almost clicking his heels. 'For in this workshop is being sounded the death-knell of the whole of the rest of the factory. My transport, my horseless carriage, will make the steam engine as obsolete as the train made the stagecoach.'

'Horseless carriage?' said the Count, drawing out the words, rolling the idea around his mind.

'It's a wonder, sir,' said Gerald, eyes shining. Foley tousled the boy's already-greasy bird's nest of hair, proud of his loyal lackey.

Massingham suppressed a bitter laugh.

Foley led them past the still-shaking engine on its fixed trestle, to a dust-sheeted object about the size of a small hay-cart. The inventor and the nimble Gerald lifted off the canvas sheet and threw it aside.

'This is my combustion carriage,' said Foley, with pride. 'I shall have to change the name, of course. It might be called a petroleum caleche, or an auto-mobile.'

The invention sat squarely on four thick-rimmed wheels, with a small carriage-seat suspended above them to the rear of one of Foley's combustion engines.

116

'There will be a housing on the finished model, to keep the elements out of the engine and cut down the noise. The smoke will be discharged through these pipes.'

'The flat wheel-rims suggest this will not run on rails,' said the Count.

'Rails,' Foley fairly spat. 'No, sir. Indeed not. This will run on roads. Or, if there are no roads, on any reasonably level surface. Trains are limited, as you know. They cannot venture where rail-layers have not been first, at great expense. My carriage will be free, eventually, to go everywhere.'

'Always in a straight line?'

'By means of a steering apparatus, the front wheels can be turned like a ship's rudder.'

Massingham was impatient with such foolishness.

'My dear Count,' said Foley, 'I foresee that this device, of which Mr Massingham is so leery, will change the world as we know it, and greatly for the better. The streets of our cities will no longer be clogged with the excrement of horses. No more fatalities or injuries will be caused by animals bolting or throwing their riders. And there will be no more great collisions, for these carriages are steerable and can thus avoid each other. Unlike horses, they do not panic; and, unlike trains, they do not run on fixed courses. Derailments, obviously, are out of the question. The first and foremost attribute of the combustion carriage is its safety.'

The Count walked round the carriage, eyeing its every detail, smiling with his sharp teeth. There was something animal-like about de Ville, a single-mindedness at once childish and frightening.

'May I?' The Count indicated the seat.

Foley hesitated but, sensing a potential sponsor, shrugged.

De Ville climbed up into the seat. The carriage settled under his weight. The axles were on suspension springs, like a hansom cab. The Count ran his hands around the great steering-wheel, which was as unwieldy and stiff as those that worked the locks on a canal. There were levers to the side of the seat, the purpose of which was unknown to Massingham, though he assumed one must be a braking-mechanism.

Beside the wheel was a rubber-bulbed horn. The Count squeezed it experimentally.

Poop-poop!

'To alert pedestrians,' explained Foley. 'The engine runs so quietly that the horn will be necessary.'

The Count smiled, eyes rimmed with red delight. He poop-pooped again, evidently in love. His craze for trains was forgotten. Poop-poop had trumped toot-toot.

Foreigners were a lot like children.

'How does it start?'

'With a crank.'

'Show me,' de Ville ordered.

Foley nodded to Gerald, who darted to the front of the contraption with a lever and fitted it into the engine. He gave it a turn, and nothing happened. Massingham had seen this before. Usually, the dignitaries summoned to witness the great breakthrough had retreated by the time the engine caught. Then it would only sputter a few moments, allowing the carriage to lurch forward a yard or two before at best stalling and at worst exploding.

If Foley's folly blew up and killed the Count, Massingham would have to answer for it. The man clearly had an impulse towards death.

Gerald cranked the engine again, and again, and . . .

. . . nipped out of the way sharpish. Small flames burst in the guts of the machine, and the pistons began to pump.

The carriage moved forward, and the Count poop-pooped the blasted horn again. He would have been as happy with the noise-maker alone as the whole vehicle.

Slowly, the carriage trundled towards the open doors of the workshop. Foley looked alarmed, but didn't protest. Picking up more speed than usual, the carriage disappeared out of the doors. The Count's straw hat blew off and was wafted up towards the roof by the black smoke that poured thickly from the pipes at the rear of the machine.

Massingham, Foley and Gerald followed the carriage to the doorway. Astonished, they saw the Count piloting the machine, with growing expertise, yanking hard on the steering-wheel and turning in ever tighter circles, circumnavigating the pile of rails, weaving in and out between sheds and buildings.

A cat shot out of the way, its tail flat. Workmen passing by stopped to stare. A small crowd gathered, of idle hands distracted from their appointed tasks. Some of the directors poked their heads out, silk hats held to their heads.

It was a ridiculous sight, but somehow stirring. The Count was very intent, very serious. But the machine just looked silly, not majestic like a steam engine. Still, Massingham had a glimpse of what Foley saw in the thing.

The Count poop-pooped the horn. Someone cheered.

Gerald, delighted, danced in the wake of the carriage.

The Count made a hard turn and suddenly the boy's legs were under the front wheels. Bright blood spurted up into the oily engine, as if it were Moloch demanding sacrifice.

Foley shouted. Massingham felt a hammer-blow to his heart.

The Count seemed not to have realised what he had done, and drove on, grinding the boy under the carriage, merrily poop-pooping the damnable horn. The wheel-rims were reddened, and left twin tracks of blood for twenty feet in the rutted earth. Workmen rushed to help the boy, who was yelling in pain, legs quite crushed, face white under the dirt.

De Ville found the brake and brought the carriage to a halt.

Foley was too shocked to speak.

The Count stepped down, exhilarated.

'What a marvellous transport,' he declared. 'It will indeed be the machine of the future. I share your vision, Mr Foley. You will make the world a swifter, purer place. These vehicles will be armoured, making each driver a warrior apart from others, a knight whose mind is one with that of his steed. You have invented a movable castle, one which can be equipped for assault and defence. The carriage can serve as refuge, land-ironclad, vehicle of exploration and finally casket or tomb. I shall be among the first purchasers of your wonderful carriage. You may number me as a sponsor of its manufacture. I shall not rest until the whole world runs on infernal combustion.'

He reached up into the air, and his straw hat was returned to his long fingers through the swirling smoke. The quality of Gerald's screaming changed, to a low, whimpering sob. The Count appeared not to notice the noise, though Massingham remembered the sharpness of his ears.

The Count de Ville tapped his hat on to his head at a jaunty angle, gave the bulb-horn a final, fond poop-poop and walked into the black clouds of smoke, which seemed to part for him and then closed around him like a cloak.

Massingham thought about the future. There was probably money in it.

A risk of theme anthologies is that if you write a story for one and don't get in (or, as I think is the case here, the book doesn't happen), you're stuck with a very specific piece which won't suit other markets. This was solicited by P. N. Elrod for a collection of stories which purport to fill in the gaps in Bram Stoker's *Dracula* by showing what the Count was doing on his trip to London when he is only glimpsed by the novel's many narrators. When he heard about this premise, Steve Baxter quite rightly suggested that he was probably taking in the shows, visiting the tourist spots and asking for directions like any other foreigner in London. Another risk of theme anthologies is that everyone has the same idea and you get a clutch of stories which read very similarly: so I resolved to do a Dracula story in which he didn't bite anyone, and which focused on another aspect of the character Stoker gave him than bloodlust.

Though the primary purpose of 'Dead Travel Fast' was to fit in with Stoker's text, there is nothing here that contradicts the timeline I have established in the *Anno Dracula* novels: *Anno Dracula*, *The Bloody Red Baron* and *Dracula Cha Cha Cha*.

UNE ÉTRANGE AVENTURE DE RICHARD BLAINE

'Go, my darling, and God bless you, Ilsa.' It's like a hammer to the back of the head.

In an instant, everything good is gone.

The world is hell.

Ink running in the rain. A wet letter in my hands. Water pouring off the brim of my fedora. An insistent tug at the sleeve of my trenchcoat. Clouds of steam. A train, about to leave.

'That's the last call, Mr Richard,' Sam says. 'Do you hear me? Come on, Mr Richard. Let's get out o' here.'

It's hard, but I can do it. My guts are lying on the rain-soaked platform, but I can walk without tripping in them. Sure, I can. It's easy.

Forget Ilsa.

Get out of Paris.

Now.

'En voiture,' the man shouts.

This is the last train out. The one we were supposed to take together. To freedom and safety.

Damn her. Damn her rotten silky hide. Damn.

'Come on, Mr Richard. Come on.'

Yeah. Let's go. Fade.

Clicking heels. A bark of gunfire. Men in grey uniform advance down the platform, pushing through panicky would-be passengers. The train lurches, wheels screaming. Sam is up in the carriage door, humping our cases.

I step up, resolved.

I can live without her. I can go on. Dead inside, maybe, but moving.

A hand closes on my shoulder.

'Mr Richard Blaine?'

It's a harsh voice, rasping. German.

The train shifts, moving off. I see more than panic in Sam's eyes as he slides away.

This just puts the cherry on top of the day. The Germans are in Paris. And so am I.

'I'm an American citizen,' I tell the Nazi. 'Neutrality is my religion.'

'That was not how you conducted yourself in Spain or Ethiopia, my friend.'

I shrug, stomach plunging. My dossier is evidently extensive and annotated.

'SS Standartenführer Professor Doktor Franz Six,' says the officer. I believe him.

Six is a small man, almost bald but still young, blue eyes cold behind steel-rimmed spectacles, uniformed in black with silver lightning-flash insignia. His trenchcoat is the colour of midnight. His cap-peak is like the razor-bill of a predatory bird.

Field-grey goons close around me. The train has gone.

It doesn't really matter. The way I feel, summary execution would be a blessing.

Damn Ilsa.

'Your assistance is required by the Third Reich,' says Six.

'The Third Reich seems to be doing quite well on its own.'

The station is being occupied. German soldiers search through the unlucky crowds, looking for faces they've memorised, matching identity papers against names on a list. French railwaymen are standing down, their duties assumed by military policemen. All further trains are cancelled.

Someone makes a break for it. There are shots.

'Indeed, this is an encouraging day for the Reich, Mr Blaine. However, I'm charged with an especial mission for the Führer, one with which you can be of great help.'

'With which? Fine grammar.'

Six smiles, showing sharp little teeth. It would be a mistake to think him soft or stupid.

The station is emptying of civilians. Rain washes down over deserted platforms. Abandoned suitcases are soaked. Someone has left behind a double-bass.

Filtering out the excess people reveals who it was that spotted me for Six. A wiry youth, with an impertinent forelock that stands up stiff as a wood-shaving. He has piggy little eyes and baggy plus-fours. With him is an annoying little white dog.

I recognise him vaguely, from around the cafés and cabarets. Though just a kid, he's some sort of a reporter. Though French, he's a fascist. Six nods, and he scurries over, dog at his heels.

'Our young friend has been of some help,' Six tells me, 'but he doesn't have the sensitivities for the job. Unlike you.'

The kid's eyes glitter. I have no friends here. He must have wanted to be Nazi Puppet Number One, and now he's just one of the gang.

We're all standing in the rain, which doesn't seem to bother Six. It's as if he has an invisible shield around him, a bubble of warmth and confidence. Hitler gives these monkeys something special.

'My friend, I'm responsible for the apprehension of certain individuals. Well, not so much individuals as types. Until they are in our hands, we cannot truly say we have taken Paris.'

'I should think that, about now, you could say what you want and nobody will holler.'

Six giggles. It's like needles scraping your skull.

'You are on my list, Mr Blaine. Paris is important to you, and you to her.'

Her. Yes, the city is a woman. Ten minutes ago she was a sweetheart. Now I know she's a whore.

The damned letter is a wet lump under my shoe.

'You're too late for that. I don't care about Paris. I don't care about anyone.'

'You only think that, Mr Blaine. Paris is a part of you. In your sentimental fugues, you may think it the better part of you, but it is your weakness. It is why you are, as it were, surrounded.'

'This is a waste of time,' the kid hisses, in French.

'I think not,' says Six. 'I think we have an understanding.'

Whatever. I'm not doing anything else. Any principles I had have been washed away by the rain. Without Ilsa, I might just as well be a Nazi. I'll make a good one. I'll have just the right attitude.

I nod.

'Excellent,' the Nazi smiles. 'We three shall round them up, all the types on our list, all the creatures of the city. When we have them, we shall have taken Paris body and soul.'

The kid's dog barks. I kick it in the head.

Just like a Nazi.

The first individual on Six's little list isn't even a human being. That doesn't matter. Rick Blaine, dog-kicker extraordinaire, isn't afraid of anything that crawls or climbs, swims or slouches.

The ape is half-way up a building, waving a straight razor and jabbering in what sounds like Hungarian. Its gums are a scarlet wound. Its long limbs and round body are covered with a thick, bristly black pelt.

'Have Göring get into a biplane and shoot King Kong off his perch,' I suggest.

Six giggles again.

They want the ape alive. It figures.

I shrug, and walk into the empty street. An armoured car is parked at the kerb. The ape throws chunks of masonry at it. It could pitch for the Dodgers, hits the swastika on the hood every time.

I've got an automatic in my pocket. I could do better with a banana.

'Hey, Ingagi,' I yell, getting the monkey's attention.

Strictly, it's an orang-outan. It waves its razor.

I catch the ape's eye. It's not stupid. It doesn't recognise me, but it knows me, senses that we have something in common. We're both foreigners in this city, but we both have a connection with it that runs deep.

'Come down,' I shout, feeling dumb.

The ape tenses, and I think it's about to launch itself into space and crash down on me in a tumble of scrabbling hands and slicing blade. My strength is that I don't care. My guts have already been torn out, and they might as well be strewn in the gutter of the rue Morgue as anywhere else.

Meekly, the orang-outan climbs down to the street. It folds its razor closed with a neat click and gives it up to me. Six's stormtroopers rush in with a net and wrap the ape up into a chattering ball.

Six and the kid reporter watch me. The Nazi applauds, slowly. I am being mocked but I don't care.

The ape is miserable, betrayed, chewing at the wires of the net, struggling with the six goons who are loading him into the armoured car. I don't care. Something tiny and hot and nasty is growing where my heart used to be.

If this is what the world (Ilsa) wants me to be, then fine. I'll be the best damn Nazi in Paris, *Sieg heil* and *Über alles*.

'You've done well, my friend,' purrs the doctor.

Give me a medal, buddy.

Our expedition under Paris is a major adventure. In a motor-launch requisitioned from the river police, we whizz through the sewers, bowed low so as not to scrape our hats off on the tunnel roofs, leaving waves of disturbed shit in our wake. None of the maps the Germans have dug up is of much help: the city sits atop an uncharted labyrinth of interconnecting tunnels, sewers, caverns, catacombs, hide-outs and lost worlds that date back to the Romans and beyond. Down here, we're relying on my mysterious and new-found instincts.

I have talents I didn't know about. I've always lived half in and half out of the world. Dr Six has chosen me well. I can home in on the individuals on his list because I have a kinship with them but am estranged from them. I can thank Ilsa for that, at least.

I wonder if she's on the list too. Six has never let me see it, if indeed it is written down and not just in his head. She'd fit in with some of the others. We have rounded up a good many women: a barefoot gypsy dancer reputed to be a sorceress, with a goat for a familiar; an Irish singer with a blank face and a bell-pure voice, along with her terrified and terrifying Hebrew manager; a consumptive artists' model, spitting blood into her handkerchief; a beautiful commissar, seduced by silk undies. Sweethearts and whores, gamines and adventuresses, royal mistresses and gutter-waifs. All on the list, all in custody.

We chug through the tunnels, casting cones of light ahead and aft. Six, the reporter, the white dog, and a platoon of standard-issue stormtroopers. The soldiers don't like being down under the streets, in the dark, in the shit. They mutter together, heedless of their boss's enthusiasm for the chase.

Six tried to persuade the pipe-puffing policeman who surrendered so meekly to join us on this trip under the city. The inspector regretfully declined, saying that though he was forced to recognise the authority of the new masters of the city he could not lend himself to such an enterprise.

Damn the flic. He was elaborately almost sorry for me, and I didn't need his pity. No wonder the city fell. Everyone was so weak, so frail. Most of the creatures we were hunting were crippled by their desperate, illusionary loves. Paris is the city of the Insanely Romantic.

I sense a presence.

'There,' I say, pointing ahead.

Searchlights are directed. There is a man in the water, swimming.

'It's the ex-convict,' says the reporter. 'The fugitive thief.'

Six giggles.

Our boat gains on the man. Waves of sewage drag at him.

He flails. Is he trying to drown himself rather than be recaptured? He's been on the run most of his life, in and out of the Château d'Yf and Île du Diable.

He is hauled out of the water in a sorry state. He lies in the boat, breathing heavily, stinking.

We emerge into a cavernous space, an underground lake in a cathedral-arched chamber. The searchlights play upon a vaulted roof hundreds of feet above us. Six whistles in awe.

The lake is big enough to harbour an island. It is a long shape, like a sea-monster lying on the surface. We pass by, and I see it's not a true island but a man-made thing. Rows of rivets stand out on its metal hide. A serrated, horn-like protrusion juts out between eye-like green windows. It is abandonded, I sense. Left here to distract us. I wave us on.

'Keep going,' I say. 'It's just a lost toy.'

Music sounds. Thin, reedy organ-tones.

I know this is one of the prizes of Paris, one of the types at the head of the list. Six smiles at me. The Opéra Ghost is nearby, driven out of the extensive cellars of the Paris Opéra into the larger catacombs. I know something of this creature's story. His tragedy is an impossible love, too.

The boat crosses the lake, our lights playing on the far shore.

'Be careful,' I say. 'This guy is known for devilish trickiness. There'll be traps.'

One of Six's troopers, having conquered the world, begins to sneer and his head is sheared in two just below his eyes. A flying guillotine. The Nazi crumples and splashes into the water, leaving behind the top of his head, still in its helmet, rolling in the flat bottom of the boat.

I kill the searchlight. We all crouch in the dark.

The music swells in mocking triumph.

It occurs to me that the ex-convict has led us into a trap. It was only a matter of time before the names on our list caught on to what we were doing and began cooperating. How many others are out there?

We collide with the shore and pile out of the boat. A jagged ripping and a scream. Some new, clever device. There is a gleam of gloom up ahead, through a tunnel. I blink and get night vision. The organ chords pour at us. The musician has lost the tune, and is improvising in a frenzy.

I tap Six on the epaulette and nod ahead.

We are to proceed, with caution.

The journalist steps into the tunnel first, and is yanked off his feet. I hear him gurgling as he dangles. A noose is cinched round his throat.

His white dog leaps up round his kicking heels, yapping.

My arm up to protect me, I run into the tunnel. Six and his men are behind me.

I know there are enemies up ahead.

Not just the Opéra Ghost, but the masked Master Thief, the Poet Swordsman, the Vengeful Count, the Pianist With the Knife-Thrower's Hands, the Tramp From the River, the Children of Paradise, the Queen's Musketeers. A full swoop of Six's types. With them apprehended, there would only be a few very small fish – boulevardiers and ex-patriates – to gather.

'Friends, friends,' I shout. 'I have led them to you. I'm one of you, not one of them. Vive la France! Liberté, égalité, frat—'

A cold hand closes on my mouth and yanks me from the tunnel. A nose pokes at my face. Cold steel lies across my Adam's apple.

The duellist wears a huge hat and a froth of lace round his throat. But it is impossible to look away from his prodigious nose, which sprouts from his face like a swollen bulb. If I look at his eyes, the tip of his nose goes out of focus and seems even bigger.

'What are you staring at, American?' he asks.

I try to shrug, but am held firm.

'You have such lovely eyes,' I say.

He laughs, lustily.

'Take me to your leader,' I say.

'We've no leader,' he replies. 'We're too rowdy a lot for leaders.'

I understand. 'Take me to him, to the master of the machine in the lake.'

A smile curls in the shadow of the nose. 'He is dead. The spectre plays for his funeral.'

I am pulled through a secret door. Candelabra light up the space all around. I see the thin black back of the man at the organ. Bone-white hands play over the keys. He turns and I see his skull-face, enormous eyes active in a white mask of death.

Others are here.

A thief in immaculate evening dress, face half-masked. His companion, a sylph-like woman in a black body-stocking that shows only her eyes. A hollow-eyed aesthetic adventurer, delighted at last to have sunk as low as is possible in Paris. A young girl, trained from infancy to be a courtesan. A lazy-eyed *apache* loafer, cigarette dangling from his snarl, a tight-skirted floozy at the end of his leash. The captain of the good ship *Atalante* and his child wife. A young man with the look of a philosopher who has discovered futility or has been nauseated by the wallpaper of the world. And the older ones, older even than my big-nosed friend. A couple of Englishmen, one dashing in disguise, the other ready to go to the tumbril for a friend. A woman cackling bloodily over her knitting. The swordsmen and the gallants, the ones whose legends have grown with the city. Shambling in the shadows is a form more twisted than the ape of the rue Morgue, hiding behind pillars, face hidden in shame.

'We are Paris,' says my captor.

He is right. These people are the heart of the city. When you think about Paris, you have to think about one or two or all of them. You may not find them there when you arrive, but they are why you go there.

I'm one of them.

Yet not.

I can forget Paris. I want to, in fact. Ilsa saw to that.

When all these people are gathered up in the pens under the Théâtre du Grand-Guignol where Six has been assembling them, and are shipped out in cattle-trucks to some death camp of the spirit the Nazis have built in the East, then I'll be free of Paris. The city will mean nothing to me.

I'm not sorry.

'You are all under arrest,' I say.

My automatic is under the gallant's nose. A gun trumps a sword.

'Don't anybody move.'

The organ wheezes to silence.

'Six,' I shout. 'Through here!'

Eyes fix on me with hate. They expected me to side with them, I see. They misread my story. Or came in at the wrong reel.

'I stick my neck out for no one,' I explain.

The deformed boy pokes his head out of the shadows. His misaligned eyes look up at me, full of tears. If I had a heart left, his ugly lost face would reach it.

But . . .

Six and his surviving goons arrive.

'I believe we have a full house,' he says.

'I thought you'd want to be here, my friend,' Six says. 'To see the job through.'

It is an overcast day. Three trucks are parked outside the Théâtre du Grand-Guignol. Soldiers stand around, waiting. Orders are posted everywhere. Passers-by don't want to know what is going on here.

The prisoners, shackled together, are herded into the trucks. Some are unused to showing their faces by day. The Opéra Ghost, in drab prison pyjamas rather than evening clothes, is less fearsome in thin daylight; not a demon lover, just a hairless, noseless old man. Without his domino mask, the Master Thief is a dull bourgeois in handcuffs.

'Where will you execute them?' I ask, empty inside.

'We would not waste so valuable a resource, Mr Blaine. We shall keep our catch safe. Away from the city, perhaps, but carefully unharmed.'

I wonder if they can live away from the city.

'Only now do we really have Paris, you understand. With these people in custody, we control this city's soul. All great cities have a collective soul, an über-mythic collective heart. The Führer understands this. What is London without the Demon Barber and the Consulting Detective and the Mayor's Cat? Or Prague without the Golem, the Alchemist, the student who sells his soul? These are our real enemies in Europe, Mr Blaine. Not armies and politicians and populations. Those can be overcome, crushed, destroyed, absorbed. It is these individuals, who in some sense are not even real people, these creatures who stand against our Nazi dream. We understand and believe in über-myths too. But there is room for only one vast myth now, a German myth that has no time for the squabbling, petty, monstrous, feeble-hearts we see before us. With these people gone, our myth can truly occupy the city. Who knows, maybe some of them can come back. The reporter understood, was willing to let himself vanish into the larger story.'

'Like me,' I say, hollowly.

'No, Mr Blaine. Not you. You have helped us not out of conviction but out of spite. All very well. We understand spite, too. You may go, because it is not important that you be here. You are a part of another city's myth-pool. It is important that you have a memory of Paris, but be estranged from the city itself. That is why you were so perfect for our purposes.'

The reporter's dog is still hanging around, sullen and angry. Its white coat is muddied, almost the colour of a German uniform.

It's hard for the soldiers to get the weeping hunchback into the truck, which holds up the rest of the coffle. Chains clank. The orang-outan is already inside, drugged for travel. Last into the truck is the policeman, grumpy because he is not allowed his pipe.

I can walk away safely now. Join Sam, and get on with my life. My myth, as Six would have it.

131

One last prisoner is too delicate to be chained with the others. She is brought out on a stretcher, thin shoulders shivering, cold white hands crossed on her breast. She won't last the journey.

Six shrugs sadly.

'We Germans love her, too,' he says. 'This girl and her type and her city. But we have iron in our soul. New-forged. We have the strength to strip the city of her.'

One of the soldiers loses his grip, and the feet-end of the stretcher hits the pavement. The girl coughs blood, and her huge eyes catch mine.

She looks like Ilsa. Every damn woman in Paris looks like Ilsa, somehow.

I'm neutral. I've done a job, in exchange for freedom. These people mean nothing to me. Less than nothing. Paris is overrated anyway. Nothing but whores and pimps and murderers. All these people have blood on their hands.

The girl is close to death, always has been.

My heart starts beating again.

'Shall we see them off, Mr Blaine?'

I put my hands in my pockets, and bring one of them out again.

'That is an automatic pistol, Mr Blaine.'

'And a very fine one, Six.'

The Nazi is disappointed in me. He makes a tiny signal. I am to be shot.

Then that blasted dog darts in and nips the heel of Six's jack-boot, sinking sharp teeth into the black leather. The SS man is surprised and looks down.

I plug him in the chest. Twice.

'Doktor Six has been shot,' I shout, to the soldiers. 'I'll guard the prisoners. Search the theatre. I saw a man with a gun, up on the roof. A jackal, running.'

Six is on his knees, dying. He doesn't understand why. He never will.

The girl smiles, thinly, blood on her lips.

The soldiers stand around, looking dumb. They were distracted by the dog and didn't see my gun spit death.

'Up on the roof,' I insist, waving my gun. 'Mach schnell!'

It gets through. They clatter into the theatre, shouting.

I take the keys from Six's pocket, and roll his corpse into the gutter. I wonder if he realised how close he came himself to an archetype, the Sardonic Nazi Officer. Of course, he was different from us. He was a real person. You can look him up in the books.

I toss the keys to the Master Thief, who gets everyone off the chain in double-quick time. I had an idea he would have the fastest fingers in the group.

'Quick,' I say, 'into the sewers.'

The ex-convict groans, 'Not again,' but his fellows hurry him along. A manhole cover is wrenched up, and the escapees plunge into the darkness. I watch the last of them – the Jewish singing-master with the scraggle of beard and the neon-glowing eyes – disappear, and pick up the girl from the stretcher. She is frozen, but I carry her underground.

Inside, the submersible device is a riot of leather upholstery and polished brass. Its captain may be gone, but it has been maintained in perfect working order. There is even a pipe organ, and the Opéra Ghost plays a Bach fugue on it as we sink below the waters of the underground lagoon.

At the helm, the captain of the *Atalante* scratches his head and tries to understand the unfamiliar controls. He is the master of Paris's waterways, and will soon learn how to manoeuvre this marvellous contraption.

We are all cramped here, but there is a joy in freedom.

I don't want anyone's thanks. It's due to me that Six got as far as he did with his project. There have been casualties. The model girl died in the sewer, and is stowed somewhere. But she'll always be here, in Paris.

I'll leave now. Hook up with Sam, head for Marseille, cross the sea. After all this French rain, I'd like to live in a desert for a while, have my own place. Six was right about me. I have a story to finish.

They are arguing, this leaderless crowd. The braggart with the nose and one of the Queen's Swordsmen butt heads over the charts, each certain of the course they should be plotting but neither with any experience of navigation. The captain smokes his pipe and carries on regardless.

The orang-outan is waking up. The *apache* has stabbed his mistress. The ex-convict is outside, in the filthy waters again. The Opéra Ghost has criticised the Irish girl's voice, and enraged the Jewish manager. A whore and a dancer are competing for the affections of the white dog. Cigarette and pipe smoke makes a pestilential cloud in the enclosed space.

There is a din of life here.

Despite Ilsa, despite everything, it's in me. Paris, and all it means. I'll never escape it entirely.

I'll leave these people soon. There's a lazy-eyed thief here who dreams of Algiers and the Casbah; I shall follow his example, and light out for North Africa. They'll break up, return to their hiding-places, play catch'em with the Gestapo. Their city will be underground for a while, but a secret victory has been gained.

The Germans won't always have Paris. But I will.

This was written for *The Time Out Book of Paris Short Stories*, edited by Nicholas Royle. If Hitler had successfully invaded, Dr Six would have been Governor of Nazi-occupied Britain. The rest of the characters aren't real, but at least they aren't might-have-beens.

Cleared paths were no good for Allie. She wasn't supposed to be after rabbits on Squire Maskell's land. Most of Alder Hill was wildwood, trees webbed together by a growth of bramble nastier than barbed wire. Thorns jabbed into skin and stayed, like bee-stings.

Just after dawn, the air had a chilly bite but the sunlight was pure and strong. Later, it would get warm; now, her hands and knees were frozen from dew-damp grass and iron-hard ground.

The Reeve was making a show of being tough on poaching, handing down short, sharp sentences. She'd already got a stripe across her palm for setting snares. Everyone west of Bristol knew Reeve Draper was Maskell's creature. Serfdom might have been abolished, but the old squires clung to their pre-War position, through habit as much as tenacity.

Since taking her lash, administered under the Village Oak by Constable Erskine with a razor-strop, she'd grown craftier. Wiry enough to tunnel through brambles, she made and travelled her own secret, thorny paths. She'd take Maskell's rabbits, even if the Reeve's Constable striped her like a tiger.

She set a few snares in obvious spots, where Stan Budge would find and destroy them. Maskell's gamekeeper wouldn't be happy if he thought no one was even trying to poach. The trick was to set snares invisibly, in places Budge was too grown-up, too far off the ground, to look.

Even so, none of her nooses had caught anything.

All spring, she'd been hearing gunfire from Alder Hill, resonating across the moors like thunder. Maskell had the

135

Gilpin brothers out with Browning rifles. They were supposed to be ratting, but the object of the exercise was to end poaching by killing off all the game.

There were rabbit and pigeon carcasses about, some crackly bone bundles in packets of dry skin, some recent enough to seem shocked to death. It was a sinful waste, what with hungry people queuing up for parish hand-outs. Quite a few trees had yellow-orange badges, where Terry or Teddy Gilpin shot wide of the mark. Squire Maskell would not be heartbroken if one of those wild shots finished up in her.

Susan told her over and over again to be mindful of men with guns. She had a quite reasonable horror of firearms. Too many people on Sedgemoor died with their gumboots on and a bullet in them. Allie's dad and Susan's husband, for two. Susan wouldn't have a gun in the house.

For poaching, Allie didn't like guns anyway. Too loud. She had a catapult made from a garden fork, double-strength rubber stretched between steel tines. She could put a nail through half an inch of plywood from twenty-five feet.

She wriggled out of her tunnel, pushing aside a circle of bramble she'd fixed to hinge like a lid, and emerged in a clearing of loose earth and shale. During the Civil War, a bomb had fallen here and fizzled. Eventually, the woods would close over the scar.

When she stood up, she could see across the moors, as far as Achelzoy. At night, the infernal lights of Bridgwater pinked the horizon, clawing a ragged red edge in the curtain of dark. Now, she could make out the road winding through the wetlands. The sun, still low, glinted and glimmered in sodden fields, mirror-fragments strewn in a carpet of grass. There were dangerous marshes out there. Cows were sucked under if they set a hoof wrong.

Something moved near the edge of the clearing.

Allie had her catapult primed, her eye fixed on the rabbit. Crouching, still as a statue, she concentrated. Jack Coney nibbled on nothing, unconcerned. She pinched the nail-head, imagining a point between the ears where she would strike.

A noise sounded out on the moor road. The rabbit vanished, startled by the unfamiliar rasp of an engine.

"S'blood,' she swore.

She stood up, easing off on her catapult. She looked out towards Achelzoy. A fast-moving shape was coming across the moor.

The rabbit was lost. Maskell's men would soon be about, making the woods dangerous. She chanced a maintained path and ran swiftly downhill. At the edge of Maskell's property, she came to a stile and vaulted it – wrenching her shoulder, but no matter – landing like a cat on safe territory. Without a look back at the 'TRESPASSERS WILL BE VENTILATED' sign, she traipsed between two rows of trees, towards the road.

The path came out half a mile beyond the village, at a sharp kink in the moor road. She squatted with her back to a signpost, running fingers through her hair to rid herself of tangles and snaps of thorn.

The engine noise was nearer and louder. She considered putting a nail in the nuisance-maker's petrol tank to pay him back for the rabbit. That was silly. Whoever it was didn't know what he'd done.

She saw the stranger was straddling a Norton. He had slowed to cope with the winds of the moor road. Every month, someone piled up in one of the ditches because he took a bend too fast.

To Allie's surprise, the motorcyclist stopped by her. He shifted goggles up to the brim of his hat. He looked as if he had an extra set of eyes in his forehead.

There were care-lines about his eyes and mouth. She judged him a little older than Susan. His hair needed cutting. He wore leather trews, a padded waistcoat over a dusty khaki shirt, and gauntlets. A brace of pistols were holstered at his hips, and he had a rifle slung on the Norton, within easy reach.

He reached into his waistcoat for a pouch and fixings. Pulling the drawstring with his teeth, he tapped tobacco on to

137

a paper and rolled himself a cigarette one-handed. It was a clever trick, and he knew it. He stuck the fag in his grin and fished for a box of Bryant & May.

'Alder,' he said, reading from the signpost. 'Is that a village?'

'Might be.'

'Might it?'

He struck a light on his thumbnail and drew a lungful of smoke, held in for a moment like a hippie sucking a joint, and let it funnel out through his nostrils in dragon-plumes.

'Might it indeed?'

He didn't speak like a yokel. He sounded like a wireless announcer, maybe even more clipped and starched.

'If, hypothetically, Alder were a village, would there be a hostelry there where one might buy breakfast?'

'Valiant Soldier don't open till lunchtime.'

The Valiant Soldier was Alder's pub, and another of Squire Maskell's businesses.

'Pity.'

'How much you'm pay for breakfast?' she asked.

'That would depend on the breakfast.'

'Ten bob?'

The stranger shrugged.

'Susan'll breakfast you for ten bob.'

'Your mother?'

'No.'

'Where could one find this Susan?'

'Gosmore Farm. Other end of village.'

'Why don't you get up behind me and show me where to go?'

She wasn't sure. The stranger shifted forward on his seat, making space.

'I'm Lytton,' the stranger said.

'Allie,' she replied, straddling the pillion.

'Hold on tight.'

She took a grip on his waistcoat, wrists resting on the stocks of his guns.

Lytton pulled down his goggles and revved. The bike sped off. Allie's hair blew into her face and streamed behind her. She held tighter, pressing against his back to keep her face out of the wind.

When they arrived, Susan had finished milking. Allie saw her washing her hands under the pump by the back door.

Gosmore Farm was a tiny enclave circled by Maskell's land. He had once tried to get the farm by asking the newly widowed Susan to marry him. Allie couldn't believe he'd actually thought she might consent. Apparently, Maskell didn't consider Susan might hold a grudge after her husband's death. He now had a porcelain doll named Sue-Clare in the Manor House, and a pair of terrifying children.

Susan looked up when she heard the Norton. Her face was set hard. Strangers with guns were not her favourite type of folk.

Lytton halted the motorcycle. Allie, bones shaken, dismounted, showing herself.

'He'm pay for breakfast,' she said. 'Ten bob.'

Susan looked the stranger over, starting at his boots, stopping at his hips.

'He'll have to get rid of those filthy things.'

Lytton, who had his goggles off again, was puzzled.

'Guns, she means,' Allie explained.

'I know you feel naked without them,' Susan said sharply. 'Unmanned, even. Magna Carta rules that no Englishman shall be restrained from bearing arms. It's that fundamental right which keeps us free.'

'That's certainly an argument,' Lytton said.

'If you want breakfast, yield your fundamental right before you step inside my house.'

'That's a stronger one,' he said.

Lytton pulled off his gauntlets and dropped them into the pannier of the Norton. His fingers were stiff on the buckle of his gunbelt, as if he had been wearing it for many years until it had grown into him like a wedding-ring. He loosened the belt and held it up.

Allie stepped forward to take the guns.

'Allison, no,' Susan insisted.

Lytton laid the guns in the pannier and latched the lid.

'You have me defenceless,' he told Susan, spreading his arms.

Susan squelched a smile and opened the back door. Kitchen smells wafted.

A good thing about Lytton's appearance at Gosmore Farm was that he stopped Susan giving Allie a hard time about being up and about before dawn. Susan had no illusions about what she did in the woods.

Susan let Lytton past her into the kitchen. Allie trotted up.

'Let me see your hands,' Susan said.

Allie showed them palms down. Susan noted dirt under nails and a few new scratches. When Allie showed her palms, Susan drew a fingernail across the red strop-mark.

'Take care, Allie.'

'Yes'm.'

Susan hugged Allie briefly, and pulled her into the kitchen.

Lytton had taken a seat at the kitchen table and was loosening his heavy boots. Susan had the wireless on, tuned to the Light Programme. Mark Radcliffe introduced the new song from Jarvis Cocker and His Wurzels, 'The Streets of Stogumber'. A frying-pan was heating on the cooker, tiny trails rising from the fat.

'Allie, cut our guest some bacon.'

'The name's Lytton.'

'I'm Susan Ames. This is Allison Conway. To answer your unasked question, I'm a widow, she's an orphan. We run this farm ourselves.'

'A hard row to plough.'

'We're still above ground.'

Allie carved slices off a cured hock that hung by the cooker. Susan took eggs from a basket, cracked them into the pan.

'Earl Grey or Darjeeling?' Susan asked Lytton.

'The Earl.'

'Get the kettle on, girl,' Susan told her. 'And stop staring.'

Allie couldn't remember Susan cooking for a man since Mr Ames was killed. It was jarring to have this big male, whiffy from the road and petrol, invading their kitchen. But also a little exciting.

Susan flipped bacon rashers, busying herself at the cooker. Allie filled the kettle from the tap at the big basin.

'Soldier, were you?' Susan asked Lytton, indicating his shoulder. There was a lighter patch on his shirtsleeve where rank insignia had been cut away. He'd worn several pips.

The stranger shrugged.

'Which brand of idiot?'

'I fought for the South-East.'

'I'd keep quiet about that if you intend to drink in the Valiant Soldier.'

'I'd imagined Wessex was mostly neutral.'

'Feudal order worked perfectly well for a thousand years. It wasn't just landed gentry who resisted London Reforms. There are plenty of jobless ex-serfs around, nostalgic for their shackles and three hot meals a day.'

'Just because it lasted a long time doesn't mean it was a good thing.'

'No argument from me there.'

'Mr Ames was a Reformist too,' Allie said.

'Mr Ames?'

'My late husband. He opened his mouth too much. Some loyal retainers shut it for him.'

'I'm sorry.'

'Not your problem.'

Susan wasn't comfortable talking about her husband. Mr Ames had been as much lawyer as farmer, enthusiastically heading the Sedgemoor District Committee during the Reconstruction. He didn't realise it took more than a decision made in London Parliament to change things in the West. London was a long way off.

141

Allie brought Susan plates. Susan slid bacon and eggs from the pan.

'Fetch the tomato chutney from the preserves shelf,' she said.

Outside, someone clanged the bell by the gate. Lytton's hand slipped quietly to his hip, closing where the handle of a revolver would have been.

Susan looked at the hot food on the table, and frowned at the door.

'Not a convenient time to come visiting,' she said.

Hanging back behind Susan, Allie still saw who was in the drive. Constable Erskine was by the bell, vigorously hammering with the butt of his police revolver. His blue knob-end helmet gave him extra height. His gun-belt was in matching blue. Reeve Draper, arms folded, cringed at the racket his subordinate was making. Behind the officers stood Terry and Teddy Gilpin, Browning rifles casually in their hands, long coats brushing the ground.

'Goodwife Ames,' shouted the Reeve. 'This be a court order.'

'Leave your guns.'

'Come you now, Goodwife Ames. By right of law . . .'

Erskine was still clanging. The bell came off its hook and thunked on the ground. The Constable shrugged a grin and didn't holster his pistol.

'I won't have guns on my property.'

'Then come and be served. This yere paper pertains to your cattle. The decision been telegraphed from Taunton Magistrates. You'm to surrender all livestock within thirty days, for slaughter. It be a safety measure.'

Susan had been expecting something like this. 'There are no mad cows on Gosmore Farm.'

'Susan, don't be difficult.'

'It's Mrs Ames, Mr Reeve Draper.'

The Reeve held up a fawn envelope.

'You'm know this has to be done.'

'Will you be slaughtering Maskell's stock?'

'He took proper precautions, Susan. Can't be blamed. He'm been organic since 'fore the War.'

Susan snorted a laugh. Everyone knew there'd been Mad Cow Disease in the Squire's herd. He'd paid off the inspectors and rendered the affected animals into fertiliser. It was Susan who'd never used infected feed, never had a sick cow. This wasn't about British beef, this was about squeezing Gosmore Farm.

'Clear off,' Allie shouted.

'Poacher girl,' Erskine sneered. 'Lookin' for a matchin' stripe on your left hand?'

Susan turned on the Constable. 'Don't you threaten Allison. She's not a serf.'

'Once a serf, always a serf.'

'What are they here for?' Susan nodded to the Gilpin brothers. 'D'you need two extra guns to deliver a letter?'

Draper looked nervously at the brothers. Terry, heavier and nastier, curled his finger about the trigger-guard of his Browning.

'Why didn't Maskell come himself?'

Draper carefully put the letter on the ground, laying a stone on top of it.

'I'll leave this here, Goodwife. You'm been served with this notice.'

Susan strode towards the letter.

Terry hawked a stream of spit, which hit the stone and splattered the envelope. He showed off his missing front teeth in an idiot leer.

Draper was embarrassed and angered, Erskine delighted and itchy.

'My sentiments exactly, Goodman Gilpin,' said Susan.

She kicked the stone and let the letter skip away in the breeze.

'Mustn't show disrespect for the law,' Erskine snarled. He was holding his gun right way round, thumb on the cock-lever, finger on the trigger.

143

From the kitchen doorway, close behind Allie, Lytton said, 'Whose law?'

Allie stepped aside and Lytton strode into the yard. The four unwelcome visitors looked at him.

'Widow Ames got a stay-over guest,' Erskine said, nastily.

'B'ain't no business of yourn, Goodman,' said the Reeve to Lytton.

'And what if I make it my business?'

'You'm rue it.'

Lytton kept his gaze steady on the Reeve, who flinched and blinked.

'He hasn't got a gun,' Susan said, voice betraying annoyance with Lytton as much as with Maskell's men. 'So you can't have a fair fight.'

Mr Ames had been carrying a Webley when he was shot. The magistrate, Sue-Clare Maskell's father, ruled it a fair fight, exonerating on the grounds of self-defence the Maskell retainer who'd killed Susan's husband.

'He'm interfering with due process, Mr Reeve,' Erskine told Draper. 'We could detain him for questioning.'

'I don't think that'll be necessary,' Lytton said. 'I just stopped at Gosmore Farm for bacon and eggs. I take it there's no local ordinance against that.'

'Goodwife Ames don't have no bed and breakfast licence,' Draper said.

'Specially *bed*,' Erskine added, leering.

Lytton strolled casually towards his Norton. And his guns.

'Maybe I should press on. I'd like to be in Dorset by lunchtime.'

Terry's rifle was fixed on Lytton's belly, and swung in an arc as Lytton walked. Erskine thumb-cocked his revolver, ineptly covering the sound with a cough.

'Tell Maurice Maskell you've delivered your damned message,' Susan said, trying to get between Lytton and the visitors' guns. 'And tell him he'll have to come personally next time.'

'You'm stay away from thic rifle, Goodman,' the Reeve said to Lytton.

'Just getting my gloves,' Lytton replied, moving his hands away from the holstered rifle towards the pannier where his pistols were.

Allie backed away towards the house, stomach knotted.

'What's she afraid of?' Erskine asked, nodding at her.

'Don't touch thic fuckin' bike,' Terry shouted.

Allie heard the guns going off, louder than rook-scarers. An apple-sized chunk of stone exploded on the wall nearby, spitting chips in her face. The fireflashes were faint in the morning sun, but the reports were thunderclaps.

Erskine had shot, and Terry. Lytton had slipped down behind his motorcycle, which had fallen on him. There was a bright red splash of blood on the ground. Teddy was bringing up his rifle.

She scooped a stone and drew back the rubber of her catapult.

Susan screamed for everyone to stop.

Allie loosed the stone and raised a bloody welt on Erskine's cheek.

Susan slapped Allie hard and hugged her. Erskine, arm trembling with rage, blood dribbling on his face, took aim at them. Draper put a hand on the Constable's arm, and forced him to holster his gun. At a nod from the Reeve, Teddy Gilpin took a look at Lytton's wound and reported that it wasn't serious.

'This be bad, Goodwife Ames. It'd not tell well for you if'n it came up at magistrate's court. We'm be back on Saturday, with the vet. Have your animals together so they can be destroyed.'

He walked to his police car, his men loping after him like dogs. Terry laughed a comment to Erskine about Lytton.

Allie impotently twanged her catapult at them.

'Help me get this off him,' Susan said.

The Norton was a heavy machine, but between them they

hefted it up. The pannier was still latched down. Lytton had not got to his guns. He lay face-up, a bright splash of red in his left upper arm. He was gritting his teeth against the hurt, shaking as if soaked to the skin in ice-water.

Allie didn't think he was badly shot. Compared to some.

'You stupid man,' Susan said, kicking Lytton in the ribs. 'You stupid, stupid *man*!'

Lytton gulped in pain and cried out.

It wasn't as if they had much livestock. Allie looked round at the eight cows, all with names and personalities, all free of the madness. Gosmore Farm had a chicken coop, a vegetable garden, a copse of apple trees and a wedge of hillside given over to grazing. It was a struggle to eke a living; without the milk quota, it would be hopeless.

It was wrong to kill the cows.

Despair lodged like a stone in Allie's heart. This was not what the West should be. When younger, she'd read Thomas Hardy's Wessex novels, *The Sheriff of Casterbridge* and *Under the Hanging Tree*, and she still followed *The Archers*. In story-book Wessex, men like Squire Maskell always lost. Alder needed Dan Archer, the wireless hero, to stride into the Valiant Soldier, six-guns blazing, and lay the vermin in the dirt.

There was no Dan Archer.

Susan held all her rage in, refusing to talk about the cows and Maskell. She always concentrated on what she called 'the job at hand'. Just now, she was nursing Lytton. Erskine's shot had gone right through his arm. Allie had looked for but not found the bullet, to give him as a souvenir. He'd lost blood, but he would live.

Allie hugged Pansy, her favourite, and brushed flies away from the cow's gummy eyes.

'I won't let they hurt you,' she vowed.

But what could she do?

Depressed, she trudged down to the house.

*

Lytton was sitting up on the cot in the living-room, with his shirt off and a clean white bandage tight round his arm. Allie saw he had older scars. This was not the first time he'd been shot. He was sipping a mug of hot tea. Susan, bustling furiously, tidied up around him.

When he saw Allie, Lytton smiled. 'Susan's been telling me about this Maskell character. He seems to like to have things his way.'

The door opened and Squire Maskell stepped in.

'That I do, sir.'

He was dressed for church, in a dark suit and kipper tie. He knew enough not to wear a gunbelt on Gosmore Farm, though Allie guessed he was carrying a small pistol in his armpit. He had shot Allie's dad with such a gun, in a dispute over wages. Allie barely remembered her father, who had been indentured on Maskell's farm before the War and an NFU rep afterwards.

'I don't remember extending an invitation, Squire,' Susan said evenly.

'Susan, Susan, things could be so much more pleasant between us. We are neighbours.'

'In the same way a pack of dogs are neighbours to a fox gone to earth.'

Maskell laughed without humour. 'I've come to extend an offer of help.'

Susan snorted. Lytton said nothing but looked Maskell over with eyes that saw the gun under the hankie-pocket and the knife in the boot.

'I understand you have BSE problems? My condolences.'

'There's no Mad Cow Disease in my herd.'

'It's hardly a herd, Susan. It's a gaggle. But without them, where would you be?'

Maskell spread empty hands.

'This place is hardly worth the upkeep, Susan. You're only sticking at it because you have a nasty case of Stubborn Fever. The land is worthless to anyone but me. Gosmore Farm is a wedge in my own holdings. It would be so convenient if I could take down your fences, if I could incorporate your few acres into the Maskell Farm.'

'Now tell me something I don't know.'

'I can either buy from you now above the market value, or wait a while and buy from the bank at a knock-down price. I'm making an offer now purely out of neighbourly charity. The old ways may have changed, but as Squire I still feel an obligation to all who live within my bailiwick.'

'The only obligation your forefathers felt was to sweat the serfs into early graves and beget illegitimate cretins on terrorised girls. Have you noticed how the Maskell chin shows up on those Gilpin creatures?'

Maskell was angry now, but trying to keep calm. A vein throbbed by his eye.

'Susan, you're upset, I see that. But you must be realistic. Despite what you think, I don't want to see you on the mercy of the parish. Robert Ames was a good friend to me, and—'

'You can fuck off, Maskell,' Susan spat. 'Fuck *right off*.'

The Squire's smile drained away. He was close to sputtering. His Maskell chin wobbled.

'Don't ever mention my husband again. And now leave.'

'Susan,' he pleaded.

'I think Goodwife Ames made herself understood,' Lytton said.

Maskell looked at the wounded man. Lytton eased himself gingerly off the cot, expanding his chest, and stood. He was tall enough to have to bow his head under the beamed ceiling.

'I don't believe I've had . . .'

'Lytton,' he introduced himself.

'And you would be . . . ?'

'I would be grateful if you left the house as Goodwife Ames wishes. And fasten the gate on your way out. There's a Country Code, you know.'

'Good day,' Maskell said, not meaning it, and left.

There was a moment of silence.

'That's the second time you've taken it on yourself to act for

148

me,' Susan said, angrily. 'Have I asked your help?'

Lytton smiled. His hard look faded and he seemed almost mischievous. 'I beg pardon, Goodwife.'

'Don't do it again, Lytton.'

By the next day, Lytton was well enough to walk. But he couldn't ride: if he tried to grip the Norton's left handlebar, it was as if a red-hot poker were pressed to his bicep. They were stuck with him.

'You can do odd jobs for your keep,' Susan allowed. 'Allie will show you how.'

'Can he come feed the chickens?' Allie asked, excited despite herself. 'I can get the eggs.'

'That'll be a start.'

Susan walked across to the stone sheds where the cows spent the night, to do the milking. Allie took Lytton by the hand and led him round to the chicken coop.

'Maskell keeps his chickens in a gurt prison,' Allie told him. 'Clips their beaks with pliers, packs they in alive like sardines. If one dies, t'others eat her. They'm *cannibal* chickens.'

They turned round the corner.

The chicken coop was silent. Tears pricked the backs of Allie's eyes. Lumps of feathery matter lay in the scarlet-stained straw.

Her first thought was that a fox had got in.

Lytton lifted up a flap of chicken-wire. It had been cut cleanly.

The coop was a lean-to, a chicken-wire frame built against the house. On the stone wall was daubed a sign in blood, an upside-down tricorn fork in a circle.

'Travellers,' Allie spat.

There was a big Gypsy site at Glastonbury. Since the War, Travellers were supposed to stay on the sites, living off the dole. But they were called Travellers because they didn't like to keep to one place. They were always escaping from sites and raiding farms and villages.

Lytton shook his head.

'Hippies are hungry. They'd never have killed and left the chickens. And smashed the eggs.'

The eggs had been gathered and carefully stamped on.

'Some hippies be veggie.'

The blood was still fresh. Allie didn't see how this could have been done while they were asleep. The killers must have struck fast, or the chickens would have squawked.

'Where's your vegetable garden?' Lytton asked.

Allie's heart pounded like a fist.

She showed him the path to the garden, which was separated from the orchard by a thick hedge. Beanpoles had been wrenched from the earth and used to batter and gouge the rest of the crops. Cabbages were squashed, young carrots pulped by boot-heels, marrows exploded. The greenhouse was a skeleton, every pane of glass broken, tomato plants strewn and flattened inside. Even the tiny herb patch Allie had been given for herself was dug up and scattered.

Allie sobbed. Liquid squirted from her eyes and nose. Hundreds of hours of work destroyed.

There was a twist of cloth on the frame of the greenhouse. Lytton examined it: a tie-dyed poncho, dotted with emblem badges of marijuana leaves, multi-coloured swirls and cartoon cats.

'Hippies,' Allie yelled. 'Fuckin' hippies.'

Susan appeared at the gate. She swayed, almost in a swoon, and held the gate to stay standing.

'Hippies didn't do this,' Lytton said.

He lifted a broken tomato plant from the paved area by the greenhouse door and pointed at a splashed yellow stain.

'Allie, where've you seen something like this recently?'

It came to her.

'Terry Gilpin. When he spat at thic letter.'

'He has better aim with his mouth than his gun,' Lytton commented, wincing. 'Thankfully.'

*

150

Lytton stood by his Norton, lifting his gauntlets out of the pannier.

'Are you leaving?' Allie asked.

'No,' Lytton said, taking his gunbelt, 'I'm going down the pub.'

He settled the guns on his hips and fastened the buckle. The belt seemed to give him strength, to make him stand straighter. Susan, still shocked, didn't protest.

'Are you'm going to shoot Squire Maskell?' Allie asked.

That snapped Susan out of it. She took Allie and shook her by the shoulders, keening wordlessly.

'I'm just going to have a lunchtime drink.'

Allie hugged Susan fiercely. They were on the point of losing everything, but gave each other the last of their strength. There was something Maskell couldn't touch.

Lytton strolled towards the front gate.

Allie pulled away from Susan. For a moment, Susan wouldn't let her go. Then, without words, she gave her blessing. Allie knew she was to look after Lytton.

He was half-way down the street, passing the bus shelter, disused since the service was cut, when Allie caught up with him. At the fork in the road where the Village Oak stood was the Valiant Soldier.

They walked on.

'I hope you do shoot him,' she said.

'I just want to find out why he's so obsessed with Gosmore Farm, Allie. Men like Maskell always have reasons. That's why they're pathetic. You should only be afraid of men without reasons.'

Lytton pushed open the door, and stepped into the public bar. This early, there were few drinkers. Danny Keogh sat in his usual seat, wooden leg unslung on the floor beside him. Teddy Gilpin was swearing at the Trivial Pursuit machine, and his brother was nursing a half of scrumpy and a packet of crisps, ogling the Tiller Girl in the *Sun*.

Behind the bar, Janet Speke admired her piled-up hair in the long mirror. She saw Lytton and displayed immediate interest, squirming tightly in an odd way Allie almost understood.

Terry's mouth sagged open, giving an unprepossessing view of streaky-bacon-flavour mulch. The Triv machine fell silent, and Teddy's hands twitched away from the buttons to his gun. Allie enjoyed the moment, knowing everyone in the pub was knotted inside, wondering what the stranger – her friend, she realised – would do next. Gary Chilcot, a weaselly little Maskell hand, slipped away, into the back bar where the Squire usually drank.

'How d'ye do, Goodman,' said Janet, stretching thin red lips round dazzling teeth in a fox smile. 'What can I do you for?'

'Bell's. And Tizer for Allie here.'

'She'm underage.'

'Maskell won't mind. We're old friends.'

Janet fetched the whisky and the soft drink. Lytton looked at the exposed nape of her neck, where wisps of hair escaped, and caught the barmaid smiling in the mirror, eyes fixed on his even though he was standing behind her.

Lytton sipped his whisky, registering the sting in his eyes.

Janet went to the juke-box and put on Portishead. She walked back to the bar, almost dancing, hips in exaggerated motion. Music insinuated into the spaces between them all, blotting out their silent messages.

The door opened and Reeve Draper came in, out of breath. He had obviously been summoned.

'I've been meaning to call again on Goodwife Ames,' he said to Lytton, not mentioning that when last he had seen Lytton the newcomer was on the ground with a bullet-hole in his shoulder put there by the Reeve's Constable. 'Tony Jago, the Traveller Chieftain, has escaped from Glastonbury with a band of sheep-shaggin', drug-takin' gyppos. We'm expecting raids on farms. Susan should watch out for them. Bad lot, gyppos. No respect for property. They'm so stoned on dope they'm don't know what they'm doin'.'

152

Lytton took a marijuana-leaf badge from his pocket. One of the emblems pinned to the poncho left in the ravaged garden. He tossed it into Terry Gilpin's scrumpy.

'Oops, sorry,' he said.

This time, Terry went for his gun and fumbled. Lytton kicked the stool from under him. Terry sprawled, choking on crisps, on the floor. With a boot-toe, Lytton pinned Terry's wrist. He nodded to Allie, and she took the gun away. Terry swore, brow dotted with cider-stinking sweat bullets.

Allie had held guns before, but not since Susan took her in. She had forgotten how heavy they were. The barrel drooped, even though she held the gun two-handed, and accidentally happened to point at Terry's gut.

'If I made a complaint against this man, I don't suppose much would happen.'

Draper said nothing. His face was as red as strawberry jam.

'I thought not.'

Terry squirmed. Teddy gawped down at his brother.

Lytton took out his gun, pointed it at Teddy, said, 'Pop,' and put it back in its holster, all in one movement, between one heartbeat and the next. Teddy goggled, hand hovering inches away from his own gun.

'That was a fair fight,' Lytton said. 'Do you want to try it again?'

He let Terry go. Rubbing his reddened wrist, the Maskell man scurried away and stood up.

'If'n you gents got an argument, take it outside,' Janet said. 'I've got regulars who don't take to ruckus.'

Lytton strolled across the room, towards the back bar. He pushed a door with frosted glass panels, and disclosed a small room with heavily upholstered settees, horse-brasses on beams and faded hunt scenes on the wallpaper.

The Squire sat at a table with papers and maps spread out on it. A man Allie didn't know, who wore a collar and tie, sat with him. Erskine was there, too, listening to Gary Chilcot, who had been talking since he left the bar.

153

The Squire was too annoyed to fake congeniality.

'We'd like privacy, if you please.'

Lytton looked over the table. There was a large-scale survey map of the area, with red lines dotted across it. The corners were held down by ashtrays and empty glasses. The Squire had been illustrating some point by tapping the map, and his well-dressed guest was frozen in mid-nod.

Lytton, stepping back from the back bar, let the door swing closed in the face of Erskine, who was rushing out. A panel cracked and the Constable went down on his knees.

Allie felt excitement in her water.

Terry charged but Lytton stepped aside and lifted the Maskell man by the seat of his britches, heaving him up over the bar and barrelling him into the long mirror. Glass shattered.

Janet Speke, incandescent with proprietary fury, brought out a shotgun, which Lytton pinned to the bar with his arm.

'My apologies, Goodwife. He'll make up the damage.'

There was nothing in the barmaid's pale-blue eyes but hate. Impulsively, Lytton craned across and kissed her full on the lips. Hot, angry spots appeared on her cheeks as he let her go. He detached her from the shotgun.

'You should be careful with these things,' he said. 'They're apt to discharge inconveniently if mishandled.'

He fired both barrels at a framed photograph of Alder's victorious skittles team of '66. The noise was an astounding crash. Lytton broke the gun and dropped it. Erskine, nose bloody in his handkerchief, came out of the back bar with his Webley out and cocked.

This time, it was different. Lytton was armed.

Despite the hurt in his left shoulder, Lytton drew both his pistols in an instant and, at close range, shot off Erskine's ears. The Constable stood, appalled, blood pouring from fleshy nubs that would no longer hold his helmet up.

Erskine's shot went wild.

Lytton took cool aim and told the Constable to drop his Webley.

Erskine saw sense. The revolver clumped on the floor.

In an instant, Lytton holstered his pistols. The music came back, filling the quiet that followed the crashes and shots. Terry moaned in a heap behind the bar. Janet kicked him out. Erskine looked for his ears.

Lytton took another sip of Bell's.

'Very fine,' he commented.

Janet, lipstick smeared, touched her hair, deprived of her mirror, not knowing where free strands hung.

Lytton slipped a copper-coloured ten-shilling note on to the bar.

'A round of drinks, I think,' he said.

Danny Keogh smiled and shook an empty glass.

Outside, in the car park, Allie bubbled over. It was the most thrilling thing. To see Terry hit the mirror, Teddy staring at a draw he'd never beat, the Reeve helpless, Janet Speke and the Squire in impotent rage and, best of all, Barry Erskine with his helmet-brim on his nose and blood gushing on to his shoulders. For a moment, Alder was like *The Archers*, and the villains were seen off.

Lytton was sombre, cold, bravado gone.

'It was just a moment, Allie. An early fluke goal for our side. They still have the referee in their back pocket and fifteen extra players.'

He looked around the car park. 'Any of these vehicles unfamiliar?'

Maskell's ostentatious Range Rover was parked by Janet's pink Vauxhall Mustang. The Morris pick-up was the Gilpins'. The Reeve's panda car was on the street. That left an Austin Maverick Allie had never seen before. She pointed it out.

'Company car,' he said, tapping the windshield.

The front passenger seat was piled with glossy folders that had 'GREAT WESTERN RAILWAYS' embossed on their jackets.

'The clouds of mystery clear,' he mused. 'Do you have one of your nails?'

155

Puzzled, she took a nail from her purse and handed it over.

'Perfect,' he said, crouching by the car door, working the nail into the lock. 'This is a neat trick you shouldn't learn, Allie. There, my old sapper sergeant would be proud of me.'

He got the door open, snatched one of the folders, and had the door shut again.

They left in a hurry, but slowed by the bus stop. The rusting shelter was fly-posted with car-boot-sale announcements. Lytton sagged. His shirt-shoulder spotted where his wound had opened again. Still, he was better off than Earless Erskine.

'It's choo-choos, I'll be bound,' he said. 'The track they run on is always blooded.'

There was activity at the pub as Maskell's party loped past the Village Oak into the car park. Maskell was in the centre, paying embarrassed attention to his guest, who presumably hadn't expected a bar brawl and an ear-shooting to go with his ploughman's lunch and a lecture on local geography.

The outsider got into his Maverick and Maskell waved him off. Then, he started shouting at his men. Allie smiled to hear him so angry, but Lytton looked grim.

That evening, after they had eaten, Lytton explained to Susan, showing her the maps and figures. Allie struggled to keep up.

'It's to do with railway privatisation,' he said. 'The measures that came in after the War, that centralised and nationalised so many industries, are being dismantled by the Tories. And private companies are stepping in. With many a kickback and inside deal.'

'There's not been a railway near Alder for fifty years,' Susan said.

'When British Rail is broken up, the companies that have bits of the old network will be set against each other like fighting dogs. They'll shut down some lines and open up others, not because they need to but to get one over on the next fellow. GWR, who are chummying up with the Squire, would like it if all trains from Wessex to London went through Bristol. They can up the fares, and cut off the South-Eastern company. To do that, they need to put a branch line here, across the southern edge of Maskell's farm, right through your orchard.'

Susan understood, and was furious.

'I don't want a railway through my farm.'

'But Maskell sees how much money he'd make. Not just from selling land at inflated prices. There'd be a watering-halt. Maybe even a station.'

'He can't do the deal without Gosmore Farm?'

'No.'

'Well, he can whistle "Lilliburlero".'

'It may not be that easy.'

The lights flickered and failed. The kitchen was lit only by the red glow of the wood fire.

'Allie, I told you to check the generator,' Susan snapped.

Allie protested. She was careful about maintaining the generator. They'd once lost the refrigerator and had a week's milk quota spoil overnight.

Lytton signalled for quiet. He drew a gun from inside his waistcoat.

Allie listened for sounds outside.

'Are the upstairs windows shuttered?' Lytton asked.

'I asked you not to bring those things indoors,' Susan said, evenly. 'I won't have guns in the house.'

'You soon won't have a choice. There'll be unwelcome visitors.'

Susan caught on and went quiet. Allie saw fearful shadows. There was a shot and the window over the basin exploded inwards. A fireball flew in and plopped on to the table, oily rags in flames. With determination, Susan took a flat bread-board and pressed out the fire.

Noise began. Loudspeakers were set up outside. Music hammered their ears. The Beatles' 'Helter Skelter'.

'Maskell's idea of hippie music,' Lytton said.

In the din, gunshots spanged against stones, smashed through windows and shutters.

157

Lytton bundled Susan under the heavy kitchen table, and pushed Allie in after her.

'Stay here,' he said, and was gone upstairs.

Allie tried putting her fingers in her ears and screwing her eyes shut. She was still in the middle of the attack.

'Is Maskell going to kill us?' she asked.

Susan was rigid. Allie hugged her.

There was a shot from upstairs. Lytton was returning fire.

'I'm going to help him,' Allie said.

'No,' shouted Susan, as Allie slipped out of her grasp. 'Don't!'

She knew the house well enough to dart around in the dark without bumping into anything. Like Lytton, she headed upstairs.

From her bedroom window, which had already been shot out, she could see as far as the treeline. There was no moon. The Beatles still screamed. In the orchard, fires were set. Hooded figures danced between the trees, wearing ponchos and beads. She wasn't fooled. These were not Jago's Travellers but Maskell's men.

Allie had to draw the line here. She and Susan had been pushed too far. They'd lost men to Maskell, they wouldn't lose land.

A man carrying a fireball dashed towards the house, aiming to throw it through a window. Allie drew a bead with her catapult and put a nail in his knee. She heard him shriek above the music. He tumbled over, fire thumping on to his chest and spreading to his poncho. He twisted, yelling like a stuck pig, and wrestled his way out of the burning hood.

It was Teddy Gilpin.

He scrambled back, limping and smouldering. She could have put another nail in his skull.

But didn't.

Lytton was in the hallway, switching between windows, using bullets to keep the attackers back. One lay still, face-down, on the lawn. Allie hoped it was Maskell.

She scrambled out of her window, clung to the drainpipe, and squeezed into shadows under the eaves. Like a bat, she hung, catapult dangling from her mouth. She monkeyed up on to the roof, and crawled behind the chimney.

If she kept them off the roof, they couldn't get close enough to fire the house. She didn't waste nails, but was ready to put a spike into the head of anyone who trespassed. But someone had thought of that first. She saw the ladder-top protruding over the far edge of the roof.

An arm went around her neck, and the catapult was twisted from her hand. She smelled his strong cider-and-shit stink.

'It be the little poacher,' a voice cooed.

It was Stan Budge, Maskell's gamekeeper.

'Who'm trespassin' now?' she said, and fixed her teeth into his wrist.

Though she knew this was not a game, she was surprised when Budge punched her in the head, rattling her teeth, blurring her vision. She let him go. And he hit her again. She lost her footing, thumped against tiles and slid towards the gutter, slates loosening under her.

Budge grabbed her hair.

The hard yank on her scalp was hot agony. Budge pulled her away from the edge. She screamed.

'Wouldn't want nothing to happen to you,' he said. 'Not yet.'

Budge forced her to go down the ladder, and a couple of men gripped her. She struggled, trying to kick shins.

Shots came from house and hillside.

'Take her round to the Squire,' Budge ordered.

Allie was glad it was dark. No one could see the shame tears on her cheeks. She felt so stupid. She had let Susan down. And Lytton.

Budge took off his hood and shook his head.

'No more bleddy fancy dress,' he said.

She had to be dragged to where Maskell sat, smoking a cigar, in a deckchair between the loudspeakers.

'Allison, dear,' he said. 'Think, if it weren't for the Civil War, I'd *own* you. Then again, at this point in time, I might as well own you.'

He shut off the cassette-player.

Terry Gilpin and Barry Erskine – out of uniform, with white lumps of bandage on his head – held her between them. The Squire drew a long, thin knife from his boot and let it catch the firelight.

Maskell plugged a karaoke microphone into the speaker.

'Susan,' he said, booming. 'You should come out, now. We've driven off the gyppos. But we have someone you'll want to see.'

He pointed the microphone at her and Terry wrenched her hair. Despite herself, she screamed.

'It's dear little Allison.'

There was a muffled oath from inside.

'And your protector, Captain Lytton. He should come out, too. Yes, we know a bit about him. Impressive war record, if hardly calculated to make him popular in these parts. Or anywhere.'

Allie had no idea what that meant.

'Throw your gun out, if you would, Captain. We don't want any more accidents.'

The back door opened, and firelight spilled out. A dark figure stepped on to the verandah.

'The gun, Lytton.'

A gun was tossed down.

Erskine fairly slobbered with excitement. Allie felt him pressing close to her, writhing. Once he let her go, he would kill Lytton, she knew.

Lytton stood beside the door. Another figure joined him, shivering in a white shawl that was a streak in the dark.

'Ah, Susan,' Maskell said, as if she had just arrived at his Christmas Feast. 'Delighted you could join us.'

160

Maskell's knife-point played around Allie's throat, dimpling the skin, pricking tinily.

In a rush, it came to her that this had very little to do with railways and land and money. When it came down to it, the hurt Maskell fancied he was avenging was that he couldn't have Susan. Or Allie.

Knowing why didn't make things better.

Hand in hand, Lytton and Susan came across the lawn. Maskell's men gathered, jeering.

'Are you all right, Allison?' Susan asked.

'I'm sorry.'

'It's not your fault, dear.'

'I have papers with me,' Maskell said, 'if you'd care to sign. The terms are surprisingly generous, considering.'

Lytton and Susan were close enough to see the knife.

'You sheep-shagging bastard,' Susan said.

Lytton's other gun appeared from under her shawl. She raised her arm and fired. Allie felt wind as the bullet whistled past. Maskell's jaw came away in a gush of red-black. Susan shot him again, in the eye. He was thumped backwards, knife ripped away from Allie's throat, and laid on the grass, heels kicking.

'I said I didn't like guns,' Susan announced. 'I never said I couldn't use one.'

Lytton took hold of Susan's shoulders and pulled her out of the way of the fusillade unleashed in their direction by Budge and Terry Gilpin.

Allie twisted in Erskine's grasp and rammed a bony knee between his legs. Erskine yelped, and she clawed his ear-bandages, ripping the wounds open.

The Constable staggered away, and was peppered by his comrades' fire. He took one in the lungs and knelt over the Squire, coughing up thick pink foam.

In a flash of gunfire, Allie saw Lytton sitting up, shielding Susan with his body, arm outstretched. He had picked up a pistol. The flashes stopped. Budge lay flat dead, and Gilpin gurgled, incapacitated by several wounds. Lytton was shot again too, in the leg.

He had fired his gun dry, and was reloading, taking rounds from his belt.

Car-lights froze the scene. The blood on the grass was deepest black. Faces were white as skulls. Lytton still carefully shoved new bullets into chambers. Susan struggled to sit up.

Reeve Draper got out of the panda car and assessed the situation. He stood over Maskell's body. The Squire's face was gone.

'Looks like you'm had a bad gyppo attack,' he said.

Lytton snapped his revolver shut and held it loosely, not aiming.

The Reeve turned away from him. 'But it be over now.'

Erskine coughed himself quiet.

Allie wasn't sorry any of them were dead. If she was crying, it was for her father, for the chickens, for the vegetable garden.

'I assume Goodwife Ames no longer has to worry about her cows being destroyed?' Lytton asked.

The Reeve nodded, tightly.

'I thought so.'

Draper ordered Gary Chilcot to gather the wounded and get them off Gosmore Farm.

'Take the rubbish, too,' Susan insisted, meaning the dead.

Chilcot, face painted with purple butterflies, was about to protest but Lytton still had the gun.

'Squire Maskell bain't givin' out no more pay packets, Gary,' the Reeve reminded him.

Chilcot thought about it and ordered the able-bodied to clear the farm of corpses.

Allie woke up well after dawn. It was a glorious spring day. The blood on the grass had soaked in and was invisible. But there were windows that needed mending.

She went outside and saw Lytton and Susan by the generator. It was humming into life. Lytton had oil on his hands.

In the daylight, Susan seemed ghost-like.

Allie understood what it must be like. To kill a man. Even a man like Squire Maskell. It was as if Susan had killed a part of herself. Allie would have to be careful with Susan, try to coax her back.

'There,' Lytton said. 'Humming nicely.'

'Thank you, Captain,' said Susan.

Lytton's eyes narrowed minutely. Maskell had called him Captain.

'Thank you, Susan.' He touched her cheek. 'Thank you for everything.'

Allie ran up and hugged Lytton. He held her, too, not ferociously. She broke the embrace. Allie didn't want him to leave. But he would.

The Norton was propped in the driveway, wheeled out beyond the open gate. He walked stiffly away from them and straddled the motorcycle. His leg wound was just a scratch.

Allie and Susan followed him to the gate. Allie felt Susan's arm round her shoulders.

Lytton pulled on his gauntlets and curled his fingers round the handlebars. He didn't wince.

'You're Captain *James* Lytton, aren't you?' Susan said.

There was a little hurt in his eyes. His frown-lines crinkled.

'You've heard of me.'

'Most people have. Most people don't know how you could do what you did in the War.'

'Sometimes you have a choice. Sometimes you don't.'

Susan left Allie and slipped round the gate. She kissed Lytton. Not the way Lytton had kissed Janet Speke, like a slap, but slowly, awkwardly.

Allie was half embarrassed, half heartbroken.

'Thank you, Captain Lytton,' Susan said. 'There will always be a breakfast for you at Gosmore Farm.'

'I never did give you the ten shillings,' he smiled.

Allie was crying again and didn't know why. Susan let her

fingers trail through Lytton's hair and across his shoulder. She stood back.

He pulled down his goggles, then kicked the Norton into life and drove off.

Allie scrambled through the gate and ran after him. She kept up with him, lungs protesting, until the Village Oak, then sank, exhausted, by the kerb. Lytton turned on his saddle and waved, then was gone from her sight, headed out across the moors. She stayed, curled up under the oak, until she could no longer hear his engine.

This takes place in an alternate version of the Somerset village that appears in my novel *Jago*, hence the reappearance of some of that book's cast in unfamiliar roles. Obviously, its plot and deployment of cowboy archetypes owe a debt to Jack Schaefer and George Stevens – writer and director of *Shane* – but I was also thinking of the underrated John Wayne vehicle *Hondo*, directed by John Farrow from a story by Louis L'Amour. It appeared in David Garnett's *New Worlds*, the latest (but I would wager not the last) incarnation of the long-running British science fiction magazine, albeit transmogrified into an American paperback anthology. Given the overlapping of American myth and British landscape, there's something appropriate about the scrambling of nationalities in the book.

ALTERNATE MAJORS

Slow News Day

John couldn't work out how the black leather straps attached to his Horst Wessel belt. Michael, the Minister for War, slapped away his fumbling fingers and examined the problem, like John's mother tying his school tie for him when he was eleven and couldn't penetrate the mysteries of the knot.

'You've got the holster on the wrong side,' the Minister sighed. 'It must be arse-backwards.'

John felt his face burn with blush as he got untangled and sorted out.

'I hope that Webley isn't loaded,' the Minister said. 'You might shoot yourself in the foot again.'

'I've never shot myself in the foot.'

'That's not what the foreign press say.'

The Minister was comfortable in full combat gear and field marshal's helmet. He gave a heel-clicking salute and a sly I-want-your-job chuckle. Most days, John would be happy to give away his job, but with the foaming example of the Iron Duchess before him, he knew that in United Britain the lot of an ex-Prime Minister was even worse than being a serving PM.

Clocking himself in a monitor, John thought he looked silly in uniform, a prat dressed as a tin stormtrooper. It had been worse when he was a lad doing his mandated year in the Mosley Youth, knock-kneed in lederhosen. Some of the Cabinet loved climbing into tight black britches and hanging decorations on their bulging black chests, but John had wanted the D-Day celebrations informal. He had hoped he would be allowed to get away with his nice grey suit. Maybe a colourful anorak if history repeated and the 5th was unseasonably rainy.

The Duke of Edinburgh went up the line of uniformed ministers, grinning ferociously like an inspection sergeant, noting each mismatched button or smudged jackboot. The Royal Family were really into the spirit of the 50th Anniversary of the D-Day landings. The Duke's brothers strutted around London in their old SS uniforms, mainly let

167

out around the waistlines. The Duke plainly hoped to embrace the Reichskanzler on the beaches, reenacting the famous photograph of Edward hugging Hitler.

The only people out of uniform in the marquee were Security Service men, who favoured long black coats which billowed over their holstered machine-pistols, and the press contingent. Drops of rain fell like pennies on the canvas canopy, which made the SS people jumpy. John had ordered there be no repetition of the unfortunate incidents of the Royal Funeral, when fire was opened on a dignified row of dissenting parsons.

The President came in, smiling and laughing, surrounded by pretty girls in Otter Guide uniform who held umbrellas over his head like an honour guard. Until last week, the President had not been coming but the troubled administration, needing to cement new European trade deals, opted to remove the human-rights issue from the negotiations. John had not met the President before. Americans always wanted to talk straight to the head honcho. Whenever they needed to sort something, the Yanks got into a huddle with the Reichskanzler. It had been different under the Duchess. Then United Britain's voice was at least as shrill as Greater Germany's.

John was in two minds about remembering the past, recent or remote. He was half afraid the Duchess would turn up in her flamboyant uniform, a blue-haired Boadicea (Boudicca they were now supposed to call her), and make speeches to journalists, dropping acid hints about her successors. The Minister of Internal Security was only partly joking when he suggested it would be fit if the Duchess were taken up on her oft-repeated desire to return to the Iron Values of the Occupation and be allowed to vanish into Night and Fog.

'John,' the President said, sticking out a crushing hillbilly bear-paw, 'good to see ya. Have you been ill?'

'Just a touch of hay fever.'

'Better take it easy. That's a killer.'

Cameras clicked as John and the President smiled. Britain had come close to severing relations with the States when the leader of Old England did the rounds of American talk shows, promoting his memoirs. Under broadcasting restrictions, OE representatives were dubbed by actors in British news bulletins. John was mightily browned off that OE people were invited to the White House but the Reichskanzler had vetoed any formal reprisals. It had taken long enough to get the Americans to the table, and Greater Europe couldn't afford whingeing little Britain scuppering the deal. There was a big Old English lobby in the States, though there was a crack-down on the smuggling of funds and weapons to terrorists in Europe.

The President's smile broadened as he passed on from John to the Duke of Edinburgh. They went into a huddle, almost like schoolgirls. John had no idea the two knew each other. He wondered if they were talking about him. If they were, SS microphones would pick it up. He doubted a report would get further than Michael, the Minister of Internal Security. He usually suppressed information that might upset his PM. John supposed he should be grateful someone thought of his feelings.

The President and the Duke went, arm in arm, over to that corner of the marquee where the veterans clustered, proud in uniforms they had worn and medals they had earned. They were all very old. Specialist nurses stood behind their wheelchairs. Those who had served in the Occupation were exempt from the Elderly Persons Act, and entitled to places in State Heroes' Homes. UB War Pensioners were the envy of Europe. German veterans were lucky to get their cyanide pills sugared.

'Blind old gits,' said Michael, the Home Secretary. 'If they were weasely enough to join the Fifth in '43, they were all out for the main chance. Some of the sneaks probably faked records. Everybody was doing that when I were a lad. If you had the SS grill a couple of codgers, you'd find half of 'em were on the beaches resisting the Invasion of Liberation, not joining in the liberating.'

The Home Secretary was a notorious cynic. As a schoolboy, he had begun his political career by informing on his father, an OE Group Leader.

'"They don't like it up 'em",' the Home Secretary quoted.

If anyone thought of the Heroic Fifth Column these days, it was as they were in *Dad's Nazis*, the popular BBC comedy programme which made figures of fun of the dedicated but buffoonish patriots who assisted the Germans during the Occupation, wiping out the last traces of the Traitor Regime.

The Home Secretary hummed the *Dad's Nazis* theme tune, 'Who Do You Think You Are Kidding, Mr Churchill?' He'd been drinking steadily in the hospitality suite.

'Watch out, the mikes will pick you up.'

'Don't panic, don't panic,' the Home Secretary continued.

A rustle of excitement whispered through the marquee. The Reichskanzler's helicopter had been sighted over the Channel. Time to go outside.

It was still not really raining but high wind turned droplets of stray water into liquid bullets that splattered against uniforms. There was a complex protocol as to who was allowed to troop out when. Doddery veterans, under their own steam or aided by nurses, were given precedence.

Crowds thronged outside, on the downs that bordered the cliffs of Dover, and below, on the pebble beach. UB and swastika pennants were held high. A tide of fish 'n' chip papers swarmed around everybody's knees.

Nearby, the almost completed Channel Tunnel terminal was swathed under thick sheets. The original idea was that the Reichskanzler should arrive for the Anniversary on the first bullet train through the Tunnel. But there had been delays.

There was a huge cheer as the wheelchair brigade appeared, followed by a warm welcome for Royalty and the President, and some modest clapping for the PM and Cabinet. John thought a TV personality with a frosted hairdo got a slightly bigger hand than he did. That was possible: Susan, who did a news show for housewives, was very popular, especially since her well-publicised announcement that she would bear an extra son for Britain.

Cloud was so heavy that the Reichskanzler's helicopter could not be seen. It had been sighted only on radar. Everyone looked out over the flat, grey Channel, waiting.

It was time to think of those who, fifty years ago, had also looked out, waiting. In fear of their lives, the Fifth Column had readied for the Invasion of Liberation, clearing the way for the German army to bring Britain into Europe, to exterminate the traitor elements that had usurped the government of the day.

John was expected to make a speech, praising these heroes. His PPS had written something down, but for the life of him he couldn't remember where. He had checked his pockets but found only the speech he had made last week, attacking indigents who were begging in the streets and clogging up the British autobahns with their caravans. It was notably the first time in forty years the word 'gypsy' had been used in public. John had not expected that to cause the kerfuffle it did.

If he were to be skipped over among all the speeches, no one would notice. The ceremony was bound to run over time. Kenneth, the Minister of Propaganda, had passed on a message from Rupert, the DG of the BBC, that it was vital the ceremony be concluded in time for the telly to switch back to coverage of the snooker finals.

The helicopter surged out of the cloud, a giant insect bristling with impressive weapons. The Reichskanzler insisted on flying a Messerschmitt Assault Ship, as deployed with such devastating effect in the recent Oil War.

The crowd gasped enormously as the chopper swooped overhead. One touch of a button and they would all be dead. If the Luftwaffe of 1943 had had such marvellous machines, the landing which had lasted a bloody thirteen hours would have been executed in seconds, the Invasion of Liberation would have been over within a week.

The helicopter made a landing precisely on the swastika

staked out on the grass of the downs. The Reichskanzler bounded out, arms spread, tummy wobbling, fists waving. The crowds cheered. Despite his problems at home, the Reichskanzler was always popular in the UB. The British loved a jolly fat man.

John was conscious of his own meagreness. His sunken chest was not served well by his snug black shirt. In uniform, the Reichskanzler looked like a victorious sumo wrestler.

The Royals swept forward to greet the German leader. This was the image of the anniversary that would be transmitted around the world. The embrace of Edward VIII and Hitler had been not in 1943 but two bloody years later. Edward had returned from exile, not stood on the beaches to greet the liberator who restored him to the throne.

The President and the Reichskanzler bowed formally, and shook hands. The American was officially 'someone we can do business with', despite his sabre-rattling about conditions in the Eastern European Homelands.

After the speeches, the Reichskanzler officially said hello to John. It was the least he could do.

'A shame about the Tunnel, hein?'

John shrugged.

'There will be an Inquiry into the delays?'

John mumbled. There was, by now, an Inquiry into the Inquiry about the delays.

'Maybe the Tunnel will be open by Atom Day, in 1995.'

That would commemorate the bombing of Leningrad, which ended the War in Europe.

'Or maybe we should wait for the centenary.'

The Reichskanzler laughed, agitating his entire enormous frame. Liking his joke more and more, he slapped his thighs, and repeated it in German to his entourage, then in English again to the President and to the media. The Reichskanzler's laughter spread as he restated the remark, infecting the crowing crowd. John tried to look amused.

The Duchess would have faced the Reichskanzler down, and

reminded him it was German insistence on adherence to rigid schedules that had jerry-built the first third of the Tunnel and caused the delays, as leaks were shored up, in the first place.

Three snake-shapes appeared out on the sea, surfacing U-boats. Bubble rafts popped up like corks, bearing stormtroopers. A handful of crack troops were to re-enact the initial landing.

The crowds on the beaches would have cheered but rain suddenly poured down, prompting a swift retreat towards canopies. Most of the VIPS had their own shelter, but John and the Michael-heavy Cabinet were squeezed out.

'We forgot Fatty takes up as much room as our entire government,' the Home Secretary said, nodding at the dry Reichskanzler. 'Then again, he combines all our offices and jobs. That's one thing about proper non-parliamentary fascism.'

Wetsuited stormtroops in lightweight scuttle helmets paddled up to the pebbles, a little bewildered. They had expected a better reception than cringing holidaymakers.

The Home Secretary had a fit of giggles.

A platoon of goose-pimpled Page 3 girls darted out to pose with the Germans, polythene sheets held over their hair. They were led by Mr Spotty, an inflatable children's TV character. Hardy paparazzi followed to record the moment. Quite a few people were laughing in the rain.

'Mustn't grumble,' one of the nurses said to her wheezing charge. 'Lovely weather for ducks.'

The veteran, Iron Cross and Order of St George on his woolly jumper, was trying to say something.

Smudge pots went off on the beach and simulated battle-smoke wafted past soldiers and Page 3 girls. Mr Spotty mimed panic.

'If we'd had those in '43,' the Home Secretary said, nodding at the topless lovelies, 'Fritz would never have got past the beaches.'

'If Mr Spotty had been PM instead of Churchill, Hitler would have crumbled,' said John.

'If Mr Spotty were PM now, we'd be a more popular government,' rumbled the Home Secretary.

There was a controversy in Germany. Some surviving veterans of the Invasion of Liberation were unable to attend the commemoration because all the accommodation was taken by politicians and generals and newspeople. The tabloids, who had more than their share of pre-booked hotel rooms, ran stories about little old ladies in the Home Counties cheated of a reunion with the now-shaky Aryan superman they had welcomed with open cami-knickers in 1944.

John privately wondered if things might not have been better if the Traitor Regime had put up a better resistance and beaten off the Invasion of Liberation. Maybe he wouldn't have had all these problems to deal with. He briefly considered resigning and appointing Mr Spotty his successor.

'You're popular now you're just a fathead in a blow-up suit,' he thought. 'Let's see how you do in the polls when you're closing down British mines and importing coal from the Ruhr.'

Mr Spotty comically ran away from the stormtroopers, who waved guns at him.

It was time for John's speech. His PPS had kept it safe and gave it to him when he needed it.

'We must remember we are celebrating not a British defeat but a British victory,' he began, 'a victory over that part of ourselves which was inefficient, was heartless, was impure, was ignoble . . .'

Even he didn't listen to the rest of what he said. Mr Spotty was distracting everyone.

The ceremony swept past. As John spoke, news cameras turned away, following the Reichskanzler and the veterans back towards the cliffs, where the stormtroopers were to demonstrate the proper use of scaling-ladders.

He finished his speech. There was some helpful applause.

The rest of the Cabinet left him near the water's edge and went to join in the fun. John felt empty and wet. Sodden socks squelched in his jackboots. His glasses were smeared with rain.

The day was so overcast he couldn't see marker buoys two hundred yards out, let alone the land beyond the Channel. The U-boats submerged, leaving cigar-shaped fast-vanishing whirl-pools.

He snapped the button off his holster, pulled out the Webley and looked out to sea. He hadn't fired a shot since his Patriotic Service. The pistol was heavy and oily.

John pointed his empty gun towards the rest of the world and said 'bang bang'.

The Germans Won

At the Enfield bus depot, off-shift crews let out a beery cheer. John clocked off just as an extra-time penalty put England into the World Cup Final in Los Angeles. The whistle blew and the cheer rose to an exultation.

The staff were watching the match on a colour telly bought especially. Four years ago, on the depot's Rediffusion, the *Mondial* had seemed played in thick snow between teams fielding subtle variations of black, white and grey strip.

On screen now, Bobby Robson was chair-lifted across the pitch by jubilant supporters. The BBC commentator talked about how much better the game was now than when he had been playing.

'Oor Bobby sits at God's right hand,' claimed Tommy, the Geordie driver on the 43 route. Tommy took football seriously, risking reprimand by wearing a Newcastle United scarf with his LT uniform. He patriotically switched to England for the duration of the World Cup.

'We used to think that way about Alf Ramsey,' muttered Stan, conductor on the 73. 'Till nineteen-sixty-bloody-six.'

In the Final, England would face West Germany. Again.

John had been on the 134 route, the long haul from Brixton all the way to the Frozen North. He took off his ticket-machine and cashed out with his supervisor, Jeffrey.

Every day, he thanked God for the GLC's Fares Fair policy, which had, since the early 1980s, made the sums so much easier. He had almost failed, all those years ago, the mental arithmetic test. He dreaded to think what would have become of him, and Norma, if he hadn't been able to go on the buses and get a job for life.

'Excellent, John,' purred Jeffrey, who liked to think himself a financial mastermind, as he weighed up the neat rolls of coins. 'Not a penny more, not a penny less.'

John was proud of his ability to keep track of change. Other conductors mistakenly accepted Irish 50p pieces or New York subway tokens, but he was scrupulous.

He took the roll of pound notes from his satchel and handed them over. A healthy wad. Regardless of policy, he could always make change for a £20 note on a 30p single from Tottenham Court Road to Muswell Hill.

Margi told him the tea was fresh-brewed and he took a mug of thick, sweet tea and a pasty. Norma would have gone to bed long ago, after the Wednesday Play; he might as well unwind with the other crews before going home to his council house in Gordon Hill. It was snug, sound and rent-controlled; he thought of it as his council castle.

As the post-match discussion recapped England's four goals against Holland's two, most of the staff opened cans of Double Diamond. Stan, who had scooped the pool on the result, was generous with the bottle of Bell's he had won.

John resisted temptation: he didn't want to go home with whisky breath. He immediately regretted turning down Stan's kind offer. He felt a bit out of it with the other staff. They were matey, of course, but sometimes he felt he shared little with them. Once in a while, he thought the others were making fun of him and he was missing the joke.

In his satchel, he found the book he was rereading, *Phineas Redux*. Jeffrey clocked the Trollope immediately and sidled over, smirking. He knew the supervisor was about to tell him – for the fourth or fifth time – that he had once written a book.

He wondered if the crews thought he was in too tight with Jeffrey, brown-nosing. Actually, he wasn't sure if he really liked the supervisor. Jeffrey seemed to feel superior not only to staff under him but to the job as a whole.

'I wrote a book once, John,' Jeffrey said, as always. 'I made bad investments, found myself enormously in debt. I thought: I know, I can get out by writing a best-seller. You know, a real page-turner. Everyone I submitted the manuscript to sent it back with a form rejection. I expect they thought it was unpublishable crap. It probably was. Still, I wrote a book once.

Not so different from your Trollope, John. Not so different at all.'

Jeffrey was still in debt, working at a job he looked down on, moving his money around in a variety of dodgy get-rich-quick schemes that always fell apart. He had invested in VHS video recorders and been wiped out by the success of Betamax. John couldn't understand Jeffrey's obvious desire to get out of London Transport. There was nothing better than helping the public, meeting people, travelling. Everyone had a smile for a bus conductor. Every route was an adventure.

He relished his pasty, home-baked at Marks & Spencer's this morning, warmed in Margi's trusty gas oven. Though the others might swig Bell's, he was content with a mug of Lipton's.

'How's the tea, love?' Margi asked.

'Warm and wet – that's what counts.'

On telly, Robson – face fringed with purple and green thanks to slightly amateurish tuning – was cagey about prospects for the trophy. He conceded that the West Germans, having thrashed Brazil in their semi-final, were favourites but slyly hinted that there might be a surprise or two coming. The interview was ended prematurely by enthusiastic fans clamouring for the beloved manager.

Stan, pleasantly glowing, reckoned England's chances were pretty good. He was hopelessly optimistic, a trait John envied. To groans, Stan produced statistics, goal averages.

'Also, the German lads will be worried about what's going on back home, with rioting along the Berlin Wall and Russian tanks massing at the border. They'll be thinking of their families.'

'It'd be a shame to win like that,' said John, who had read John Pilger's sensitive analysis of the German crisis in this morning's *Sun*. 'I'd be surprised if Robson accepted the cup under those circumstances. Honour is more important than winning.'

The cheeriness lasted a while. Then Jeffrey said, 'Of course, it'll be a different story in the final. Like in sixty-six. The Krauts may lose wars, but they win World Cups.'

John remembered the 1966 World Cup. He had been twenty-three, new to the buses. No grey in his hair. Bobby Moore's boys were unconquerable, overwhelming all opposition. People in the streets wore England scarfs and armbands as if they were the insignia of a nascent totalitarian state.

During the host team's cup run, John noticed something around him that he didn't like: an arrogance, a xenophobia, a cruelty. It was sneering in the tub-thumping of commentators, politicians, union leaders, businessmen. Everything was adversarial, setting worker against boss, North against South, England against the World. There was even talk of troubles in Ulster.

Trollope would have been able to express it better than he could, but the initial success of Alf's Commandos pricked something buried since the War. At the beginning of the Final, which he watched with his parents at the postman's house, English supporters chanted, 'Two world wars and one World Cup', jeering as the Germans jogged on to the pitch at Wembley.

That wasn't the attitude. That wasn't the game.

He remembered thinking that, if this was what England felt, then England deserved to lose. No matter how staunch Moore, the Charltons and the rest of the glory-covered team were, if the fans saw football as an excuse for expressing prejudice, it wasn't worth winning.

Three–three by the whistle. Four–three to the Germans in extra time.

He felt like a traitor, but John thought the result was fair. And after that, something changed.

'You'll see,' Jeffrey announced. 'It'll all go pear-shaped in the Final. That's the trouble with bloody Britain. Never finishes the job. We're just not ruthless enough, too concerned with seeing the other fellow's point of view. Our players will feel so sorry for poor old Fritz, with his divided country falling under commie tank-treads and four hundred and fifty per cent inflation wiping out their wages. We'll let 'em have a couple of goals just so they feel better. And before you know it, some kraut will be holding up the World Cup and blowing raspberries at us all.'

There was a lot of grumbling, but the supervisor was capable of finding an excuse to fire anyone who argued with him.

'We'll lose. You know why? Because we like bloody losing. It makes us feel warm and fair-minded and decent. Remember in sixty-nine, when we tried power-sharing in Ulster rather than send in the troops? Or eighty-two, when we had the *Belgrano* under our guns and let it sail back to port? It's as if nothing matters enough to us to fight for.'

'Oor Bobby won't let the lads lie back on the pitch,' said Tommy. 'England'll play to win, fair and square.'

'That's right, Geordie. Fair and square. If it's worth winning, it's worth cheating for. Remember the last final. In Italy.'

England had been in that too. Against Argentina. The final result found England losing two–one.

'The Argies put three of our blokes in hospital. And Maradona scored the winning goal with his hand while their midfield distracted the ref. Was that fair and square?'

'We don't play like that,' John said. 'If other people do, that's their problem. In the end, you'll see, it's better to be on the up and up, Jeffrey. Maradona may have won that match, but I very much doubt he's happy these days. I understand Argentine jails aren't very comfortable.'

'But we should have shelled the fuck out of the *Belgrano*.'

It wasn't just about football. In '66, with Wilson throwing his weight about and thinking of committing British soldiers to Vietnam, it had been about everything. The country was riding high, and looking around for someone to trample. The

Germans had tripped that up. Better it should happen at Wembley than on some battlefield.

That arrogance, the bossy brutality of the '60s, faded a bit, with the arrival of the gentler 1970s. Wilson gave way in bad temper to Heath and the bridge-building policies which took the United Kingdom happily into Europe. Heath stayed in office long enough to open the Channel Tunnel and conduct John Lydon's Youth Orchestra in an all-Elgar promenade concert to celebrate the Queen's Silver Jubilee.

Subsequent prime ministers, Tory and Labour, were peace-makers not jingoists: Jim Callaghan, Denis Healey, Peter Walker, Chris Patton. Good blokes all. John, a born floater, had voted for the lot of them. Next year, for a change, he would give a woman a chance, and put Harriet Harman in Number 10 Downing Street. She had such a sympathetic face, and made a point of travelling everywhere on public transport.

It was true that England had never won the World Cup, but they had played in four finals since 1966 and never been knocked out before the semi-finals. The record was nothing to be ashamed of. West Germany, winners in '66, had collapsed in Mexico in '70 and not even qualified for '74 or '82.

In other countries – like Holland or Spain – football was the focus of riots, violence, even mass murder. Families could enjoy British football every Saturday, either at thronging arenas up and down the country or on BBC 1's *Match of the Day* after the news. Everyone said British football was the safest, most exciting in the world. And there was no chance of being under a petrol bomb if the away side lost. What with Berlusconi's satellite channel robbing Italian terrestrial viewers of their own league games, British football was even being screened to huge ratings in Italy.

'You're wrong, Jeffrey,' John piped up, courage swelling. 'There's nothing wrong with losing in a final. Being Second Best in the World means something. There's nothing wrong

181

with being top of League Division Two. There's nothing wrong with being honestly Second-rate.'

'Second place is no place, John.'

'We always come second in the Eurovision Song Contest,' Stan muttered, spieling to break up the argument. 'It's because we always try to find a good group and get them to do a good song. We never put in some crass glitter bird like the Luxembourgers. All those la-la bing-bang songs that sound the same in any language always win. We should never have let Lennon and McCartney write all our entries in the seventies.'

'Show me a good loser, John, and I'll show you a loser.'

Jeffrey made soft little fists. John knew he had to argue, job or no job. This struck to the core of his being. Every man can be pushed so far into a corner, but there he will find the thing he truly believes.

'Results don't matter, Jeffrey,' said John. 'Playing the game does. Life isn't results. When you die, they don't calculate your goal average and judge whether you should be promoted or relegated. Life is the game, the process of the game, moment to moment. If you do your best, no one can blame you. If you play fair, no one can argue with you. Better to be a successful dustbinman than a wash-out field marshal.'

A deadly, viperish calm fell on Jeffrey's face. Measuring his words with venom, he said, 'Maybe that's why you've been a bus conductor all your life, John.'

The staff fell silent. Only the telly – *Whistle Test*, with John Peel – made a sound. Everyone looked at Jeffrey, feeling the contempt of his words, trying to wipe from their minds the slight of what he had said.

John felt the others fall in behind him. Margi, who always had a soft spot for him, held her rolling-pin like a club. Tommy clapped a matey hand on his shoulder. Stan quietly turned off the telly and crossed his arms.

Tomorrow, Jeffrey would resign or request a transfer. He would not be able to keep working with these men and women. He could never be part of the crews.

'Jeffrey,' John said, pride in his backbone, 'there's nothing wrong with being a bus conductor.'

Removed from the immediate context of their first appearances, this pair of alternate visions may seem a bit bewildering, not least because as time passes it becomes necessary to remind people who John Major actually was. Remember that blank bit of history between Margaret Thatcher and Tony Blair? Yes, him. I recall a piece in *Interzone* that suggested life after John Major's unexpected election victory in 1992 was like an alternate world, with everything somehow wrong. I certainly felt that way, since I'd just published 'SQPR' (which can be found in my first collection, *The Original Dr Shade and Other Stories*), which was a vision of a future Britain under a Labour government and predicated on him losing that election. Years on, my reputation as a prophet is restored – all the policies I suggest in 'SQPR' have been adopted by New Labour.

'Slow News Day' was prompted by the fiftieth anniversary of the D-Day landings. Harry Turtledove, on an alternate history panel at a convention, suggested that it was the most despairing of all Nazis-won-the-War variants – and I would concur with that. Part of the comfort of the sub-genre is that you are forced to conclude things could have been worse than they are. 'The Germans Won' is not another Nazis-won-the-War tale, but takes off in a left-handed manner from the sub-genre. It was written for another Nicholas Royle anthology, the football-themed *A Game of Two Halves* (which was, itself, partly inspired by 'SQPR') and perhaps stands as the utopian mirror image of the dystopian 'Slow News Day'.

NB: one of the facts everybody knew about John Major – the only boy who ran away from the circus to become an accountant – was that he once failed to get a job as a bus conductor because he couldn't manage the mental arithmetic. If you've forgotten the trivial personalities who inspired the characters of Mr Spotty and Jeffrey, you're better off and I won't sully your mind by reminding you.

COMPLETIST HEAVEN

I'm plumbing additional channels, homing on signals from as far away as Hilversum and Macao. With each twiddle, the dish outside revolves like Jodrell Bank stock footage from the *Quatermass* serials. Lightning crackles above the garden, approximating a Karloff–Lugosi mad lab insert shot from the '30s.

Unimaginable images and sounds are pulled down from the skies. With the new reflectors, this satellite system can haul in not only everything being broadcast but anything that has ever been broadcast. Shows listed as lost or wiped are beaming out to Alpha Centauri; now those signals can be brought unscrambled back to Earth.

This is my creation. Fuelled by coffee-bags and custard creams, I have substantially made the system myself, like Rex Reason assembling the Interocitor in *This Island Earth*. It was an interesting technical excercise, jacking in all the signal-boosters and calibrating the dish to the minutest fraction. My redundancy money was well spent, despite what Ciaran said when she left for the last time.

I admit it's true: I could spend the rest of my life eating biscuits and watching repeats on television. There is so much to see, so much to discover . . .

Just tuning the first channels, I come across a Patrick Troughton *Doctor Who* which does not officially survive, and a stumbling, live *Sherlock Holmes* from the late '40s. If anyone on Mars or Skaro makes television programmes, this dish will pick them up. To be honest, there is no need ever to leave the house except for groceries. Everything ever hurled out over the airwaves, on film or videotape, will turn up eventually. The full listings edition of *What's On TV* looks like a telephone directory.

This is Completist Heaven.

Whoever assigns frequencies has a sense of humour, though it often takes minutes to get the joke. Channel 5 is a perfume infomercial. Chanel No. 5. Channels 18 to 30 are *verité* footage of drunken Brits being obnoxious on holiday in Greece, with 'The Birdy Song' on a tape-loop soundtrack. Channel 69 is Danish porno. Channel 86 is *Get Smart* reruns. Maxwell Smart was Agent 86. I clock a Martin Kosleck cameo in a vampire episode and make a mental note to list it on Kosleck's file card. Channel 101 is disgusting true-life mondo horror, rats and bugs and atrocity and burial alive; in a minute, I remember that in *Nineteen Eighty-Four* Room 101 is where you face the most frightening thing in the world.

What does that leave for Channel 1984?

Channel 666 is either a director's cut of *The Omen* or a Satanic televangelist. In the thousands, most of the channels are date-tied: Channel 1066 is a historical drama in unsubtitled Norman French, Channel 1492 is a collage of Columbus movies with Jim Dale being tortured by Marlon Brando, Channel 1776 is that *Bilko* episode set during the Revolutionary War. Channel 1789 is a mini-series about the French Revolution: Jane Seymour goes nobly to the guillotine while Morgan Fairchild knits furiously in the first row. It's not in Maltin, Scheuer or Halliwell, so it must be new. I don't count mini-series as movies, so I don't have to watch further, though I'm sure that's Reggie Nadler dropping the blade.

I hit Channel 1818. Dyanne Thorne, a couple of melons down the front of her SS major's uniform, tortures someone in black and white. A girl in a torn peasant blouse squeals unconvincingly as a rat eats cold lasagne off her exposed tummy. I figure this is a print of *Ilsa, She-Wolf of the SS* that I've never seen. I get out the file card for the film and my notes make no mention of a rat torture quite like this. This is the sort

186

of revelation I pay the monthly fee for: it is possible no one has ever seen this version of the movie before. I take up my red ball pentel, and prepare to jot down any information. The store of human knowledge must always be added to.

The crowning moment of my life was when my letter in *Video Watchdog* finally corrected all previous misinformation and established, beyond a shadow of a doubt, the correct German running time of *Lycanthropus*, aka *Werewolf in a Girls' Dormitory* or *I Married a Werewolf*. Ciaran was especially cutting about that. Many people don't understand, but without accuracy all scholarship is meaningless and the least we can do is lay down the parameters of what we are talking about. Now, my mission in life is to force all periodicals and reference books to list *Matthew Hopkins, Witchfinder General* (the title as it appears on the screen) under M for *Matthew* rather than W for *Witchfinder*. Ignorant souls, starting with the film's distributors, have been committing this error since 1968. Heathens who list the Michael Reeves movie under C for *The Conqueror Worm* are, of course, beneath contempt and not worth considering.

The Ilsa movies are in colour, so I fine-fiddle the knobs. Snow crackles across the image as the victim screams. No colour appears. Ilsa gets out her nipple-clamps, sneering in a bad accent, 'Vellcome to SS Experiment Kemp Sex!' The camera pulls back, and on the next slab over from the abused girl lies the unmistakable bulk of a flat-headed, clumpy-booted, electrodes-on-the-neck, Universal-copyright Pierce-Karloff-Strange Frankenstein Monster.

Puzzled and intrigued, I gnaw a chocolate-coated ginger snap.

An ident crawl along the bottom of the picture identifies the film: Channel 1818 Feature Presentation *Frankenstein Meets the She-Wolf of the SS*.

Obviously, this must be some new retitling of a familiar movie. If the colour came on, I could identify it. More twiddling is to no avail.

I dig out Weldon's *Psychotronic Encyclopedia*, Glut's *The Frankenstein Catalog* and Jones's *The Illustrated Frankenstein Movie Guide*. *Frankenstein Meets the She-Wolf of the SS* does not make these standard reference tools. I venture further: consulting Lee's sadly outdated *Reference Guide to the Fantastic Film*, Willis's three-volume *Horror and Science Fiction Films*, my bound collection of Joe Bob's *We Are the Weird* newsletter, some back issues of *Shock Xpress*, and such variably reliable sources as the Phantom's *Ultimate Video Guide* and the mysterious *Hoffmann's Guide to SF, Horror and Fantasy Movies*. No one lists a Frankenstein–Ilsa crossover. This is exciting, a discovery. I feel a thrill in my water, pull out a fresh file card, and write down the title. I curse myself for having missed the credits.

To celebrate, I hold a cheddar thin in my mouth and suck gently, until saliva seeps through the biscuit and dissolves it. With my tongue, I work the paste bit by bit into my gullet. The sensation is exquisite.

Officially, there are only three Ilsa movies (*Ilsa, She-Wolf of the SS*, *Ilsa, Harem Keeper of the Oil Sheiks*, *Ilsa, Tigress of Siberia*) but Jesús Franco's *Greta, Hause ohne Männer* aka *Wanda the Wicked Warden* or *Greta the Torturer*, with Thorne in the title role of Greta–Wanda, is sometimes spuriously roped into the series. Could this be a hitherto-undiscovered entry in the *Ilsa* series, or some apocryphal adventure of a lookalike Greta, Gerta, Irma, Helga, Erika or Monika? The sync is just off, but I'm sure this is shot in English, not dubbed. A heel-clicking subordinate salutes and snaps, 'Heil Hitler, Major Ilsa', establishing this as indeed part of the Ilsa canon. The black and white bothers me still. Is this a flashback within a colour film? That would be a bit artsy for Ilsa.

The Nazi Bitch Queen is in an office, ranting. It's definitely Dyanne Thorne (once seen, those melons are unmistakable) and from the relative lack of lines on her face, the movie has to be from the mid-'70s. Oddly, it looks good in black and white:

188

less like a bad dupe which has lost colour than a film lit for monochrome. The shadows gathering in the office as night falls make the scene look better than the cheesy images I remember from other Ilsa movies. Not James Wong Howe good, but at least George Robinson good.

I look through Glut and Jones, trying to find a Thorne credit in a '70s Frankenstein movie. Of course, just because a film is called *Frankenstein Meets the She-Wolf of the SS* doesn't mean it's a Frankenstein movie. *Frankenstein's Bloody Terror* is a werewolf movie and several Japanese giant monster films have Frankenstein forced into their titles for German release, since Frankenstein is a generic term for monster in Germany. This must have been retitled since Glut came out, since he lists non-Frankenstein Frankenstein titles. With the proliferation of fly-by-night cable and video, some movies have multiple titles into double figures. I need three file cards just to list the alternate titles of *Horror of the Blood Monsters* or *No profanar el sueño de los muertos*. However, that Monster, noted in occasional cutaways, leads me to identify this tentatively as a genuine Frankenstein movie as well as an unknown Ilsa.

As the film plays on, I eat several bourbons, almost whole, chewing them like dog biscuits.

Something is definitely strange about *Frankenstein Meets the She-Wolf of the SS*. I'm convinced it was shot in black and white. Ilsa strides through what looks like the Universal Studios Middle European village (built for *All Quiet on the Western Front*, it shows up in all their monster movies), accompanied by pudgy SS extras. Wherever she stands in the shot, her mammoth breasts seem to be the centre of the frame.

The plot involves Ilsa establishing a Nazi experiment camp in a ruined castle. Cringing villagers avoid Ilsa's goose-stepping buddies. The village is called Visaria. I guess it's supposed to be in Czechoslovakia or Poland. It's hard to tell, because it seems more like generic Eastern Europe than a real country. The burgomeister wears lederhosen and an alpine hat with a peacock feather.

Visaria.

I flip back in Glut and Jones, trying to track down a niggling memory. I am right. Visaria is the name of the village in the latter Universal horror films: 1940s monster rallies like *Frankenstein Meets the Wolf Man* and *House of Dracula*. Whoever wrote *Frankenstein Meets the She-Wolf of the SS* must be a monster trivia junkie. I assume Forry Ackerman will get a cameo, and the Ken Strickfaden lab equipment will be dusted off. That suggests the auteur touch of Al Adamson, who always liked to borrow leftover props from the Universals for atrocities like *Dracula Vs Frankenstein*. This looks too good to be an Adamson (no acid trip, no Russ Tamblyn, no bikers) but I feel I'm getting this movie pinned down. Maybe it's from about the same vintage as *Blackenstein*, the one with the Karloff-style monster sporting a flat afro.

I write: '1972 to 1975? American. Stars Dyanne Thorne (as Ilsa). The tortured girl looked like Uschi Digart.'

Then Lionel Atwill shows up as a police inspector with a prosthetic arm and an eagle-crested cap, with Dwight Frye and Skelton Knaggs as the most cringing of cringing villagers. They are from the '40s, like the sets and the photography, and I'm lost.

Bourbon biscuit crumbs turn to ashes in my mouth.

Even if – and it's inconceivable – I'm wrong and the leading woman is not Dyanne Thorne but a lookalike, the scene with the rat and the nipple-clamps could never have been shot in the '40s. Even for the private delectation of Lionel Atwill's houseguests. Ilsa doesn't have the lipsticky, marcelled look of the women in '40s horror films. Her hippie eye make-up and butch haircut are '70s to the bleached blonde roots.

I swallow and am forced to assume this is a *Dead Men Don't Wear Plaid* gimmick, mixing footage from different films. Perhaps it has been overdubbed with wisecracks by *Saturday Night Live* regulars. I listen to the dialogue as Ilsa dresses down Inspector Atwill, and can't catch any deliberate camp. One-shots of Ilsa and Atwill alternate and I try to see inconsistencies in the backgrounds. The match is good.

Then Ilsa peels off one elbow-length black leather glove and slaps Atwill across the face with it. Thorne's Ilsa, from the '70s, is in the same shot with Atwill's Inspector, from the '40s, and their physical interaction is too complicated to be faked. Ilsa rips apart Atwill's many-buttoned uniform, yanking off his artificial arm, and squats on him, hip-thrusting against the stump that sticks out of his shoulder. Thorne's orgasmic moaning is as unconvincing as ever but Atwill looks as though he's getting something out of the scene. Unsatisfied, Ilsa gets up and rearranges her SS skirt, then has Atwill summarily executed. Black blood squirts out of his burst eye. The ketchupy '70s gore looks nastier, more convincing in hand-me-down '40s expressionist black and white.

The telephone rings and the answering-machine cuts in. It's Ciaran, complaining about maintenance. She jabbers on, an uncertain edge to her voice, and I concentrate on important things.

This is definitely a crossover movie. I fervently wish I had seen it from the beginning so I could tell whether the title-card was original or spliced in. Actually, trying to track this one down is pointless. Whatever it's really called, it's impossible.

It's the usual Ilsa story but the supporting characters are from the Universal monster series. Major Ilsa is the last grand-daughter of the original Henry Frankenstein and the castle is her ancestral home. That would make her the character played by Ilona Massey in *Frankenstein Meets the Wolf Man*. Dyanne Thorne is even wearing an Ilona Massey beauty mark, which shifts alarmingly around her mouth from scene to scene with typical Ilsa continuity. She is supposed to be working on the creation of a race of super-Nazis for Hitler, but spends more time having weird sex and torturing people than contributing to the war effort.

To help her out around the laboratory, where Glenn Strange lies supine on the table, Ilsa drags Dr Pretorius, Ernest Thesiger's swish mad scientist from *Bride of Frankenstein*, and

Ygor, Bela Lugosi's broken-necked gypsy from *Son* ... and *Ghost of Frankenstein*, out of their concentration camps. Pretorius keeps adjusting his pink triangle to set off his lab coat and Ygor leers gruesomely at Ilsa, tongue dangling a foot or so out of his mouth.

The sex scenes are near hardcore, but extremely silly. Ilsa needs a man who can sustain an erection for a whole night and most of the next morning if she is to achieve full satisfaction. She thinks she is in luck when virile Larry Talbot tears off his clothes as the full moon rises. In an unprecedented shot, yak hair swarms around the Wolf Man's crotch. Jack Pierce must really have given Lon Chaney Jr a hard time with that lap dissolve. Ilsa and the Wolf Man go at it all over the castle, with ridiculous grunting and gasping and Franz Waxman's Wedding Bells score from *Bride of Frankenstein*, but there's big disappointment at dawn as the moon goes down and the werewolf turns back into dumb old flabby Larry–Lon. Ilsa yells abuse at the befuddled and limp American, and batters him to death with a silver cane.

After this, Ilsa is so crabby she shoves the burgomeister's irritating daughter into the sulphur pits below the castle. As the little girl goes under, we cut to Ygor–Bela snickering over a lamp positioned under his chin to make him look scary.

In theory, Universal's creature features have contemporary settings. *Dracula* and *The Wolf Man* clearly establish 1931 and 1941 for the dates of the action, so their sequels must take place in the years of their production. *Ghost of Frankenstein* (1941), *Frankenstein Meets the Wolf Man* (1943), *House of Frankenstein* (1944) and *House of Dracula* (1945), the Visaria movies, are all set in an unspecified Eastern Europe of torch-bearing peasant mobs, gypsy musicians and saluting policemen. Though Atwill in *Son of Frankenstein* complains that he missed out on the First World War because the monster tore his arm off when he was a boy, no one ever mentions the then-current War. In its crazed way, *Frankenstein Meets the She-Wolf of the SS* is more 'realistic'. The war, as reflected in the

Nazi pornos of the '70s, has leaked into the enclosed world of Universal horror.

I mix Kettle Chips and Jaffa Cakes, washing them down with Appletise.

Predictably, at sunset, a distinguished visitor arrives at the castle, nattily dressed in top-hat, white tie and tails, peering hypnotically over his long nose. John Carradine announces himself as Baron Latos. As Ilsa escorts him to her boudoir, Carradine's floor-length cloak sweeps into a wing shape. An animated bat lands on Ilsa's breasts and writhes, pushing her back on to a canopied four-poster bed. Reverting to human form, Dracula nuzzles his moustache between Ilsa's thighs. The Count unbuttons his immaculate trouser fly to uncurl a white length of vampire manhood and pleasures Ilsa all through the night. The end, though, is inevitable. At sunrise, Dracula turns to ashes on top of an unsatisfied and infuriated Ilsa.

A sunburst of realisation: Channel 1818 is showing not movies that were made, but movies that can be imagined.

Appletise blurts out of my nose at the conceptual breakthrough.

The ending is guessable: Dr Pretorius charges the Monster and he gets up off his slab in time to be the insatiable stud Ilsa has looked for throughout the picture. Glenn Strange, naked but for asphalt-spreader's boots, pounds away at Ilsa's tender parts for what seems like hours as revolting partisan peasants burn down the castle around their ears. The Monster's tool is in proportion with the rest of him, scarred with collodion applications. As Ilsa finally comes like a skyrocket, burning beams fall on the bed and an end title flickers.

As usual on cheapo movie channels, the film fades before the end credits so there's no chance of noting down the copyright date. I howl in frustration and throw away the file card. With no concrete information, I might just as well not have watched the film.

In anger, I batter the cushions of my sofa. Then I'm drawn back to the television. Over a frozen frame of Boris Karloff as

193

the Monster in a Beatle wig, Channel 1818 announces the rest of the evening's movie programme.

King Kong Meets Frankenstein. Willis O'Brien's dream project.

The Marx Brothers Meet the Monsters. Through the bungling of Igolini (Chico), Professor Wolf J. Frankenstein (Groucho) puts the Monster's brain into Harpo's skull. Margaret Dumont is Dracula's Daughter.

House of the Wolf Man. A 1946 Universal, directed by Jean Yarbrough. Otto Kruger and Rondo Hatton tamper with the brains of Lon Chaney, Bela Lugosi and Glenn Strange.

Dr Orloff, Sex Slave of Frankenstein. Directed by Jesús Franco, with Howard Vernon and Dennis Price, plus hardcore spliced in a decade after Price's death.

Frankenstein Meets the Space Monster: The Director's Cut. The three-hour extended version, with additional beach party numbers.

My bladder is uncomfortably full but I can't get up to pee lest I miss anything irreplaceable. Channel 1818 is a treasure trove. If I keep watching, I'll be able to note down credits. I'll be the true source of information. Weldon, Glut and Jones will have to beg me for credits. My interpretations will be definitive. Hardy's *Aurum Encyclopedia: Horror* will have to be junked entirely. The history of horror is written on shifting sands.

Then come trailers: Peter Cushing sewing new legs on to disco queen Caroline Munro in Hammer's *Frankenstein AD 1971*; an hour-long print of the 1910 Edison *Frankenstein!*; Baron Rossano Brazzi singing 'Some Lightning-Blasted Evening' in Rodgers and Hammerstein's *Frankenstein!*; Peter Cushing and Boris Karloff in the same laboratory; W. C. Fields as the Blind Hermit, sneering, 'Never work with children or hunchbacked assistants'; James Whale's 1931 *Frankenstein*, with Leslie Howard as the doctor, Bette Davis as Elizabeth and a still-living Lon Chaney, all staring eyes and glittering teeth, as the Monster; John Wayne and a cavalry troop tracking the

Monster through Monument Valley in John Ford's *Fort Frankenstein*; a restored 1915 *Life Without Soul*, with Percy Darrell Standing; *Frankenstein 1980* in 3-D, with a better script; James Dean and Whit Bissell in *I Was a Teenage Frankenstein*.

1818 was the year in which Mary Shelley published *Frankenstein, or The Modern Prometheus*. This is the Frankenstein Channel.

My bladder lets go, but I don't mind. I can't make it to the kitchen without looking away from the screen, so I'll have to improvise food. As always, I have enough munchies to keep me going. Sleep I can do without. I have my vocation.

My wrist aches from writing down titles and credits. I have responsibilities.

David Cronenberg's *Frankenstein*. Dario Argento's *Frankenstein*. Ingmar Bergman's *Frankenstein*. Woody Allen's *Frankenstein*. Martin Scorsese's *Frankenstein*. Walerian Borowczyk's *Frankenstein*. Jerry Warren's *Frankenstine*. Akira Kurosawa's *Furankenshutain*. Ernest Hemingway's *Frank Stein*. Troma's *Frankenslime*. William Castle's *Shankenstein*. Jim Wynorski's *Wankenstein*. Wayne Newton's *Dankenshane*. Odorama's *Rankenstein*.

I watch, reference books strewn around the floor, all useless, all outdated. On and on, monsters and mad doctors, hunchbacks and mobs, blind men and murdered girls, ice floes and laboratories.

Channel ident 1818 flickers. I fight pangs in my stomach and eat the crumby paper which was wrapped around my last pack of digestive biscuits. Sammy Davis Jr slicks hair across his flat-head in a *Rat Packenstein* picture, as Dino and Frank Sinatra fix up the electrodes.

I recognise the strange smell as my own. There are enough crumbs behind the cushions of the sofa to sustain life. I pick them out like a grooming gorilla and crack them between my teeth.

Badly dressed black musicians rob the graves of blues singers in the endless *Funkenstein* series. Ridley Scott directs a run of *Bankenstein* ads for Barclays, with Sting applying for a small business loan to get his monster wired. Jane Fonda works the scars out of her thighs in the *Flankenstein* video.

I am transfixed. I would look away, but there is a chance I might miss something. I'm dreaming the electronic dream, consuming imaginary images made celluloid.

Brides, sons, ghosts, curses, revenges, evils, horrors, brains, dogs, bloods, castles, daughters, houses, ladies, brothers, ledgers, lodgers, hands, returns, tales, torments, infernos, worlds, experiments, horror chambers . . . of Frankenstein.

I hit the exhaustion wall and burn through it. My life functions are at such a low level that I can continue indefinitely. I'm plugged into Channel 1818. It's my duty to stay the course.

Abbott and Costello, Martin and Lewis, Redford and Newman, Astaire and Rogers, Mickey and Donald, Tango and Cash, Rowan and Martin, Bonnie and Clyde, Frankie and Annette, Hinge and Brackett, Batman and Robin, Salt and Pepa, Titch and Quackers, Amos and Andy, Gladstone and Disraeli, Morecambe and Wise, Block and Tackle . . . Meet Frankenstein.

I can barely move, but my eyes are open.

Credits roll, too fast to jot down. These films exist for one showing and are lost. Each frame is unique, impossible to recreate. I daren't even leave the room to get a pack of blank videotapes. It is down to me. I must watch and I must remember. My mind is the screen on which these Frankensteins perform.

The Frankenstein Monster is played by . . . Bela Lugosi (in 1931), Christopher Lee (in 1964), Lane Chandler, Harvey Keitel, Sonny Bono, Bernard Bresslaw, Meryl Streep, Bruce Lee, Neville Brand, John Gielgud, Ice-T, Rock Hudson, Traci Lords.

The experience is priceless. A red sun rises outside, and I draw the curtains.

'Now I know what it feels like to be a God,' croaks Edward G. Robinson.

I will stay with the channel.
'We belong dead,' intones Don Knotts.
I will watch.
'To a new world of Gods and monsters,' toasts Daffy Duck.

This first appeared in Stephen Jones's *The Mammoth Book of Frankenstein*. It may well be the most pointlessly over-researched story ever written by someone other than Howard Waldrop. Steve, incidentally, does keep file-cards on films and actors (and has updated his Frankenstein volume as part of his *Illustrated Monster Movie Guide*). I've written for *Video Watchdog* and edited *The BFI Companion to Horror*, so I know all about the pressures of getting facts right amid a blizzard of misinformation. I also realise how close you come to obsessive-compulsive disorder in doing that kind of work.

COASTAL CITY

From the window of his 38th-floor office, Francis X. Riordan could see the Statue of Freedom out in the bay, his torch held high; the Allied Nations HQ, reflecting the city like a giant black mirror; and the Imperial State Building, still the tallest skyscraper in the world.

In the rare moments when Coastal City was not in crisis, Chief Riordan liked to stand before his panoramic window and look out at the metropolis, at the thin mists drifting round the spires of the highest structures, at the blimps making doughnut-holes in low clouds, at the flying folk.

Riordan could remember when there were no flying folk.

He couldn't put a date on it, or even a decade, and his head buzzed a little if he tried. But there had been a time before the miraculous. Some things had changed enormously, beyond belief in fact, but others, ordinary things you expected to change, had stayed the same.

He had no idea any more of his age.

At the beginning, he had been only a few years away from retirement. Somewhere in his late fifties, hair iron-grey, moustache white, pipe clamped in his teeth. He was still there, caught in that moment. Wars had come and gone, radio given way to television, books of mug-shots and sketch artists replaced by tap-ins to the Federal Bureau of Inquiry's national database and interactive imaging computers, man had reached the moon and beyond. But Police Chief Frank Riordan still hadn't retired. He was a ticking clock, stuttering on a moment in personal time, straining forward but pulled back.

A golden jet shot across the sky. It was the first of the flying folk, the most beloved, Amazon Queen.

She had come to Coastal City before the War – WWII, the Big One – and declared her own war, on criminals and fifth columnists and other evildoers. Riordan remembered his first sight of her, after the averting of a major elevated-railway sabotage incident. She was a goddess in a golden cape and bathing-suit, a streetcar lifted over her head, gently drifting downwards, tiara shining in the sunlight.

They coined a word for her: hyperhero.

Soon there were others: some flew, some didn't. The Streak, who could run faster than sound. Green Masque, who dressed like a Ziegfeld girl and broke up rackets with high kicks. The Darkangel, who haunted the night in search of miscreants. Gecko Man, the wall-scaling, wise-cracking youth. Teensy Teen, the Shrinking Cheerleader, and her sidekick, Blubber Boy. The Outcasts, high-schoolers with hyperpowers and acne. Vindicator, the cyborg avenger remade in Vietnam as an implacable enemy of evil.

The hypers brought out the best and worst of Coastal City. They set an example, protected the innocent, kept the peace. But there were equally powerful, equally hyper, villains; gimmick gang bosses like Max Multiple, Circe and Mr Bones, mad scientists like Dr Megalomaniac and Comrade Atomic Man, freaks like Dead Thing and the Creech, mystery men like the Dealer and Shadowjack, flamboyant sociopaths like Pestilence and Hexfire. And that was only the more-or-less human ones.

Giant monsters from beneath the seas or the earth: Tentaclo, the ten-armed titanic octopus; Ssquarrq, the living earthquake; the Anti-Human Wave. Alien invaders from Mars, Mercury, Planet Q, Aldebaran, Dimension Terror and Zandorr. Demons from Hell: Asmodeus Jr, Lillyth, the Jibbenainosay.

Coastal City had been levelled more times than Riordan could count. It seemed each of the hyperheroes spent ten months of the year pairing up with a rotating succession of hypervillains, demolishing city blocks in their fights. Sometimes, hypers formed tag teams and knocked down whole streets. And once a year, there would be a crossover free-for-all, frequently involving something enormously powerful from another galaxy, and all the hypers would destroy the city while saving the universe.

Chief Riordan, whom some called the city's heart and guts, had lived through medieval plagues, alien invasions, month-long nights, demonic manifestations, nuclear fires, transportation of the whole city back to the age of the dinosaurs or one of the moons of Zandorr, and a thousand one-man hyper-crimewaves. He had personally been possessed by Asmodeus Jr, temporarily granted all the powers of Gecko Man and had a million-dollar contract put on his head by Max Multiple. Always, he'd sustain a few bruises, wrap a bandage round his head or put his arm in a splint, then be back in his office and on the job.

The city could be rebuilt overnight, and often had been.

In the beginning, it wasn't even called Coastal City. For the briefest moment, during Amazon Queen's battle with Lady Nazi, it had been New York, and there had been a Statue of Liberty and a Brooklyn Bridge. Then, when the Streak came to town, the city was revised, the buildings grew taller and shinier, the shadows became deeper and darker.

Amazon Queen saved President Roosevelt from Lady Nazi's poison kisses. And the Streak began his decades-long persecution of the crazy crime boss Max Multiple. Suddenly, everyone was calling the place Coastal City and things became more hectic.

That must have been 1939 or '40.

Then, there had been a framed photograph in Riordan's office of him in France, posed by his biplane after his famous victory over Hans von Hellhund, the Demon Ace. Later, the picture showed him with the crew of the bomber *Eudora Fae*, after dropping the third atomic bomb on Samurai Satan's private army. Now, his younger self, flashing Nixon Vs, was beside his experimental hypersonic Stud Fighter on a carrier off the coast of Vietnam. He knew that if he sat here much longer the picture would show him in the Gulf War.

Floating about twenty years in his past was a war. But that war kept pace with the present, always lagging the same distance behind him.

That was just one of the things that changed.

He had no real memories, he thought sometimes, just polished anecdotes, flashbacks that faded. If he concentrated on the framed photograph, he saw all the images at once, all the wars, all the planes. Only his face was always the same, albeit with different moustaches: from Douglas Fairbanks to Clark Gable to Dennis Hopper.

There were firebursts over the city.

Amazon Queen was dancing in the air with three small, swift, insect-like humans. Flameflowers blossomed and streamers fell towards the streets, where people looked up and pointed. They were rarely hurt by falling debris. It was another day in Coastal City.

Only a moment ago it had been the '30s. There was a Depression finishing and a War to come. That was always the moment in Coastal City, though the Depressions and the Wars changed.

Now, it was . . . what year was it?

It was always Next Year in Coastal City, just far enough ahead for the hyperinventions to be off the drawing-board. But not so far that the President of the day was out of office.

A green shape swept upwards across the building, crossing the window in a green flash, leaving those sucker-marks that were hell to wipe off. Riordan craned to look, but Gecko Man was gone.

Riordan was more comfortable with Amazon Queen and the Streak, beyond human comprehension as they were, than with youngsters like Gecko Man or the Outcasts. Amazon Queen and the Streak, the first generation of hypers, were of his vintage and had his attitudes. They were clean-cut, good-humoured, even-tempered, unswervingly confident in their own rectitude.

Gecko Man never seemed to take anything seriously but was plainly knotted with neurosis; he was just a mixed-up kid, though he had been around since the Brittles came out of Liverpool and Kennedy was shot by that alien in Dallas. And even Gecko Man was weirded out by the Vindicator, who had been a hypervillain the first time he showed up with his blockbustergun but had become popular enough to be classed as one of the good guys. The old hypers always trussed up even the most powerful menaces and left them for the cops, but the Vindicator collected severed heads.

The department had cops, newer men and women, who understood the world of the Vindicator. But Chief Riordan would always be a New Deal man. Hyperheroes with capabilities that put them in the demigod class looked to him for fatherly advice, and accepted his judgments as final.

And the city rose and fell. Again and again.

Ginger, his assistant, brought in a report. The three creatures Amazon Queen was zapping were the latest conjurings of her arch-enemy, Lillyth. Amazon Queen could handle that.

Ginger had been with him since the beginning.

At first, she was a scatty secretary, and looked like Ginger Rogers. Now, she was Assistant Chief, and looked like Sharon Stone. Along the way, she had resembled Lauren Bacall, June Allyson, Jane Fonda and Meryl Streep. She had been an undercover femme fatale, a starched housewife, a counterculture radical, a feminist overachiever.

But she was still stuck with a name from the '30s.

Riordan told Ginger to pass on a routine alert to Colonel Gritsby of COMMAND (Central Operation to Maintain Massive American National Defense) that hyperhumans were engaged in a firefight over a populated area.

'Lillyth?' Ginger mused. 'Is she a supernatural entity or an extra-terrestrial being?'

203

'She's a demon sorceress from Dimension Terror. Check both boxes.'

Ginger shrugged, and left the office.

For decades, Coastal City had been almost cosy. Buildings might be destroyed, but innocent bystanders were rushed out of the way. Casualties were amazingly light, limited to hyper-villains who unwisely made final stands on perches above the bay – the torch of the Statue of Freedom was very popular – and accidentally fell to their usually temporary deaths in the waters below.

Hyperheroes never so much as gave them a shove, though it was quietly agreed that no one should ever hold the Streak, who could accomplish anything in a fragment of a second, responsible for not darting out and saving Dr Megalomaniac from a fatal fall in the way he would if Ginger, on whom he was kind of sweet, were tottering on a ledge. As it happens, dozens of falls, fires, explosions, executions, banishments to Dimension Terror and Mittel European lynch mobs had failed to do any permanent harm to Dr Meggo.

A few months – years? – ago, that had started to change. A few minor hypers, mostly those who had not been heard of for a while, got killed in the odd big brawl. Peers gathered for funerals, though they could hardly be expected to remember much about the fallen.

At first, when Iridium Man was destroyed by Mr Bones, Riordan had expected I-Man to be back within the month, but it seemed his death was more permanent than most. In life, he hadn't been much of a name – just a second-stringer in a short-lived group, the Atom Age Teens, who had been around for a while before Gecko Man turned up. But, as a dead hyperhero, he took on a totemic position. If Iridium Man could die, so could anyone else.

About that time, Vindicator started seriously collecting heads. The mood of the city changed, even its look. Edges were sharper, shadows thicker. The Depression spread, affecting more than the picturesque and grateful orphans who received Christmas presents in the Streak's annual Santa Claus act. There were homeless persons, mentally ill veterans, even the odd teenage hooker. A few street cops turned out to be dirty.

Riordan couldn't understand it.

Once, he found himself picking up the phone and asking to speak with President Roosevelt.

Then, in his mind, he asked himself: which one?

The silver spires and the elegant dirigibles were still there, in the world of the flying folk. But down in the labyrinthine streets and alleys, the Darkangel kept the fragile peace through terror. Even Vindicator started to seem soft. Nightgaunt, the city's newest 'hyperhero', was a demon turncoat who ate the entrails of slain foes.

Once, the city had been an American Ideal. All problems were solved quickly and with good cheer. Even the worst of the worst were like naughty children, sent to their rooms until the next scrape. And the hyperheroes were all big kids, enjoying themselves.

What had changed?

Now Coastal City was America's Nightmare.

The old city was still there, if you looked.

Riordan realised the problem was in himself. Like Max Multiple, he hopped between personalities. He was different with different people: fatherly with Amazon Queen, irascible with Darkangel, a buffoon with Gecko Man, sad but stern with Vindicator, almost senile with Nightgaunt.

He was in everyone's world, and they were all inside him, tearing him apart.

Only months till retirement.

But months were eternal in Coastal City. It was just months since Watergate (when Dr Meggo replaced the President with an evil robot), since the Bay of Pigs, since Anzio.

Riordan wondered. I-Man was gone and even poor sweet dumb Teensy Teen had been stomped flat by the Dealer. For a while, it seemed Amazon Queen had actually died, sucked into the Nevergone Void, but she came back, reborn and rejuvenated and with a more revealing costume, and a meaner streak. But Green Masque, who had been around almost as long as Amazon Queen, fell victim to a serial killer, Pestilence, and was actually gone from continuity, rarely seen even as a ghost.

It could happen.

He could die. Ironically, on the eve of retirement. He would be greatly mourned and swiftly avenged.

But he was an anachronism. The times would be served better if Coastal City's police chief were a woman or a psychopathic hypervillain or a black man. There was more potential in any of those, more chance for conflict or crisis.

It was all about stories, about plot material.

He wasn't one of the immortals.

Dr Megalomaniac was out there, a one-time nuisance reworked as a mass murderer. And so many others. With grudges, with hyperpowers.

Living through months that spanned decades, only noticing the gradual changes when they were well established, always careering from crisis to crisis, Frank Riordan was wearing out. At first, slowly; now, rapidly.

How long would this go on?

He looked out of his office window as night fell. The torch of the Statue of Freedom burned bright, its fires reflected in the frontage of the Allied Nations HQ.

A giant, ten-armed octopus was pulling itself painfully up the Imperial State Building, tentacle by tentacle. Futile shellbursts were exploding all around. Crowds in the streets were running in panic.

Riordan forgot his troubles and used the gold phone. It was answered at the first ring, but as usual she didn't speak, just listened.

'There's a crisis in Coastal City,' he told the silent party. 'If ever we've needed you, we need you now.'

COASTAL CITY

This was written for *The Time Out Book of New York Short Stories*, edited by Nicholas Royle. There is no truth in the rumour that he's soliciting for *The Time Out Book of Birmingham Short Stories*, but if he were I'd probably come up with something.

A sub-plot of my novel *The Quorum* deals with a made-up publisher called ZC Comics. 'Coastal City' takes place inside the wholly-owned, copyrighted ZC universe, and reflects sixty years of imaginary comic books like *All-Streak Monthly* and *Sergeant Grit and His Gorilla Guerrillas*. I wrote the story before I'd heard of Kurt Busiek's excellent continuing comic series *Astro City*, which parallels my line of thought about the superhero medium.

QUETZALCÓN

'The Kingston Dunstan Convention'

PROGRAMME BOOKLET

Guest of Honour
KINGSTON DUNSTAN

Leech Pyramid Plaza, London Docklands
31 October–1 November 1997

Introduction: A Message from Coatlicue

It's hard to believe it, but organised Kingston Dunstan fandom has been around for less than a year. It seems so long ago that 'the Kingston' arrived in style and established himself as the greatest tragi-comic fantasy writer of 1996–7, but last November you could have asked me what a smoking mirror was and I'd not have been able to tell you. Back then, let's face it, we were all reading Jonathan (Whatever Happened To) Monahan.

With the publication by Real Press of *Popocatépetl Popsy*, the world – and little me – took notice. Since then, a new Dunstan winner has launched every two months, each taking a more commanding position at the head of the best-seller lists. Two feature films, an animated TV series and a West End pantomime (with Philip Scofield) are in the works, and you, the devoted, have reached deep into your pockets to purchase Dunstan-related figurines, jewellery, role-playing games, underwear and costumes.

This weekend, I look forward to mingling among you in the feathered headdress and macramé-and-semiprecious-stones robes of a worthy High Priestess of Tezcatlipoca (much like the original Coatlicue, of KD's *Chimborazo Chippie*) and I trust that I will encounter in the corridors of the Leech Pyramid Plaza many a strapping Centzon Huitznáue, fluttery Tlaloc, humming Huitzilopochtli and sinister Quetzalcóatl.

Everyone here, I expect, will be a Kingston Dunstan character. By special dispensation, the hotel will allow true fans proudly to display their obsidian knives, and drink peyote-sprinkled chocolate in the several bars. Our con will be a riot of parrot plumage, and I hope you'll take the opportunity to mingle with your fellow-fans and, of course, with 'the King of the Smoking Mirror' himself.

A few words about our most esteemed special guest of honour. Without Kingston Dunstan, we wouldn't be here. He has graciously taken time out at the end of what has been for

211

him a whirlwind year, admitting to me that he knows it's time he gave back something of himself to those who have done so much to make his reign a roller-coaster of bliss. He has asked me to pass on the fact that he will always be available for anyone (especially anyone female between the ages of twelve and twenty-five dressed in the ankle-bells, ceramic-bead thongs and body-oil of one of the fragrant handmaidens of Xilonen from *Tenochtitlán Tootsie*) who might wish to shower rose-petals on his head or buy him drinks. Of course, with me at the convention, you'll have to get at the back of a long queue which I will be at the head of.

I know that Kingston will give generously of himself, and that you will all take away with you a warm, personal piece of the great man's greater heart.

So, remember, let's get fannish out there!

Coatlicue, Chairperson and High Priestess

212

Friday Night

18.00. Opening Ceremony.
Coatlicue and her handmaidens welcome you to Quetzalcón.
Singing, dancing, sweetmeats, offering of a small goat.
Trumpets, zithers, filking.

19.00. Registration Opens.
Pick up your bag of Kingston Dunstan goodies. Includes new
book, old book and, if you're one of the lucky few, toenail-
parings. You can have your Aztec or ordinary name on your
badge. No stupid jokes, please.

20.00. Party. Meet Kingston Dunstan.
A buffet of honeyed serpent-meat, jellied condor tongue and
pepper wine, courtesy of Real Press. This is your first chance to
get near the Kingston as he is borne into the ballroom on a
jewelled throne by four acolytes, descending from the hotel's
luxurious Apex Suite to be among us. If you find a peacock
feather in your goody bag, you're the lucky winner picked to
heft the shovel-sized fan and ensure not a drop of sweat starts
out on Kingston's forehead when the central heating cranks
up.

22.00 Panel: 'Why We Love Kingston Dunstan'.
Coatlicue (High Priestess), Lucy Julie Fancey (Real Press
publicist), Kevin Goode (editor of *Smoking Mirror*, the official
Kingstondunstanzine) and Chalchiuhtlicue (winner of the
Kingston trivia contest in *SFX Magazine*) explain for the
marginally initiated just what it is the Kingston has to offer his
loyal fans. Kingston Dunstan remains on his throne, elevated
so he can look down benevolently on the panel, and modestly
accepts their well-deserved oblations.

Midnight. Party. Meet Kingston Dunstan (Again).
Frank Conklin, editor of *Feathered Serpent*, the alternative
Kingstondunstanzine, has cashed in his last five giros to pay for
a sumptuous feast laid at the feet of the Kingston, who strips
off his shoes and socks and leaves footprints in a trough of
pâté, that fans can then eat. Kingston has promised not to
wash his feet or change his socks for a month before this
evening, so the fare should be tasty.

Film Programme: *The Fan* (US, 1981, Edward Bianchi. With
Lauren Bacall, James Garner, Michael Biehn); *King of Comedy*
(US, 1983, Martin Scorsese. With Robert De Niro, Jerry Lewis,
Sandra Bernhard).

Guest of Honour Biography
by Jack Yeovil

As a child, the Boy Who Would Be Kingston was unexceptional, always picked last in games; as a youth, he was middling in social circles, known mostly for his remarkable crop of skin blemishes; and as a young man, he was hardly distinguished in his chosen profession of council clerk.

Kingston Dunstan's first taste of success came at last year's Quetzalcón, when he was fired up by the generous heart of the then-best-selling fantasist Jonathan Monahan and saw that a bright future could be his. Suddenly, the novels piling up under his wonky desk were issued by Real Press (formerly Monahan's publisher) and broke through to unprecedented success: *Popocatépetl Popsy*, *Chimborazo Chippie*, *Tenochtitlán Tootsie*, *Cotopaxi Cutie*, *Machu Picchu Mucho Peaches*.

Few authors have been so instantly acclaimed. 'Kingston Dunstan is funnier than I am – by miles!' – Terry Pratchett. 'Kingston Dunstan is the Dostoyevsky of heroic fantasy, the Shelley of sword and sorcery.' – J. R. R. Tolkein (via spirit medium). 'Kingston Dunstan is the golden youth of his genre, a bright candle that burns brighter and faster than any of his predecessors.' – Neil Gaiman. 'If Kingston Dunstan is going to keep writing this stuff, I might as well go home.' – Michael Marshall Smith. 'Kingston Dunstan makes my stuff look like a festering pile of shit!' – A. S. Byatt. At the small funeral of Jonathan Monahan, John Clute toasted Kingston Dunstan with 'The king is dead, long live the Kingston!'

Twelve months ago Kingston Dunstan was living in a bedsit in Birmingham, filing forms for a living. Now he divides his time between residences in Hampstead, Beverly Hills and Puerto Vallarta. Twelve months ago, bookshops had huge displays of Jonathan Monahan books where there are now Kingston Dunstan sections, offering all his novels as books, talking books, colour-in books, join-the-dots books, cookbooks, videos, CD-ROMs, cassettes, graphic novels and in tablet-form. More than one Smiths branch has opted to stock only Kingston Dunstan books: giving shelf space to anything else is a waste of time when KD Klassics are guaranteed to shift faster than the Flash with a rocket up his arse.

Those who know him say success hasn't changed Kingston Dunstan. His parents admit they haven't seen much, if anything, of him since he sold his first book, but will proudly tell you of his generosity in paying off the mortgage on their family home with his first royalty cheque, giving them jobs as curators of the Living Museum of Kingston Dunstan that their small terraced house has been turned into. His first wife looks forward to a reunion this weekend with the beloved husband who popped out for a packet of fags shortly after his Hollywood payment came through and has naturally been too busy to go back home, especially since his recent remarriage to the winner of a 'What I Would Do With Kingston Dunstan on a Weekend in Rio de Janeiro' competition held by the *Sunday Sport*.

This has been the Year of Kingston Dunstan. Enjoy it while it lasts.

Saturday All Day

10.00. Kids' Korner.
What does the future hold for you? Bring along a small child and our resident haruspex will foresee your fortune. Note: You are required to sign a disclaimer.

12.00. Paper: 'The King and the Kingston'.
Professor Peter Atkins of Liverpool University delivers his PhD thesis on the similarities between the King – Elvis Presley – and the Kingston. Should the Professor inadvertently commit sacrilege, he is available for the cut and thrust of a post-paper question-and-answer session. One thing is certain: Kingston Dunstan can sing 'Wooden Heart' a lot better than Elvis could write a tragi-comic fantasy.

14.00. Panel: 'The Care and Feeding of Kingston Dunstan'.
Coatlicue (High Priestess), Brenda Trout Dunstan (the first Mrs D), Mysti Kristle Dunstan (the current Mrs D) and Barry the Barman theorise about the sort of treatment required to keep a best-selling tragi-comic fantasy author as happy as Catherine the Great at the Horse of the Year Show. Expect chocolate, alcohol, backrubs and school uniform to be mentioned quite often.

16.00. Hot Chocolate.
Kingston Dunstan judges the hot chocolate competition, and bestows chocolate kisses upon the winner. When you've finished, make sure the cups and pans are given to Frank Conklin, the gopher in charge of washing-up.

Film Programme: *Trance* (West Germany, 1982, Eckhart Schmidt. With Desiree Nosbusch); *Q: The Winged Serpent* (US, 1982, Larry Cohen. With Michael Moriarty, David Carradine, Candy Clark); *The Cook, The Thief, His Wife & Her Lover* (UK–Holland–France, 1989, Peter Greenaway. With Michael Gambon, Helen Mirren, Alan Howard, Richard Bohringer).

I'm the Kingston, Me

Coatlicue has asked me to provide a few words for the convention booklet. Naturally, my agent turned the Coat Person down flat since Quetzalcón could obviously not cough up my usual fee. However, I have generously decided to write this piece in exchange for a simple Jaguar XKE in eggshell blue.

Anyone who knows me well can tell you that nothing is as important to me as the love of my fans. Every day, over and over again, I am reminded of the selfless devotion of those tireless young men and women who feel honoured to clean my house without ever asking for any more than an occasional pat on the back (or other place) from *moi*. It doesn't even matter much that Frank, the CF* who scrapes the disgusting build-up from under the rim of my solid platinum toilet bowl, doesn't exactly do an A-Number-One job of it. Nothing makes me more grateful for my deserved success than to wake up between silk sheets and find cooked breakfast laid out for me on the taut brown stomach of a sixteen-year-old Filipina pearl-diver.

I've been fortunate. Not all writers have their brilliance recognised so consistently by the public. Few are lucky enough to have fans so devoted that they would stage a suicide raid on the offices of a newspaper that dared to publish a spiteful, envious, malicious review. I cannot condone the murder by explosive device of innocent people, even if they are hate-filled critics, but it's hard not to be touched by the love of those so dedicated to the perfection of my life that they will sacrifice theirs merely to settle a petty grudge.

Believe me, nothing would please me more than to have my new short story appear in this booklet to share *gratis* with my most devoted fans, but the realities of publishing and the demands of money-management require me to pull the story and give first serial rights to the *New York Times* for a record-

*Cringing Fanboy

218

breaking fee. Nevertheless, while I drive my new Jag, I shall transmit fond thoughts into each and every one of your minds. Even if you are one of those fat fans with beards.

I hope that at the con I will get a chance to meet each and every one of you, and give you all the honour of buying me a drink, presenting me with a small Picasso etching, abasing yourself at my feet or demonstrating your trufan devotion by carving my cover designs into your chest with a scalpel.

I can only hope my heart is big enough for you.

Kingston Dunstan

Saturday Night

18.00. Raffle.
Stephen Jones, of the Kingston Dunstan Appreciation Society, raffles valuable items donated by fans, publishers and film companies. The funds raised will be used to buy a fabulous feathered headdress, which will be presented to the Kingston at . . .

20.00. Ceremonial Anointment of Kingston Dunstan.
Kingston Dunstan, robed and perfumed, is again be borne into the ballroom and anointed with oils and unguents by handmaidens. Regional chapters of the KDAS will stage dances in the Kingston's honour, competing for his favour. Outcome to be settled by single combat.

22.00. Masquerade.
Your chance to show off your costuming skills. Dress up as your favourite Kingston Dunstan character, and revel into the night. This event open only to female fans between the ages of twelve and twenty-five. Body-painting is encouraged; goats should not be employed unless absolutely necessary.

Midnight. Judging.
Kingston Dunstan selects the winners of the masquerade, who are be freshly oiled and despatched to the Apex Suite, to receive their prizes from the hand (and other body parts) of the Kingston himself.

Film Programme: *Misery* (US, 1990, Rob Reiner. With Kathy Bates, James Caan, Lauren Bacall); *The Wicker Man* (UK, 1973, Robin Hardy. With Edward Woodward, Christopher Lee, Britt Ekland).

Kingston Dunstan: An Appreciation
by Kim Newman

Popocatépetl Popsy is more than just the best tragi-comic fantasy novel ever written. It is also a profoundly moving discourse upon the phenomenon of 'perfect sacrifice', which clearly has a relevance beyond the pre-Conquest Mexican setting so richly evoked by Kingston Dunstan's pellucid prose.

Of all the gods of the Aztecs, none was more loved and feared than Tezcatlipoca (Smoking Mirror). He is the personified form of the summer sun, bringing both ripe harvests and bitter drought. Each year, to appease the sun, one of the tribe's captives would be elevated as an incarnation of the Smoking Mirror. He was instructed in singing and flute-playing, and his music was always of the highest, most potent kind. The priestesses had him wear flowers and taught him to smoke elegantly. He was dressed in the finest costumes, and servants waited upon his every wish and desire. For a whole year, he was heaped with honours and pleasures.

Twenty days before the date fixed for the sacrifice, he received four beautiful girls as wives, and then began a series of festivals and dances. When the final day arrived, the young god was taken out to a step-pyramid by the priests and escorted in procession to the highest level. With one cut of his obsidian knife, the priest would rip out the sacrifice's heart and offer it to the sun, knowing this would ensure the tribe's fortunes for another year.

Kingston Dunstan makes this story the stuff of high comedy – who can forget the scene with the four fiancées and the avocado – but also a true tragedy. For do we not still treat our best and brightest, our most beautiful and talented, as little more than wretched stuff to be torn apart as a propitiation of the ghastly gods of the marketplace?

Kingston Dunstan always gives us food for thought. This weekend, he will give us so much else.

221

Sunday

08.00. Levee. Breakfast with Kingston Dunstan.
Kingston Dunstan is brought down to breakfast by the lucky
masquerade winners. The highest-bidding fans not only sit
with him as he scarfs down bacon and eggs but are allowed
into the bathroom of the Apex Suite to watch him shit, shave
and cough up phlegm. This opportunity will not be repeated,
so be prepared to pay over the odds.

10.00. Panel. 'A Gift to the Gods'.
Coatlicue (High Priestess) discusses the belief-systems of
ancient Mexico with Kingston Dunstan (Guest of Honour),
paying special attention to their relevance to the world of
today. This might be quite a surprise. Especially to the Guest
of Honour.

12.00. Guest of Honour Roast.
Derek Leech, owner of Real Press, serves as High Priest for this
humorous event, in which the Kingston is hauled over the
coals, takes his turn on the spit and opens his heart to all.

14.00. Banquet.
A choice cut for everybody. Kingston Dunstan, as usual, is the
centre of attention. A vegetarian menu is not available, though
those with high blood pressure will be pleased to note that our
fare is definitely of the 'healthy heart' persuasion.

16.00. Dead Dog Party.
We send you all home with a warm inner glow, certain your
prosperity and health are assured for another year.
We'll see you again at next year's Quetzalcón, which will, of
course, be dedicated to now-up-and-coming, soon-to-be-top-
of-his-profession fantasy trilogist Franklin Conklin.

QUETZALCÓN

This was originally put out (by Stephen Jones's Airgedlámh Publications) as a chapbook, designed by Michael Marshall Smith, given away at the 1997 World Fantasy Convention in London. It went in the delegates' bags with a ton of flyers, press releases and kipple and was often thought to be a programme for a real con no one had ever heard of, and discarded. They're now quite rare items.

RESIDUALS
(with Paul J. McAuley)

On his way out, the motel guy switches on the TV and the AC without bothering to ask if I want either. The unit over the door rattles and starts to drip on the purple shag carpet. On a dusty screen, a cowboy hunkers down over the Sci-Fi Channel station ident, squinting from under a Stetson. It ought to be like looking at myself, because the cowboy is supposed to be me. But it's not.

The Omega Encounter is always playing somewhere on a rerun channel, I guess, but here and now it's like an omen.

I'm still living off the *Omega* residuals because it's *my* version of what went down, officially adapted from the 'as told to' book Jay Anson did for me. Nyquist sold *Starlight*, the book Tom Fuckin' Wolfe wrote with him, for twenty times as much to Universal.

There's a little skip where there used to be a shot of a fly-blown, bloodied rubber cow carcass. It could be a censor cut or a snip to reduce the running time. When E. W. Swackhamer directed *Omega*, there were thirteen minutes of commercials in an hour of TV; now there are eighteen, so four minutes of each hour have to be lost from everything made before the '90s.

I don't unpack, except for the bottles of Cuevero Gold Tequila I bought at the airport, and sit up on the bed, watching two days of my life processed and packaged as a sixteen-year-old movie of the week.

It's gotten to the part where I find the first of the mutilated cattle. I'm showing one to Mr Nyquist, played by Dennis Weaver the way he plays McCloud, shrewd and upright. To tell the truth, Nyquist was always half bombed even before it all started, and he had a mean streak in him that was nothing to do with drink. The bastard would hit Susan when he was in the bag, going off like a firecracker over the slightest thing and stomping out, banging the screen door hard, leaving her holding her cheek and me looking down at my dinner. He was crazy even then, I guess, but still able to hold it down.

The movie makes me a lot more talkative than I ever was around Nyquist. Susan is Cybill Shepherd in her post-*Last Picture Show*, pre-*Moonlighting* career slump. I am Jan-Michael Vincent in his post-birth, pre-death career trough.

I watch until I follow the slime-trails in the grass and see the lights of the mother ship off in the distance hovering above the slough, and then I flip channels because I can't stand to watch any more.

They didn't have the budget to do the aliens right on TV and only used long shots, but I still don't want to watch. I can take the expensive computer-controlled models in the movie because they're too real in the way Main Street in Disneyland is too real. So perfect a reproduction it doesn't fool anyone for a second. But show me a couple of out-of-focus midgets jumping around inside silvered plastic bags in slow motion with the setting sun behind them, and my imagination fills in the blanks. The sour reek. And the noise the things made as they hopped around, like they were filled with Jello and broken bones.

QVC is less of a blow to the heart. I drink tequila out of the bathroom glass and consider calling a toll-free number to order a zircon chandelier. Then I drink some more and decide against it.

Despite Steven Spielberg, Harrison Ford (as Nyquist) and five million pre-inflation bucks of ILM, *Starlight: The Motion Picture* was a box office disappointment. By the time the effects were developed, *Omega* had spun off a mid-season replacement series with Sam Groom (as me) and Gretchen Corbett that got cancelled after three episodes. The aliens were old

news, and everybody knew how the story came out. In
Starlight, I'm rewritten as a codger farmhand who sacrifices
himself for Boss Man Ford, stealing the film with a dignified
death scene. Richard Farnsworth got an Oscar nomination for
Best Supporting Actor, but lost out to the gook in *The Killing
Fields*.

I give up TV and call my agent, using the room phone
because my mobile doesn't want to work out here in the desert,
all that radar, or the microwave signals they send to the secret
Moon colony (ha ha), and I tell him where I am. He says to
watch my ass, and that when I get back he thinks he might have
another hardware-store commercial lined up ('Fix your
starship, lady?'). It's just for New York cable but it'll pay the
rent a while. He doesn't think I can pull off this reunion, is
what it is, and I tell him that and then I hang up and I watch
an old *Saturday Night Live* for a while.

I was on one show for about five minutes, in a Conehead
episode with Dan Ackroyd and Jane Curtin. Can't hardly
remember that night – I was drunk at the time – but now I
guess those five minutes are always showing somewhere, just
like everything else that ever went through a transmitter. If
aliens out there have been monitoring our broadcasts like they
did in old movies to explain why they speak perfect English,
just about the first question we'd ask them was if they taped
those lost episodes of *The Honeymooners*. I watch Chevy
Chase do Gerry Ford falling over just about everything on
the studio set, and drink some more tequila and fall asleep a
while.

It's been a long day, the flight out from New York delayed
two hours, then a long drive through Los Angeles, where I've
never driven because I was chauffeured around when all the
deals were in the air, and which is ten times more packed with
traffic than I remember, and out into the high desert along
Pearblossom Highway with all the big trucks driving in bright
sunlight and blowing dust with their headlights on.

The phone wakes me up. I use the remote to turn down Dave

Letterman, and pick up. A voice I haven't heard for twenty years says, 'Hello, Ray.'

At first, only the *Enquirer* and the *Weekly World News* were interested. But when the reports came back and the FBI slapped a security classification on them, and Elliot Mitchell started making a fuss because he was transferred to the Texas panhandle and his field notes and his twenty rolls of film and six hours of cassette recordings were 'lost', *Newsweek* and *Rolling Stone* showed up. Tom Wicker's piece in *Rolling Stone* said it was all part of a government plot stretching back to Roswell, and that the US Army was covering up tests with hallucinogenic weapons.

Then the artefacts went on view, and ten types of expert testified they were 'non-terrestrial'. It wasn't a government conspiracy any more, it was a goddamn alien invasion, just like Nyquist and me had been saying. Mitchell had rewritten his field notes from memory, and sent photocopies to *Science* and *Nature*. He even got his name as discoverer on the new hyper-stable transuranic element, which along with the bodies was one of the few tangible residues of the whole thing. I wonder how he felt when Mitchellite was used in the Gulf War to add penetrative power to artillery shells.

Then the *Washington Post* got behind the story, and all the foreign press, and the shit hit the fan. For a while, it was all anybody talked about. We got to meet President Carter, who made a statement supporting our side of things, and declared he would see that no information was withheld from the public.

I was on *The Tonight Show* with Johnny Carson, back when that meant something. I did Dick Cavett, *CBS News* with Walter Cronkite, *60 Minutes* with Mike Wallace, *NBC Weekend News* with Jessica Savitch. Me and Nyquist were scurrying to get our book deals sorted out, then our screen rights. People were crawling all over, desperate to steal our lives, and we went right along with the feeding-frenzy.

We wrapped each other up with restraints and gag orders, and shot off our mouths all the time. Mitchell was out of the loop: instead of deals with Hollywood producers and long lunches with New York publishers, he got tied up in a civil-liberties suit because he tried to resign from the US Geological Survey and the government wouldn't let him.

Then the Ayatollah took the hostages, and everyone had something else to worry about. Carter became a hostage in his own White House and most of the artefacts disappeared in the C-130 aircrash the conspiracy theorists said was staged. Reagan never said anything on record, but the official line changed invisibly when he became President. The reports on the reports questioned the old findings, and deposits of Mitchellite showed up on Guam and somewhere in Alaska.

I did *Geraldo* with Whitley Strieber and Carl Sagan, and came off like a hick caught between a rock and a hard place. I had started drinking by then, and tried to punch out one or the other of them after the show, and spent the night in a downtown holding tank. I faced a jury of sceptics on *Oprah* and was cut to pieces, not by reasoned scientific arguments and rationalisations but by cheap-shot jokes from a studio audience of stand-up wannabes.

I told my side of it so many times that I caught myself using exactly the same words each time, and I noticed that on pre-recorded shows, the presenter's nods and winks – always shot from a reverse angle after the main interview – were always cut in at exactly the same points. An encouraging dip of the head laced with a concerned look in the eyes, made in reaction to a cameraman's thumb, not an already-forgotten line from me.

Besides *The Omega Encounter* and *Starlight*, there were dozens of books, movies, TV specials, magazine articles, a Broadway play, even a music album. Creedence Clearwater Revival's 'It Came Out of the Sky' was reissued and charted strongly. Some English band did a concept album. John Sladek and Tom Disch collaborated on a novel-length debunking, *The*

Sentients: A Tragi-Comedy. That's in development as a movie, maybe with Fred Ward.

Sam Shepard's *Alienation*, which Ed Harris did on Broadway and Shepard starred in and directed for HBO, looked at it all from the dirt farmer's point of view, suggesting Nyquist and me were looking for fresh ways of being heroes since we'd lost touch with the land. The main character was a combination of the two of us and talked in paragraphs, and the scientist – Dean Stockwell on TV – was a black-hatted villain, which displeased Mitchell no end. He sued and lost, I recall.

By then I was looking at things through the blurry dimple at the bottom of the bottle, living off the residuals from commercials and guest appearances in rock videos and schlock direct-to-video horror movies shot by postmodernist *auteurs* just out of UCLA film school, though I recall that Sam Raimi's *The Color out of Time* was kind of not bad.

Then I read in *Variety* that Oliver Stone has a treatment in development raking the whole thing all up, blaming it on J. Edgar Hoover, Armand Hammer and Henry Kissinger. There was an article in the *New York Times* that Norman Mailer had delivered his thousand-page summation of the phenomenon, *The Visitation*. And that's where I got the idea to get in touch with Mitchell and make some cash on the back of Stone's and Mailer's publicity, and maybe Mitchell had been reading the same articles, because before I can begin to think how to try and track him down, he calls me.

I drive past the place I'm to meet Mitchell and have to double back, squinting in the glare of the big rigs which roar out of the darkness, all strung up with fairylights like the spaceship in *Closer Encounters*. I do what sounds like serious damage to the underside of the rental when I finally pull off.

The ruins are close to the highway, but there's a spooky feel which makes me leave the car's headlights on. Out across the dark desert basin, where the runways of Edwards Air Force Base are outlined in patterns of red and green lights a dozen miles long, some big engine makes a long-drawn-out rumble that rises to a howl before cutting out.

I sit in the car and take a few pulls on my bottle to get some courage or at least burn away the flutter in my gut, looking at the arthritic shapes Joshua trees make in the headlights. Then I make myself get out and look around. There's not much to the ruins, just a chimney-stack and a line of pillars where maybe a porch stood. People camping out have left circles of ash in the sand and dented cans scattered around; when I stumble over a can and it rattles off a stone I realise how quiet the desert is, beyond the noise of the trucks on the highway. I get a feeling like the one I had when the three of us were waiting that last night before we blew up the mother ship, and have to take another inch off the level of the tequila to calm down.

That's when my rental car headlights go out and I almost lose it, because that's what happened when they tried to kidnap me, the lights and then the dashboard of my pickup cutting off and then a bright light all around, coming from above. That time, I had a pump-action shotgun on the rack in the cab, which is what saved me. Now I have a tequila bottle with a couple of inches sloshing in it, and a rock I pick up.

A voice behind me says my name, and I spin and lose my balance and fall on my ass, the tequila bottle emptying over my pants leg. A flashlight beam pins me and behind it Elliot Mitchell says, 'This was the last socialist republic in the USA, did you know that? They called the place Llano del Rio. This was their meeting-hall. They built houses, a school, planted orchards. But the government gave their water rights to the local farmers and they had to move out. All that's left is the orchards, and those will go because they're subdividing the desert for housing tracts to take LA's overspill.'

I squint into the light, but can't see anything of the man holding it.

'Never put your faith in government, Ray. Its first instinct is to protect not the people it's supposed to serve but its own self.

People elect politicians, not governments. Don't get up. I'm happier to see you sitting down. Do you think you were followed here?'

'Why would I be followed? No one cares about it any more. That's why I'm here.'

'You want to make another movie, Ray? Who is it with? Oliver Stone? He came out to see me. Or sent one of his researchers anyway. You know his father was in the Navy, don't you, and he's funded by the UN Counterpropaganda Unit, the same one that tried to assassinate Reagan. The question is, who's paying you?'

'Crazy Sam's Hardware back in Brooklyn, if I do the ad.'

I have a bad feeling. Mitchell appears to have joined the right-wing nuts who believe that little black helicopters follow them everywhere, and that there are secret codes on the back of traffic signs to direct the UN invasion force when it comes.

I say, 'I don't have any interest except the same one that made you want to call me. We saved the world, Elliot, and they're ripping off our story . . .'

'You let them. You and Nyquist. How is old Nyquist?'

'Sitting in a room with mattresses on the walls, wearing a backwards jacket and eating cold creamed corn. They made him the hero, when it was us who blew up the mother ship, it was us who captured that stinking silver beachball, it was us who worked out how to poison most of them.'

I put the bottle to my lips, but there's hardly a swallow left. I toss it away. This isn't going the way I planned, but I'm caught up in my anger. It's come right back, dull and heavy.

'We're the ones that saved Susan, not her lousy husband.'

'We didn't save her, Ray. That was in your TV movie, *The Omega Encounter*. We got her back, but the things they'd put inside her killed her anyway.'

'Well, we got her back, and if fuckin' Doc Jensen had listened we *would* have saved her, too.'

I sit there, looking into the flashlight beam with drunken tears running down my face.

'How much do you remember, Ray? Not the movies, but the real thing? Do you remember how we got Susan out of the mother ship?'

'I stay away from shopping-malls, because they give me flashbacks. Maybe I'm as crazy as Nyquist. Sometimes, I dream I'm in one of those old-fashioned hedge mazes, like in *The Shining*. Sometimes, I'm trying to get out of the hospital they put us in afterwards. But it's always the same, you know.'

Mitchell switches off the flashlight. I squint into the darkness, but all I see is swimming after-images.

'Come tomorrow,' Mitchell says, and something thumps beside me.

It is a rock, with a piece of torn paper tied to it. Under the dome light of the rental car, I smooth out the paper and try to make sense of the map Mitchell has drawn.

Two days. That's how long it took. Now, my life is split into Before and After. What no one gets is that the thing itself – the event, the encounter, the invasion, the incursion, the whatever – was over inside two days. I've had head colds and belly-aches that lasted a whole lot longer. That's what marks me out. When I die, my obits will consist of three paragraphs about those two days and two sentences about everything else. Like I said about Jan-Michael, I have a post-birth, pre-death rut for a life. Except for those two days.

After about a decade, it got real old. It was as if everyone was quizzing me about some backyard baseball game I pitched in when I was a kid, blotting out all of the rest of my life – parents, job, marriages, kid, love, despair – with a couple of hours on the mound. I even tried clamming up, refusing to go through it all again for the anniversary features. I turned my back on those two days and tried to fix on something else worth talking about. I came close to making it with Adrienne Barbeau, didn't I? Or was it Heather Locklear? Maybe it was just in one of the scripts and some actor played me. I was doing harder stuff than alcohol just then.

233

That phase lasted maybe three months. I was worn down in the end. I realised that I needed to tell it again. For me, as much as for everyone else. I was like those talking books in that Bradbury novel – yeah, I admit it, I read science fiction when I was a kid, and doesn't that blow my whole story to bits, proving that I made it up out of half-remembered bits of pulp magazine stories – my whole life was validated by my story, and telling it was as necessary to me as breathing. Over the years, it got polished and shiny. More than a few folks told me it sounded like Bradbury.

'A million years ago, Nyquist's farm was the bottom of the ocean,' I would always begin, paraphrasing the opening of my book. 'Susan Nyquist collected sea-shells in the desert. Just before I looked up and saw the spinning shape in the sky, I was sifting through the soft white sand, dredging up a clam-shaped rock that might once have been alive . . .'

No, I'm not going to tell it all again here. That's not what this is about at all.

Do you know what a palimpsest is? It's old parchment that has been written on once, had the writing rubbed out, and been written on again. Sometimes several times. Only, with modern techniques scientists can read the original writing, looking underneath the layers.

That's my story. Each time I've told it, I've whited out the version underneath. It's built up, like limescale on a dripping faucet. In telling it so many times, I've buried the actual thing.

Maybe that's why I've done it.

Regardless of the movies, it wasn't a B picture, with simple characters and actions. Okay, there were aliens (everyone else calls them that except Strieber, so I guess I can too), a woman was taken, and we poisoned most of them and dug out dynamite and blew up their spaceship (I've never liked calling it that – it was more like one of Susan's shells blown up like a balloon, only with light instead of helium or air). We saved the world, right?

Or maybe we just killed a bunch of unknowable Gandhis

from the Beyond. That's what some woman accused me of at a book-signing. She thought they'd come to save us, and that we'd doomed the world by scaring them off.

That gave me a shock. I tried to see the story the way she might.

It didn't play in Peoria. The woman – pink bib overalls, bird's-nest hair, Velma-from-*Scooby-Doo* glasses, a 'Frodo Lives!' badge – hadn't seen the visitors, the aliens.

She hadn't seen what they'd done to Susan.

But I was up close.

The little fuckers were evil. No, make that Evil. I don't know if they were from outer space, the third circle of Hell or the Land of Nod, but they weren't here to help anyone but themselves.

What they did to the cattle, what they did to Susan, wasn't science, wasn't curiosity. They liked taking things apart the way Mikey Bignell in third grade liked setting fire to cats, and Mikey grew up to get shot dead while pistol-whipping a fifty-two-year-old married lady during a filling-station hold-up. If the visitors ever grow up beyond the cat-burning phase, I figure they could do some serious damage.

I am not just trying to justify what we did to them.

Now, without trying to tell the story yet again, I'm tapping into what I really felt at the time: half scared, half enraged. No Spielberg sense of wonder. No TV movie courage. No Ray Bradbury wistfulness.

'Inside the ship was all corridors and no rooms, criss-crossing tunnels through what seemed like a rocky rubber solid stuff. Mitchell went ahead, and I followed. We blundered any which way, down passages that made us bend double and kink our knees, and trusted to luck that we'd find where they'd taken Susan. I don't know whether or not we were lucky to find her or whether they intended it. I don't know if we were brave and lucky, or dumb rats in a maze.

'Mitchell claims the thing told us where to go, flashed a floor-plan into our minds, like the escape lights in an airliner.

235

I guess that's his scientific mind talking. For me it was different. I had a sense of being myself and being above myself, looking down. We didn't take a direct route to Susan, but spiralled round her, describing a mandala with an uneven number of planes of symmetry. It was like the New Math: finding the answer wasn't as important as knowing how to get there, and I think Mitchell and I, in our different ways, both flunked.'

I didn't say so in the book, but I think that's why what happened to Susan afterwards went down. When we dragged Susan, alive but unconscious, out of the hot red-black half-dark at the heart of the ship we were too exhausted to feel any triumph. We went in, we found her, we got her out. But we didn't get the trick quite right.

Here's how I usually end it:

'Nyquist was shaking too bad to aim the rifle. I don't amount to much, and while I can't shoot good enough to take the eye out of the eagle if you toss a silver dollar in the air, nine times out of ten I'll at least clip the coin. Mitchell was shouting as he ran towards us with two of the things hopping after him. The reel of wire was spinning in his hands as he ran. Nyquist snapped out of it and tossed me the gun' – in his version, he gets both of the critters with two shots, bing-bang – 'and I drew a bead, worried that Mitchell would zigzag into the line of fire, then put a bullet into the first alien. Pink stuff burst out of the back of it in mid-leap, and it tumbled over, deflating like a pricked party balloon.

'Even from where I was I could smell the stink, and Nyquist started to throw up. The second critter was almost on Mitchell when I fired again, the hot casing stinging my cheek as I worked the bolt, and fired, and fired, and kept shooting as Mitchell threw himself down in a tangle of wire while the thing went scooting off back towards the ship. My hands shaking so bad I sliced my hand when I trimmed the wires back to bare copper. Mitchell snatched them from me and touched them to the terminals of the truck's battery.

'We didn't have more than a dozen sticks of low-grade dynamite for getting out tree-stumps, and Mitchell hadn't had time to place them when those things came scooting out like hornets out of a bottle. And Mitchell hadn't even wanted to do it, saying that the ship must be fireproofed, like the Apollo module, or it wouldn't have survived atmospheric entry. But it was our last best hope, and when the sticks blew the ship went up like a huge magnesium flare. I put my hands over my eyes, and saw the bones of my hands against the light. The burst was etched into my eyeballs for months. It hardly left any debris, just evaporated into burning light, blasting the rock beneath to black crystal. You can still see the glassy splash where it stood, if you can get the security clearance. There was a scream like a dying beast, but it was all over quickly. When we stopped blinking and the echo was dead, there was almost nothing where the ship had been. They were gone.'

Is that an ending? If it is, what has the rest of my life been? An epilog, like on some Quinn Martin series episode, with William Conrad reporting that I am still at large, still running off my mouth, still living it down?

Or has it just been an interlude before the sequel?

I wake up the next morning with the shakes. There's not even fumes in the tequila bottle I clutched to my chest all night, and nothing but warm cans of Dr Pepper's in the motel vending-machine, so I drive the mile into town and buy a twelve pack of Bud, giving thanks to California's liberal liquor licence laws. I'm coming out of the 7–11 when two men in sunglasses fall in step with me either side, and I don't need to see their badges to know what they are.

They make me leave my beer in the car and take me across the dusty highway to the town's diner, an Airstream trailer with a tattered awning shading one side. The older guy orders coffee and pancakes and grins across the table while his partner crowds me on the bench. I can't help looking through the greasy window at my car, where the beer is heating up on the front seat, and the older guy's grin gets wider. He gets out a hip-flask and pours a shot into my coffee and I can't help myself and guzzle it down, scalding coffee running down my chin.

'Jesus,' the young guy, Dale Bissette, says, disgusted. He's the local field agent, blond hair slicked back from his raw-boned face. He hasn't taken off his mirror shades, and a shoulder harness makes a bulge under his tailored suit jacket.

'Judge not,' the other guy says, and pours me another shot, twinkling affably. He has curly white hair and a comfortable gut, like Santa Claus's younger brother. He has hung his seersucker jacket on the back of his chair. There are half-moon sweat stains under his arms, and sweat beads under his hairline. 'Ray's living out his past, and is having a hard time with it. Am I right, or am I right?'

I ignore the rye whiskey in the coffee mug. I say, 'If you want to talk to me, talk to my agent first. Murray Weiss, he's in the Manhattan directory.'

'But you're one of us,' the older guy says, widening his eyes in mock innocence. 'You got your badge, when? Seventy-seven? Seventy-eight?

It was 1976 and I'm sure he damn well knows it, done right out on the White House lawn, with a silver band playing and the Stars and Stripes snapping in the breeze under a hot white sky. The Congressional Medal of Honour for me and Nyquist, and honorary membership of the FBI. I'd asked for that because if it was good enough for Elvis it was good enough for me. It was the last time I saw Nyquist, and even then he was ignoring me with the same intensity I'm right now ignoring that rye.

I say, 'Your young friend here was polite enough to show me his badge. I don't believe I know you.'

'Oh, we met, very briefly. I was part of the team that helped clean up.' He smiles and holds out his hand over the coffee mugs and plates of pancakes, then shrugs. 'Guerdon Winter. I'll never forget that first sight of the crater, and the carcass you had.'

'You were all wearing those spacesuits and helmets. 'Scuse me for not recognising you.'

The FBI agents looked more like space aliens than the things we killed. They cleared out everything, from the scanty remains of the mother ship to my collection of tattered paperbacks. I still have the receipts. They took me and Nyquist and Mitchell and put us in isolation chambers somewhere in New Mexico and put us through thirty days of interrogation and medical tests. They took Susan's body and we never saw it again.

I think of the C-130 crash and I say, 'You should have taken more care of what you took, Agent Winter.'

Guerdon Winter takes a bite of pancake.

'We could have had that alien carcass stuffed and mounted and put on display in the Smithsonian, and in five years it would have become one more exhibit worth maybe ten seconds' gawping. The public doesn't need any help in getting distracted, and everything gets old fast. You know better than me how quickly they forget. You're the one in showbiz. But we haven't forgotten, Ray.'

'You want me to find out what Mitchell is doing.'

'Mitchell phoned you from a pay phone right here in town ten days ago, and you wrote him at the box number he gave you, and then you came down here. You saw him last night.'

Dale Bissette stirs and says, 'He's been holed up for two years now. He's been carrying out illegal experiments.'

'If you were following me you could have arrested him last night.'

Guerdon Winter looks at Dale Bissette, then looks at me. He says, 'We could arrest him each time he comes into town for supplies, but that wouldn't help us get into his place, and we know enough about his interrogation profile to know he wouldn't give it up to us. But he wants to talk to you, Ray. We just want to know what it is he's doing out there.'

'He believes you have the map,' Dale Bissette says.

239

I remember the scrap of paper Mitchell gave me last night and say, 'You want the map?'

'It isn't important,' Guerdon Winter says quickly. 'What's important is that you're here, Ray.'

I look out at my rental car again, still thinking about the beer getting warm. Just beyond it, a couple of Mexicans in wide-brimmed straw hats are offloading watermelons from a dusty Toyota pickup. One is wearing a very white T-shirt with the Green Lantern symbol. They could be agents, too; so could the old galoot at the motel.

I know Dale Bissette was in my motel room last night; I know he took Mitchell's map and photocopied it and put it back. The thing is, it doesn't seem like betrayal. It stirs something inside me, not like the old excitement of those two crystal-clear days when everything we did was a heroic gesture, nothing like so strong or vivid, but alive all the same. Like waking up to a perfect summer's day after a long, uneasy sleep full of nightmares.

I push the coffee away from me and say, 'What kind of illegal experiments?'

If Mitchell hadn't been a government employee, if they hadn't ridiculed and debunked his theories, and spirited him off to the ass end of nowhere – no Congressional Medal ceremony for him, he got his by registered mail – if they hadn't stolen the discovery of Mitchellite from him, maybe he wouldn't have ended up madder than a dancing chicken on a hotplate at the state fair. Maybe he wouldn't have taken it into his head to try what he did. Or maybe he would have done it anyway. Like me, he was living in After, with those two bright days receding like a train. Like me, he wanted them back. Unlike me, he thought he had a way to do it.

Those two agents don't tell me as much as I need to know, but I suspect that they don't know what it is Mitchell is doing. I have an idea that he's building something out in the desert that'll bring those old times back again.

Driving out to Mitchell's place takes a couple of hours. The route on the map he gave me is easy enough: south along Pearblossom's two-lane blacktop, then over the concrete channel of the aqueduct that carries water taken from Washington State – did you see *Chinatown*? Yeah, there – and up an unmade track that zigzags along the contours of the Pinon Hills and into a wide draw that runs back a couple of miles. The light in the draw is odd. Cold and purple, like expensive sunglasses. Either side of the road is nothing but rocks, sand, dry scrub and scattered Joshua trees.

I start to feel a grudging sympathy for Agent Bissette. No matter how he hangs back, it's impossible to tail a car out here without your mark knowing. I have the urge to wait for a dip that puts me momentarily out of his sight and swerve off into a patch of soft sand, sinking the rental like a boat in shallows, creating another unexplained mystery.

Mitchell's place is right at the top of the draw, near the beginning of the tree-line. In the high desert, trees grow only on the tops of the mountains. The FBI parks under a clump of stunted pines and lets me go on alone. I'm lucky they didn't want me to wear a wire. They'll just wait, and see if I can cope with Crazy Elliot. For them, it'll be a boring afternoon, with maybe an exciting apprehension about nightfall.

Me, I'm going back to the Days of Sharp Focus.

The rye in the coffee has burned out and I've not touched the soup-warm beer on the passenger seat. I can feel the heat steaming the booze out of my brain. I'm going into this alone.

I get out of rental, aware of Winter and Bissette watching me through the tinted windshield of their Lincoln Continental. Of Mitchell there's not a trace. Not even footprints or tyre tracks in the sandy soil. I crouch down, and run a handful of warm sand through my fingers, making like an Indian tracker in some old Western while I ponder my next move.

There are tine-trails in the sand. The whole area has been raked, like a Japanese garden. I can imagine Mitchell working by night, raking a fan-shaped wake as he backs towards the paved area I see a dozen yards away.

I walk across the sand, and reach the flagstones. This was the floor of a house that's long gone. I can see the fieldstone hearth, and the ruts where wooden walls used to be.

Beyond the stone is a gentle incline, sloping down maybe twenty feet, then levelling off. Down there, protected from sight, Mitchell has been building. I look at his paper, and see what he means. The FBI think it's a circuit diagram, but it really is a map. Mitchell has made himself a maze, but there's nothing on his map that shows me how to get through it.

I know now where the old timbers of the house have gone. Mitchell has cannibalised everything carriable within a mile, and some things I would have sworn you'd need a bulldozer at least to shift, but he must have had a few truckloads of chicken-wire, wood and just plain junk hauled out here. The archway entrance is a Stonehenge arrangement of two '50s junkers buried hood-first like standing stones, with their tailfins and clusters of egg-shaped rear lights projecting into the air. A crosspiece made of three supermarket shopping-carts completes the arch.

There are other old cars parked and piled in a curving outer wall, built on with wire and wood. And all over the place, sticking up through the sand, are sharp spars and spines that sparkle in the sun.

I know that glittery look, a glinting like the facets of an insect's eye or 1970s eye make-up under fluorescent disco lights. It's Mitchellite.

I walk up to the gateway and stop, careful not to touch the spars. They dot everything – stone, wood, metal – like some sort of mineral mould. Crusty little alien points that seem to be growing out of the ordinary Earth stuff. About ten years ago, a couple of crazy English physicists claimed you could use Mitchellite to get unlimited energy by cold fusion and end up with more Mitchellite than you started with, but they were debunked, defrocked and for all I know defenestrated, and that was the end of it. But maybe they were right. It looks like the Mitchellite is transmuting ordinary stuff into itself.

There's an iron crowbar, untouched by Mitchellite, propped against a stone. I pick it up, heft it in my hands. It has a good weight. I always felt better with a simple tool, something you could trust.

Planks are set between the half-buried cars, a path into the interior of the maze. They are pocked with Mitchellite spars that splinter the rotten wood from the inside. I smash the crowbar down and split a plank, scraping away bone-dry wood fragments from the Mitchellite nerve-tangles that have been growing inside, sucking strength from the material.

It looks fragile, but it doesn't crumple under my boots.

On the other side of the arch hangs a shower curtain that leaves a three-foot gap beneath it. I push it aside with the crowbar and step into the maze.

The structure is open to the sky, mostly. The walls are of every kind of junk, wood, lines of rocks or unmortared concrete blocks, even barbed wire, grown through or studded with Mitchellite. A few yuccas rise up from the maze's low walls, their fleshy leaves sparkling as if dusted with purplish snow. The floor is made of Mitchellite-eaten planks. There are stretches of clean, unmarked sand. But by each of them is propped a rake, for obscuring footprints. By the first rake is a pane of glass in the sand, and in the hollow under the glass is a handgun wrapped in a plastic baggie, and a handwritten note: 'In case of F(B)IRE smash glass.' So that's what the crowbar is for. I leave the gun where it is and turn and stare at the maze again.

After a while I fish out the map and look at it. It takes me a while even to work out where I am, but with a creepy chill I realise I'm standing on the spot where Mitchell has drawn a stick figure. In the centre of the map is a white space, where there's another, bigger stick figure. Dotted throughout are smaller figures, drawn in red. I know what they're supposed to be. Some are drawn over black lines that represent walls.

I call out Mitchell's name.

The maze funnels my own voice back to me, distorted and empty.

'Ray, come on, what are you waiting for?'

It was obviously a doorway. Mitchell bent down low – the round opening was the creatures' size – and squeezed into the ship.

I hesitated, but thought of Susan, and the things that had taken her.

'I'm coming, Mitchell.'

I followed the geologist. Inside was another world.

'I'm coming, Mitchell.'

I know at once what he's done. This isn't really a maze. It's a model, twice as big again as the real thing, of the aliens' ship.

My knees are weak and I'm shaking. I'm back on the mandala path. I'm above myself and in myself, and I know where to go. I know the route, just as I know the ache that sets into my knees after a minute, an ache that grows to a crippling pain. Just as I remember finding Susan. And finding out later what they'd done to her.

Mitchell took the lead, that time. I followed, forgetting Nyquist chicken-heartedly frozen at the entrance and not daring to go further.

Remembering, I follow Mitchell's lead again. Round and inwards, a spiral across a DNA coil or a wiring diagram, a bee-dance through catacombs. The route is a part of me.

The deeper inside the maze I get, the more Mitchellite there is. The original wood and stone and wire and concrete have been almost completely eaten out. Purple light glitters every-where, dazzling even through my sunglasses. Without them I'd be snow-blind in a minute.

When the process is finished, when there's nothing more of Earth in the maze, will this thing be able to fly? Will Mitchell carry the war to the enemy?

'Ray,' someone – not Mitchell – shouts, from behind me.

It's the FBI. I thought I was supposed to haul Mitchell out on my own. Now the pros are here, I wonder why I've bothered.

I feel like a sheep driven across a minefield. A Judas goat.

I got into the maze and I'm still alive, so Guerdon Winter and Bissette know it's safe.

I turn, shading my eyes against the tinted glare that shines up from everything around me. The agents are following my footprints. Bissette doesn't duck under the crossbar of an arch nailed up of silvery grey scraps of wood, and scrapes his forehead against a Mitchellite-speckled plank.

I know what will happen.

It's like sandpaper stuck with a million tiny fishhooks and razor-blades. The gentlest touch opens deep gashes. Bissette swears, not realising how badly he's hurt, and a curtain of blood bursts from the side of his head. A flap of scalp hangs down. Red rain spatters his shades.

Bissette falls to his knees. Guerdon Winter plucks a handkerchief from the breast pocket of his sweat-stained seersucker jacket. A bedsheet won't staunch the flow.

'You can't go on,' Guerdon Winter tells the junior agent, who can't protest for the pain. 'We'll come back for you.'

Naturally, Guerdon Winter has his gun out. When Mitchell and I went into the mother ship, we didn't even think of guns. I left my shotgun in the pickup, and Nyquist held on to his rifle like it was a comforter blanket and wouldn't give it up to us. Some heroes, huh? Every single version of the story rectifies the omission, and we go in tooled up fit to face Bonnie and Clyde.

The FBI has made a bad mistake.

They've changed the story again. By adding the guns, and maybe themselves, they've made me lose my place.

I don't know which way to go from here.

My feet and my spine and my aching knees were remembering. But the memory's been wiped.

Bissette is groaning. His wound is tearing worse – there are tiny particles of alien matter in it, ripping his skin apart as they grow – and the whole right side of his head and his suit-shoulder are deep crimson.

'Ray,' prompts Guerdon Winter. There's a note of pleading in his voice.

I look at the fork ahead of us, marked with a cow's skull nodding on a pole, and suddenly have no idea which path to take. I look up at the sky. There's a canopy of polythene up there, scummy with sand-drifts in the folds. I look at the aisles of junk. They mean nothing to me. I'm as blank as the middle of the map Mitchell gave me.

Then Winter does something incredibly stupid. He offers me a hip-flask and smiles and says, 'Loosen up Ray. You'll do fine.'

I knock the flask away, and it hits a concrete pillar laced with Mitchellite and sticks there, leaking amber booze from a dozen puncture-points. The smell does something to my hindbrain and I start to run, filled with blind panic just the way I was when I followed Mitchell, convinced alien blimps would start nibbling at my feet.

I run and run, turning left, turning right, deeper and deeper into the maze. The body remembers, if it's allowed. Someone shouts behind me and then there's a shot and a bullet spangs off an engine-block and whoops away into the air; another turns the windshield of a wheelless truck to lace, which holds its shape for a moment before falling away. I leap over a spar of Mitchellite like an antelope and run on, feeling the years fall away. I've dropped the map but it doesn't matter. The body remembers. Going in, and coming out. Coming out with Susan. That's the name I yell, but ahead, through a hedge of twisted wire coated with a sheen of Mitchellite, through the purple glare and a singing in my ears, I see Mitchell himself, standing in the doorway of a kind of bunker.

He's older than I remember or imagined, the boy scout look transmuted into a scrawny geezer wearing only ragged oil-stained shorts, desert boots, and wraparound shades, his skin tanned a mahogany brown. I lean on the crowbar, taking great gulps of air as I try and get my breath back, and he looks at me calmly. There's a pump-action Mossbauer shotgun leaning on the wall beside him.

At last, I can say, 'This is some place you got here, Elliot. Where did you get all the stuff?'

'It's a garden,' Mitchell says, and picks up the shotgun and walks off round the bunker. He has half-healed scars on his back. Maybe he brushed a little too close to something in his maze.

I follow. The bunker is a poured-concrete shell, a low round dome like a turtle-shell half-buried in the dry desert dirt. There's a battered Blazer parked at the back, and a little Honda generator and a TV satellite dish. A ramp of earth leads up to the top of the bunker, and we climb up there and stand side by side, looking out over the maze. It extends all around the bunker. The sun is burning over our shoulders, and the concentric spirals of encrusted junk shimmer and glitter, taking the light and making it into something else, a purple haze that shimmers and glitters in the air, obscuring more than it reveals.

'How long have you been doing this, Elliot? It looks like you've been here years.'

Elliot Mitchell says, 'You ever been to South America, Ray? You should have. They're very big on flying saucers in South America. Out in Peru there are patterns of stones in the deserts that only make sense from the air. Like landing-strips, parking-aprons.'

A chill grips me. 'You're building a spaceport?'

'We never had any evidence they came from outer space,' Mitchell says.

'What are you saying, they're from Peru? There's some bad shit on Earth, but nothing like those things. What are you doing here, Elliot? Trying to turn yourself into one of them? Listen, if you've found anything out, it'll mean a shitload of attention. That's what I—'

'More chat shows, Ray? More ten-line fillers in *Time*? I had some guy from the *National Enquirer* a month or so. He tried to get in. Maybe he's still in here, somewhere.'

I remember the red marks on Mitchell's map, in the otherwise blank space of the maze.

I say, 'You let me in, Elliot.'

'You understand, Ray. You were there, with me. You know what it was like. Only you and me really know what it was like.'

I see why he wants me here. Mitchell has built this for a purpose, and I'm to tell the world what that is. I say, 'What are you planning, Elliot? What are you going to do with all this?'

Mitchell giggles. 'I don't control it, Ray. Not any more. It's more and more difficult to get out each time. When we went to get Susan, where did we go?'

He's setting me up for something. I say dumbly, 'Into the ship. That's how I knew to get to you here. This is like the ship.'

'It's how I started it out. But it's been growing. Started with a bare ounce of Mitchellite, grew this garden over the template I made. Now it grows itself. Like the ship. We went in, and we went somewhere else. Not all the way, because it hadn't finished growing, but a good way. Back towards where they came from. Wherever it was.'

'You're saying the ship didn't come from outer space?'

'It *grew* here. Like this.' Mitchell makes a sweeping gesture with the shotgun, including everything around him. He's King of the Hill. 'Once a critical density had been reached, the gateway would have opened, and they would have come through.'

'They *did* come through. We poisoned them, we shot them, we blew up their fucking ship.'

'Mitchellite is strange stuff, Ray. Strange matter. It shouldn't exist, not in our universe, at least. It's a mixture of elements all with atomic weights more than ten times that of uranium. It shouldn't even get together in the first place without tremendous energies forcing the quarks together, and it should fly apart in a picosecond after its creation. But it doesn't. It's metastable. It makes holes in reality, increases quantum

248

tunnelling so that things can leak through from one universe to another. That's how they probed us. Sent a probe through on the atomic scale and let it grow. Maybe they sent millions of probes, and only one hit the right configuration. Before we sent up astronauts, we sent up chimps and dogs. That's what they did. They sent through seeds of the things we saw, and they lodged and grew.'

'In the cows.'

Great chunks had been ripped out of the cows I found. Nyquist thought it was chainsaw butchers, until I dug around and found the blisters inside the meat. Like tapeworm cysts. And Susan, Susan, when we got her out . . .

'In the cows,' Mitchell says. 'That was the first stage. And then they took Susan. That was the second stage, Ray. First chimps, then the astronauts. But we stopped it.'

'Yeah. We stopped it.'

Mitchell doesn't hear me. He's caught up in his own story.

He says, 'They gave the first *astronauts* ticker-tape parades down Wall Street, but what happened to the chimps? First time around they picked us up and husked us of our stories and forgot us. *Second* time is the ticker-tape parade.'

Susan never came round. That was a blessing at least. Doc Jensen wouldn't believe me when I told him that I figured what had happened to the cattle was happening to her. Not until that night, when the things started moving under her skin. He tried to cut them out then, but they were all through her. So I did the right thing. Doc Jensen couldn't, even though he saw what was inside her. He'd still stuck with his oath, even though he had a bottle of whiskey inside him. So I did what had to be done, and then we went out and blew up the ship.

Mitchell tells me, 'You have to believe it, Ray. *This* time they won't forget us. This time we'll control it. They tried to discredit me. They stole my records, they said I was as crazy as Nyquist and tried to section me, they made up stories about finding terrestrial deposits of Mitchellite. Well, maybe those were real. Maybe those were from previous attempts. It's a matter of configuration.'

He gestures with the shotgun again, and that's when I cold-cock him.

He thought I'd be on his side. He thought I wanted nothing more than fame, than to get back the feeling we had in those two days. He was right. I did. His mistake was that he thought I'd pay *any* price. And forgetting to put on a shirt.

The crowbar bounces off his skull and he falls like an unstrung puppet. I kick the shotgun off the domed roof and then he looks up at me and I see what he's done to himself. The sunglasses have come off, and his left eye is a purple mandala.

When I finish, there isn't much left of the top of his head. In among the blood and brains: glittering purple-sheened strands, like cords of fungus through rotten wood. A couple of the things inside him try to get out through the scars on his back, but I squash them back into Mitchell's flesh.

After I kill Mitchell I take the gasoline from his generator and burn the dome without looking to see what is inside it, and smash as much of the whole centre of the maze as I can. I work in a kind of cold fury, choking in the black smoke pouring out of the dome, until I can hardly stand. Then I toss the crowbar into the flames and walk out of there.

There's no sign of the FBI agents, although their car is still there when I get out. Winter and Bissette are still back there, incorporated. I hope to God they're dead, although it isn't likely. But the maze has stopped growing, I know that. The light's gone from it. There's a cell phone in the glove compartment, and I use the redial button and tell the guy on the other end that Winter and Bissette are dead, that the whole place has to be destroyed.

'Don't go in there to look for them. Burn it from the air, it would give them a kindlier death. Burn it down and blow it up. Do the right thing. I made a start. They won't come back.'

When I say it, for the first time it sounds finished.

Authors who talk shop, which is to say bandy ideas for stories, often wind up collaborating. This spun out of a conversation Paul McAuley (author of *Pasquale's Angel*, *Fairyland* and the *Confluence* trilogy) and I had about invasion stories, wondering what might happen, in the rest of their lives, to ordinary people who had saved the world from aliens. Neither of us uses the first person often, but we wound up doing so here – an odd technical challenge for a story written in alternating chunks. It appeared first in *Asimov's Science Fiction*.

TEDDY BEARS' PICNIC
(with Eugene Byrne)

Bob splashed tap-water into his eyes, and tried to blink away the throbbing in his head. He wasn't supposed to be hung over till tomorrow, but everyone and his uncle was buying him drinks. In the Ladies' Lounge he'd gone easy, knocking back only the sweet sherry his Mam and Thelma drank. He wished now he'd stuck to the Back Bar and brown ale.

Then again, Terry had just put a couple of gallons through his kidneys, on top of a fish and chip buttie tea, and he was in a worse state than Bob. Terry was in one of the stalls, hands jellyfish on the floor, chinning the porcelain rim as he spewed.

Bob went over and hooked his hands into Terry's armpits, lifted him up and aimed his mouth at the toilet bowl. He felt the racking of reverse peristalsis – a term remembered from school – run through Terry's ribs. The last of the chips and Mother's Pride came up as beery sludge.

'She let you tup her last night,' Terry said. 'Tight-drawers Thelma.'

That was true.

'She thought you were going to die in foreign parts, so she dropped 'em for you.'

That was arguable.

Yet more came up out of the bottom of Terry's stomach. It must be the last of it.

'She'll never understand, that one.'

Bob hauled Terry upright and wiped his face with a rough paper towel, getting off the worst of the sick.

'You smell like a tramp's dustbin.'

Terry touched a fist to his chest and lightly thumped Bob over the heart.

'She'll never get in here, Bob. Not bloody Thelma.'

'I should hope not. It's the Gents.'

'Ahh get on with you, you know what I mean.'

Bob did.

'Come on, Bob. Back to the battlefront. King, country and Strongarm Ruby Red Bitter are calling.'

Terry lurched out of the toilets. Bob followed, as he had been following his mate since St Godric's primary school.

Thelma had been furious when he volunteered. She'd screamed at him that he didn't have to go in the Army – he could have had a medical exemption from National Service for his flat feet – and that now he'd passed his City & Guilds he should make a career for himself, but oh no, he had to sign up just because his best pal Terry had.

The smell of piss was worse in the corridor outside the Gents. There was a sound, as if someone had left a tap running. Bob ran into Terry's back. By the stairs stood a fat bloke in a dark suit. It took a moment to realise he was piddling against the wall.

'I don't much like flock wallpaper either,' said Terry, 'but this is taking it a bit far.'

The man turned and zipped the fly on immense trousers.

'It's me own fookin' club, y'daft get,' he snorted in broad Mancunian. 'I can take a burst where I fookin' like.'

Bob recognised the fat man. The Comedian was chairman and secretary of the club. He was in with Jack Carter, and in this part of town Jack Carter ran everything.

The Comedian looked at them. 'I know you lads. It's your party tonight, in't it? Do or die, king and country?'

Bob didn't want to admit it, but Terry took an unsteady bow.

'Daft bastards,' the Comedian said, not without admiration. He pulled out a wad of notes. With pee-smelling fingers, he peeled off four blue fivers and shoved them into Bob's hankie pocket.

'Buy yourself some slant-eyed scrubber in Saigon, lads.'

Terry tried to thank him but spasmed again, bending double to drool thin bile on the already-stained carpet. Bob held him up.

'That's a fookin' pretty picture.'

The Comedian's enormous mouth opened in a bark of laughter that shook all his mounds of fat. Terry coughed again, hawking stomach-lining.

'Fare thee well, lads,' said the Comedian. 'And when you get to the Bloody 'Chine, kill some fookin' treens for the Wheel-tappers and Shunters Social Club. Bring us back a necklace of ears we can hang on the darts trophy.'

He put his hand round the full glass and left it there. He told Bet Lynch to have one herself.

'Don't mind if I do, Bob,' said the barmaid, looking him up and down. He'd lost a lot of weight. 'A vodka-tonic. That'll be four and ninepence please.'

1965 seemed a long time ago. Prices had doubled in two years. Everything in Indo or the NAAFI was dirt cheap. It was as well he had a wedge of back-pay from the months when he couldn't spend it.

Bet gave him change, peering at him from under vast false eyelashes like hideous jungle insects. He could hear her thinking, 'Poor love, the things you've been through . . .'

At quarter to two on a wet Sunday in February, the club was almost empty. The few customers were old lads, men with no missus at home to do them Sunday dinner. They looked up from the *News of the World* and eyed him. Word of his adventures had obviously come home ahead of him.

He'd sent a telegram saying he'd be back Monday, but had made it a day earlier. The taxi had dropped him off at the house an hour ago, but there was no one in and he didn't have a key. Mam and Dad must have gone to Auntie Glad's in Hartlepool. He went over to Thelma's and found she'd gone on the bus to visit a schoolfriend in Thornley. Walking by

Terry's parents' house, he noticed a boarded-over window. There was a red paint splash like blood on the front door.

He looked at the beer. Foam ran down the sides of the glass. He strained to hear the fizz. Hundreds of tiny bubbles burst. A pint of Whitbread Trophy Bitter! The pint that thinks it's a quart! He'd liked the IPA in the NAAFI and Tiger Beer in Saigon, but Trophy was the taste of home, the taste of before.

Maybe because he was a sort of hero or someone further up the chain of contempt thought he was cute, or maybe it was just procedure, but they'd decided to Blighty him fast. After a few days' check-up at a base hospital at Cam Ranh Bay, he was on the gozome bird.

The RAF had a few ancient, hideously noisy, Sunderland flying-boats to shuttle quacks and Blighty Ones from Cam Ranh Bay to whatever troopship was nearest home. In a few days T-for-Tommy flew him from Indo to Rangoon, Calcutta, Karachi and Aden. He was dropped off at Port Said to join the SS *Uganda*. Nobody from his unit was on board, but some of the blokes had heard about him. Before they passed Malta he'd been awarded honorary extra stripes and invited to join the sergeants' messdeck.

The door opened with a blast of damp air, chilling him to the bone. An old man with a toothbrush moustache, flat cap and stained overcoat ambled in, shouting to Bet that he'd have 'Just the usual 'alf.' Further down, a man and a woman had an animated argument about whether someone's car was blue or green.

On the boat, a Welsh Sergeant-Major called Williams took a shine to him. Old as the hills, he'd even been out in Burma during the Real War. Now he was coming home from his third tour in Indo.

'You get 'ome, it's a lot smaller than it used to be,' he'd said. 'Not just the size of the 'ouses. Things people are worried about are smaller, too. You'll be dying for a pint of the local brew. I bet you've been dreaming about this foaming glass of Newcastle Brown or whatever muck it is you drink up there.

For two years you've imagined that dirty great 'andful of beer you'll down in one the minute you get off the train. Queer stuff, beer. Wherever you go, the first pint's no bloody good. Especially at 'ome. The last pint you 'ave is always the best one.'

The top of the pint had almost gone flat. Only a thin line of white foam ringed the brown liquid's surface.

He patted the pockets of his battledress trying to find a cigarette. One thing about the Army was they gave you plenty of pockets. Not like the tight bell-bottoms the younger blokes were wearing these days. The fashion came from Russia, like most daft things. He found a battered pack of Guards in the Penguin Pocket on his trousers. He took it out, along with the paperback Williams had given him, *The Edge of the Sword* by Anthony Farrar-Hockley. The author had been captured in Korea and tortured. Farrar-Hockley had guts, but his book was very stiff-upper-lip, officerly and British and matter-of-fact. If Bob wrote up his story, he wouldn't be nearly so polite.

They had docked at Avonmouth late last night. Troopships never landed at Southampton, Pompey, London or even Liverpool any more because it was 'bad for morale'. Indo hands returned furtively to a dock miles from anywhere, preferably in the middle of the night. It was not a heroes' welcome: no lord mayors, no military bands. They were greeted by glaring yellow sodium lamps, cranes, a knot of dock-workers huddling in grimy, glistening oilskins, a few MPs glowering from under the peaks of their red caps and a couple of dozen Queen Alexandra nurses in khaki cloaks. No anthems or hymns were sung; there was only the hiss of the rain on concrete, the clanking of chains, the occasional shout. There were no cigars, only the smell of bunker-oil and damp clothes, and the diesel fumes from the Deltic loco hauling the hospital train waiting on the quay for *Uganda*'s less fortunate passengers.

The tab burned his throat, reminding him he'd not had anything to drink since a mug of tea at the WRVS caravan on the docks. Sod it, he thought. He lifted the glass and necked the lot in one go.

'Worth waiting for, was it?' asked Bet.

'To be perfectly honest, no. It tastes of nowt much, doesn't have enough alcohol in, and is full of gas.'

He theatrically placed the empty glass by the pump-handle in front of her.

'But it is nonetheless what we drink round here, and here is home. So I'll have another pint please, Bet, love.'

Off the boat, Williams saw to it that Bob was marched through demob on the double. Everyone was frightened of sergeant-majors, especially officers. He'd sorted Bob's pay and made sure he didn't have to bother with the nonsense of giving up his uniform and kitbag and signing for every little bloody thing. He even wangled first-class express rail warrants.

They travelled together as far as Bristol Temple Meads, then Williams had to get off to change for Swansea. He was going to spend a few weeks with his sister, then he'd be back in the Army again.

'Listen to me, lovely boy,' he'd said. 'Going 'ome is hard work, but you got to stick it out, see.'

The next pint was a little better.

'What are you going to do, Bob?' asked Bet.

'Reckon I'll hang around till you close, then find a caff that's open and read the Sunday papers till me Mam and Dad get back home.'

She looked at him, knowing he was kidding her.

'I'll go back to accountancy I suppose,' he admitted. 'I can count with both sets of fingers and me toes, you know.'

Aye, so it's just as well you didn't get any of them shot off, isn't it? Sorry to butt in like this, man, but I had to introduce meself sooner or later. Me name's Survivor-Guilt. You and me, we're about to get to know one another right canny well, young Robert.

'You are a card, Bob,' said Bet. 'And after everything you've been through and all.'

Obviously there were stories going around town: how he'd suffered, how heroic he'd been. Maybe he should write a book so everyone would know the truth. He was lucky. He'd come back in one piece. The firm had even taken the trouble to find his BFPO address and write him that his old job was waiting. He was all right. Better than most.

Awright, Bob, whatever you say, marra.

'And what about Terry, eh?' Bet said. 'Who'd have thought he'd be that big a bastard? Pardon my French. If he come in here, the only pint he'd get'd be flung in his bloody rotten face.'

'*Do I look like a fanny?*' yelled Sergeant Grimshaw, face up close against Terry's. 'I repeat, do I look like a fanny?'

'No, Sergeant,' Terry said, wide-eyed.

'Then *why* are *you* trying to *fuck* me? You 'orrible Northern bollockbrain scum-filth snot-gobbling shit-faced granny-shagger.'

Bob, backbone rigid, swivelled his eyes. Terry seemed to be blasted by the Sergeant's breath.

'And what are *you* looking at, tart?'

Grimshaw loomed up against Bob, eyes huge.

'Are you his girlfriend? Are you two nancy-boys homos of the botty-banging jessie persuasion? I'll have no unauthorised buggery in my barracks.'

There were thirty or so young men on the parade-ground, still in civvies, suitcases beside them. They were almost all National Servicemen, barely willing to heed the call of their country. Someone sniggered.

A weight was lifted from Bob and Terry, as the sergeant wheeled off to shout at someone else.

'Let me make myself perfectly clear, ladies. These two poove puddings may be lower than the shreds of toe-cheese I scrape out of my socks, but you are all equally worthless in my eyes. You are all, I repeat all, less than nothing. You are merely the fanny-discharge of your miserable whores of mothers. After nine weeks, you may, and I underline *may*, be elevated from the mud to the position of Private Soldier in the service of His Majesty the King. You, do you love His Majesty the King?'

The Sergeant addressed a London lad called Butler, whose permanent grin could not be wiped away. Bob and Terry had met him at the station, en route to Basic Training Depot No. 9, which was near Walmington-on-Sea, a small town on the south coast.

'Yes, Sergeant, I love His Majesty the King.'

'If His Majesty the King needed to wipe his bottom after a royal shit, would you rip the tongue out of your head and humbly offer it to him as toilet paper? If His Majesty the King needed a holder for his candle-stick would you bend double from the waist and open your arsehole? If His Majesty the King required you to gob in your father's face, tit-fuck your mother and run a lawnmower over your virgin sister, would you reply, "At once, Your Majesty, anything you say, Your Majesty"?'

'Is that a rhetorical question, Sergeant?'

The Sergeant's hand latched on to Butler's crotch like a vice. Butler's eyes went red.

'Sing soprano, you spunk-eating splash of spew. Sing "The Happy Wanderer".'

Butler screeched, tears pouring down his cheeks. Grimshaw literally squeezed the tune out of him, wringing his balls as if they were a musical instrument.

'I love to go a-wandering . . .' Butler yelped, stumbling through the song, '. . . with my knapsack on my back . . . fol-de-ree, fol-de-rah, fol-de-rah-hah-hah-hah-*aaarrgh*!'

Grimshaw gripped, white-knuckled, protracting the final note.

'Above us all is Lord God Almighty, who takes no interest in our affairs. Directly below God is His Majesty the King. Loyal to His Majesty the King are His Majesty's Armed Forces. His Majesty's Armed Forces have bestowed upon me absolute power of life and death over you, Butler. When I speak, it is not merely myself, Sergeant Grimshaw, speaking, but it is the voice of God, transmitted through His Majesty the King and down through every honoured echelon of His Majesty's Armed

Services direct to your pustulant earholes. Can you hear me, Butler?'

The Londoner nodded through agony. Grimshaw eased his grip, then kissed him full on the lips.

'I love you, Butler. You are the best, the only, man in this whole squad. You are promoted to honorary Corporal for the duration of your basic. In my eyes, you are still the drippings from a syphilitic rat's knob-end. But, in comparison with them, you are a demi-god. You walk with giants, and you carry a Bren gun.'

The Sergeant stood back to survey the recruits, who stood like trees next to their suitcases and duffel bags. Bob realised the man had managed in five minutes to make a cohesive unit of young men who were mostly still strangers to each other. They were united in their utter hatred of Sergeant Grimshaw.

'In a moment, you will all get a cheap thrill,' Grimshaw shouted. 'Corporal Butler here will order you to strip naked. The last man out of his kit will be cleaning the bogs with his toothbrush for the next month. Then, you will be examined for hideous diseases and disgusting parasites, be given a proper haircut with scissors the size of sheep-shears, and be issued with uniforms, boots and other essential kit. You will be required to care for these with your worthless lives. Remember, these are not presents. These are lent to you for the duration of your service. Each and every bootlace and jockstrap is the personal property of His Majesty the King. If an item is damaged or lost, the rules of war require me to inflict merciless and disproportionate punishment. Butler, give the order to disrobe, now.'

'Men,' Butler squeak-shouted, then dropping his voice an octave, 'at the double, kit *off*!'

Bob unlaced his shoes first, and began neatly to get out of his civvies, folding and piling every garment as his Mam had taught him.

Some of the others were stark naked before he had his shirt and trousers off.

Buttons pattered on the asphalt. Terry was ripping off his clothes as if invited in for late-night coffee with Sabrina. It began softly to rain.

Grimshaw wove in and out of struggling lines. It was not easy to undress standing up. Men hopped from foot to foot as they fought with socks and shoes.

Bob knew he would be last. He tried to hurry, but he could not break the habit of neatness. At last, he folded his underpants and put them on the pile. He supposed he would have to learn how to clean toilets.

Grimshaw walked past and looked down, first at his shrivelled genitals, then at his perfectly folded square of clothes.

'Very neat, Nancy.'

Bob was astonished and relieved. There were other men still trying to undress.

In the end, there was only Frank Spencer, the squeaky-voiced semi-imbecile who had been at the station with Butler. He had started undressing with his cap and worked down, and got his trousers stuck on his shoes.

Spencer fell over, sobbing silently.

'Butler, over here,' Grimshaw shouted. 'Piss in this man's eyes.'

Bob saw Butler pause, realise how precarious his position was, and trot over to his friend. He pointed his knob, but couldn't get a flow going.

The rain was pissing down for him. Finally, he managed a pathetic dribble. He missed Spencer's face. Bob would have liked to think that was deliberate.

Spencer was crying out loud, scrabbling round like a crab, ripping his trousers apart at the seams in a last, desperate attempt to get them off.

'Rest of you, line up,' Grimshaw shouted.

The rain was stinging cold, with a January wind pelting it against bare skins. Bob felt needles of ice against his back and buttocks. Like everyone, he was shaking, dripping rain droplets with every shiver.

'Best bath you've 'ad in years, you dirty beggars.'

They huddled in a line, hugging themselves. Their clothes were forgotten, soaked through by the rain.

'Nobody gets a towel or a uniform until Spencer has well and truly been pissed on. And I mean by every man here.'

Dread closed on Bob's heart. He had never been able to use a public urinal. He would point and feel pressure in his bladder, but it just didn't happen. He always waited for a sit-down to be free and pissed in private.

And now he didn't even need to take a slash.

Grimshaw, this elemental force of malign nature, would skip to Bob as quixotically as he had from Terry to Butler to Spencer. When he failed to produce the thinnest squirt of piss, Bob would be on the ground where Spencer was. The Sergeant would probably order the rest to shit on him.

This was a nightmare that would never end. Nothing could be worse than this.

And it was only his first day in the Army.

'Sod this for a game of soldiers,' Terry said through chattering teeth.

William Casper, who claimed to be eighteen but looked four years younger, was in line after Butler. He was the only other 'volunteer' in the squad. He hardly had hair on his pubes. And he couldn't manage a piddle.

Bob thanked His Majesty the King and God. The wrath of Grim would not descend next on him.

'Pathetic, the lot of you.'

The Sergeant picked up Spencer, who was now at last free of all clothes but his socks and shoes.

'You all right, lad?' he asked, tenderly, smiling. 'Could do with a cuppa rosie lee, I'll bet.'

Spencer cried out and nodded.

'You'd love to be inside, warm. Wrapped up. Jam bun. Bourbon biscuits. *Sing Something Simple* on the wireless.'

Spencer looked wistful, cracked an idiotic longing smile, and sagged, almost leaning on the Sergeant, a cat cuddling up to a loving owner.

'Well, you can forget that, Private Piss-Stain Spencer!' Grimshaw yelled, raping the moment to bleeding bits. 'You've not earned a uniform yet. None of you human-shaped lumps of shit have. Fall in in formation, and start running.'

Naked and delirious, Bob collided with Terry as they tried to stand in an orderly group. Grimshaw took his swagger-stick to shins, then started whipping buttocks.

The Sergeant jogged, and Bob tried to run along after him. His feet bled on the rough asphalt, and his ankles jarred with every step. The rain was bucketing down on them.

After half an hour, Grimshaw called enough and directed them to the baths where, he delighted in telling them, they could get the filth off their feet with a nice cold shower.

Bob thought it was a wonder no one had died. He and Terry leaned against each other and limped, moaning, towards the bath-house.

Inside, immaculately uniformed, plumply pink and comfortable, was an officer. He took a look at the stumbling men, who must have seemed like survivors of some war atrocity, and his look of composure vanished. He pantomimed appalled sympathy and wheeled on Grimshaw, red-faced.

'It looks as though these men have been tortured,' he shouted.

'That is correct, *sah*!'

All anger vanished and the officer smiled indulgently.

'Well done,' he said. 'Carry on, Sergeant.'

Grimshaw looked at the men and shouted, 'Into the showers, girls. And be sure to scrub behind your ears.'

Bob read it over again.

Some will tell you the greatest hero the British armed forces have ever produced was Admiral Nelson, some will put up Monty, some General Gordon. But to any National

Serviceman who went through Basic Training Depot No. 9, the only real hero is Private Arthur Seaton. They didn't give Seaton the Victoria Cross. In fact, they hanged him and buried him in an unmarked grave. If I knew where it was, I'd smother the plot in wreaths, and so would a hundred others. Seaton, you see, was the soldier who killed Sergeant Grimshaw. Grim would have been proud of him. One shot, straight to the head, just the way he liked it. Sometimes, when I wake up thinking I'm back in Walmington-on-Sea or Khe Sanh, I sob at the injustice. Seaton wasn't in our mob. He came along months after we'd shipped out. There's not a man who trained at Walmington who wouldn't swap tickets for the Cup Final for the chance to see Sergeant Grimshaw's brains shot out. It's a tragedy it wasn't captured on film. I hope they buried Grim at a crossroads with a bayonet through his heart and a tin of bully beef rammed up his arse.

He handed the page to Thelma. Frown-lines crinkled her forehead, and she was unable not to look as if she smelled something bad.

'What do you think?'

Thelma struggled to find words. 'It's a bit . . . hard. Really nasty.'

'I can't write a soft book, love. Not about the Army, not about the war.'

'It's so bitter, Bob. This poor man Grimshaw was just trying to . . . well, to toughen you up, make men of you. You can't still hate him.'

'Thelma, Frank Spencer had eleven thumbs. He was a walking disaster. He couldn't cross the road without causing an accident. He couldn't boil a kettle without burning the water. When he got through his basic, Grimshaw wrote up a report on him and got him assigned to the REME, recommended him for *bomb-disposal*. How long do you think he lasted? There are bits of him they still haven't found.'

*

'Have you noticed,' Terry said, 'how Grim fixes everything according to the weather? We get PT or beasting or cross-country runs or assault-courses only if it's cold and wet.'

'Right,' Bob agreed. 'If the weather outside is half-way decent, we're indoors, learning how to use Blanco and Brasso, or how to clean a rifle, or how to break someone's neck with our bare hands.'

''Olds and rolls and throws and breakfalls,' Butler snapped, getting the Sergeant's voice perfectly. 'I'd like to try some 'olds on Grimmy.'

'He's not such a bad bloke underneath,' Casper put in.

Everyone looked at him as if he'd just admitted he fancied Hitler.

Casper was a strange one. The grand obsession of his life was bird-watching. Birds of prey.

'He's a bleedin' monster, birdy-boy,' Butler said. 'I tell you, when I'm out of this, back behind the wheel of a bus where the Lord intended I should be, I'll be dreaming of the day Grim steps out on that zebra crossing in front of my double-decker. Bump! Oh! Have I killed you, Grim? Bloody shame! Never mind, eh?'

'But he likes you, Corporal Cockney Get,' said Terry.

'Sing "The Happy Sodding Wanderer", Geordie Shite.'

'Fol-de-reeeee, fol-de-*raaaarrgh-my-bollocks*!' sang Terry.

Butler smiled. Bob couldn't get used to the way Butler and Terry tossed unforgivable insults at each other, yet had become friends for life within days.

Bob wondered if he wasn't getting a bit jealous. He was starting to feel Butler getting in the way of Bob and Terry, just as Terry always resented Thelma.

'Cheer up,' Bob said. 'It's a half-holiday tomorrow.'

After two months, they were finally getting leave to visit the town for Saturday night. Apparently, there wasn't much to do besides visit the pier that almost got blown up in the Real War and hang around Walker's Palais de Danse. Walker's was where the local girls would be. Butler had been talking about it all week. South Coast Girls were legendary in London. Butler was full of stories about knickers lost under the pier.

Bob wondered if he'd be better for Thelma if he were more experienced. He could imagine what she'd think, especially if he caught something. Still, he'd be away for two years.

'You'll never get any birds again, Butler,' said Terry. 'Not after they've had some proper Northern cock. Me and Bob'll run through 'em like a dose of salts.'

'I jus' want to see somewhere that's not this bloody cage,' said Casper.

There were moans of assent from up and down the hut.

'Snap inspection,' someone shouted.

Grimshaw burst in like the Federal Bureau of Inquisition, flanked by hard-faced corporals, pace-stick under his arm.

Everyone stood to attention by their lockers. Grimshaw started examining gear, passing brusque comments on the state of socks and confiscating copies of *Health and Efficiency* and *Tit-Bits*.

Two lockers down from Bob was Frank Spencer, a ticking bomb. His mother, one of those smothering, protective sorts, was always sending him parcels of things like vests, hot-water-bottles, and tracts on the evils of drink. She also sent tins of corned beef. He told them he'd always liked it, and that his mum must have assumed they didn't have it in the Army.

Grimshaw opened Spencer's locker, and two tins of Fray Bentos fell out.

'What's this, cuntface?'

'Two tins of c-corned beef, Sergeant. From my mother.'

'His Majesty's rations not good enough for you, spastic? These foreign objects are an insult to the Crown. You are aware of the regulation that says you can only eat Army bully beef?'

'My mum—'

'I'm not interested in the pox-rotted slag who birthed you between Saturday-night shag sessions with Sheffield Wednesday's second team.'

Irrepressible anger sparked in Spencer's eyes.

'Don't you pick on my mum,' he squeaked.

In the silence, Bob's spirit shrank. Spencer, the cringing reed, had snapped and talked back. Grimshaw would show no mercy.

'So you're missing your mum's cooking? Have to do something about that, won't we? How'd you like a forty-eight-hour pass so's you can visit your mum for a slap-up feed?'

Spencer was as surprised as anyone but still mistrustful. This must be a prelude to a punishment so ghastly it would go in the record books.

Bob prayed Spencer would turn down the offer.

'Nice,' Spencer said.

Bob knew the abyss had just opened up,

'Very well, Spencer, your wish shall be granted. Fairy Godmother Grimshaw will see to it that you spend this weekend in the bosom of your family. However, to compensate, all other leave is withdrawn.'

Twenty-nine hearts turned to stone. Even Butler's smile vanished.

'While you, Spencer, are eating home cooking, we shall endeavour to change the situation here, so the grub comes up to your high standard of cuisine. The rest of you slags will spend the weekend peeling spuds.'

Spencer could still get out of it, and turn down the leave, but he was too addle-headed to see ahead more than a few minutes. Bob knew even Frank Spencer would hardly enjoy his time at home, knowing what was waiting when he got back.

They spent Saturday in a freezing shed next to the cook-house peeling an Everest of potatoes. Grimshaw insisted each be peeled like an apple, in a single stroke that produced a perfect spiral of peel and a completely skinless potato. Bob's fingers were cut ragged. They were so chilled and shrivelled that he couldn't feel them, but he knew agony would set in over the next few days.

Throughout it all, they talked about Frank Spencer. Terry

kept up a bitter running commentary, about the warm tea and hot food he was eating.

'That Betty of his'll be giving him one right now,' he said. 'I bet she has to put the rubber johnny on for him, or he'd get it over his head.'

There were grumbles.

Just now, much as Bob hated Grim, he hated Frank Spencer worse.

'How about a song to cheer us up?' Casper suggested, feebly. '"Boiled Beef and Carrots"?'

He was pelted with potatoes.

At last, it was done. To one side was a heap of peelings as high as a man's waist. To the other, tubs of naked potatoes, streaked with blood.

They sat in the hut, too exhausted to move.

Grimshaw arrived, fresh from the mess, and examined the work.

'A job well done, men.'

He picked up a potato and tossed it into the air, catching it again like a cricket-ball. Then, he picked up a peeling and delicately wrapped it round the potato. It didn't quite fit.

'While you've been working, I've given some thought to the matter of your diet. Choosy types like your friend Spencer have made me wonder if the staple fare in our cookhouse is fine enough for your poor delicate tummies. After consideration, I've decided to take potatoes off the menu for a month. Tighten your bellies. Give you variety.'

Bob was numbed. He couldn't follow Grimshaw.

'So,' the Sergeant continued, 'we shan't need the fruits of your labours. This mess must be tidied away. Butler, get some flour and some buckets and make up some paste. The rest of you, pay attention. By morning, you will have glued the peelings back in place. All neat and tidy. Tomorrow, we shall do the decent thing and bury the spuds with full military honours.'

*

The next night, Butler and Terry held Frank Spencer down while the rest of the squad lined up, raw potatoes in their frostbitten fingers. They forced him to eat the cold, hard spuds. Frank sobbed, mouth bleeding, as he chewed. His teeth cracked on the stringy potato mulch.

Bob held Spencer's chin and forced him to swallow. He felt nothing.

'Come in, come in, dear boy. We meet at last!'

The Bloomsbury office was just as he had imagined a literary agent's would be: thick carpet, heavy mahogany furniture, a few cardboard boxes (manuscripts, no doubt), an occasional table with a bottle of sherry. The only things out of place were framed pictures, messy collages made of pictures scissored from books and magazines.

Kenneth Halliwell looked the part, too, wearing a silk dressing-gown, smoking a pink Sobranie in a cigarette-holder.

He pressed a desk buzzer, 'Joseph, could you delight us a moment with your presence.'

A man popped in. Joseph wore Russian-style bell-bottoms and a white vest. In his thirties, he was trying to look younger. His glossy hair was down over the tops of his ears.

'Bob and I are in need of some refreshment. Would you procure some tea?'

'Earl Grey, Lapsang Souchong or Ty-Phoo?'

Halliwell's assistant had a thin voice, with a little Leicester in it somewhere. Bob chose Earl Grey. It wasn't Ty-Phoo and was easier to pronounce than Lapsang Souchong. Joseph flounced out.

'I am sorry about the boy,' said Halliwell. 'Sometimes I think, "If only I had a hammer . . ." It's so hard to get the help. Poor Joe fancies himself a writer, but he just hasn't got it. He keeps turning out silly little plays, daft experimental stuff full of obscenities. How does he imagine he'd ever get by the Lord Chamberlain?'

Halliwell picked up what Bob realised was his manuscript.

'This, on the other hand, is good. Needs a polish, but I think we have something very saleable. It's raw, it's immediate, direct. Above all it's angry, without being unpatriotic. I shouldn't think we'll have too much trouble with the censors, though I hope to Heaven we have a little.'

'Why do you want trouble with the censors?'

Even a publishing novice like Bob knew how heavily the Lord Chamberlain could come down on a book. The *Lady Chatterley* trial had all but bankrupted Penguin, and the upholding of the obscenity verdict by Lord Chief Justice Goddard had forced everyone to play safe.

'Because, dear boy, every time the papers report that a book worries the censors, it means an *extra ten thousand copies*.'

Ten thousand copies! An *extra* ten thousand copies! But only if they weren't pulped by the Post Office.

'I also took the liberty of getting a Roneo of your manuscript sent to Gelbfisch.'

'Schmuel Gelbfisch? The Russian film-producer?'

'He's Polish actually. Well, Jewish really. Gelbfisch won't read your book himself. He has people to do that for him. Sam dodders into London every year to buy books and plays. I know he's mad keen to do a film about the Indo-China War. The Russkies are just as mired in it as we are, and the right story could be terrific box office.'

He knew he was being a prat, but Bob couldn't help but imagine Albert Finney playing him, and Larushka Skikne as Terry, with Michael Caine maybe as Stan Butler. Julie Christie as Thelma, William Pratt as Grimshaw, Jack Hawkins as Molesworth, Peter O'Toole as Fotherington-Thomas. A Royal Film Premiere, with the King and the Tsarina. Queues outside the Regal, with his name up in lights.

'We're going to have to think of a title. Joseph suggested *It Ain't Half Hot, Mum*. I quite like it. Conjures the insolent cheeriness of the ordinary soldier, but also suggests sentimentality and yearning for home. What do you think?'

'Actually, Mr Halliwell—'

'Kenneth, please.'

'Actually, er, Kenneth, I don't like that at all. It's the sort of thing a Londoner would say. I'm from the North-East.'

'Oh. Pity.'

'Mortar!' yelled Bob 'Hit the deck!'

A second shell fell with an ill-tempered crump into a paddy field. A ten-foot column of water rose.

Everyone yelled at everyone else to take cover. Bob threw himself at the dirt next to a wooden hut. He took the safety off his SLR and chanced a peep over a low wall of baked mud. Lieutenant Gurney paced up and down about thirty yards away, right out in the open, scanning the tree-line with binoculars.

'Bloody toff,' said Terry, crawling up beside Bob.

'He's trying to draw their fire so's we can get some idea where they are.'

'He's showing off is what he's doing,' said Terry. 'He's a belted earl. He has to prove he's got more guts than us proles.'

A ball of oily flame engulfed the Lieutenant.

'Christ in Heaven,' said Terry. 'I didn't mean that!'

Burning pieces of Jack Gurney filled the air. They were breathing him, choking on him.

Casper squirmed up next to them. 'See any small-arms?'

'Nowt yet. Only mortars. They just hit Lieutenant Gurney.'

'That was no mortar. He trod on a mine.'

Bob's stomach clenched. This wasn't a chance encounter with the treens. The platoon had been drawn into a trap.

He flinched as a machine-gun opened up from the tree-line about three hundred yards away. Tracer churned up the ground a comfortable distance beyond the wall. Earth pattered on them.

'Aye, this spot'll do,' said Casper.

He unslung a long leather case from his back and drew out a lovingly oiled Lee-Enfield. From one of his ammunition-pouches, he took a telescopic sight wrapped in oilcloth. Neatly, he fixed the sight to the rifle.

Casper was the platoon sniper. He'd been in Indo ten days when he took the brigade trophy for skill-at-arms.

Butler came over.

'Snudge says we're to set up along here with whatever cover we can. He's put one of the Brens over to our right. He says you're to set up here too, Casper. If you clock anything wearing pyjamas, slot it and pray it's Ho Chi Mekon himself.'

'Willco,' Casper breathed. His mind was already miles away, willing victims to wander into his cross-hairs.

Bob was starting to be afraid of little William Casper, with his hawk-eyes and ever-mounting kill score. He was an ancient child, more bird of prey than man.

Bob, Terry and Butler sat with backs to the wall and heads well down. If Vic tried to come at them across open rice paddies, they'd hear about it soon enough.

'What are we in for?' asked Terry.

'Dunno,' said Butler. 'Snudge is dialling nine nine nine.'

A shell burst very close to the wall. Bob's ears hurt. Nobody said anything for a while.

At the morning briefing, Captain Fisher, the battalion intelligence officer, had said this would be a routine Bryant & May raid. Everyone home in time for tea and the football results on the Forces Broadcasting Service. It was only as the platoon was rattling along a dirt road in a couple of old Matadors that Butler told Bob why the old sweats had groaned when Captain Fisher walked into the tent.

Bob had liked Fisher. He had a soft West Yorkshire accent, not a wireless announcer drawl like Gurney's. He seemed an ordinary bloke. But behind his back, he was called Billy Liar. In his head the Indo-China War was long over and he was mopping up before the Victory Parade. Nothing he said bore any relationship to the truth. The way Fisher told it, all they had to do was come out here and burn down this village.

The civilians and their livestock had already been moved to a protected compound (which was what Fisher insisted they call concentration camps). This was in keeping with the policy in the British sector of depriving the Viet-Cong or any NVA infiltrators of help from the civil population.

The tactic had worked in Malaya in the 1950s, prompting Anthony Eden, the Saviour of Suez, to commit himself to the Relief of Indo-China. Eden hoped to replay World War II, with himself as Churchill and Ho Chi Minh, 'that little Indo-Chinese upstart', cast as Hitler. When France went communist after the War, it pulled out of its former colonies, leaving a few idealogues – 'Red Jesuits', they called them – behind. A 'democratic' regime sprouted, puppeteered by French colonial die-hards who refused to follow the Paris line, but that collapsed after the humiliation visited on all those battle-hardened Maurices at Dien Bien Phu. It fell to Britain and her Empire and Commonwealth to disinfect Indo on behalf of the free world. Naturally, Russia couldn't let that happen, so Premier Kissinger got up in the Duma and pledged to match the Brits man for man and gun for gun. Eden and Kissinger both claimed to have made the first commitment to South-East Asia. The British and Russian armies each referred to their allies as 'reinforcements'.

It had been bloodless enough to start with, merely a matter of sending a few technicians and instructors to help the regimes in the Republic of South Vietnam. Now the commies were on the march again, with the support of plenty of folk fed up with the corrupt and incompetent succession of governments in Saigon. What had started as a 'limited police action' with a few Gurkhas had in seven years become so popular it was keeping 100,000 British and 20,000 Anzac troops in work, not to mention the 150,000 (and rising) Russians who'd come along, too. Enoch Powell, Eden's successor as Prime Minister, would gladly give the whole bloody shooting-match to the Ivans – *anyone dammit*! – and get Britain out. But a British Government's word was its bond, and the Russians couldn't be allowed win the war on their own.

The British were supposed to be fighting American-backed communists, but strategists spent more time jockeying for position with the Russians. A *Punch* cartoon showed King Edward VIII and Tsarina Tatiana in full state uniforms standing over a map of Indo-China, squabbling about who would administer which regions 'when the victory was won', while a tiny, ragged Ho said, 'What do you mean, "when"?'

The treens found their range. One of the eggs landed somewhere behind them, in the village. Someone yelled, 'First aid!'

It all happened in slow motion. Bob reckoned he should have been deafened by the racket from the explosions. Somehow, he wasn't. He was in mortal danger here and realised he was enjoying it, savouring it. It was something to write home about. This was making a man of him.

'The condemned men are entitled to a last smoke,' said Terry, offering round Capstans.

They all lit up. Someone scurried over at a low crouch.

'Put those fuckers out, you stupid fucks!' shouted Sergeant Snudge. 'Fucking treens can see your fucking smoke a fucking mile away. Then you fuckers'll be fucking fucked.'

Bob stubbed the cigarette. He knew Snudge – bloody silly name – didn't like him. None of the old lags did. They were new bugs, the sprogs, and as such bad joss. Regulars despised National Servicemen, claiming that they tended to get themselves and others killed, but the one time Bob snapped and declared himself as a volunteer, he was scorned even more openly.

'The Mekon's got us pinned,' said Snudge. 'We can't rush him because we don't know where he is or how strong he is, and it's over nearly open ground. We can't do a runner because the little bastards have cut the fucking road as well. I've radioed for help, but we've to wait here until Billy Liar finds the bottle to tell Lieutenant-Colonel Windrush he's fucked up afuckinggain. Then we have to wait until Windrush finishes dithering and gets Brigade's permission to call for assistance. Just pray it's the dropshorts and not the fucking Raf. If you see any aircraft, for fuck's sake, fucking hide. Now get dug in. If a firework comes your way before you've got a hole, flatten yourself on the dirt face-down. And keep your gob open. It'll stop you going deaf. Butler, report to Popeye, collect some spare ammo, and a crate of gold-tops and pineapples. Get yourselves nice and fucking comfy. It's going to be a fucking long day.'

Bob wasn't enjoying this any more.

Terry had the spade, a crummy little thing with a handle no longer than his forearm. Eighteen inches down he hit water. Not surprising, with a paddy field close by.

'Bollocks!' said Terry.

Two shells landed in front of them in rapid succession, spattering loose change against the wall.

Bob's ears were ringing.

'They're comin',' said Casper quietly, from behind his rifle-sight. 'Usin' t'mud banks in t'paddy for cover. I see at least five. Can't get a bead on any yet.'

'I'll tell Snudge and get the ammo,' said Butler, crawling at speed towards the middle of the village.

Moments later, a vast cage of hot metal enveloped them. Mortar shells exploded all round, machine-gun bullets hammered the dirt wall. Any more and the wall would simply disintegrate.

Bloody Yanks.

The Mekon's communist allies, the United Socialist States of America, were pledged to support North Vietnam and the Viet-Cong to the hilt. Except there were no actual Yanks in Indo. They'd learned a lesson invading Japan in '45 and liked to get others to do their fighting on the Pacific Rim. There was a supply route – the Casey Jones Trail – running through the warring statelets that used to be China, all the way down to Cambodia. By the feel of it, all that Yank ordnance was being delivered right here.

Casper fired, smoothly slid his rifle-bolt back, then forward, and bit his lower lip. He'd got one.

Butler came back, dragging two wooden boxes behind him. 'Help yourselves,' he said. One box contained smooth, round phosphorus grenades – gold-tops. In the other were the Mills bombs – pineapples – beloved of the Commando comics Bob and Terry had read as kids.

They spaced out behind the wall, laying out grenades and spare magazines. They'd lost interest in digging in.

There was a bigger than usual explosion behind them. Black smoke. Popping and zipping noises. The Mekon's mortars had brewed up one of the lorries, and plenty of spare ammunition by the sound of it.

Bob was breathing too fast. Was this what a panic attack felt like?

'Terry?' he shouted.

'Kiddo?' said Terry, tightening the chin-strap on his helmet.

'Nothing,' said Bob.

'Aye, mate,' said Terry, smiling. 'Me too.'

At the far end of the wall, the Bren opened up. Short, intense bursts hammered like a pneumatic drill. Casper fired over and over again, working his rifle-bolt like the pistons of the Flying Scotsman.

Bob peered over the wall, saw the top of a head – a shock of black hair – over a little mud-bank a hundred yards off. He aimed, squeezed the trigger – almighty bang! – and missed. The Bren tore up water and mud. Bob jammed himself against the wall, head well down, and held the rifle over his head with both hands, working the trigger with his thumb, trying to stop the thing flying out of his hands, firing in the general direction of the enemy.

A gold-top exploded like some pure white blossom, sending thin trails zipping out in every direction, searing squiggles into his eyeballs. Gleaming aluminium roared overhead. Trees burned like a Guy Fawkes bonfire.

'Canberras!' shouted Butler.

'*English Electric* Canberras,' said Bob.

The napalm and the heat of the engines made the air look like the clear, freezing water of a brook in the Yorkshire Dales.

*

The main humanities lecture hall of the University of Sussex was packed to capacity. Students even sat cross-legged in the aisles. There were nearly a thousand of them out there, all impossibly young and fresh. Bob had only a couple of years on the older ones, but they looked as if they came from another world. Clean-cut girls in college scarves and duffel-coats; Beetniki aping Russian style in goatee beards, bell-bottoms and Afghan coats; clever, angry lads from pit villages and factory towns; ironic, waspish waifs who had failed Oxbridge entrance and were going the plateglass route.

'Settle down, please,' said Dr Dixon from the podium.

Bob hadn't wanted to come, but Kenneth had pleaded. It would get into the papers, it would sell more books.

He glanced across the stage at the men with whom he would debate. Francis Urquhart, the local MP, was talking down to the bewildered Jim Hacker, a former Eden protégé serving his time as a junior minister. The government spokesmen sat unsubtly to the right, while Bob was next to Howard Kirk, reader in Sociology, who took the extreme left. Author of *The Russians Can Bloody Have Constantinople*, a book about radical opposition to British imperialism, the long-haired academic smoked a roll-up with casual arrogance.

'I suppose this is as quiet as it's going to be,' said Dixon nervously. 'Perhaps we can get started.'

There was uproar and cheering as a group of students unfurled a long banner. They wore American-style broad-brimmed hats and sleeveless leather jackets with red tin sheriff star badges. Dixon attempted an apologetic smile which came out as a grimace. The thirty-foot-long banner declared, 'WORKERS AND INTELLECTUELS UNITE AGAINST ANGLO-RUSSIAN IMPERIALISM IN INDO-CHINA.'

Urquhart sneered at the misspelling. Hacker asked to have it pointed out, then laughed loudly. Men with cameras – press? – took pictures of the banner.

His book had been out for five weeks and garnered good reviews. Bernard Levin, Malcolm Muggeridge and Christopher

Booker praised him in *The Times*, *Punch* and the *Statesman*. Even a blimp called Brigadier Alistair Lethbridge-Stewart, drafted by the *Daily Telegraph* to pass comment, acknowledged Bob had 'seen a thing or two', though he finally dismissed the book as 'a rather insolent eructation from the ranks'.

Dixon introduced the panel. The politicians were hissed, which upset Hacker but steeled Urquhart's contempt for young people. Kirk grinned and waved at the regimented clapping that greeted him. This was not an impartial crowd.

'And finally,' said Dixon, 'an Indo-China veteran who, as author of *It Ain't Half Hot, Mum*, has done much to bring into the public arena questions about British involvement in the war.'

Students cheered and whistled. For him! They kept on cheering. Kirk was a bit put out. Bob was puzzled, but thrilled. At last, he had his hero's welcome, from people who had looked down at him all his life.

'Perhaps we could begin,' said Dixon, 'by asking Bob for an assessment of the feelings of the ordinary soldier about service in Indo-China. Do the troops feel as though they don't belong there?'

Over and again, Captain Vinh had asked the same question, between punches, slaps, and blows from rifle-butts. Bob never did have an answer. For Vimto or anyone else.

'To be honest,' he said, 'most squaddies have no strong opinion on whether they should be there or not. They've been called up—'

'What I think Bob's trying to say,' interrupted Kirk, 'is that our soldiers have been lied to by the British and Russian governments. Well over ninety per cent of our servicemen in Indo-China are conscripts—'

'What I think Bob's trying to say,' interrupted Urquhart, 'is that our splendid lads are doing their duty like honest, loyal patriots—'

'What I think Bob is saying is—' interrupted Hacker.

He never got the chance to finish. The hall erupted. Some students jeered and whistled, the others chanted, 'Heavens no, we won't go!'

Most boys here would have National Service deferred so they could complete their education. Then they'd be called up. At least half would end up in Indo during their two years. Bob wasn't sure how he felt about the politics, but he couldn't blame them for not wanting to go. He'd been stupid enough to volunteer.

'This war is none of our business,' shouted Kirk above the din, to huge cheers. Urquhart tried to say something about an international duty to save the world from the evils of American communism. Hacker looked queasy.

At the side of the stage, a tall, muscular middle-aged bloke in a suit, short hair, thin lips, definitely ex-military – Hacker's bodyguard? – spoke into a walkie-talkie.

A knot of men in brown corduroy trousers and polo-neck sweaters moved rapidly down the left-hand edge of the hall towards the stage. Bob knew at once these were serious people, not like the rich poseurs wearing Red Chic slouch-hats and tin stars.

He reached for the commando-knife taped as always to his ankle. Then he remembered he was the hero here. They'd be after the MPs.

Objects flew.

Bob's entire body flinched, and he fought the urge to throw himself flat on the stage. He heard explosions and gunfire, but it was just the slamming of spring-hinged wooden seat-bottoms as kids stood up.

He looked at Hacker and Urquhart, who were cringing behind a human wall. The bodyguard's broad back was splattered with egg-yolks.

Bob shook, uncontrollably.

With a straight face, Captain Fisher assured us our action had been an outstanding success. We had killed fifteen

Viet-Cong, wounded another twenty and captured two machine-guns and 42 assorted small-arms, all American-made. We listened in astonishment. There was only our platoon involved and as soon as the Raf pounded what may or may not have been enemy positions, the treens just faded away. I only saw a single dead enemy – the one Casper hit – and we certainly didn't carry off any weapons. Our score was one dead lieutenant – post-humous VC, of course, for the 14th Earl – and three men wounded. Nevertheless 'Billy Liar' wrote it up as a victory. I don't know if anybody higher up the chain of command really believes him, but my impression is that we are sinking further into the mire of Indo because 'Fisher' is too soft-hearted to tell his superiors how badly we're doing. In turn, they are too timid to tell the generals, who keep the worst of it from Enoch Powell, who tells the King we won the War in 1964. The only people who realise we're losing are sergeants, and they're as inscrutable as hateful Buddhas. If they had any opinions of their own, they'd die rather than let them out. Believe me, I've seen that happen.

In the senior common-room Bob drank whisky with Dixon, Kirk and a few others. After the Minister and the MP fled, Kirk had turned the meeting into an anti-war rally, hijacking Bob's book for his political ends. Bob got flustered and turned red at first, but part of him enjoyed the hero-worship of a thousand passionate and intelligent young people. And it was hard to argue with Kirk's line that Britain had no business in Indo-China.

Dixon came over, evidently half-cut. 'You know, old man, we tried to get your pal to come along.'

'Terry?' The name was a stone in Bob's mouth.

'He's controversial, isn't he? Does he mean it?'

He was vaguely surprised Terry hadn't come up earlier.

'Yes, Dr Dixon.'

'Jim, please.'

'Yes, Jim. Terry means what he says.'

Bob hadn't seen Terry since coming back, and Terry had made no attempt to contact him. Most people thought what Terry had done was treasonable, but Bob hadn't written it that way. The least he could do was give his oldest friend the benefit of a doubt.

Would Terry have got three cheers from the students? Yes, he probably would.

'Hello,' said a woman. Bob looked into startling eyes. She was in her late teens or early twenties and slim, with long straight hair and an elfin face. She wore blue corduroy bell-bottoms and an embroidered *Afghantsy* coat.

'Bob, this is Diana. Diana Scott.'

'I'm a drama student,' she said. 'I'm with Howard. Dr Kirk.'

Bob guessed what that meant. Lucky bastard.

A woman in early middle age bustled into the room, all smiles and theatrical kisses.

'Who's that?' said Bob.

'Howard's wife,' admitted Diana. 'Probably come to collect him. It's her birthday. They're going to the theatre. The latest Rattigan. Howard's looking forward to shredding it.'

He looked funny at her, trying to work it out. She sighed and smiled indulgently. Bob must seem amazingly provincial to her. He was painfully conscious of his accent.

'It's an open marriage. They're well known for it. They regard wedlock as patriarchal and exploitative.'

Bob had read about this kind of thing in the *Observer*. He and Thelma would be in bed together of a Sunday morning, with the papers. He'd make fun of it, but secretly be envious; she'd be disgusted, but be secretly threatened.

That was back when they were still sharing a bed. Recently, Thelma was losing interest in sex, and objected to him screaming in his sleep. Then there was the business of keeping the commando-knife under the pillow. Just in case burglars came in when they were asleep, he said.

Everybody nagged them both about having kids.

'Come on, Bob,' said Diana. 'I don't want to spend the rest of the evening drowning in sherry with these tweedy codgers. There's a wine bar just opened in town. From there we can go on to a discotheque.'

They had seventy-two hours' leave. Lieutenant Noote, the padre, had tried to muster a team for 'a game of footer against our ARVN friends'. Bob was deputed to tell him that the platoon would rather spend time in Saigon.

It was hard to explain without mentioning whores. Bob knew Noote understood the situation exactly, but still felt guilty for disappointing the poor man. The padre was okay.

He tried not to think about Thelma.

During awkward pauses in the conversation, Noote's office rattled with skiffle from his wireless. Mostly, the Forces Broadcasting Service played ballads and big band, but there was one anarchic announcer – Simon Dee – who played Lonnie Donegan, Chas McDevitt and Ray Ellington, and was starting to give needle-time to radical new music coming out of Russia and Ireland and even Great Britain.

You never heard Lulu or Cilla Black, who sang as if they were desperate for a shag, on *Two-Way Family Favourites*, and certainly you never heard Alan Price or the Quarrymen, or Newcastle's own People's Balladeer, Alan Hull. Those songs made Bob feel things he'd couldn't say out loud. Angry, joyous, sexual, Northern things. He couldn't hear Price's 'Kalinka' without wanting to explode, and there was something dreadful in the Quarrymen's 'gallant cossack horsemen in their thousands dying' he couldn't get out of his mind.

Saigon would be wonderful if there wasn't a war on. All the mystery of the orient combined with the chic of France, the former colonial power. Many of the buildings are elegant, the food – if you can be bothered to wander beyond the NAAFI – is a marvellous mixture of French and

283

oriental, the streets are full of bustle and life. Whole families riding on Russian motorbikes, street traders selling cigarettes and souvenirs, kids asking for buckshee ... and the women. But before a squaddy could find himself a nice girl and exchange ten shillings for three or four minutes of true love, he had to get tanked up. That was easy in Saigon, if dangerous. Walking into a bar where the Anzacs were drinking was asking to be duffed up. When Aussies get more than two 'tubes' of Fosters in them, they start wondering what they are doing in Indo. Then they reason Britain got them into the war. Their next impulse is to find a Pom and knock his teeth out.

The air was thick with screeches: 'I want you give me one, Tommy.' 'Bet you fancy me, Brian.' 'Sucky-fucky, ten-bob note!'

As Terry negotiated with a fifteen-year-old street angel, her younger sister was draping herself round Bob, fingers fluttering against his fly.

'I love you long-time, Tommy,' she cooed in his ear. 'Do you fine knee-trembler.'

Butler came along and unpeeled the girl.

Bob wanted to deck the cockney bastard. But he was also grateful. The longer he was in Indo, the harder he found it to be unfaithful to Thelma. At first, like everyone, he had been on holiday; all arrangements were suspended, all bets were off. Sex was affordable and available all the time, and no one thought less of you for whoring.

Every time, he thought more about Thelma and disappointed himself. The funny thing was that sometimes he couldn't even remember what Thelma looked like.

All round him were tiny, pretty faces. Almond eyes dark as night, tiny teeth sharp as pins.

'Watch the door, our kid,' Terry said, as he and Butler went upstairs.

Bob nodded.

Often, soldiers were interrupted *in flagrante* by chopper-waving young men claiming to be brothers or fiancés of supposedly nice girls. It took a lot more than ten bob to square them.

Down the street, a radio was playing 'A Mouse Lived in a Windmill in Old Amsterdam' by Ronnie Hilton. All signs were in faded French and Vietnamese, battered English and new-painted cyrillic. Everywhere, there were posters for Vimto. Some of the whores believed douching with the stuff prevented conception and VD.

The Russians were taking over in Indo-China, relieving the British in the south, particularly the Mekong and Piedmont areas. The Brits ran the show on the coastal plains and the highlands, where most guerrilla activity was. HM Forces had had more practice at dealing with that than Ivan. Popeye Popplewell said the year before you could get 'sucky-fucky' in Saigon for half a crown. The Russkies drove prices up, and wore girls out. They did everything to excess. Including, so dark rumour had it, commit war crimes.

A staff car cruised by, scattering children. In the back, an ARVN officer sat bolt upright, with more braid on his uniform than a cinema usher. With him sat a veiled Dragon Lady, one of the daughters of Fu Manchu.

An ox-cart got in the way and the car stopped. The officer stood up to shriek at a peasant, who shrugged. The officer ordered his driver to reverse. The Dragon Lady leaned forward to whisper in the driver's ear and something flashed. The driver's head tilted back, a red yawn opening in his throat. Bob saw, but the officer didn't.

A tiny gun went off, and the top of the officer's head came off in his hat. He tumbled out of the car like an unstrung Muffin the Mule.

The Dragon Lady vaulted out of the car, *ao dai* riding up to reveal bare and boyish calves. She paused, pointing a gloved hand at Bob. Her ladylike gun was almost swallowed by her velvet fist.

His guts were ice. The sound was turned way down.

A breeze lifted the veil and he saw a man's face. A European face. The world wasn't making sense.

Then he was gone and noise fell in on Bob. Ronnie Hilton was still singing that a windmill with mice in was hardly surprising. The staff car's engine was still turning over.

Terry and Butler came down, buttoning up, big grins on their stupid faces. Bob was still shivering.

Whistles sounded. Bob looked at faces in the street. No one had made any more attempt than he had to detain the assassin. No one seemed even to notice anything unusual.

Terry took charge and got them out of there before the police arrived.

'Blimey, Bob,' said Butler. 'Can't leave you alone for a minute.'

On our last evening in Pay-Gone there was an ENSA concert hosted by Simon Dee in an aircraft-hangar on the edge of town. The comedian was supposed to be Terry Milligan, but he was cancelled by the Ministry of Defence because he'd thrown a batter pudding at 10 Downing Street in protest at the war. Instead, we got Arthur Askey dressed as a bumble-bee. Cliff Richard came on and brought the house down with 'I've Got Sixpence', Britain's Eurovision entry that year. I think even he was surprised at the way everyone sang along, but he probably wasn't aware of the superstition among troops in Indo. On the exact date when you have just six months' service left, you start a 'chuff chart'. Thereafter, you tick off each day as it passes. This gave rise to a song popular in camps and barracks throughout South-East Asia:

I've got six months, lousy ****ing six months,
Six months to hang on to my life,
I've got two months to whore, two months to be sore,
And two months to get cured for my wife.

286

You won't have read in the papers about what happened next. The censors like you to think our troops are whole-some chaps who suspend their sexual desire for the duration of hostilities until they can go home and get married. That night, as a troupe of go-go dancers called Pan's People kicked into their routine, two thousand battle-scarred squaddies rushed the stage. Vietnamese girls are beautiful, but they don't look like the girls back home. We'd none of us seen a girl from back home for quite a while. In their spangled Union Jack shorts and halters, with long white legs and bulging breasts, Pan's People were the girls from home we had all been imagining every night. Any man in the audience would have raped the pack of them – seeing on each the faces of his fiancée, girlfriend, some shopgirl, a meter maid – while the rest of us cheered him on.

Redcaps came in with firehoses and doused our ardour. I understand two blokes were crushed in the chaos. I wonder what they told the families.

Diana had a rich father and a Triumph Spitfire. It made getting to Avening a lot simpler. All morning they'd driven through the Cotswold countryside, stopping for a pub lunch of cheese, beer and fresh bread. No scampi and chips in a basket here. This was England as everyone wanted it to be. With the aid of the AA map, they'd finally found Avening and asked a man at the local garage for directions to the Powell place.

In the back garden, next to a heap of uncut firewood, was a battered Land-Rover. The cottage was tiny, cut into the side of a hill at the top of a country lane. It seemed surprisingly modest for the home of the director of *A Matter of Life and Death*.

Bob knocked. Somewhere a dog barked. The door opened. A small man in his sixties answered. He wore a cardigan and frayed carpet-slippers. He had a small, meticulously groomed moustache, a large, bony, bald head and huge, bright eyes.

For a moment, he said nothing. Then he noticed Diana. He smiled at her. 'Who's your agent, then?'

Diana giggled. 'Haven't got one.'

'But you are an actress?'

'How did you guess?'

'With your looks it would be a sin not to be an actress, or perhaps a King's mistress.'

Bob cleared his throat.

'In you come, then,' said Powell to Diana. 'You as well,' to Bob. 'I suppose you're the chap who had the memorable adventures in Indo-China.'

'That's right,' said Bob. 'Have you been sent my book?'

'Unfortunately, yes,' said the old man, leading them into a small, cosy living-room. 'Earl Grey or Lapsang Souchong?'

'Lapsang Souchong,' said Bob.

'And you, my dear? You remind me of a pre-Raphaelite model. Cup of tea?'

'PG Tips'll do me fine,' said Diana, taking off her coat and flopping on to a sofa.

'Good girl. I'm all out of the posh teas, anyway. Temporary financial embarrassment. Haven't made a movie for three years. And that was a nudist flick for a Greek friend.'

Powell went off to busy himself with the kettle. Bob took off his crombie and sat next to Diana. She had never heard of Michael Powell and barely recollected the films he had made with his Hungarian partner, Imre Pressburger. But she was an actress and a movie-director was a movie-director. No wonder the cunning little vixen had insisted on driving him down here.

Until two weeks ago, Bob hadn't heard of Michael Powell either. He and Terry had gone to the pictures twice a week for fifteen years and knew all the actors and actresses, but couldn't imagine why anybody would read credits. Kenneth had to explain to him the difference between a producer and a director. However, when given a list of Powell's films, Bob realised he had seen most of them back when they were kids, though Terry had insisted they not go to see *The Red Shoes*, which Thelma had been interested in, because it was a girlies' film, about ballet.

When the Gelbfisch corporation bought the rights to *It Ain't Half Hot, Mum*, Bob had gone to London to meet one of Gelbfisch's producers, a hyperactive young Italian (actually he insisted he was Sicilian) called Martino Scorsese. Through the producer's excited discourse Bob gathered Gelbfisch thought it best to have a British director for this subject, and he, Scorsese, had just the man in mind.

A man who hadn't worked for three years, had been rude about his book within moments of meeting him, and was now trying to seduce his girlfriend.

'Sugar, anyone?' shouted Powell from the kitchen.

'No thanks,' said Diana.

'Three for me, please,' said Bob.

'Only joking,' said Powell. 'I'm afraid I don't have any.'

In a tiny cinema at an advertising agency's offices in Soho, Scorsese had shown him *The Red Shoes*. It was about a young ballerina and a ruthless White Yank impresario, played by John Barrymore, who told her she could be happy in love or be a great artist but not both. Scorsese sighed with pleasure every time Barrymore appeared. Terry had been right about it being a daft girlie film, but Bob found himself in tears at the end when the company performed the ballet without Moira Shearer, who had just killed herself. Maybe it was Scorsese's enthusiasm, but Bob was moved – perhaps even upset – by the film. He couldn't forget it, even if he didn't like it.

Thelma said something similar about Bob's book.

Powell's career stalled in 1960, when his *Peeping Tom* was refused a certificate by the Lord Chamberlain's office and the negative impounded by the police. It was allegedly the most disgusting picture ever made in Britain, but of course no one would ever know. Since then, he had only shot 'glamour' films – silent strip-off shorts lasting one reel or, more bluntly, the length of the average wank – and *Nakeder Than Nude*. Scorsese desperately wanted to get Powell working again.

Powell came back with the tea. 'Didn't bring any Scotch, did you?'

'No, I'm sorry,' said Bob.

'Pity,' said Powell. 'I asked Gelbfisch's representative on earth to get you to bring me a bottle. It's the least I deserve for having waded through your book.'

Bob was burning at this persistent rudeness.

'I noticed a pub in the village,' said Diana. 'They won't have called time yet. I'll go and get a bottle.'

'There's no need.'

'It won't take a minute. I insist.'

She pulled on her coat and disappeared.

'Sit at the table,' said Powell, 'and I'll explain what I'm going to do.'

Bob did as he was told, and accepted a cup of sugarless tea.

'I'll make this movie,' said Powell, fixing him with inquisitor's eyes. 'Not because of your wretched book. I'll do it for the money, but mainly I'll do it for little Scorsese. He's watched all my films, dozens of times. He was quoting great lumps of dialogue to me over the phone the other day. I've been here for years. The phone wouldn't ring for weeks at a time. Then this crazy Sicilian calls.'

On the table was the figure of a winged lion, painted gold. Powell picked it up and fidgeted with it for a moment, drifting off into a personal reverie.

'Look . . .' Bob started

'You didn't come all the way down here to be insulted?'

'If you don't like the book, why don't we just forget it?'

'Should never have put it between hard covers, Bob. It's a penny-dreadful, a poorly written compendium of clichés. Some nice yarns in it, I admit, but there are two reasons I dislike it. First, there's no magic, no poetry. Second, and this is far more important, there's a great dishonesty at the heart of it. Haven't got a fag on you, have you?'

Bob fished a packet of Strands and his new Dunhill lighter from his pocket and flung them on to the table. Powell put a cigarette in his mouth and offered one to Bob. Bob refused. Powell lit his cigarette, passed the lighter back, and stuffed the packet into the pocket of his cardigan.

'Now,' said Powell, 'you're feeling hard-done-by. You're probably trying to think of a way of saying how dare I insult you, after all you've been through, that won't sound petulant.'

Bob shook his head. 'I don't care whether you like the book or not.'

'Of course you do!' he smiled. 'You're being dishonest again. Now, what we need is a shopping-list.'

Powell took an envelope from a letter-rack and produced a stub of pencil.

'Unpaid rates bill. Should be big enough to make the list of the things we're going to have to change.'

'That's enough!' said Bob, standing up. 'I'm a frigging war-hero, me. I don't have to put up with this.'

'Sit down!' snapped Powell. 'Have one of your cigarettes.'

Do as the man says, Bobby, or thee and me'll have a major falling-out. Survivor-Guilt again.

There was plenty in the book that was dishonest, Bob knew. He couldn't go on too much about the whores with Thelma reading over his shoulder as he typed. Not that that mattered any more. She'd found out about him carrying on with Diana. All the train-trips to London and overnight stays, pretending he was on business to do with the book. The marriage had been in trouble anyhow. Compared to his new friends, Thelma was just so trivial in her concerns, so boring. They wanted to change the world, she wanted to change the curtains.

Bob took a Strand without lighting it.

I wasn't talking about Thelma, Bobby lad. This rude old get here has tumbled the Other Thing, hasn't he? The unfinished business.

'As it happens, I had another offer yesterday. The reputation, no matter how unearned, of having made the most shocking film ever shot in Britain can sometimes be helpful. So, either I film your book, or I make *Confessions of a Radiogram*

291

Repair Man, a sex comedy which has precious little sex and isn't funny. But it's British, and our cinemas are swamped with Russian police films, Australian musicals and German horror movies. I do have yet another choice, to starve, but I don't much fancy that.

'Bob, you rightly believe you've had hard times and have earned certain rights. So you have. Fair enough. But you can't expect medals from an audience. They don't automatically care about your suffering. They'll buy their tickets and want something in return. Two hours of magic, wonder, terror, laughter and tears. Gelbfisch bought your book, and Martino, bless him, is giving it to me. You now forfeit any rights you have in this work, and gracefully pass them on to the experts. It'll be an exploration. We'll find out things you don't know about yourself. Maybe things you don't want to know.'

Bob was afraid, but couldn't let it show. He sighed, smiled and shook his head in resignation.

'Whatever you say, Mr P.'

'Call me Micky.'

Diana returned with a bottle of Johnnie Walker.

'Just the ticket, my dear,' said Powell, patting the chair next to him. 'Come sit. Bob, are we on exes?'

'Eh?'

'Expenses. Did Martino float you any of Sam Gelbfisch's wonga for development?'

'Couple of hundred quid.'

Powell's eyes twinkled. 'Excellent. We must adjourn to somewhere more amenable. Bob, be a good fellow and toddle into the village and get a jerrican of three-star. Then we can take the Land-Rover. Harvey's in Bristol, I think. Imre tells me great things about the new chef.'

As Bob left, he noticed Powell patting Diana's knee. There was no resemblance, physical or vocal, but Micky Powell reminded him of Terry.

'You lot, get out to the mortar-pits and piss on them.'

'Come again, Sarge?'

'Water's low and the mortar-tubes are overheating. Your piddle'll cool them down for a while. Get cracking.'

'Why-nor,' said Terry, 'me grandbairns'll never believe I passed water for King and Country.'

Bob and Butler laughed a little too loud, a little too long. They pulled on helmets and their new Russian-made flak-jackets and ran out of the bunker at a crouch to the battalion mortar-pits.

This was Day 67 or 68 of the siege of Khe Sanh, depending on which reckoning you used. By chuff-chart, it was Day 42, exactly six weeks before Bob was due to ship home. And Terry, Butler and Casper. If they got out of this place. There wasn't an airstrip any more. The Viet-Cong and the NVA had pushed the perimeter in that close. It was ten days since the last transport, a Blackburn Beverley, had attempted a landing. It lay in a blackened, twisted heap inside what had become enemy territory two days ago.

Behind the mortar-pits, a small queue of men lay on their bellies. A corporal ushered them in, one at a time, to have a burst on the tubes. Bob had got over being piss-shy after about two minutes in Indo-China.

As the perimeter shrank, eight thousand men and sixty artillery pieces were noosed into a smaller and smaller area of rocky, messed-up orange soil. Every enemy shell had been carried over the mountains on the back of a peasant, but now every shell was pulling its weight. There were dozens of casualties each day and they could only be evacuated by helicopter. The Army and Air Force were overstretched and the Navy was pressed into service, taking the wounded out to HMS *Bulwark* somewhere out off the coast.

The brass were getting edgy about sending the wokkas. You could tell when they were coming, not by the sound of their engines or rotors but by the enemy machine-guns and ack-ack opening up on them all along the valley. Now they only flew in in the thick fog that covered everything until the late morning,

UNFORGIVABLE STORIES

but the treens had the range of the landing-strip, and threw everything they had at it, anyway.

'You next,' said the corporal. Bob scuttled into the sandbagged pit where half a dozen men, stripped to the waist, worked the mortars.

'Over here,' said a squat little bloke with fair hair and a black beard. Everyone had a beard now. If there'd been water for shaving they wouldn't have to Jimmy Riddle on the artillery. 'Try to give it a hosing from the middle down to the bottom. If you've not got enough, concentrate on the bottom.'

They'd been here more than two months. At first, they'd been on 'offensive patrols' but found nothing. In the dense elephant-grass and bamboo thickets, you couldn't see anyone not hold-ing a gun to your nose. Mostly, they'd been holding a shrinking perimeter, living in holes in the ground covered in sandbags and oil-drums and empty shell-casings full of dirt, trying to ignore the rats, being shelled and shot at by snipers every hour of the day, wondering if they'd ever be able to sleep again.

Bob undid his fly and pissed. The mortar-tube hissed and a cloud of toxic steam billowed up from it. The little bloke studied his work with interest. The poor sod was only doing his job.

It was bad enough that the wokkas couldn't get casualties out, much worse that they couldn't get supplies in. Food and ammo were low. Three divisions were supposed to be fighting their way up to break the siege, but no sign of them yet. The Raf dropped HE and napalm all over the jungle to no effect. The treens moved their big guns to new positions every night.

'Nice one, son,' said the blond bloke. 'Cover your ears.'

A round was dropped into the tube. Bob put his hands to his ears and turned away with his cock still hanging out. The shell went away with a nasty, loud 'boink!'

'I'd put that away if I was you,' said the blond bloke. 'Send in the next one, would yer?'

Bob buttoned up and scrambled out of the pit. 'You're in, Butler – Ha ha! You're in – urine – get it?'

294

Captain Fisher had given a compulsory lecture, which was supposed to convince the men that there was no comparison between the British position at Khe Sanh and the Free French debacle at Dien Bien Phu. No, Captain Fisher said, this was more like the British at Kohima–Imphal, where General Slim lured the Japs into wearing themselves out by attacking a strong position, then defeated them. That night, someone finally settled Billy Liar's hash. Person or persons unknown sneaked into Fisher's billet and cooked off a gold-top in his sleeping-bag. 'White-saucing' was by no means an uncommon fate for unpopular officers and NCOs. Lieutenant-Colonel Windrush didn't even bother to start an enquiry. The bush telegraph had it that the CO was crackers or hitting the bottle, or simply just as pleased as everyone else that his intelligence officer had vaporised.

Crackers or not, Windrush had more important things to worry about.

Crouching behind the sandbags of the mortar-pit, Bob wondered whether to make a run for the billet. Along with food, water and ammo, cover was in short supply.

Khe Sanh was, in Army parlance, a 'super-sangar', a fort and artillery base on a plateau deep in the Annamite mountains, surrounded by other mountains, near the border with North Vietnam and Laos. Its artillery covered the main NVA infiltration route into South Vietnam. Billy Liar aside, the Viet-Cong and the NVA – and their friends in Debs DC – certainly saw it as Britain's Dien Bien Phu. Its loss might force the British to pull out of Indo-China. That would prompt the Australians and New Zealanders to leave too. The Russians might be unwilling to stay on by themselves. Potentially, the future of communism in South-East Asia hung on this rat-infested, rust-coloured shit-hole on top of a mountain in the middle of a load of bigger mountains.

The big NVA guns, 155mm, opened up from their positions on the Co Roc Ridge about four miles away. In Laos. In another country.

'Best stay put for a bit, eh?' Butler sniggered. 'Bloomin' marvellous, innit? I've been taking diarrhoea pills for the last month so's I can get good and constipated and keep the number of bog-trips I have to make at an absolute minimum. Now we get orders to evacuate bodily wastes. I'm going to write to my MP about this.'

'Well stick me in the envelope along with the letter. I've had enough of this now. I want to go home,' said Terry.

Three 155mm shells crashed on to the airstrip in rapid succession.

'Hell's bells,' said Terry. 'Anyone got a tab?'

'Only these,' said Bob, fishing a packet of Players No. 6 from a pocket at the side of his flak-jacket. 'I was reading in the *Mirror* the other week that the fag company makes these specially as going-to-work gaspers. You have your nasty cheap little Number Sixes at the factory or the office. Then, when you go out in the evening, to the pub or club, like, you have your proper king-sized fags.'

'Wouldn't mind being down the club this evening. What day is it?'

'Saturday, man.'

'Never mind!' said Butler. 'That means there'll be a film show in the parish hall tonight. Wonder what it'll be?'

'Same as it's been for the last five weeks,' said Terry. 'The Reverend Noote will run *The Browning Version*, a travelogue called *This is Belgium* and Cliff Richard in *Summer Holiday*.'

''Spect you're right,' said Butler. 'Never thought I'd get sick of the sight of a bus.'

'You think you've got problems?' said Terry. 'I'm having strange erotic fantasies about shoving a Mills bomb up Melvin Hayes's jacksie.'

Casper emerged from the mortar-pit.

'Getting a bit crowded this side,' said Butler. 'Shall we make a run for it?'

Casper gazed at the sky, thought for a moment, then nodded. He hadn't said anything in two weeks. People dealt with the strain of the constant shelling in different ways. Casper was no crazier than anyone else. To Butler, Bob and Terry, he was becoming something of a lucky charm. There was no logical reason, it was just that everyone was getting superstitious.

Before he stopped talking, Casper explained that if he looked at the jungle down a rifle-sight, his spirit soared like a kestrel over the trees, enabling him to see treens hidden from ordinary men's eyes. He popped off shots regularly, but there was no way of knowing if he scored any kills. Casper was satisfied that each bullet told.

Casper led off and the rest followed, separated by a couple of paces, making for the big underground bunker known as the Parish Hall. It was the battalion briefing-room, storage-space and place of entertainment. The flicks would be starting in an hour or so, and there was no sense in going back to their billet only to have to run over here again later. They'd just have to be early.

'Ah fuck! Ah fuck, fuck, fuck!' said Terry as they scurried through the bunker's entrance.

'What's up, our kid?' asked Bob.

Terry pointed to a blackboard. TONIGHT'S LECTURE. 'ESCAPE AND EVASION TECHNIQUES'. ALL ATTEND. Terry took a piece of greying paper from his bum pocket. His chuff-chart. He tore it to confetti.

'I'm going to be played by *Rodney Bewes*?'

Bob had been hoping for someone like Albert Finney. Rodney Bewes was the star of *Wish You Were Here*, a television series set in a Morecambe guest-house run by Thora Hird (his mother-in-law) and wife Rita Tushingham, dreaming of a better life than cooking miserly fried breakfasts and rationing the toilet-paper.

'Yes,' said Powell. 'He was recommended by the screen-writers, Clement and La Frenais. Ideally I'd have wanted Imre, but our relationship is still a little, ah, encumbered by the past.

You should know about that. Still, Clement and La Frenais have done an excellent job.'

They sat in a bare office at Pinewood Studios. Rusting, metal-framed window, several layers of bland green paint over the brickwork of the walls and flaking off a big, barely warm radiator.

'For Terry, we have a young man named James Bolam. Also an actor from the television, I believe.'

Powell was no longer the rude, shabby old man in the Cotswold cottage. In a sharp suit, he was as abrasive as ever, but every discourtesy seemed part of a relentless drive towards a distant but attainable goal. He was just like John Barrymore in *The Red Shoes*.

'Aye, I think I know him,' said Bob. 'Little bloke. Terry is big and coarse. This fellow has the right accent, mind. I suppose he'll do at a push. Is it too late to get rid of Rodney Bewes? There's Albert . . .'

Powell smiled. 'Now, for Thelma, we've got Brigit Forsyth.'

'*Thelma*! You can't put her in the film! I only mentioned her a few times in the book. It doesn't seem decent, bringing personal business in like that.'

If Powell put Thelma in his bloody film, her dad would probably belt him. Bob would lose the house in the divorce settlement.

'How is that charming girlfriend of yours, by the way?'

'You mean Diana? I'd've thought you could tell me, Micky. It's a while since I've seen her.'

'Oh,' said Powell wistfully. 'I took her to a press do in Wardour Street a couple of weeks ago. Last I saw of her she was talking to a trendy young director with mutton-chop whiskers and a spotty hankie tied round his neck.'

Bob had been at the same party. Diana had wandered over to say hello, given him a peck on the cheek and run off with her director, who wanted to put her in something called *Devil Bride of Dracula*. He couldn't honestly say he was too upset; he'd been out with four women (an actress, a painter and two models) in the last month.

'Now we've got Reg Varney to play Butler,' said Powell. 'He's a little on the old side, but he can put a lot of cheek into it. Hartnell's a little long in the tooth as well, but I have to have him for Sergeant Grimshaw.'

'You've cast *Doctor Who* as Grim? Micky, that man was a monster, a bloody psychopath with stripes. Not some doddering old eccentric.'

'Padre Noote will be played by Derek Nimmo.'

Bob smiled. 'Now that's good. Nimmo for Noote is spot-on, Micky.'

Oh he is now, is he?

'But, er . . .'

'But what, Bob?'

Tell him, kidder. Tell him how that chinless clown of a sky-pilot turned out to be the best man in the battalion.

'Noote wasn't just a caricature. He was a very courageous man.'

'Don't worry,' said Powell, shuffling through sheets of paper, scribbling his initials on some.

Bob was at Pinewood as a technical adviser. He'd been there two days, showing the extras how a British soldier wore his kit and how to slouch the right way. For this, he was getting an exorbitant £150 per week, with £15 of that going to Kenneth. He'd been shocked to find the jungle sequences would all be shot in the studio.

A knock at the door. 'Come!' snapped Powell. A woman came in, dressed from neck to toe in an immense fur costume. She held more fur under her arm.

'Want to see this now?'

Powell nodded. She put the fur thing under her arm and on to her head. She was a giant teddy-bear.

'Jump up and down a bit,' said Powell.

The teddy-bear did as it was bid.

'Good,' said Powell. The woman took off her bear's head. 'Is it easy to move around in?'

'I'll use nylon for the fur,' she said. 'Cheapest and lightest. It'll be uncomfortable under the lights. You'll need to damp everyone down between takes.'

Powell sniggered. 'Let 'em suffer for their art. Run off two dozen. All different styles and sizes. Make some of them quite battered. Miss out the odd ear and eye. They should look as if they've been loved for a long time.'

'All in shades of brown?'

Powell gave her the thumbs-up. She left.

Bob didn't know quite what to say. 'The Viet-Cong dress in black pyjamas, generally, Micky.'

Bob had long since given up asking to see the script. Powell kept making excuses.

'I said your book had no magic in it,' said Powell. 'Well, I may have been mistaken. I managed to find some.'

'I still don't get it. Why teddy bears?'

'You will.'

Another knock at the door. A bespectacled woman clutching a clipboard popped her head in.

'Just thought I'd let you know, Micky, that the young man from the Lord Chamberlain's office is still waiting outside. You've kept him for seven hours, now.'

'Poor little lamb,' he said. 'What's his name?'

She consulted her clipboard. 'Puttnam.'

'"Puttman". Good.'

'No, I said "Putt-Nam".'

'And I said "Putt-Man". Make sure it gets spelled that way on all correspondence. Shall we let him in?'

The woman shrugged.

'Go on, then.'

She left.

'Bob, for the next ten to twelve weeks I'm going to be doing one of the most stressful jobs in the world. If I get more than four hours' sleep a night, I'll be lucky. The reason I'm not going to show you a script is that I don't want to have any more arguments than are strictly necessary.'

300

'I understand, Micky, but . . .'

Powell stared him in the face. The intense stare of an angry headmaster.

'Good. Now I need a big favour from you. The usual drill with the Lord Chamberlain's office is that you show them a completed film. If they want anything cut, they ask for it. Things are a bit different with me. Ever since I made *Peeping Tom*, I've been on the blacklist. I get my own personal censor for the duration of principal photography. You don't have a huge amount to do on the set all day. I'll get someone to let you know which days you'll be needed. For the rest of the time, I'd be greatly indebted if you were to keep young Puttman as far out of the way as possible. Give him *la vie bohème*, take him to parties, introduce him to loose women. Bloody hell, try and get him addicted to black bombers or the white mischief. Only thing is, there's a restaurant near here called Les Oiseaux. For God's sake, don't ever take him there. I promise you, Bob, by all I hold dear: the more you keep this cretin out of my hair, the better our film will be.'

His shoulders started to shake. It was a moment before it became clear he was laughing.

'Not that I've got a lot of hair any more. Ah, young Mr Puttman from the Lord Chamberlain's office! Come in! Come in! I want you to meet Bob . . .'

The official version is that fourteen hundred men surrendered at Khe Sanh. Actually, on the day Major Lampton, the highest-ranking surviving officer, ran up the white flag, I'd say that there were about two thousand of us left, though a lot of them were stretcher-cases. Of the original garrison of eight thousand I've no idea how many were killed or wounded, but it was a lot.

When the situation became hopeless, we took advantage of three mornings of exceptionally heavy fog to try and scuttle the place. The Raf, the Army and the Navy threw in every aircraft they could. While the bombers and fighter-bombers tried to keep the enemy artillery busy, helicopters and light aircraft zoomed in, filled up as fast as possible and got out again. Regular Dunkirk, it was. Orders were to abandon everything but helmets and flak-jackets and just get aboard.

The Loamshires – us – were to hold the perimeter, along with a West African Commonwealth unit and a few companies of Gurkhas. We were bitter about this. Three Para had been got out, as had the Greenjackets, the Somerset Light Infantry, Princess Wallis's Own Royal Borsetshires and most of the gunners and engineers. The powers-that-be decided a mixed bag of non-Brits were expendable. And us? One of the blokes in the platoon, Eddie Booth, put into words what we were all thinking: 'We've been tossed in so's the f***ing government isn't seen to be saving the white cream and just leaving the wogs.'

'Well, they've bloody left me, white honky,' said Eddie's best mate, Bill Reynolds, who came from Jamaica. Strange pair, Bill and Eddie. They used to insult one another's skin-colour all the time, but they were inseparable.

It was our bad luck to be in an unfashionable foot-and-mouth regiment that didn't have anyone fighting its corner in Whitehall.

We wondered where the ARVN were. It was their bloody country we were fighting for, after all. The word was that most of them were so useless that the top brass didn't want them in the way. But the big question was: where were the Russians? The Russian Air Force would have been big enough to provide plenty of cover and helicopter more of us out. It seems HM government was too proud to ask for help, but we heard a whisper they actually refused a Russian offer of help. Was a little national humiliation too much to ask to save hundreds of lives and hundreds of men from the horrors of captivity?

Day four of the evacuation dawned bright and sunny. A

few wokkas tried to come in, but without cover it was hopeless. Three were shot down and only two made it out again. The next day was the same, only I got promoted to Lance-Corporal. The day after, the enemy were on top of us, anyway. We surrendered.

Captain Vinh was tall for a treen – five foot ten, maybe six foot. He wore a spotless olive-green uniform, unembellished by insignia. Only the red star on his pith-helmet broke the anonymity. And the livid purple scars on the left side of his face.

Vinh noticed Bob was trying not to stare.

'Does my face offend you? My unit was attacked by your British Air Force two years ago, just north of the Demilitarised Zone. I lost a lot of comrades.'

'I'm sorry,' said Bob. A mistake: rule one of interrogation was to keep it polite but neutral. Give away no information, no emotions, no nothing.

Vinh looked him in the face, nodded slightly and offered a cigarette from a red and white packet. There were three other men in the room, guards with American-made Garand rifles. No cameras. Bob accepted the cigarette and a light.

Noote warned against pictures of the NVA being nice to their captives. One tab might make Bob a propaganda snapshot: see how nice we are to the European imperialists?

The interrogation room was half the interior of a wooden hut on bamboo stilts. They were not in a prison-camp as such, but an ordinary village the NVA had taken over and fenced in with barbed wire for the temporary storage of prisoners. They'd been split into smaller groups. Just two companies of the Loamshires were billeted here. He was still with Terry, Butler and Casper. And Noote, who was the CO.

The cigarette tasted surprisingly good. American Virginia tobacco. Two draws on it and Bob felt quite light-headed. It was a week since he'd last had a smoke.

Vinh consulted a buff folder on his desk. There was a single sheet of paper in it.

They'd all been kicked around by the guards, and by civilians, when they were being marched here. They were fed more or less regularly – rice and bits of vegetables. Everyone had the shits, of course.

'Lance-Corporal, Second Battalion, Loamshire Regiment,' said Vinh. His English had a heavy American accent. A lot of NVA officers had studied at American universities.

Bob said nothing. Name, rank, serial number, date of birth. That was all you had to give them.

'I understand everybody calls you "Bob"?'

Bob tensed. How had he found that out? Probably no big deal. Captain Vinh was 'interviewing' everyone. Someone had probably dropped his name in an unguarded moment. Or had it beaten out of him, more like.

'You come from an industrial area of England? Many people work in factories, often in unhealthy and unpleasant conditions.'

Bob tried to look pleasant and accommodating without saying anything.

'Your government conscripts its working men and sends them to the other side of the world to burn the homes of peasants, to bomb women and kids. Bob, you have studied at night-school to better yourself. You are, I am sure, an intelligent man. Have you ever asked what in tarnation you and your, ah, mates, are doing here?'

Aye, you're right enough there, Captain Vinh. How the hell do you know all this about me, Captain Vinh? Who's been blabbing?

Vinh turned suddenly and banged his fist on the table.

'Why are you in Indo-China?'

Bob shrugged.

'Let me level with you, Bob,' said Vinh, sounding all reasonable again. 'You can't give me any military intelligence. The entire active strength of the Second Loamshires was captured. I'm not interested in what platoon or company you belong to, or your tactics or weapons or operating-procedures, or any of that shit. All I want is the answer to that one question. It's not for my superiors, it's just something I cannot understand, something that keeps me awake. Why the hell are working men from Britain oppressing working men in Indo-China?'

Terry would have said, 'That's the British working man all over, Captain Vinh. Can't resist a scrap.' But Terry always had to be carried away from interrogations.

Bob shrugged.

'Bob, do you want to go home?'

Bob nodded. No point in lying.

'Here's some literature.'

He pushed leaflets across the desk. Pictures of British PoWs getting off a plane in Switzerland. The catch was that you had to sign a statement condemning British imperialism in South-East Asia. And embrace international socialism, and convince the treens you meant it.

'Thank you,' said Bob. He'd wipe his arse with them.

'You have a good think about it, huh?' said Vinh. 'I know some of your comrades are certainly considering this offer very carefully.'

Though he walked with the aid of a stick since 'Vimto' Vinh broke his ankle, Lieutenant Noote led the morning stroll around the camp. I fell in with Terry, beside the padre, ambling along. Butler – just out of the cage after a week's punishment – leaned on Casper, who hadn't spoken to anyone in months. Whistling through cracked lips, we made a racket out of 'Colonel Bogey'. Behind us, Eddie Booth and Bill Reynolds had suspended their colour-prejudiced bickering to poke fun at our yellow captors. 'Ugly little treen f***ers,' they muttered in agreement. Water dripped from the thatch of the huts, and gushed out of the nearby trees. There had been a hell of a storm the night before.

Noote greeted each guard personally, calling him by the nickname that had been agreed on.

'Good morning, Herman. Good morning, Prof. Good morning, Gertie. Lovely weather we're having. Lovely for ducks, that is.'

The guards grinned humourlessly at the absurd Englishman, hobbling with pride as if he ran the camp.

It was Noote's idea to give all the guards nicknames to rob them of their dignity. It made us less afraid of them. He organised a series of meetings to democratically elect names for all the goons, and to establish routines.

Noote, of course, was Escape Officer. Early on, he had gathered us all and announced, 'I'm asking each hut to appoint a representative to the Escape Committee. We also need an adjutant, an intelligence officer and a quartermaster. You're QM, Butler. I've got you marked as a scrounger who can rustle up larcenous miracles. We have to take a crack at getting some men over the wire soon, because the longer we wait the more beaten-up and malnourished we're going to get. We can't be more than five or six days' march from the Demilitarised Zone. With the Lord on our side, we stand a fair chance of making a home run. What we need to do is pool our resources. Think about what kit you have, and about what you know, what skills you have, what information you may possess. It's all for one, here.'

I wasn't entirely sure about Noote's optimism. This wasn't Colditz, with tunnels and Red Cross parcels and forged papers. But it was true that we had a fair bit of equipment; with a few days' warning that we might be captured, every man had concealed something useful. Razor-blades were sewn into trouser turn-ups; rat-packs, maps and water-purification tablets stuffed into jacket-linings; compasses hidden in boot-heels; groundsheets tucked away in waistbands; cigarette lighters, pencils and pocket-knives shoved up where the sun don't shine.

This morning, the padre was chipper. The storm had knocked down several stretches of wire in the night, and none of the guards was making any effort to repair the perimeter. It was clearly time to put Plan Wooden Horse into action. It involved no subtle deception. Simply, the plan was to break through the wire and walk to safety. The only clever part was that Noote would spend hours running the remaining prisoners around the village so energetically that a head-count was impossible.

The observation tower leaned on three bamboo stilts, battered by the storm. There was no one manning it and the machine-gun had fallen down and been carried away.

Terry and I had drawn lots and were ready for the go. Butler had scrounged the compass out of a broken penknife, and we were kitted out with a hand-drawn map on the back of one of Vinh's propaganda leaflets, a lighter and six cigarettes (for burning off leeches), a groundsheet, two sachets of vegetable soup and four Durexes.

'A, er, prophylactic appliance in a sock makes a very serviceable water-canteen,' Noote had explained. 'In the jungle, you can't risk drinking river or stream water if you can avoid it. Collect rain from the plants.'

'They never taught us about rubber johnnies in the Scouts,' said Terry.

Now, with everything sopping wet, there was a rare surfeit of potable water.

'The Lord is conspiring,' Noote commented.

It was nearly time for the break. With double rations in my belly to build my strength, I felt stuffed rather than nervous. Terry was eager, dancing a little, like a boxer.

Butler sat down, exhausted, unsupported.

I saw Billy Casper wheeling round, arms outstretched and flapping, tweeting scratchily. The kid had been acting like that for a while, turning his head like a bird, squatting everywhere as if perching.

'Good man,' Noote said, assuming this was a diversion.

Casper climbed the rickety tower. Guards gathered round, shouting up at the prisoner, their language as

307

birdlike as his screeches. Rifles were raised.

Terry and I drifted towards the wire.

Casper spread his arms in an 'I can fly' gesture, and the tower collapsed under him. He pulled himself into the air, stretching. For a moment, it was as if he really could fly. He would soar above the village and flap lazily over the jungle, migrating to freedom.

Gertie the guard shot Billy. He fell to Earth like Icarus, broken.

Terry was ready to go, but I froze, staring at Billy's dead face. He was just a kid. A crazy kid.

'Come on, kidder,' Terry said.

I couldn't move. My nerve was shot.

Captain Vinh marched up. Noote said, 'Captain, I wish to protest most strongly at this atrocious . . .'

Vinh swatted the padre to the ground with a backhand. Then he drew his revolver and shot Noote in the head, twice.

'There will be no escape this morning,' he announced. 'Bob, Terry, bury your dead.'

Vinh's adjutant had brought shovels.

He couldn't stand up straight, couldn't lie down properly. All he could do was crouch. Any attempt at stretching brought him up against bamboo and barbed wire. Bob had been in this little cage, roasting by day, freezing by night, for half a week. The pain wasn't usually physical, apart from the times you got cramps. But it was still agony. He wanted to scream, give Vimto whatever he wanted. Terry was in the other cage, within sight.

'Times like this I wish you were a woman,' said Terry, making calf-eyes through the wire.

'I wish I was a bloody woman,' said Bob, 'then I wouldn't bloody be here.'

When every scrap of him wanted to chuck it, Bob would think that, if Terry was taking it, so could he. They recited

Newcastle United squads from all the years they'd been following the team. They sang songs together, always the filthiest versions.

> 'My old man said go to Viet-Nam,
> I said "Fuck off, bollocks, you're a cunt".'

In the dead of night when the guards were asleep, Bob and Terry talked about those shovels Vinh had brought for them to bury Casper and the Lieutenant. Vimto had known about Plan Wooden Horse. Someone was being talkative.

When fear and pain and despair set in, there was always hate. Only their hut had known more than half an hour before that Wooden Horse was a goer.

They had a traitor among them. Someone had grassed them up.

If it wasn't Bob or Terry – and, since Bob had frozen, he was petrified Terry would think it was him – and it couldn't have been poor Billy Casper because he was no longer able to talk, that left only one man.

Bob and Terry realised at exactly the same moment who the traitor was.

'I hate you, Butler,' Terry breathed.

Terry (James Bolam) was being interrogated by Captain Rambo (Raymond Massey), the American communist agent who ran the camp, issuing orders to the NVA and Viet-Cong.

'Absurd Englishman,' Rambo said, in close-up. 'You force us to such things. But then, the British have always been the world's fools. You are like children who will never leave the nursery, who still have rules about telling tales, who want to cry but can't be seen with tears on their faces. Oh no, mustn't show emotion, mustn't "let the side down".'

White leader ran across the screen, flashing scribbles and blips. Lights came up in the projection room.

'Ray is spot-on, isn't he?' said Powell cheerfully. 'It was difficult to get a sufficiently eagle-faced Yank. In the old days,

Imre and I would have used Barrymore, but poor John's drunk
dead.'

Three weeks into filming, these rushes were the first Bob had
seen of *It Ain't Half Hot, Mum*. He'd been busy keeping the
man from the Lord Chamberlain's office out of the way. This
evening, Puttnam was off at the ICA, watching a fashionable
new movie from America, *Seven Brides for Seven Comrades*.
Bob had tried hard to appreciate these left-wing art movies, but
still preferred British comedies or Italian police thrillers.

'Do I have to tell you I never saw any Americans in Indo?'
said Bob. 'Plenty of American guns and shells, but no actual
Americans.'

'I know, I know,' said Powell, 'but it's an article of faith
among our political masters that the enemy war effort is
directed from Debs DC. This is horse-trading. Little Puttman
appreciates a splash of transatlantic evil. It's funny: he's
supposed to be the guardian of good taste and morality, but he
came over all excited yesterday and insisted we shoot a scene
where Rambo forces Butler to play Russian roulette. My
Rambo would never do that.'

'Did you have to give Rambo all the best lines? He's
obviously your favourite character in the film.'

'Balance, Bob. You have to make your villains a little heroic
and your heroes a little villainous. It adds spice.'

Bob felt out-manoeuvred.

Everyone else in the projection-room left their seats. About
half of them clustered around Powell wanting decisions,
signatures, orders.

'Have you eaten?' Powell asked Bob. 'Hang around and
we'll go to Les Oiseaux. Restaurant near here, run by a chap
who used to make films before the War. Kept falling foul of the
censors and had to pack it in. I want to talk about the scene
we're doing tomorrow, where Terry murders the traitor.'

Bob was aghast. 'That's not in the book.'

Powell smiled, eyes hard. 'Ah, but it should have been,
shouldn't it?'

*

Butler cradled the broken Billy Casper in his arms, tears pouring down his cheeks, sobbing.

'You didn't 'ave to do that,' he said to Vinh. 'Billy was just a kid. Poor little sod 'ad gone soft in the 'ead.'

I couldn't see which of the guards shot Stan. He fell backwards, a look of peace on his face.

Terry and I crawled close.

I remembered Butler from Walmington-on-Sea, a million years ago. The spivvy lad who could always get fags and sweets, who could recite bus routes like scripture, who laughed like Sid James.

That lad was dying.

Terry held his hand. Vimto stood over us, sneering contemptuously.

'Don't cry, lads,' Butler said, 'I'm goin' 'ome. I'm drivin' the number 42 straight to the Cemetery Gates.'

He died smiling.

Butler squirmed against the wall of the hut, tears pouring down his cheeks, sobbing.

Terry and Bob crawled close.

Butler didn't try to deny or explain or justify himself. Most likely, he'd sold them out because he couldn't stand the idea of being put back in the cage. Maybe he did it for chocolate or extra ciggies.

'I never did like cockney cunts,' said Terry.

Butler snivelled.

Terry held his throat. Bob concentrated his hatred, focusing, willing Terry's fingers to be strong.

There was a loud crack as Butler's neck snapped. Inside the hut, it sounded like a gunshot.

'That's done the bastard,' Terry said.

'Ey, look here,' muttered Bob. 'He's got three packs of tabs and a bar of chocolate stowed in his corner.'

Terry spat in Butler's dead face.

*

INT. HUT. NIGHT.

BUTLER sits, waiting, dead inside. Monsoon rains pour down, rattling in the thatch. The door opens. TERRY and BOB stand in the doorway, water pouring off their coats. BUTLER has been expecting them, he is almost relieved.

> TERRY
> You know why we're here, Stan. You know what we have to do.

> BUTLER
> In your shoes, I'd do the same. I'm just so sorry. For everything.

BOB watches as TERRY steps towards BUTLER. He doesn't understand the bond between the two men. BUTLER opens his arms in a cruciform pose. Water and moonlight make his face beautiful. TERRY gently puts his hands round BUTLER's neck.

> TERRY (with love)
> I hate you, Butler.

BOB shuts his eyes. We hear the rain pouring down. BUTLER doesn't struggle. TERRY lays him out on his cot, at peace. TERRY wipes BUTLER's face.

> BOB (v.o.)
> In the end, everyone wanted Butler dead, himself most of all. The prisoners, the guards, his mates, his enemies. Even the jungle wanted him dead. There'd be no medals for Terry, but he was a hero all the same.

Through the noise of the storm, we hear helicopters. And music: 'The Teddy Bears' Picnic'.

'Good eeee-vening,' said the restaurateur. He was an immense, jowly man with a deep, rich London voice. 'If it isn't Micky Powell!'

'Alfred, you old devil,' said Powell. 'How are you?'

Alfred shrugged. 'Come and have the best table, chum.'

In the taxi, Powell had explained that Alfred had also been a director, rising from 'quota quickies' at about the time Powell had done. Bob remembered many of the films he had done: *The Thirty-Nine Steps*, *Fanny by Gaslight*, *The Trouble with Harry*, *The Third Man*. Like Powell, Alfred was black-listed on the strength of a single picture. *Nutter* cast the Lithuanian star Larushka Skikne as a young man who kept the mummified corpse of his mother (Margaret Rutherford) in the attic of his boarding-house in Skegness. 'They never forgave him for the scene where Sylvia Sims is murdered in the bathing-machine,' Powell said. Crucified by critics, bishops and politicians, Alfred quit the business.

'This restaurant is my way of getting my own back,' Alfred said as he showed them to their table. 'To my knowledge, I've killed two MPs and three clergymen, not to mention that dreadful woman. Let me get you a wine list.'

Bob sat down. As befitted a restaurant near a studio, the walls were covered with framed film stills. It took him a while to realise Alfred was in all the pictures, often peeping out from behind the scenery.

Powell chuckled. 'The queer thing is, I don't think he's joking . . .'

'Sorry?'

'About killing people. Alfred was ruined by do-gooders and God-botherers. No one's ever proved anything, of course. He was questioned by the police a few years ago. This ghastly suburban woman – Whitewash? Whitewall? – started a campaign to get piano-legs covered, that sort of thing. Wanted to clean up smutty movies. Said *Brief Encounter* was immoral and undermined the family. J. Arthur tried to calm her down by inviting her to the studios, giving her the VIP treatment. He made the mistake of getting Les Oiseaux to do the catering. Three days later, she was dead of a "mystery stomach bug". I hope you like poultry and game-birds. That's Alfred's speciality. Shall we order?'

After three excellent courses, during which Powell astounded Bob with funny stories about famous actresses he had slept with, the coffee arrived and Powell's eyes turned to neons again.

'Now, about Terry and Butler,' he began. Bob writhed in his seat, coffee gritty in his mouth.

'You can't show Terry killing Butler. They've both got families.'

Powell smiled, sharp teeth showing. 'Every time you see an extra with his kit slung incorrectly, you whine. Whenever we combine or manufacture characters to distil a greater truth from the morass of reality, you complain. And yet, you lie throughout your book. And you feel threatened when we diverge from your lies to tell the truth.'

'You weren't there. You don't understand.'

'No, Bob, I wasn't and I don't. But you were there, and you don't understand. You have no excuse.'

'Thelma was reading the manuscript over my shoulder as I was typing it. There were things I couldn't put in the book.'

'Did you write the book for Thelma?'

'It's dedicated to her.'

'Why not to Terry?'

'You know . . . what he did afterward . . . the terrible thing. Some say he's no better than a traitor himself.'

'Some? Do you?'

Bob took another swallow of coffee. It wasn't helping.

He had scuppered Plan Wooden Horse by freezing up. He hadn't killed Butler, but had let Terry do it for him. And, in Fotherington-Thomas's compound, where severed heads were kicked about like footballs, he had lost it again.

'When you came to visit me in Avening, I told you there was a great dishonesty in the book. What I'm trying to do is squeeze that out of the film. Sometimes that involves making up things that didn't happen. Sometimes it involves showing things that will upset Thelma and people's families and the bloody Church of England. Now, Bob, are you with me or against me? Can I count on you for the rest of the shoot, or do I have to ask Alfred to whip up one of his special cream desserts for you?'

Bob didn't know.

'I have no time for politics,' said Powell, running a huge cigar under his nose. 'But the way I see it, your friend Terry is the honest one. Fancy a brandy?'

'I haven't seen him since. I called on his parents. His Dad's disowned him. Yes, please.'

'He could have changed his name, gone to earth, maybe moved to another country.'

'But your film, Micky, is going to make it worse for him. He'll never be able to get on a bus again without worrying that one of Stan Butler's mates will recognise him.'

Powell shook his head. 'Your unfinished business with your friend is between you and him, Bob. Nobody else.'

He was right, of course. Even in the rare moments when he was being civil, Micky Powell had a way of making Bob feel a total wanker. He was like a combination of Captain Vinh and Terry.

There was a commotion at the door. A small man in an immaculately cut overcoat stormed in like a raging bull.

'Mee-keey!' he yelled through a jet-black beard, 'Mee-key Powell! Wonderful news!'

Powell rose and engulfed the little Sicilian in a hug.

'I am so happy,' said Scorsese. 'I have been to see Gelbfisch,' – he crossed himself – 'he like rushes. He say you get extra twenty thou for the, you know . . .' He made circular motions with both hands.

'Helicopters?' suggested Powell.

'Helicopters! *Si*! All helicopters you need! Is great news, no?'

Vinh was incandescent with fury. All the prisoners were lined up as if for inspection. His reasoning was that, since the head-count was one short and he knew no one had breached the perimeter, someone was playing hide-and-seek.

'Very well. If Butler does not show himself within ten minutes, I shall have one of you executed.'

Bob and Terry looked at each other.

All night, they had scrabbled at the soft earth under the floor of the hut, digging not a tunnel but a grave. The idea had been that Vimto would assume Stan – strengthened by that extra chocolate and driven insane by guilt – had escaped into the jungle.

Vinh was waving his Colt .45.

Minutes passed. Some of the weaker prisoners sagged. Others got fidgety.

'Stan Butler, come out, come out,' yelled Vimto. 'Olly-olly-ox-in-free!'

'He'll be half-way to Saigon, by now,' Terry said.

Vinh marched over, furious, pistol cocked.

'Or Hanoi,' Terry allowed. 'He was a bus-driver. Terrible sense of direction.'

'Escape is not possible.'

'Captain, do you really think one of your guards would put it in his report if he fell asleep at his post?'

Vimto obviously had thought of that, but couldn't afford to lose face. Only the prisoners would suffer now. Later, he was quite capable of having some sixteen-year-old NVA peasant shot as well. The Captain put the muzzle of the gun to Terry's nose, and grinned.

'Not so uppity, eh?'

Terry stared the treen down.

Bob heard something. A boom, away in the distance, like far-off thunder. He thought it was panicked blood pounding in his ears, but he realised Terry and Vinh heard it too, and were distracted from their face-off.

It was a thrumm, now. Like a gramophone played too loud three doors down, rattling ornaments on the mantelpiece, but too distorted to make out the tune. There was just a throbbing bass line.

Vinh, strangely, was struck afraid. He backed away from Terry and looked up into the sky, clutching his gun as if it were a lucky charm.

Dum-dum-dum-dum-dum-dum-dummm-dum . . .

It was music. Ominous oom-pahs. Someone laughed in surprise. Vimto shot him in the knee.

Bob recognised the tune as the words cut in.

'If you go down in the woods today,' sang Henry Hall . . .

'It's the bloody "Teddy Bears' Picnic",' said Terry.

Accompanying the song was the slicing of helicopter rotors. Vimto issued orders in rapid Vietnamese to scurrying guards. Bob's stomach sank. Anything that scared Vinh's boys was not necessarily good for the prisoners.

The music filled the air like a hailstorm. Bob felt it in his teeth.

Tum-te-tum-te-tum-te-tum-te-tum-te . . .

'Look!' said Terry, pointing.

Above the tree-line were ten helicopters, in a loose vee formation. Westland Wessexes and Scouts. The music came from loudspeakers mounted over their cargo doors.

Some of the prisoners started waving their arms and dancing for joy. Rescue was at hand.

Vinh shouted orders up to the observation tower. For a moment, Bob was certain he'd have the machine-gun rake the exercise ground and massacre the prisoners. Instead, the gun was pointed at the sky.

Some of the men were singing along.

Bob found himself humming: dit-dit-de-de, dit-dit-de-dum . . .

Something flared from the lead wokka, burning a trail across the sky, imprinting a neon squiggle on Bob's eyeballs.

'Everybody down,' Terry yelled.

Henry Hall – mainstay of *Children's Favourites*, hosted on the BBC Light Programme by Uncle Mac throughout the halcyon decade of Bob's childhood – whispered thunderously, as the delicate sounds of his band drowned out explosions and gunfire.

The rocket detonated in the observation tower. Guards and the gun exploded out of the fireball and rained around in flaming chunks.

Today was the bloody day, the day those sodding teddy bears finally had their fucking picnic!

This was not a day anybody wanted to be in the woods!

The guards started shooting the prisoners. A bullet spanged in the dirt between Bob and Terry. They rolled backwards, towards a hut.

Machine-guns opened up from the helicopters, stitching across the village at random, killing as many prisoners as guards. Bob realised this was not a rescue mission. The men in the helicopters probably didn't realise they were attacking a prison-camp. Everyone who died was a treen. That was how you knew one Indo-Chinese from another. The ones you killed were the enemy.

Eddie Booth and Bill Reynolds jumped up and down and waved in the middle of the carnage, trying to signal the wokkas. The machines circled the village, machine-gunning and firing missiles.

Everything was on fire.

Terry had swiped a rifle from a dead guard. Bob knew he was looking for Vimto. But this was Indo-China. You didn't kill who you wanted to, you killed who you could.

Terry shot a jabbering guard.

Bob felt burning thatch fall on his legs. Terry dragged him out of the fire.

'I owe you, our kid.'

'I'm paying you back for that Stanley Matthews cigarette card.'

There was an explosion, very near. Eddie Booth was tossed up in the air and came down in flames. It was no use. The wokkas were going to blitzkrieg everyone and everything. They were going to die.

'Terry?'

'Aye?'

'When you went out with Thelma, you know, for those two weeks.'

'Forget it.'

'But did you . . . ?'

'Yes.'

Bastard, Bob thought. 'I forgive you,' he said.

'So do I.'

Then the shooting stopped. A xylophone sounded in the song's middle-eight. Crackling fires spread. A few people were moaning.

Bob and Terry were still alive.

The helicopters touched down, rotors slowing. The music faded.

A rotund officer, wearing a panama hat over earphones and cricket-pads over khaki drills, jumped out, accompanied by a small mongrel dog and juniors with guns. He strode straight under the whipping scythes of the rotors, towering over men who bent double. Pausing, he took a deep breath, and said, 'I love the smell of burning flesh in the morning. It tastes like . . . *cooked breakfast.*'

We soon realised the man who had stepped out of the sky was Major Nigel 'Mad Nye' Molesworth of the Long-Range Jungle Patrol Group. Terry was greatly dischuffed to discover the LURP hadn't made a special raid to rescue us.

What they'd seen from the air was a couple of hundred yards square of empty jungle – our exercise ground – which was the nearest thing they'd find to a cricket pitch this far up the Ulu. They even parked two of their helicopters at either end to act as sight-screens for the bowlers. Apparently, it was Sunday, and Molesworth always played cricket on Sunday. He wasn't going to let a little thing like the Indo-China War break that habit. He even insisted on breaking for tea at four sharp, and served cucumber sandwiches with the crusts cut off. He had a standing order with Fortnum & Mason's Hong Kong branch.

Terry and I were too exhausted to complain. We weren't the only survivors; of the two hundred or so of us there, perhaps fifty had been killed or injured, and a few of the guards had disappeared into the jungle to chance the snakes and their own punji traps.

So we sat there and watched the cricket. Molesworth ordered two of the helicopters to ferry survivors back to our lines south of the DMZ, starting with the most urgent casualties.

Molesworth quickly fixed on the tall and athletic Bill Reynolds, reckoning that any West Indian must be a born cricketer. He was right. Bill was a demon bowler and a handy batsman. Terry and I had always reckoned cricket was for nancies – not a proper game like football – though we both kept quiet about that. Molesworth's Gurkha wicket-keeper had a necklace of human fingerbones.

Lieutenant Darbishire, the bespectacled medical officer and the nearest thing to a sane man in the unit, got us to help him collect identity discs from the dead.

'This Noote sounds VC material,' he commented.

Late that afternoon, with Captain Jennings at the bat, an enemy patrol found us. Some of the guards must have got through to make a report. The treens could hardly miss a load of helicopters and two dozen white-clad Ruperts hitting a ball around the jungle. They opened up with small-arms and grenades. Molesworth ordered the machine-gunners to keep them at bay while the last few overs were played. I revised my opinion of cricket. Or decided that nancies were a lot harder than we had thought.

Jennings was bowled out and, since his side needed thirty off two overs to draw level with Molesworth, gracefully conceded. Molesworth considered it and accepted. I knew damn well he'd have liked to play it out to the end.

We realised that all the other survivors had been ferried out by now. Terry, Bill Reynolds and I were the last Loamshires left. We had no choice but to go along with the LURP.

Molesworth was the last aboard the bus. He strolled over to the machine Terry and I were in, bat slung over his shoulder, stumps under his other arm, pads flapping in the downdraft from the rotors. He sat down next to me and unbuckled his pads. Over the racket of the engine, the door-gunner pumping tracers into the jungle below, this time the loudspeakers were playing 'Nellie the Elephant'.

'The Mekon don't play cricket,' he shouted to me, 'chiz chiz.'

Bob had realised within moments of setting foot on the sound stage that he came at the absolute bottom of the pecking-order. Having written 'the original book' made him of considerably less interest to grips and extras than, say, being the lad from the canteen who brought down the tea-urn and biscuits.

After two months of shooting, he had learned to blend in with the many busily employed people whose jobs were hard to define. Sometimes he would be called on for an opinion that would, likely as not, be ignored or overruled by Powell. Very occasionally, he was palmed off on a journalist or television interviewer down to do a story on the film.

Puttnam had gone native and joined the effects crew. He was merrily sloshing buckets of kensington gore over people. Powell was sneakily getting shots of the man from the censors with blood up to his elbows. He was shooting ridiculously violent scenes that he would willingly sacrifice during the inevitable arguments over final cut, just so he could get away with the things he really wanted to keep.

They really did use tomato ketchup. Every time Powell shot

a battle scene, the set smelled like a chip shop.

'I love the smell of burning flesh in the morning . . .'

Bob shuddered.

At first, he had worried that he wouldn't be able to stand watching the filming. He still wore his commando knife and had nightmares. Everything had associations that took him back: noises, sights, smells, phrases.

Though the actors' guns were real-looking, they made only the feeblest of pops when they were fired. Bob understood that the rat-tat-tat sounds were added later by Dino DiCampo, the foley artist. As Rodney Bewes and James Bolam ran across the stage for the dozenth time, stepping between pre-set firework charges, firing their toy guns into the air, Bob was taken back not to Indo but to the Waste Ground where he and Terry played war as kids. The actors were doing the same thing.

He felt an almost physical ache for what was lost. They had played British and Germans. Or, during the war of 1956, British and Egyptians. Then, after they had both seen Jack Warner as the secret agent in *I Was a Communist for MI6*, they had been parachuted into America to ferret out atom secrets. Thelma had been briefly impressed into service as the Yankee temptress played by Patricia Roc.

If Bob ever had a son, and caught him playing war, he would belt him black and blue. If, as it seemed sometimes, the Indo-China War dragged on long enough for a son of Bob's to grow up and be conscripted into it, Bob would put the lad on the Paddy Boat himself, and send him off to Ireland with all the other beetniki and conchies.

His family had done its bit.

'Again,' drawled Powell, who treated actors worse than he treated anyone else, which was quite an achievement. 'Try to look more terrified, fellows. The treens are trying to kill you, after all.'

In the back of the helicopter, as 'I am a Mole and I Live in a Hole' played on a reel-to-reel tape-recorder, Bob and Terry clung to the webbing and listened to Darbishire's modest war stories. The lieutenant clearly didn't like recounting his own exploits and played everything down if he had been involved. With Captain Jennings, he had actually been to Hanoi under-cover, and blown up two American oil-tankers in Haiphong harbour. Darbishire was keener on regaling them with anecdotes about his comrades.

Molesworth and his band of merry cut-throats specialised in rescuing downed pilots, carrying out daring acts of sabotage along the Casey Jones Trail or having hair's-breadth escapes. They were supposed to be executing covert reconnaissance missions deep inside enemy territory but spent most of their time on high-profile japes and wheezes. These public school-boys seemed to be in a different war. Bob couldn't imagine them experiencing the terror, discomfort, misery and doubt that had been his lot ever since Sergeant Grimshaw first called him a tart. In peacetime they'd all be Arctic explorers, mountaineers or in prison.

'Winker' Watson, who had been captured by the enemy five times and each time had escaped in the same way most people would nip out for a packet of tabs, was the door-gunner on this ship. He periodically raked the jungle with fire, claiming to be tiger-hunting.

'Do you know,' said Darbishire, 'I think Winker's just popped someone.'

They looked out of the open door and saw two bodies sprawled in a clearing. Among them were the half-assembled parts of what looked like an American-made rocket-launcher.

'A boundary,' said Winker.

The helicopters were playing 'pub cricket', scoring runs on the number of legs possessed by their kills. It was con-sidered bad form to take pot-shots at innocent goats to get ahead.

Darbishire, trusted to keep the score, made a note.

'You're all bloody doolally,' Terry said.

Darbishire shrugged, embarrassed. 'If you think we're mad,

wait until you meet the chap at the end of our little Sunday jaunt.'

They were proceeding north-west into Laos, over mountainous country. The jungle below was thicker, more remote from the War, but primordially dangerous. Bob half-expected a long-necked brontosaurus to poke its head out of the trees, roaring at the flying-machines.

Darbishire flipped open a file folder marked 'MOST SECRET' and showed them a photograph. It was of a smooth-faced, chinless youth with a mop of curly locks, in the uniform of the Coldstream Guards, sheathed sword in one hand, bearskin in the other. He stood erect, but had a big, open smile. He looked about fourteen.

'This is Major Basil Fotherington-Thomas. Major Molesworth was at school with him.'

'Looks harmless,' Terry said.

Darbishire wiped his specs.

'Looks can be deceiving, old man. Fotherington-Thomas has more medal ribbons than Lord Emsworth's prize pig. Mountbatten called him "the finest jungle fighter of his generation", said he was the new Wingate. He's been out here since sixty-three. We haven't had official word from him in eighteen months, but intelligence suggests he is running his own show from some stone age settlement way, way up the Ulu. He's got his own war going, and has been upsetting top brass by popping off some people who are supposed to be our allies. He issues statements claiming responsibility for assassinations, always branding the dead as traitors or corrupt. He's had a few ARVN generals killed.'

'And were they traitors or corrupt?' Bob asked.

'Well, in all probability, yes. But it still doesn't do just to top them in the street, you know. Due process of law, and all that.'

'You've let this go on for a year and a half?' said Terry.

'This isn't the first attempt to, um, re-establish contact with Major Fotherington-Thomas. Have you ever heard of "Just William"?'

'The tunnel fighter?'

'That's the fellow. Captain William Brown, the solo man. Once sat in one of those enemy tunnels on his own for twenty days awaiting business, then scragged eighteen treens, armed with only a Sykes-Fairburn knife and a torch.'

Darbishire dug out another photograph. Bob looked at it.

'Brown was sent in alone to talk sense to Fotherington-Thomas. Hasn't been seen since.'

'Yes, he bloody has,' Bob said. 'I saw this bloke dragged up as a tart in Saigon. He assassinated an ARVN officer. One shot to the head.'

'I'm not surprised. Seems "Just William" has joined the other team. Frightfully bad show, really.'

Though he must have been pushing eighty, Schmuel Gelbfisch wore a violently orange kaftan over his swollen belly and a leopard-spotted fur hat on his bald head. He was propped up by a nineteen-year-old 'secretary' with the shortest skirt Bob had ever seen and soft leather thigh-boots. He had to be arranged in his seat in the screening-room like a sultan being lowered into a bath of pillows.

Born in Warsaw, Gelbfisch was the first film-producer to relocate from Berlin and establish his studio in the Ukraine, which became the global centre of the entertainment industry in the teens and was only now surrendering its pre-eminence to international co-productions shot with the cheap labour of Spain and the Philippines. The growling bear of Metropolis–Gelbfisch–Mayer, the company Gelbfisch had founded with the Czech writer Carl Mayer in 1919 to make the silent classic *The Blood Lust of Dr Caligari*, was still the most familiar trademark in the world. He had stayed in power longer than any president or monarch.

Martino Scorsese, Gelbfisch's grand vizier, sat immediately to his left and a little below. Michael Powell, a supplicant for once, had dressed up a bit with a beret, and was seated within swatting distance of the mogul. Bob was jammed in down at the front with the 'talent'.

Rodney Bewes apologetically introduced himself. 'I'm doing my best to be you, mate. Honest.'

Bob thanked him. From what he had seen, Bewes was a fine actor, even if he wouldn't last ten minutes in the Wheeltappers, let alone Indo-China. He'd still have preferred Albert Finney, who had just made *King and Country*, a film about the man who shot Sergeant Grimshaw, with Leo McKern as John Mortimer, the QC whose argument failed to save Arthur Seaton from the gallows. In *King and Country*, Grim was being played by a much more sinister actor than William Hartnell, the black-browed and scowling Patrick Troughton.

Powell got up and coughed for silence. Bob had expected him to moderate his manner in the Royal Presence, but he drawled as confidently as usual, explaining that they were about to see a fine assembly of the attack on the prison camp. It would be the last scene before the intermission.

The lights went down.

Over black leader, the first ominous thrums of 'The Teddy Bears' Picnic' played. Dread clutched Bob's heart. The scene faded up on the jungle tree-line, shot by Jack Cardiff's second unit in Queensland, as bombs exploded, turning everything into a big bonfire. Helicopter blades sliced on the soundtrack. Bob's hand crept unbidden to the knife at his ankle. His heart pounded in sync with the wokkas.

Then came a shot of the twelve helicopters in flight, music pouring out of them. Scorsese sighed in contentment. The money was on the screen. The shot pulled back, and the wokkas overflew rolling green fields. Intercut were flashes of the second-unit jungle and the elaborate studio set. Powell had explained that he wanted the artificial jungle to look like a Douanier Rousseau, and dozens of art students had been set to work painting each leaf a bright colour.

The helicopters flew over what was very recognisably Canterbury Cathedral. A family of Indo-Chinese peasants trying to repair a stalled ox-cart looked up from the main street of a small Kentish market town as the LURP passed overhead. An explosion filled the screen.

There was a close-up of Dirk Bogarde, elegantly inexpressive. He looked nothing like 'Mad Nye' Molesworth, but managed that spark in the eyes.

The green fields of England were intercut, faster and faster, with the jungles. Fires raged in both landscapes, overlapping in the editing.

Bob was covered with a jungle sweat.

He couldn't watch the actual attack scenes and turned to look at the audience. Scorsese was rapt, Powell critical. The secretary covered her eyes. The actors, who knew it was only play, were mostly shattered. Rodney Bewes breathed, 'Good God'.

The lights went up.

'So,' said Powell to Gelbfisch, 'how much did you love it?'

The mogul tilted his head to one side, as if deciding which way up a painting should be hung, and thought about it.

'Micky,' he croaked. 'One thing I understand not. The War is in Indo-China. Why you let us see you film it in England?'

'This isn't a film about Indo-China, Sam. It's about England.'

Gelbfisch thought some more.

We put down in a clearing, which turned out to be a graveyard. There were giant granite heads, with thick lips and lazy eyes, stuck all around, staring blindly at the helicopters.

'Welcome to beautiful Laos,' said Terry.

'Looks like more bloody jungle to me,' I replied.

The humid, steaming heat was almost unbearable. You could choke just by trying to breathe in a place like this.

Molesworth ordered Jennings and some others to stay with the wokkas, then organised the rest to march the short distance to the camp they had overflown. He led us all in singing 'They're Changing Guard at Buckingham Palace' to keep us in step.

As we entered the village, the locals came out from the huts to look at us. They were savages, naked except for grey mud-streaks, though some spear-carrying men had rank insignia tattooed on their arms.

The twentieth century was a long way away.

A crazy little Englishman darted out from somewhere and introduced himself as David Bailey, a news photographer on an assignment for the *Observer*. He ranted about Fotherington-Thomas, making the Major sound like a cross between Florence Nightingale and Jack the Ripper.

Molesworth had Darbishire take a look at the malarial civilian. Bailey begged us for a place on the helicopter home. He seemed concerned that he had missed his deadline by a few years.

At last, we stood in the village square. Flies buzzed all around. More dead eyes stared at us. Even some of Molesworth's Marauders were horrified.

From the largest hut, he came. A golden youth with ringlets half-way down his back, he had a tattered paperback of A. A. Milne's *Now We Are Six* in one hand and a flint axe in the other. He looked up at the world, then around at the village, then down at us.

'Hullo clouds, hullo sky, hullo pile of severed human heads,' said Major Basil Fotherington-Thomas.

Bob realised that this was what they whispered about as an XPD mission – meaning 'expedient demise'. A murder raid. But, though Fotherington-Thomas was armed only with a sharp rock and his men seemed mostly to rely on spears, Molesworth didn't unholster his Webley and shoot the blighter. Instead, he stuck out his paw and joked, 'Dr Livingstone, I presume.'

The heat was worse than ever and the stench was

indescribably ghastly. Bob and Terry huddled together for safety, instinctively recognising that they alone in this place were as yet not completely insane. The pile of heads Fotherington-Thomas mentioned was jumbled on a dais in the village square. Bob had a nasty feeling that the Major viewed his visitors as the potential raw material for another such monument.

Something snakelike and black stirred. It had been camouflaged against one of the giant heads. Bob realised it was a white man, face and clothes striped black and dark green. He smiled, showing a red tongue and white teeth against the primal background. His eyes glittered.

It was 'Just William'.

No one else had seen him. Bob nudged Terry, but Brown had blended into the scenery again. Bob looked around. How many shadow-men, armed with more than spears, were there around the village?

'Hullo, Molesworth,' said Fotherington-Thomas gaily. 'You're just in time for tea. Did you bring any tuck?'

Outside the Empire Cinema, Leicester Square was thronged. There were rival groups of beetniki peace protesters and Young Conservative patriots, both claiming the film was an insult to their causes and threatening to disrupt the performance. There was also a rumour that a mad royalist who still thought the King had been seduced away from righteousness by his White Yank wife intended to throw glue into Princess Consort Wallis's hair-do, gumming her tiara to her beehive. The word was that the King's sister-in-law, the Dowager Duchess of York, had agreed to turn up tonight on the off-chance that the glueman would strike and she could pretend to be sympathetic.

A discreet row of well-dressed but dangerous men were doubtless ready to step in if trouble started. They were under the direction of a calm chap with a bowler hat, carrying an umbrella and with a carnation in his frogged lapel, and a startlingly beautiful woman with auburn hair who wore a leather jump-suit. Bob would have fancied his chances with the security lady, but apparently she was married.

For Bob, the worst of it was the pathetic gaggle of men in wheelchairs or on crutches, with shaggily grown-out Army cuts and the remains of combat gear, holding a candle-lit vigil for the Ex-Servicemen's Peace Campaign. He had wanted to give them a donation, but the security chief discreetly hooked him with his umbrella, saving him from the fate of being photographed by the *Daily Mirror* consorting with men who were regarded as no better than conchies. He had heard that Terry was one of the underground leaders of the ESPC. That made sense.

It Ain't Half Hot, Mum was the Royal Film Performance. It was a controversial choice, but Lord Mountbatten, who liked a good war film, had seen it and advised King Edward he would enjoy the battle scenes. And the Duke of Cornwall (next in line to the throne), who had served in Indo-China and won the respect of a surprising number of cynical soldiers, was on record as saying that this was the first film to give the truth of the conflict. Bob had heard that the King would rather have seen something with an X-certificate featuring Sarah Miles or Glenda Jackson with no clothes on, but that Princess Consort Wallis had overruled him. Powell was obviously delighted at the honour, but still professed indifference. When reporters asked him about it, he responded with stories they could never print about the King's nieces.

In his new-fitted tail-coat, Bob felt like a prat, but his mam and dad were beaming, truly happy with him for the first time since he went away. They were chatting with Rodney Bewes, clucking over him as if they had adoption papers in their back pocket. Malcolm McDowell, hotly tipped to win a Best Supporting Actor BAFTA for his mad-eyed performance as Fotherington-Thomas, was being interviewed by McDonald Hobley for BBC-TV. Kenneth Halliwell trotted about with Joan Bakewell, loudly crediting himself with the discovery of

Bob. Joseph, in a violently white two-piece that left his midriff bare, attracted photographers. He poked his tongue out at Bob. Diana swanned through, cleavage down to her navel and hair like a termite hill, accompanied by the film's production-designer, Ken Russell.

Standing on the velvet carpet, alone for a moment, Bob looked over the ropes, at the pressing crowds. Most of them were here to see the Royals and the stars. But some were here to make a point, to be seen, to make trouble. Banners were waving across the square as a group of students, under the direction of the snakelike Howard Kirk, protested against the War. Two weeks ago, riot police had been sent on to the campus at Sussex, and a girl was in a coma after taking a truncheon-blow to the head during a 'sit-in'. Even the most patriotic papers seemed to think there was something wrong with bashing a pretty middle-class girl's brains in just because she was silly enough to have let her boyfriend persuade her to go to an anti-War demo. If she'd been ugly, it would probably have been all right.

Rather embarrassingly, Bob was button-holed by Noote's widow, who thanked him profusely for what he had said in his book. He didn't think she'd enjoy the film – after much back and forth argument, the censors had left in the bullet-hole in Derek Nimmo's head but taken out the blood and brains on the ground – and didn't know what to say to her. Among the showfolk, there were quite a few other VIPs. Dennis Potter, the Labour Party leader, was there, along with Clement Freud, the Liberal chairman, but the Prime Minister would not be coming until later, making his entrance shortly before the Royal Party.

Everyone he met asked him what he thought of the film. Rather than admit he still didn't understand why Micky had shot half the jungle scenes in Kent, he claimed not to have seen it yet. After the performance, he'd have to stay out of the way.

Bob looked around the crowd, passing over famous faces, and sensed acutely who was missing. Thelma must be fuming at home. Despite the divorce, he'd asked her to come, but she had seen a photograph of him with Britt Ekland in the Sunday papers and drawn unwarranted conclusions.

He thought for a moment that he saw Terry. But it was only James Bolam in a blue tuxedo, sporting the Fu Manchu moustache he had grown for his next picture.

Fotherington-Thomas sat cross-legged in the square, shaded by his pyramid of severed heads, and read aloud, his clear voice transporting them all to the Thousand Acre Wood where a boy would always be playing with his bear. Bob felt his mind stretching round the craziness of it all. Terry was laughing and crying silently at the same time. Bailey took photographs, though there was no film in his camera. The villagers gathered, lulled by Fotherington-Thomas's voice, and even chimed in with well-loved phrases and sentences.

Every time Bob felt fear crawl down his spine like a many-legged insect, he found that William Brown was looking at him. The tunnel fighter always stood in the shadows, rarely getting more than a few yards away from the jungle. In this, the worst place in the world, the worst thing was Captain Brown. Worse than Vinh, worse than Grimshaw, worse than the Devil. Because Brown had been touched by an angel. His eyes burned with a pure white light of purpose.

With a dozen men like Brown, Fotherington-Thomas could win the War. But then, which war would they find next? These men were not taking orders from Saigon, let alone London. This was a whole new country.

'Fotherington-Thomas,' Molesworth announced, 'as any fool knows, you're utterly wet and a weed.'

Tears started in the eyes of the Boy Monster God. He spread his white arms, and bared his chest. Molesworth drove a sharpened cricket-stump through Fotherington-Thomas's heart. Without a sound, he died. His face was almost beatific. He tumbled from his position and sprawled at the Major's feet.

The tribesmen looked at the murderer of their god. Bob didn't know if they'd bow down or rise up.

Brown had disappeared. Bob felt a spasm of panic. Just because he couldn't see Brown didn't mean Brown couldn't see him. In fact, that was when 'Just William' was at his most dangerous. And Bob was a left-over witness, unfinished business.

Molesworth picked up *The House at Pooh Corner* and wiped blood off its cover. The natives, filed teeth bared, hissed at the sacrilege.

'"In which Tigger is Unbounced",' he announced.

As he read, Molesworth was accepted.

There was a tug at Bob's sleeve. He expected a stab at his heart, but it was Darbishire, not Brown.

'I've called Captain Jennings on the wireless. He'll bring the helicopters over and get us out. Then we'll *flambé* this whole place, burn it to the ground.'

'Best news I've heard all week,' said Terry.

'What about him?' Bob nodded, indicating Molesworth.

'The Major? We've lost him, I fear,' sighed Darbishire, shaking his head. 'It happens sometimes. He's lived too much, seen too much. He can't take any more.'

'Too right, son.'

The helicopters were coming. A missile streaked out of the sky, burning white, and exploded.

'I thought the plan was for an air strike *after* we were evacuated,' said Terry.

'Do you chaps ever do anything but complain?' snapped Darbishire.

A hut exploded. More fire fell from above. Through the heat-haze, Bob saw one helicopter hovering low. Jennings had fired at the outskirts of the camp to provide a distraction.

People were running all over the place. Molesworth stood still and tall, still reading aloud about Owl and Tigger and Eeyore.

Some of the natives had guns. Watson went down on one knee, with a hideous leg wound which he shrugged off.

A shroud of flame enveloped the pile of heads. They must be

preserved in something flammable. Faces shrank to skulls. Eyes boiled to angry points.

A rope ladder unrolled, conking Darbishire, who clutched his head and looked irritated. Terry grabbed the ladder and secured it with his weight, nodding through the din. Darbishire was first up. Bob made it second.

A few other men scrambled up, climbing past Terry and into the cabin. Watson pulled himself up with his hands.

Tribesmen gathered, jabbing with spears, in a circle, closing on Terry. Bill Reynolds got half-way up the ladder, and took a round between the shoulder-blades. He fell backwards, boots clumping Terry, who let go of the ladder and staggered.

The helicopter lifted up.

Bob shouted at Jennings, 'There's still a man on the ground.'

The ladder dangled out of Terry's reach.

'Can't stay here for ever,' Jennings yelled over the noise.

There were explosions all around as the other wokkas poured tracer into the village. Bob, choking on hot fumes, flung himself out of the cabin door, and crawled head-first down the ladder, hooking his boots into the rungs, swaying in the wind, bullets whistling past his head.

He was caught up in the rope and couldn't go any lower. But he could reach out. He stretched his arm, popping his shoulder-joint, and held out a hand for Terry.

Terry was holding his head, bewildered. Tribesmen were within stabbing distance.

'Terry,' Bob shouted. 'Take my hand!'

His fingers brushed mine, but suddenly there was a yard of space between us. It might as well have been a million miles. I shall never forget the look of horror on Terry's face. I shall never forgive myself for not doing more.

His fingers brushed Terry's hair. Then the helicopter rose three feet. Terry looked up and saw the opportunity. He jumped, but missed his grasp. A native swung a spear at him, and he jumped again . . .

Hanging upside-down, Bob saw a black-and-green face in the native crowd, its eyes fixed malevolently on his. 'Just William' would not let him go so easily. Reflexively, he made a fist . . .

Terry's hand closed round Bob's fist, and the helicopter lifted upwards. But Terry's fingers slipped. Their eyes met and Bob saw blame in Terry's surprised glare.

It was too late to open his fist and interlock his fingers with Terry's.

In huge close-up, a hundred feet across, on the screen of the Empire, Leicester Square, James Bolam failed to get a grip on Rodney Bewes's fist. It was the first time Bob had seen the scene cut together.

How had Micky Powell known? In his book, he'd been unable to put it down. He'd taken all the blame, but not given the details.

Only two other people alive could have known.

Bob, soaked with sweat, looked around the darkness. Which of them had it been? Who was here tonight?

Terry? Or 'Just William'?

The helicopter was twenty feet from the ground. Bob was slung underneath it like an anchor. Terry sprawled among the natives, who looked up at the departing war machine. Bob saw the dark shape of William Brown closing on the writhing Terry.

He screamed and screamed, eyes shut tight, unable to watch the inevitable play out.

'It's this passage,' Halliwell had said. 'You can't let it stand and expect to be published. It's tantamount to treason.'

Bob remembered what he had written.

Somehow, Terry got out of the camp – I think Brown might have rescued him, and dumped him in the jungle – and wandered around for days in the jungle, delirious and fever-struck. He was recaptured by the treens and wound up in another prison camp, where another officer presented him with the deal Vinh had offered. I have a cutting from the *Straits Times*, an English language newspaper from Hong Kong, with a photograph of Terry getting off an airliner in Zurich and the story of the press conference he gave to denounce the War as Anglo-Russian imperialism. Now, he travels around Britain, almost a fugitive in his own country, addressing anti-War meetings, and saying that Britain has no business in Indo-China, that the peoples of the country should be left to work out their destiny for themselves. He also campaigns for the government to do more to secure the release of prisoners of war. In his place, I would have done the same thing in Indo, and would be doing the same thing at home.

Halliwell had made him change the last sentence to 'Some things can be understood but not forgiven'. He always told himself that he meant his own moment of cowardice, but he knew everyone else who read the book thought he meant Terry's 'treason'.

The film ended with another scene Bob had not seen before. The fires engulfed Fotherington-Thomas's camp and faded into a blood-red banner. There was a pan down to Rodney Bewes, with long hair and fashionable clothes, sitting in a bookshop, signing copies of Bob's book.

Filing past, with books to be autographed, were all the characters from the film. Those who had died were hideously mangled. Intermingled were life-size teddy bears. At the end of the line, making eye contact with Rodney Bewes as he neared him, was James Bolam, still in uniform.

On the soundtrack, a ragged chorus of soldiers sang 'The Teddy Bears' Picnic'.

The film ended with Rodney Bewes and James Bolam – no, damn it, Bob and Terry – looking at each other, not saying anything out loud.

Haunted faces.

The applause was still continuing, and Micky Powell was taking bows, smiling broadly at the small but significant section of the audience who were booing as loudly as the others were cheering, when Bob made it to the Gents. He was a wreck. The film had brought everything back. Now here he was in his silk shirts and his MG sports car and his poncey £2 haircut swanning around with shallow pseuds and arty-farty types who didn't care nearly as much as they pretended they did.

Who was he trying to kid?

He knelt over a toilet bowl and puked up the smoked salmon he had eaten at the reception. He had been presented to the King and now he was throwing up like a teenage drinker. He was sick until he was empty.

How could he ever face anyone? Now that everyone knew?

He staggered out of the stall and shoved his head under a running tap.

Cold water stabbed his hackles.

He looked up, rubbing paper towels into his neck. Water had seeped down into the back of his shirt.

He looked into the mirror. Eyes glittered from behind him. He wasn't afraid.

He turned.

A shape came out of one of the stalls. Bob knew it was Brown, somehow come from out the jungle hells of the other side of the world, still intent on settling accounts, silencing the witness.

This was best. At least he would die as he was supposed to have died.

It wasn't Brown.

'Hello, our kid. This time, you're the one spewing.'

Terry was thinner than he had been. In the photographs Bob had seen, he wore his hair long and beard shaggy, but now he was clean-shaven and had a severe short back and sides.

He wore a Navy uniform.

'I'm not enlisted in me own name,' he explained.

'Terry, I'm . . .'

Terry shrugged. 'Aye, I know.'

They looked at each other, just as the actors had in the film. Bob wondered if Powell were directing them.

'For a while, in the jungle, I thought you'd done it because of Thelma,' Terry said.

Bob laughed.

'I know, I know,' said Terry. 'I went daft. That's a good picture, you know. I don't know what all those English fields and teddy bears were for, but it brings it back. A lot of people are going to have their minds changed. You've done well.'

'It's not my picture.'

Terry smiled.

'How've you been, kidder?' Bob asked.

'Busy. But I can't take it any more. The speeches, the meetings, the organising. I can't do that. I'm just a Geordie piss-head, in way over my depth. You're the clever one. I'm going to sea because I can't be a hero any more. That's your job, Bobby. Know what I mean?'

Bob did, but shook his head.

'It's bloody funny when you think about it, Bob. Living through it all, from Grimshaw through Khe Sanh to Fotherington-Thomas counted for nothing. Your book made people sit up, but it's only this film that will get through. From now on, the film and our lives are mixed up in a jumble. People will ask you about things in the film they made up, and you'll start to wonder whether they happened. Eventually, the film will seem more real than the life. In the meantime, you know what you have to do.'

Bob left his tailcoat in the toilet, and joined the crowd piling out into the square. The mood was strange. He wondered what the King had thought.

A reedy young bloke shook his hand and congratulated him. Bob realised that had been Charles, Duke of Cornwall. He fancied that the Prime Minister looked at him with hatred. He couldn't get within twenty yards of Powell, who was beaming between Scorsese and a small man Bob took to be Imre Pressburger. He allowed himself to be washed out of the foyer with the surge of people.

Terry had vanished. Bob was no longer looking around for the mad eyes of William Brown.

Bob fought his way to the stand of the Ex-Servicemen's Peace Campaign. A couple of Young Conservatives were jeering at the bearded men, some of whom were in wheelchairs.

'Excuse me,' he said to a man holding a placard, 'but how do I join up with you?'

When the Berlin Wall came down, Eugene Byrne and I were in front of Eugene's television in Bristol being miserable. Eugene was flat on the floor with back trouble and I was emotionally bruised from a brief relationship. We are both interested in alternate history, and rather envied all those Eastern Europeans who were getting to overthrow their apparently monolithic and implacable governments while our pretty dismal lot in the West were still in place. We wound up writing 'In the Air' (which appeared in *Interzone*), a novella set in a timeline where America had a revolution in 1918 and Russia didn't. Our equivalent figures for Lenin, Stalin and Václav Havel were Eugene Debs, Al Capone and Kurt Vonnegut Jr; and the story was mostly set in the 1950s and about Buddy Holly, Howard Hughes and Jack Kerouac.

We returned to the world of the United Socialist States of America in further stories: 'Ten Days That Shook the World', about the Revolution itself; 'Tom Joad', about the Depression; 'Abdication Street', about a 1970s Royal Wedding in Tsarist Russia; 'Citizen Ed', about hero-of-the-people/mass murderer Ed Gein; and 'On the Road', a post-communist wrap-up to the series. Some people liked these stories a lot, while others took exactly the opposite view. As is suggested by the mixing of 'real' people with 'fictional' ones – our Depression story features Eliot Ness, Melvin Purvis, Tom Joad (from *The Grapes of Wrath*) and the Waltons (among many others) – the point is not solely to create a respectable 'might have been' of the type it is now fashionable to call 'counter-factual' but to twist history and popular culture to create a distorting mirror for the century. The whole cycle was published in America by Mark V. Ziesing as a handsome volume, *Back in the USSA*.

This story is part of the series, but stands a little aside in that it is about Britain rather than America. Eugene and I both interviewed Michael Powell, a director we both admire enormously, towards the end of his life, and Eugene actually visited the house as described here. Powell was one of the great English visionaries, and one of his major subjects – in *The Life and Death of Colonel Blimp*, most explicitly – was the nature of the British character and its various schismed self-images. In this story, we were able to touch on a great number of differing takes on the British national character, from kitchen-sink realism through sitcom (Clement and La Frenais deserve a bigger credit than they get in the story), heroic and disenchanted war film, *Carry On* comedy and public-school juveniles to semi-mystic fantasy.